The Power
of
Notes and Spells

A Teapot Cottage Tale (#2)

Annie Cook

Copyright © 2023 Annie Cook

ISBN: 978-1-916820-58-6

Acknowledgements

Huge thanks go to a handful of people who have unfailingly supported and cheered me on through the process of pulling this book together. Massive gratitude goes to:

My namesake, my grandma Annie Cook (R.I.P), continues to be my inspiration for the Teapot Cottage tales; She was an 'owd Lanky' lass through and through. Her witchery and 'funny' way of talking will make my heart smile for the rest of my days on earth.

The beautiful Rebecca Pockett, my sweet friend, is one of my most enthusiastic champions. She is also one of the most experienced Senior Neonatal Nurses in the United Kingdom. My understanding of the finer points of emergency care for pre-term babies is thanks to her.

Cumbria Police, for their expert guidance and advice about what support can be offered, and to whom, at the scene of an RTA.

Dawn Walter and Sandra Gilfillan, two more gorgeous friends, gave me safe and quiet places to keep writing at a time when my life was unusually stressful and difficult.

Jacqueline Winnell, a beautiful friend who took a massive amount of acute stress off me when it mattered most.

Liam Beale, my graphic designer, who has the patience of a saint. He's a Lancashire lad too, so how could I *not* want to work with him? I'm thrilled that he is happy to work with me!

Gwen Morrison, from Publish Nation, has bravely undertaken the challenge of managing insecurities I didn't expect to have, about the process of getting a book published, noticed and appreciated.

My husband Kerry, the love of my life, has consistently kept me fed and watered, and made sure I always had tonic for my gin. He is my number one fan.

Friends and strangers alike, from all different parts of the world, have told me how much they enjoyed my first book, No Small Change, and how much they are looking forward to this one; the second in the Teapot Cottage series. The reactions and reviews have inspired me so much. I hope you enjoy The Power of Notes and Spells just as much, if not more.

You're all amazing.

For my Uncle Jack Greenhalgh;
A proud 'Lancashire Lad' to the end.
Thank you for believing in me, all through my
life, until the very end of yours.
Rest in Peace.

Chapter One

A Spell To Attract True Love

On the night of the new Moon,
light a tealight candle and keep it near to you while you work.
Wrap a red ribbon (to represent romantic love) fully
around a white rose (to represent love everlasting) and make a
completely ribboned parcel.
Anoint it with two drops of rose otto, to represent two hearts
and souls to be joined.
While making the parcel, focus the thoughts
on love and romance.
Incantation; just once, directly into the parcel:
'Angels of Love, I Ask of You,
Bring Forth My Soul-mate, Forever True.'
Place the parcel under your pillow for
seven times seven (forty-nine) nights, repeating
your mantra just once each night before you go to sleep.

Growing up on Ravensdown farm, at the edge of a tiny town called Torley in a quiet corner of the Lake District, Seraphine Raven - better known to her family and friends as Feen - had always believed in love at first sight. The young white witch, with very strong penchants for Spoonerism and chatting with foxes in the forest, didn't really have a lot of choice; not after what had happened to her own besotted parents, Mark and Beth, around thirty years earlier.

On a wintry Saturday afternoon, in a remote country pub nestled deep in the Forest of Bowland, a fresh-faced Mark Raven had locked eyes with another young white witch by the name of Beth Brierley; a descendant of a local family of witches. In that instant, they were both convinced that even if they lived until they were a hundred and eighty, there would never be anyone else for either of them. Barmaid Beth had pulled a pint of Pendle Witches ale for farmhand Mark, and 'Boom!' Cupid skilfully shot the same arrow through them both, and two fates instantly meshed into one.

Mark and Beth had talked and joked about it often enough over the years, for everyone who knew them to be convinced too, that love-at-first sight existed. After all, Feen's father was an 'Owd Lanky' farmer; a solid, salt-of-the-earth, working-class barrel of a bloke with an accent as thick as treacle, never happier than when he had his hands in the dirt or was rounding up a mob of stubborn sheep. Pragmatic to a fault, with precisely zero in the way of airs and graces, Mark wasn't the type who had much truck with 'all that bloody woo-woo shyte,' as he termed it. He called a spade a spade, never suffered a fool for more than forty seconds, and he wouldn't have been caught dead talking about 'higher vibrations,' or other unearthly things he didn't understand - at least not in the same way his wife and child did.

But he did understand the concept of love at first sight and, as he'd said often enough, when something smacks you in the chest that hard, and your heart gets hijacked with so little hope of it ever being returned, you just have man-up and accept it. There's nothing else to be done. So, as a man who nearly always understood when he had no choice in a matter, Mark had simply shrugged his broad shoulders and surrendered to the inevitable; that he'd lost his heart, good and proper, to the strikingly beautiful blue-eyed beauty who'd served him his pint o' Pendle Witches. And from the moment that he did, he didn't mind.

Beth had often told her daughter, in describing the moment she first saw Mark Raven, that her heart had literally shifted in her chest. It had *fallen*, she said, leaving her hopelessly in love with the rough and ready young man with the broadest and most comical Lancashire twang she'd ever heard. He'd sauntered through the door, in his mud-caked boots and scruffy oilskin parka, with a smile that could melt the North Pole.

'A'reet, lass?' he'd asked, as his heart fell.

'Aye, cocker,' she'd responded with a wink, as hers did too, and within a split second she was his and he was hers and that was that.

So although Feen had never been in a hurry for it to happen, she always had the unshakeable belief that when her own true love turned up, well, she'd just *know*.

Lately though, something had shifted a little and she'd found herself feeling a bit more wistful than previously, about what might be taking him so long. More and more often now, she found herself wishing that her knight in shining armour would rock up sometime soon, please, and hopefully on a nice white horse that didn't need new shoes that she'd end up having to pay for. She'd met her fair share of spongers and losers, thanks very much, and didn't want to meet any more, but at the ripe old age of almost-twenty-four she was more than ready for romance.

Not that she'd ever admit it. While Feen Raven possessed a rather unique window into most other people's innermost thoughts, she rarely felt compelled to confess her own. Although she usually knew *exactly* what was ricocheting around in most people's heads, few were ever allowed to know what was happening in hers.

This afternoon, she was heading into Carlisle to do a couple of errands. She tooted her horn as she drove away from the farm, past Teapot Cottage; her stepmother Adie's holiday house a little further down the drive. Adie was in there cleaning it, and getting it ready for a new tenant who was due to arrive tonight.

Feen was irritable this morning, which was slightly out of character. She wasn't usually upset by much, or too disorganised to make a simple shopping list and run the risk of forgetting half of what she needed. She wasn't usually prone to strange dreams either, but last night she'd been woken several times by a series of random, disturbed thoughts, most of which she couldn't even remember this morning. It had all left her feeling fidgety and unsettled, and for once in her life she couldn't really figure out why.

Intuitively, she knew the spirits were playing with her, as they occasionally did. She wasn't yet privy to whatever hijinks they were up to but she tried to shrug it off, for now at least. She knew better than to try and second-guess the other-world influences that shaped her life in different ways, especially when they threw exasperating roadblocks in the way of her perception.

3

Knowing that whatever was being cooked up on her behalf would only be revealed when her guides and angels jolly-well thought it should, and not before, she shrugged her shoulders and kept driving. But she did feel compelled to make her feelings clear to them.

'Whatever you bunch of dingbats are up to today, please can it tot be nedious? I have enough to think about right now, without you hurling all manner of mischievous joops for me to hump through. Please don't be pixies in my head today!'

It never occurred to Feen, as she drove towards the city, that this might be the day when she'd be swept away by the very thing that had taken her goo-goo-eyed parents by storm all those decades ago. It was probably just as well that she didn't yet know what was coming; that instant flash of crystal-clear, cerebral lightning that gave a glimpse of exactly what the future was going to look like.

If she'd known in advance that she'd be ending the day finally understanding the reality of love at first sight, and how it really felt to be hit by that particular freight train, it would have created utter turmoil in her head - the kind that would have made driving impossible. Eventually, of course, she'd appreciate that her excitable angels were being deliberately obtuse until precisely the right moment, when what they'd intended all along could come to pass. She would understand that she'd been cleverly engineered to be in the exact right place at the exact right time, with no sense of anticipation to spoil things.

But within minutes of parking her car and walking into the heart of the city, all thoughts of shopping and spiritual mischief melted away completely, because being hit by a freight train didn't even come *close* to describing what happened next.

He was standing about forty feet away, next to a lamp post, talking to someone who had their back to her. She didn't even vaguely register who it was. Male, female, tall or short, old or young, she really couldn't have said. All she noticed was him. The rest of the world had simply stopped all around her. Everything, everyone else, had completely fallen away.

At about five feet ten, he was stocky with a well-proportioned body. He had a beautiful oval face, with intense, heavy eyebrows, the most wonderful hint of dark stubble around his jaw, and a generous bow-shaped mouth. He also had the most glorious head of hair; long and almost black, fanning out from his face and cascading well past his shoulders. Feen guessed he'd be in his mid-twenties.

He was dressed like a Goth, in a long black leather coat that flared from the waist. Black jeans were held up with a pewter-buckled belt, beneath a purple t-shirt that had something scribbled on it in white writing that she couldn't quite read. A black and white dogs-tooth patterned scarf was draped casually around his neck. His heavy, thick-soled, round-toed black leather boots had chunky heels, chrome toe-tips, and shiny bits hanging off the ends of the laces. He was standing with his hands in his jeans front pockets, rocking ever-so-slightly back and forth on his feet, and looking like he'd walked straight off a movie set or a rock concert stage. Feen froze, staring.

He was listening intently to whoever was talking to him, and then he suddenly threw back his head and laughed. That's when Feen's heart literally fell, just like her mother's had; irretrievably, and forever.

She wasn't even aware that she was standing stock still in the street with her mouth hanging open like a flycatcher, until he felt her gaze on him, and he stared straight back. At the exact moment his green eyes locked with her blue ones, she felt the breath being sucked out of her body. The expression on his face was one of pure shock. He looked, quite literally, as if he'd seen a ghost.

Feen abruptly turned and ran, and she didn't stop until she got all the way back to her car where she sat, shaking like a leaf, as she tried to control her breathing. Her heart was hammering fit to fly straight out of her chest. She checked behind her, and peered down both ends of the lane. There was no sign of him. She'd half expected him to chase after her, yelling for her to stop and wait for him; hoping for that, yet scared to death of it. She was immensely relieved, that he wasn't here tapping at her window, yet deeply bereft that he wasn't. What would she have said? What would *he* have said?

What if I never see him again?

The thought made her stomach lurch. After all, this was Carlisle. It wasn't Torley, her hometown, where most local people knew one another, at least superficially. He could be from anywhere. But in the instant she'd seen him, Feen knew. He was her soul mate; the

5

man she'd been waiting for, all her life. The man she wanted to be with, for all of her life.

Had he found her? Or had she found him? Had they found one another? Or had they not? Had this been a glimpse of a gorgeous future, or the cruellest impression imaginable of what would never be?

A deep, sharp pang of loss rocked Feen to the core. She knew that she would forever be condemned now to wandering the earth, looking for him, as the one missing piece she now knew existed, she now knew she *needed*, that would make the puzzle of her life complete.

'Sometimes you have to give fate a bit of a nudge, love.'

Her mother's voice, ghostly in the ether, whispered to her now. Beth didn't come to her often, but when she did, Feen always felt it, and she always knew it was important.

'Go on, silly, this is it! He is you. You are him. Get going!'

Abruptly, Feen jumped back out of the car, barely remembering to shut the door behind her, and ran as fast as her feet would carry her, back down the road towards where she'd seen him. Misery overwhelmed her as she realised he was no longer there. She scanned all sides of the wide space, as far as she could see, but he was nowhere in sight. He'd vanished. She raced around in every direction, checking all the alleys and side streets, hoping to see his retreating form down one of them, but he was gone.

Flooded with frustration, and fighting the urge to burst into an epic flood of tears right there in the street, Feen scolded herself hard.

Oh, you stupid, stupid woman! Why did you run away like a scalded cat?

Shell-shocked and bereft, she stayed rooted to the spot, until someone came past and accidentally bumped her back into reality. She shook herself mentally and checked her watch. She still had just under an hour left on her parking and despite the warmth of the early summer day, she was chilled to the bone and shaking. With all thoughts of shopping gone, and not knowing what else to do with herself, she dived into the corner café she was standing in front of, and ordered a comforting cup of hot chocolate.

She wasn't capable of driving anyway, just yet. Her thoughts were a scrambled mess. She needed time to come to terms with the fact that her world had been rocked to its core and she'd responded like a startled bird. She felt ridiculous now; childish and pathetic. Her face flamed with humiliation, at how stupidly she'd reacted to what now felt like the most important thing that had happened in her life to date.

Feen felt her thoughts sliding slowly into negative overdrive, and for once she felt powerless to stop them.

He's gone. I've lost him, and nobody else will ever come close. This was my one chance. I'm going to be alone forever!

Poor Feen had never been 'popular,' especially with boys. At school in particular, while she'd got on okay with a couple of the girls, most of them had basically ignored her, and the boys had given her a pretty tough time. None of them had ever bullied her physically, but most had relentlessly ridiculed her, particularly her diminutive size-six frame.

They also consistently savaged her natural use of Spoonerism; transposing the first letters of a pair of words. A few of the meaner boys had called her 'bad mitch' for a short while, until they got tired of the teachers telling them off. Most had eventually settled for dubbing her 'Feirdo Ween' which had stuck for pretty much her whole adolescence. Back then, lot of kids regarded her as 'spooky' and always pretended they were afraid of her, shrinking back and widening their eyes as she passed. They'd have been amazing on the stage, some of them. She'd always itched to tell them, sarcastically, what brilliant little actors they were.

Ultimately, though, she'd held her tongue. She'd made up her mind to pay *them* no mind, because it simply made life easier. But of course, with all that going on, there hadn't even been a date for her prom on offer, let alone a full-blown love-life. Even the quieter boys who hadn't indulged in the bullying had always given Feen a wide berth. The last thing they needed, she knew, was to be badgered themselves by the bullies for showing any interest in their target.

She also knew about the weekend pyjama parties she'd never been invited to, where groups of teenage girls would sit around discussing the various forms of paralysis that plagued them, as they made their first forays into the dating world.

'Does he like me? What do you think he meant when he said that? What should I do if he doesn't turn up? Would it look desperate if I texted him? Do you think this top is too tarty for a first date?'

Feen had missed out on all of that. She'd never had a single conversation about boys, even with her one close friend Josie, who'd married her childhood sweetheart without ever having to give a moment's thought to whether he'd dump her because she had a better-looking friend, or whether he'd hate her new halter-top or hairstyle. She never had to worry that he'd run out on her, if she went all the way to home base and ended up pregnant.

It wasn't that Josie wouldn't have listened, or been sympathetic to whatever dilemma Feen might have ended up in, over a boy. She absolutely would have tried but Feen knew, without a doubt, that Josie would never truly understand in a million years what had happened in the street just now. It wasn't the kind of thing *anyone* would understand, unless they had wildly romantic tendencies, or a portal into a distinctly different world. Josie, bless her gorgeous heart, had neither.

Torley wasn't exactly teeming with eligible men, and Feen wasn't interested in the motley bunch from school who *had* stuck around the area, even those who might have matured enough to see her as more than just that easy-target, 'off-the-wall chick' they'd known as kids. It meant there still weren't many prospects and sometimes, as her girlfriends were meeting boys and falling in love, Feen had quietly wondered if and when her inherent quirkiness might finally attract the affection of a nice young man, or when her own interest might eventually be sparked by one.

There had been one semi-significant lover in Feen's past; a very patient young man who, in all fairness, she could have taken or left. He'd been a friendly and sociable sort who needed like-minded souls around him, and he struggled with the fact that Feen didn't. He'd persevered for almost a full year with the dreamy young woman who would far rather spend time alone in fields picking primroses than interacting with people. But, despite his best efforts, her fluctuating interest finally got the better of him and he moved on. He eventually got engaged to one of her more outgoing acquaintances, which suited all three of them perfectly.

Feen had never been able to pretend what she didn't feel. She also knew that trying to force the hand of fate was futile. Things happened when they were supposed to, and not before, and trying

8

to ignore, force or meddle with the process never helped at all. The best example of that, in recent times, was her father Mark. He hadn't been looking for love again when it rocked up and turned him inside out, around eighteen months ago. He'd been known throughout the land as a confirmed widower, ever since Beth had lost her battle with bowel cancer almost a decade ago. She'd been the love of Mark's life, and nobody - including him - ever imagined he'd fall in love again.

But then a woman called Adie Bostock had arrived to housesit at Teapot Cottage, on the edge of Ravensdown farm. Within nine months of Mark and Adie meeting and starting off as friends, and furiously denying every last pull of mutual attraction, they'd ended up getting married. Everyone who knew them was delighted - not to mention vastly relieved that they'd finally admitted to what had been blindingly obvious to everyone else from the start. They were surprisingly well-suited, for people who'd come from different worlds.

They were blissfully happy together, and Feen adored her new stepmother. Their lovely romance had given her renewed hope for her own prospects for falling in love, whenever it might choose to happen. She was confident it would, but time was passing, and seeing everyone else having fun and starting to get settled had started to make her vaguely and uncharacteristically impatient.

The bald truth was that fate didn't give a monkey's about how keen or reluctant people might be, for their lives to be upended by Cupid. Whether it suited his targets or not, that fat little marksman showed up when he jolly-well felt like it, not when he was asked, or asked *not* to! But Feen found herself confused beyond belief, about today's not-quite-close-enough encounter of the world-rocking kind, in terms of what it meant, or what might happen next.

Surely something would?

Now, she had to acknowledge that for the very first time in her life she'd managed to tumble into in full-blown panic mode about her love-life; and not about whether Prince Charming was actually coming, but more about where he'd gone!

She deliberately chose to sit in the window of the café with her hot chocolate. She usually preferred to tuck herself away at the back, somewhere in a corner, well out of the public eye. Putting herself on display like a living mannequin was acutely uncomfortable.

But I'm still hoping to see him! If I sit at the back, I won't see him. And he won't see me. Oh, come and find me? Please? Please come and find me!

But, as the next forty minutes passed, Feen became resigned to the fact that the man who'd hijacked her heart had completely disappeared with it. She also managed to convince herself that he'd have been too startled by her unkempt appearance to be interested in pursuing her anyway.

She looked down at her light cotton, original 1950's frock, covered in a bold pattern of glorious green and blue hydrangeas. It was a retro-shop bargain she'd found on a trip to Lancaster, with a very full skirt and half sleeves. She wore a cream lace t-shirt underneath it to draw less attention to its slightly-too-wide scooped neck. She'd pinned part of the skirt up with an antique blue and green diamante brooch, revealing the heavy swathe of pleated cream lace she'd added beneath it. Her dark hair was carelessly scraped back and secured in a messy ponytail with a dark blue velvet scrunchy, and she had her little black buttoned boots on. She wasn't wearing a scrap of make-up. To an outsider, she looked quirky, charming, and completely beautiful, but she felt like a second-hand frump.

I look a mess, she thought wildly. *My hair is in such a state, and these moots are so buddy! What was I thinking, coming out looking like this? I'm a crain trash. If we ever meet again it'll be him that runs away!*

Feen had always resisted being a slave to fashion, but she wondered now if that had been a mistake. Maybe 'he' thought her idea of style was ridiculous and uninspiring. Maybe everyone else did too. The thought had never occurred to her before, that her uncultivated, purely instinctive image was hopelessly wrong. Perhaps she really did look every bit as ridiculous as she suddenly felt. For one who'd never really cared what anyone else thought of her, or how she looked, Feen was now eating herself alive with embarrassment and worry.

A profound sense of despair, not felt since her mother had died, suddenly settled like a shroud around her. So derailed was her train of thought now, it didn't occur to her that by her very own reasoning, if she was meant to be with 'him' she would be. If 'he' really was meant for her, as her mother had already confirmed from another realm, another chance would come.

But frustration and despair had unusually eclipsed Feen's normal line of logic, so she didn't think about any of that. She just stared miserably into her mug of chocolate and idly moved what was left of the pink and white marshmallows around the top with her spoon until they dissolved in the mug, leaving a sticky pink ring around the top.

After finishing her drink, she wondered if she should prolong her own agony and order another one, and sit in the window for a little longer. But, she decided, if he was still around she'd surely have reconnected with him by now. It seemed that he was long gone, and all she could hope for now was that she'd somehow, somewhere, sometime, run into him again.

Hopefully before we're crashing into each other in a hare comb somewhere, dribbling and demented, and having to try and untangle our Zimmer frames!

She wiped the mallow moustache from above her top lip and dragged herself dejectedly back to her car, where she sat for a good while, staring into the middle distance. She felt depleted and crushed, as if she'd run a marathon, only to be told it didn't count and she'd have to run it again.

It was hard to believe that fate could be this cruel; that her spirit-world protectors could have allowed this to happen. They'd never let anything disrupt her like this before, not since the death of her mother, anyway. They messed with her head a lot, yes, and played all kinds of hide-and-seek games with her logic and perspective whenever it suited them, but they'd never been vindictive before. What happened today felt indescribably, unfathomably unkind, and it simply wasn't possible for Feen, who was usually so highly intuitive, to wrap her head around the cruelty of it.

She sat quietly in her car, waiting for her mother to 'speak' to her again. She fully expected Beth to come forward and chide her gently, that she'd unwittingly thrown a spanner in her own works by running away, and had nobody to blame but herself. But nothing came, which only made her more confused about what had actually happened to her, and why. It felt as if even her own mum had spiritually abandoned her, right when she needed her the most.

11

With a heavy sigh, and pushing aside the familiar flare of grief she always felt, whenever she realised how much she still missed and needed Beth, Feen started her car and pulled out into the street. All she could think about was 'if only.'

If only I hadn't run off like that. If only I'd managed to see him when I went back. If only he'd felt the same way and had come to find me!

They could have been sitting together right now, getting to know one another, and trying to make sense of the bolt of invisible lightning that had somehow fused their futures - in Feen's mind at least!

Fighting back her tears of crushing disbelief, she drove back to Torley town and pulled into the carpark behind the local flower shop 'Heavenly Blooms.' She had a deal with Fiona Frost, the town's florist, to buy the flowers that had withered to the point where no one else wanted them. Instead of just throwing them away, Fiona let Feen have them very cheaply instead. The arrangement suited them both.

For some of the silver-backed, resin-bubble jewellery Feen made, with miniature flowers encased in it, it didn't matter that certain blooms were a little past their best of freshness. As long as the petals and leaves still had enough hue and grain that hadn't spoiled, she could still work with them to create beautiful pieces; delicate earrings, necklaces, bracelets and brooches, with trimmed or cut-down flower petals of all type and colour. She would usually find a lot growing wild, but Fiona's cast-offs gave her the opportunity to work with different colours, textures and shapes that weren't always easy to find in the local woodlands or meadows, or even in the flowerbeds at home, which were seasonal, of course.

'Hello, Fiona?' she called as she stepped into the shop. She paused just inside the door, closing her eyes and inhaling deeply, allowing the aromas to gently bring her back to herself. She adored the smell of the shop; the blend of different floral scents mixed with the more earthy fragrances of oasis, leaves and soil.

Fiona Frost was a short, rotund woman who had run her lovely little flower shop in Torley for more than twenty years. She stepped in from the back section and greeted Feen warmly.

'Hello, love!' she beamed. 'Gosh, look at you! Aren't you just the most beautiful thing in here today?' Feen flushed and modestly waved the compliment aside.

'I've got some pretty red carnations for you if you want them? I've also got a handful of orange roses that have started drooping, and a big sunflower gone a bit curly at the edges just on one side. If you're interested, you can have the lot for two quid. How does that sound?'

'It all sounds perfect for some very bold, fire-themed necklaces, I think!' Feen declared, as she handed over a two-pound coin. 'I presume you're still saving these?'

Fiona nodded vigorously. 'I certainly am. You know, last year my jars of two-pound coins paid for our holiday!'

'That's right, they did! You sold some of the less common ones for quite a good profit as I recall, and you went on an exotic coo-week truise, didn't you? I was amazed by that. So canny of you! Where are you and Alastair aiming for this year?'

Fiona pulled a face. 'Sadly, I think it'll just be a hot week in Lanzarote or somewhere like that, in the next couple of months. Very low-key this time. We've a big autumn and winter coming up with our first two grandchildren expected within three months of one another,' she explained.

'Alana and Zoe are both going to need a lot of help as first-time mums, and Zoe and her boyfriend have finally sold that poky little flat of theirs, and bought a decent house. They'll be moving right before her due date though, as it turns out, which puts a bit of extra pressure on things. So I can't go far for very long. If we can get to the Canaries for a week or so of guaranteed sun, I'll be happy.'

Feen had gone to school with Fiona's twin daughters, Alana and Zoe Frost. They'd been a couple of years ahead of her at their small school, but Feen remembered them well. They were as close as any twins could be, and nobody had been at all surprised when they'd both fallen pregnant within a few months of each other.

Fiona made a little more small talk, mostly asking about how Feen's commission work was going, providing an exclusive, limited-edition jewellery line for her stepsister's wife, the famous fashion designer Gina Giordano. 'I'd kill for one of her pieces,' she said wistfully. 'One day, when I decided to sell this place and put my feet up, I'll splurge on something from GinGio.'

13

Fiona also talked briefly about how busy her husband Alastair was, as Torley's only Funeral Director. Feen thought that he and Fiona were a great team for the town, running such complementary businesses right next door to one another, and being genuinely caring and compassionate people. They were both successful, too. It seemed that death and declarations of love or condolence were big business for Torley town.

Fiona was warm and easy to talk to. No matter how busy she was, she always made time to stop and talk properly to Feen, and actually listen to her, as if what she had to say really mattered. Few people ever made Feen feel that way, so she always enjoyed her visits to Fiona's gorgeous little shop.

She was tempted to talk about her incredible encounter with the soulmate she'd found in Carlisle, and how bereft it had left her feeling, but she knew she'd probably collapse into a sobbing heap if she did. Deciding that it really wasn't fair to put poor Fiona on the spot, to have to mop her up or find something meaningful or encouraging to say in the face of bereft hysteria, she splurged another two pounds on a bunch of bright yellow tulips for Adie, and gave Fiona a goodbye hug.

The biggest downside of being what most people would describe as 'a tad strange' she mused, as she started walking back to her car, was that there weren't many people to talk to about *anything* weird or earth-shattering that might happen to you. It wasn't just the 'boy' thing. It was everything.

Feen needed someone to help her make sense of what had happened today but, as she already knew, 'ordinary' people wouldn't understand the bizarreness of the circumstances, or the total discombobulation she was feeling in their wake, and she didn't exactly have a bulging address book of people who were as spiritually eccentric as she was herself. She didn't even know anyone left alive and *compos mentis*, who could shed any light on the day's events.

Her grandmother Alice, Beth's own mum, was also a white witch, and Feen had always found her to be of great comfort in the past, especially in times when nobody else in the world understood her. But Alice's mind was so addled now, with dementia, it would be hard to get a coherent word out of her. Most times, when Feen went to visit 'Anny Gralice' at the care home in Keswick, the poor

14

woman did little but stare at her in confusion. No matter what Alice might still understand (and Feen knew there wasn't much anymore), she'd long-since lost the ability to engage in a conversation about any of it. Even on her 'best' days, not much of what came out of her mouth could be classes as reliable anymore.

Feen could - and often did - talk to Beth, way over yonder in the spirit world. But there was always a limit to how much that helped, because it was usually a one-way conversation, with any communication from Beth coming more in the form of a *knowing*, an intuitive response that Feen could only feel. It wasn't the same as an actual exchange of words with anyone living who really 'got' her. And in any case, even though a one-way conversation was sometimes better than none at all, where was Beth right now? She rarely came when called, even when it really mattered. She simply turned up when she felt like it. Feen imagined her drifting around in the cosmos, utterly distracted, humming a happy tune and paying no helpful attention whatsoever to the fact that her daughter had been reduced to an emotionally disordered, blithering mess. It was hard sometimes, not to be angry with her mother. It was a monumental challenge, to be left to try and figure out everything all by herself.

At times like this, she felt her own oddness so much more profoundly. Being so different could sure as hell be lonely.

She spoke again to her guides, for what she decided would be the final time today. She'd run out of patience with them all. She decided she'd rip a hefty strip off them and then turn her back on the lot of them - for the time being, at least.

Thanks a bundle for pitching me into a pit I can't get out of. I guess I just have to accept the inevitable - that if I'm meant to be happy with someone I will be, but only when you all decide to see fit. How dolly jecent of you! But you put a man in front of me today and then you let him disappear. This, how I'm feeling now? It's your work, so maybe you can help me feel a bit less bereft and broken-hearted about it all, if you do feel so inclined. If you don't, then do me a <u>real</u> favour, and bugger off and leave me alone.

15

Chapter Two

A Song For Dad (R.I.P)

As time goes by I just can't see,
the meaning in much since you left me
Life can be savage, life can be cruel,
one day you wake up and all of the rules
You lived by...
Just no longer apply.
So I won't stop to look,
but I'll rewrite the book and I will find a way
Not to forget you, but at least not to cry
And one day I'll wake and my cheeks will be dry.

Gavin Black finally pulled up outside the front door of Teapot Cottage, turned off the engine of his Porsche Cayenne GTS, and allowed a surge of relief to wash over him. He checked his watch. It was nearly six o'clock. It had been a hell of a drive from London, via Carlisle, and he'd left at the crack of dawn. He was knackered, and his thoughts were all over the place.

He'd had a meeting in Birmingham and then taken the rare chance to catch up in Carlisle with a retired rock musician friend of his dad's, who'd suggested meeting for lunch and a wander around Carlisle's good music shops. Gavin had gone straight to the city, before driving to his rental cottage a few miles away in Torley. He was looking forward to having a quiet evening now, making a couple of important trans-Atlantic phone calls, and getting his thoughts together before his dreaded meeting tomorrow with his long-estranged mother. She lived with her parents, his Nanny and Bampa, in their rambling old 19th-century villa at the other end of Torley Valley on the outskirts of the town.

It would have suited Gavin just fine if he'd never had to see his morally impoverished mother again. In fact, he'd done his level best, for the last ten years, to make sure Carla Walton would stay out of his life for ever. But fate had rocked up and shown him that no matter how cleverly you think you've played your hand, you don't always get what you want.

Carla was about as easy as a razorblade to get along with, and he didn't suppose that had changed. Seeing her again, after so long with no contact, was going to be a tough gig. What he hadn't banked on happening as well, today, was having yet another hand-grenade hurled into the middle of his best laid plans.

Things came in threes, as the saying went. The untimely death of his dad, just two months earlier, had shaken his world to the core. Having to confront Carla on an errand that couldn't be avoided was a second devastating body-blow and, just as he was getting to grips with that too, a random eyeball encounter in Carlisle this afternoon with the tiniest, most startlingly beautiful woman he'd ever seen, had instantly reduced him to a gibbering wreck, incapable of coherent conversation.

He'd been almost rude, in excusing himself to his dad's friend, before bolting after the tiny woman who had scampered away at lightning speed. Despite his best efforts, which largely consisted of stampeding down different side streets like a demented bull, he'd been forced to admit defeat when he couldn't figure out where she'd gone. Several hours later, he was still a profoundly rattled, half-deranged mess of confusion about what had actually happened to him in the moment when his eyes had locked with hers. He just couldn't get her out of his head.

Somehow, the thought of never seeing that gorgeous girl again, of being haunted by her beautiful face forever, was almost more than Gavin could stand. But how the hell was he ever supposed to find her again in a city as big as Carlisle? He'd wandered around the streets for over an hour, trying to spot her, then he'd gone to sit in the window of a local café with a cup of very strong coffee, quietly cursing, and hoping he might catch sight of her. He wasn't lucky, and he left the city feeling utterly deflated and sad. He wasn't sure why, but it had become yet another thing to feel wretched about, as if his list of vexations wasn't already long enough.

He snapped back to the present, sighed heavily and dropped his shoulders, and pulled his light holdall from the back seat of his car. There wasn't much in it. He only intended to be here for a couple of days. In preference to staying in either of the town's potentially rowdy pubs, where he wondered if he'd get even less sleep than usual, he'd booked Teapot Cottage for the minimum requirement of a week. It would be peaceful, if nothing else and - on the bright side - if the miserable business he had to complete here with his mother did end up taking longer, at least he had the safety net of a few more days.

He found the key to the front door under the potted rosebush to the left of it, right where the owner Adrienne Raven had said it would be. He let himself in and was surprised to find the place completely unlike the typical sterile holiday house he was expecting. Teapot Cottage was unusually cosy, warm and welcoming, and he instantly felt as if he'd stepped into someone's private and much-loved home.

The cottage had been furnished and decorated thoughtfully, with a good eye for what worked. The living room was mostly cream and pale blue, and the battered beige leather sofa and matching armchair had been draped with blue waffle-cotton throws, with lime green cushions. Both of the multi-paned living room windows had generous seats built in front of them that looked inviting, with sumptuous pads and plumped-up lime and blue striped cushions. Two table lamps promised gentle light from cream-coloured shades. Heavy cream damask curtains hung at the two wide windows that gave a magnificent view of the valley.

A match-ready open fire was laid, but Gavin felt warm enough not to need it. It wasn't just the fact that it was early summer. He somehow felt as if Teapot Cottage was actually *hugging* him. He felt reassured somehow, like he'd stumbled into the embrace of someone who really cared about him. He pushed the thought away.

Cognitive overload. I'm thinking stupid things that don't make any sense.

He set his bag down on the coffee table, and wandered through to a compact but cosy and well-appointed kitchen. A fire-engine red Aga cooker with two chrome-covered hotplates dominated the space along one wall, with a traditional pulley-style wooden drying rack hoisted above it. A small Welsh dresser sat against the opposite wall, loaded with cups and dishes, and an old but sturdy pine table and six spindle-backed chairs filled the middle of the room.

A bottle of red wine sat on the table, along with a loaf of what looked to be home-made bread wrapped loosely in a tea towel, and a note propped up against both. It was from Mrs Raven, welcoming him to Teapot Cottage, and saying she would pop in and say hello, once he'd settled in. He opened the fridge door and was happily surprised to see that she'd stocked it with a pack of bacon, half a dozen eggs, a small block each of butter and cheese, and a litre of full fat milk.

Gavin found sugar and teabags in caddies on the bench, but was slightly disappointed that there wasn't at least some instant coffee. The glass coffee plunger on the bench seemed to be mocking him, and he pulled a face at it before stowing it away in a cupboard and firmly shutting the door.

It hadn't even occurred to him to pick up any provisions on the way here. He vaguely recalled having driven straight through Torley town, but he hadn't really noticed anything about it. That showed him how messed-up his head was; full of colliding and agitated thoughts that eclipsed his ability to see what was right in front of him or consider even the most basic practicalities. Thank God Mrs Raven had chosen to feed him, for his first night here, at least!

As he set the kettle fully on the Aga's hotplate and set about brewing himself a cup of tea, he reasoned that more coffee probably wasn't a great idea anyway, this late in the day. All things considered, he'd probably have enough trouble sleeping tonight as it was, without hurling a high dose of caffeine into the mix.

He didn't want to keep thinking about the last conversation he'd had with his mother on the phone from his flat in London, but he couldn't get it out of his head. It was like the red-raw socket in your gum-line where you'd just had a molar yanked out. Poking it with your tongue was profoundly unpleasant, yet you simply couldn't stop yourself from doing it.

Bloody woman.

If Gavin's recent phone call to her had been anything to judge by, Carla hadn't mellowed much in the ten years since he'd left home. She'd made it clear that she wasn't going to make it easy for him to see her. He sighed heavily, wondering why he was even surprised that nothing had changed.

He took his tea back to the living room, and plonked himself down on one of the window seats. The view of the valley was stunning. The small huddle of stone buildings that made up Torley town was just visible, nestled down in the distance.

He sat looking out at the view, and he let his mind drift back to the past. As painful as it all was, and as hard as he'd kept trying to push the past few months out of his mind, it was now all tapping at his brain again.

He realised tonight, for the first time, that he'd been actively trying to block out how he'd felt about *any* of what had happened to him lately, but sitting here now, he decided that he couldn't keep doing that. Whether he liked it or not, he knew he had no choice but to work through the events that had led to him coming up here in the first place.

You can't run away from yourself, mate. Its only ever a matter of time until you crash into yourself coming around a corner.

It was something his dad, Martin Black, had said more than once in the past, and Gavin was now starting to appreciate exactly what it meant.

Finally, he felt brave enough not to shy away from his anguish, as he had every other time it popped up and threatened to derail him. He rested his head against the cool glass of the window, and surrendered to his mind's determination to drag him back.

Carla had been so full of venom towards her 'wayward' son after he turned sixteen and realised that he could no longer manage her endlessly unpredictable, fearsome fury. He'd gone to live with his father instead, and for ten years he'd been safe there, knowing that his unhinged mother would never come within a mile of 'Traitor's Gate,' as she'd scathingly dubbed Martin's Mayfair flat.

20

But for many months after Gavin had left, she'd randomly plagued him with emails and texts, to wind him up about how he'd walked out on her just like his 'violent bully of a father' had done. Like a bored cat that persisted in pawing at a half-dead mouse, she'd revelled in reminding him that he'd gone overnight from hero to zero and was now, officially, 'the biggest disappointment of her life.'

He'd learned, over time, to stop her from getting the better of him. Whenever it took her fancy to pop up and pester him, he'd simply mention Martin in some domestic context and she'd scuttle back to her corner and go quiet for a while. To his surprise and great relief, she eventually stopped playing her crazy cat-and-mouse games with him altogether, and all had gone quiet on the Eastern front.

He never felt compelled to contact her. Why stir up a hornet's nest with someone who'd already told you, more times than you could count, that they didn't need you in their life because you were the biggest disappointment of it?

But Martin Black had died, leaving Gavin's previously protected flank exposed, and while Carla hadn't started up again, he half expected her to now, since she was bound to have heard of Martin's passing. It had been in all the papers, and even briefly on the TV news. Bush telegraph was surprisingly reliable too, when death came knocking, so he had to assume she knew, one way or another.

She hadn't contacted him to offer her condolences of course, or see how he was, but that had just been a relief, because the prospect of hearing from his mother *always* made him feel faintly queasy. Processing his own bereavement was already hard enough. The last thing he needed on the other end of a phone was his whining, mean-spirited nemesis, gloating in grotesque disrespect for the man who, despite her dire predictions, had actually done a damn fine job of raising him.

Carla was a piece of work. Their early years together as mother and son hadn't been too difficult, but as Gavin had moved into adolescence, she'd started to resent the fact that he was growing up and developing a mind of his own, and making future plans that didn't include her.

21

Needing her less, he supposed. One minute, she would be absolutely fine, but in the next she'd turn on him, screaming, accusing him of being fickle, selfish, insincere and unloving. He never knew what did or might set her off.

When walking on eggshells finally became too much of a challenge, he withdrew from her completely, and the communication gap that began between them eventually widened into a gulf that neither of them seemed to know how to bridge. She would explode over something, and half the time he never knew what, and he'd barricade himself in his room until she calmed down. She would then be all sweet and apologetic, like a child seeking forgiveness, and falling over herself to make him smile.

His immature, limited level of understanding didn't quite reach to recognising his situation as domestically abusive, but Gavin had known that Carla wasn't very 'together' compared with other mothers he knew. His friends had relatively normal parents, as far as he could tell. But although he realised that things weren't right, he didn't have the faintest idea about what to do, or even who to talk to without paralysing embarrassment, about his mother. Life with her was stressful but he balanced it as best he could by interacting with her as little as he could get away with, and making sure there were other more fruitful things going on in his life, such as meeting up with friends and writing songs and music.

The diversions helped, but it was like living cheek by jowl with a powder keg, with no idea what might set it off, or what the damage might be when it blew. There was a certain brittleness about Carla, a trembling, glass-like quality that continually kept Gavin anxious about saying or doing the wrong thing. He lived every day, wondering, if or when she'd lose the plot completely, and stand in front of him and scream until she shattered.

When he was sixteen they'd had a particularly vicious row, and he'd finally admitted defeat. He tracked down his father, packed a bag, and walked out of Carla's house. She'd screamed at him never to come back, and he'd vowed that he wouldn't, and he never had, in ten full years.

That day, he walked for nearly two hours from the East End to Mayfair, found Martin's flat, knocked on the door and simply asked the father he didn't even know, if he could live with him. He reasoned that if Martin did turn out to be the violent bully Carla always said he was, it wouldn't take him long to find out. If living with his father became unworkable, he could move on quickly enough and maybe crash with a mate for a while until he worked out what to do next.

But Martin Black had listened to his son's embarrassed, unrehearsed and stumbling speech, about being unable to live with his mother anymore and wanting to give his dad a chance. Then silently, with tears rolling down his cheeks Martin had reached out and taken Gavin's rucksack, opened the door wider, and stepped back to invite him in.

Over time, father and son got to know one other, and both made a solid and successful commitment to hauling themselves out from Carla's cold shadow. They became a tightly bonded pair, with lots in common, and shared many similar dreams.

Gavin's initial confusion about what kind of man his father really was, and the resentment Carla had fostered, were gradually replaced by respect and genuine admiration. Love settled firmly, and quietly prevailed. Finally, Gavin had a real home where he felt a sense of safety, acceptance and belonging. Getting to know his father left him completely unable to reconcile the Martin Black he came to know with the cruelty, violence and desertion Carla had accused him of. Martin didn't have a harmful bone in his body or a hurtful thought in his head, that Gavin could feel or see.

Instead, this allegedly 'selfish and aggressive bully with a volatile temper' gently cherished his vulnerable son, nurturing his dreams and visions, and actively supporting his education, both in and out of school. Both men were musical and entrepreneurial, and keen to build on their shared talents. They had the same sense of humour, and laughed a lot. They also came to the same decision, at more or less the same time, that even though Gavin hadn't done as well as he could or should have in college, he had a far greater destiny than to end up being caught up in a string of dead-end jobs that would take him precisely nowhere.

Martin was a highly skilled session musician, routinely playing with a variety of well-known artists and rock bands. He was also a patient and talented teacher to his son, and he quickly realised how clever Gavin was, musically. He willingly bankrolled a Business and Music degree, and introduced Gavin to the right influential contacts. Thanks to his father, Gavin was on his way to becoming a successful musician in his own right.

Finally, he was getting the encouragement he'd always needed, to really thrive. As soon as he legally could, he changed his name from Walton to Black, and he was surprised at how different it made him feel; like he had his own identity at last. Martin's long-time partner Mike lived elsewhere for most of the time but was a frequent, stable and loving presence in his life too, and was just as enthusiastic about his future. Secure, supported and safe, with two doting fathers, Gavin finally managed to stop feeling like the biggest disappointment of *anybody's* life.

Martin's untimely death from a brain tumour had slammed him sideways. The cancer had come quickly. In the space of six weeks, Martin had gone from complaining about feeling unusually dizzy and sick, and utterly exhausted by doing the smallest tasks, to being gone from the world completely. With no time for a space between shock and grief, Gavin and Mike had clung together like two men drowning, with their lifeboat gone.

The funeral - Gavin's first - had been brutal. At the same time, curiously, it had been the most wonderful, glorious, uproarious celebration of Martin's life. Mike had helped him make the simple but thoughtful arrangements for his father, which had included an ear-shattering motorcycle escort of more than forty friends with vintage machines, accompanying the beautifully restored BSA motorcycle and sidecar that carried Martin's coffin on his last journey from the funeral home, past his flat and the recording studio he'd spent so many years working in, and on to the crematorium. As terrified as Gavin was, at the thought of damaging the rarest and most expensive bike in his father's entire vintage motorcycle collection, he had ridden Martin's 1948 Vincent Black Lightning as part of that entourage, with his heart in his mouth to go with the lump in his throat.

A surprisingly cheerful wake had been held back at the flat, with Martin's favourite rock songs playing in the background and caterers supplying food and drink for the huge crowd who'd turned up. Anyone who wanted to share a special story or memory of Martin was warmly invited to do so and many people did, including a good handful of the high-profile rock stars he'd worked with. A lot of folk had clearly thought the world of Martin Black.

Later, some musician friends had taken a turn on the various instruments that were permanently set up in the flat's sound-proofed basement, with everyone cramming in to listen. Gavin played keyboards, with Mike on drums. Others stepped in with bass and rhythm guitars. One friend, the lead singer in a well-known band, happily provided vocals and the result was an impromptu jam session with an excellent rendition of Martin's all-time favourite song – Led Zeppelin's Stairway to Heaven - to top it all off. Everyone sang along with that one, some holding their mobile phones aloft to shine a light to their departed friend. It was a truly fitting musical tribute to a man much loved by many, and Gavin knew that what everyone had said was true; their dearly loved father, partner, colleague and friend would have been thrilled beyond belief about every aspect of the day that was dedicated to him in farewell, and in celebration of his extraordinary life.

Darkness had settled by the time everyone had finally gone. Mike had drawn the curtains in the living room, opened a bottle of scotch and handed a glass to Gavin. Battling with emotional exhaustion, the two men had finally been able to sit quietly, with enough space and privacy to acknowledge their own feelings about the funeral, and gently honour a man they'd both loved very deeply.

But, what Mike had gone on to share that night, had left Gavin stunned and even more bereft. While reminiscing about the past, Mike had told him about Martin's terrible nightmares in the early days of their relationship; how often Mike had tried to soothe him and reassure him he was safe.

Gavin learned that his father had suffered abuse from Carla Walton that had left him emotionally traumatized, isolated and ashamed. He heard how hard Martin had fought, in vain, to be a part of his son's life before Gavin had turned up at his door. He also learned just how heartbroken Martin had been, at being forced to leave him with his seriously unsound mother.

Martin hadn't simply deserted his family, as Carla had always maintained. He'd been forced out, with no recourse or legal access to his child, since she'd never named him as Gavin's father on the birth certificate. It was hard for a man in Martin's position, officially labelled as a violent bully and deserter, to lay claim to his son. Taking a vicious, vitriolic Carla Walton on in court was more than he could manage, already emotionally beaten, and with the limited resources available to help him fight his corner. At the time, Martin had been broke; still trying to make his name in the music world, and the pair had not been married. They'd only lived together, and Carla had gone to great lengths to prove that Martin was a violent and emotionally unpredictable, unfit father.

'He was abusive', she'd said. 'He used to hurt me, and if I'd let him stay, he'd have hurt you too.'

But as Gavin discovered from his father's lover, every last allegation Carla had made against Martin had been completely untrue. He'd only ever hurt her once, and completely unintentionally, as he'd innocently brushed past her in the garden. She'd lost her footing and fallen, hitting her face on a concrete fencepost, blacking her eye and fracturing her cheekbone. Her face had swelled up like a watermelon. It was an unfortunate, freak accident, but she'd twisted it to suit her own purposes, namely having Martin officially condemned in court as a thug and an unfit parent.

After finding out that Martin was gay and had fallen in love with another man, the accident in the garden had been the final straw for her. Punishing him in such a terrible way, for not being willing or able to commit to her, was the only weapon she had; that and the son she withheld through a court injunction and a carefully constructed tapestry of lies so damaging it had taken Herculean efforts to unpick.

Gavin had been devastated. 'Jesus, Mike! Why the fuck did he never tell me any of this?'

Mike had looked at him with eyes full of love and concern. 'He wanted to protect you, mate, to shield you from the truth,' he said quietly, in his well-rounded Cockney accent.

'Carla's your mother. He convinced himself that whatever she did, way back then, she couldn't control herself. He just wrote her off as mentally ill or something, and maybe she was. Who knows? He was kind enough to forgive her a long time ago, for what she did to him.'

Mike had laughed then, shortly, and without humour. 'I don't know how he managed to do that, to be honest, but he did. He was a far better man than I could ever be, as far as that went.'

He'd shrugged and continued. 'But she's still your mother. Martin never wanted you to know what she'd done. Because you're an only child, with no siblings to fall back on, he was hopeful that in some way you'd eventually patch things up with her and end up having a decent relationship. He thought it might help you to have that, especially because you still have *her* parents, your Nanny and Bampa, and he couldn't let anything he might tell you get in the way of your chance to maybe one day reconnect properly with them too.

'He was just a kid when his mum died, and his dad disowned him years ago. They never reconciled before the old bastard died, so there's little chance of you having any meaningful connections on his side of the family. You have to appreciate too, Gavin, that there was also a lot of shame, in the context of his situation.'

His stepfather went on to explain. 'Back in the day, domestic abuse didn't get the attention it gets nowadays. Despite what the law might've said, it was still tough enough for a woman to get good support from the authorities when she was being beaten or controlled by a man. It was unimaginable, for a *man* to admit that he was being abused by a *woman*. Your dad was already dealing with more prejudice than he should have, just for being gay. He suffered in silence over being abused because there was nowhere to go to get help, and he felt that nobody would have taken him seriously even if there was. Even his own father - who'd already written him off as an 'evil poof' don't forget - didn't believe him! You can't imagine the impact of that.'

27

Mike had taken a long swig of his whisky, and carried on. 'As far as your dad was concerned, his relationship with your mother was long dead and buried, and his relationship with you since you arrived here a decade ago was everything it needed to be. The truth about what had happened in *their* relationship would only have hurt you. He never wanted that. He thought you'd been hurt enough.'

'So, if that was what he wanted, why have you told me now?'

Mike hadn't answered straight away. Instead, he'd twirled what was left of his scotch around in his glass and started at it for a few moments, clearly considering his words carefully before he'd said them. Then he'd taken a very deep breath.

'Because while Martin could forgive your mother for what she did, Gavin, I couldn't. I was the one who sat with him though too many tough nights to count, for years, while he struggled to process and accept everything, including things he couldn't confide to me straight away. His shame was crippling. I was the one who encouraged him into therapy and went with him to most of the sessions, and some of those were incredibly painful. Brutal, Gavin, and not just for him but for me too.

'I was the one who saw and dealt with the agony he suffered from that bitch, *and* from being cut off from you. I mended him. With love, and with the patience that *comes* with the kind of love I had for your dad, I mended him.'

Mike's voice had grown slightly defensive, and Gavin had known better than to interject or ask any further questions. The man clearly had a lot of his own resentment sitting on his chest and needed to offload it.

'Your mother tried to destroy Martin's dreams, Gavin. She ruined his reputation in his local community, and a lot of opportunities he might've had were ruined along with that. He was marked as a violent thug, who wouldn't support his own child, which was bollocks because he absolutely *did* pay money to Carla, every single month for you, for the whole time you were with her. It was all she would let him do. There are bank statements to prove it, mate. He sent letters and cards too, always, at Christmas and birthdays, but they always got returned. They're all in the bottom drawer in our bedroom, if you want to see for yourself how hard he tried to reach out to you.'

Mike had shaken his head. 'So many damaging lies. So much wilful destruction. You don't know what that does to a man's chances in life. He was harshly judged. It was heart-breaking. And he had to fight like a dog to rebuild his life, but he did it.'

Mike had then put down his glass and faced Gavin squarely.

'I'm sorry, but your mother isn't just a 'bit-of-a-trick' to get along with, son. She was - and probably still is - is a bitter, twisted piece of pestilence, and I don't think you should be shielded from that anymore. You're not a child anymore, Gavin. You're a grown man in your own right, old enough to have kids of your own, in fact, and I know your dad wouldn't agree with me telling you all this.

'He'd be outraged, I imagine, but I need to do the right thing by him and tell you the truth about who he really was. He was a good man who suffered greatly, and he didn't deserve to, and I think it's only right that you know that.'

He'd picked up his glass again, and taken another sip from it.

'And what's more, I love you every bit as much as your dad did. Carla Walton is an abomination, but she's still your mother, which means she still has the power to hurt you, and I worry about that. I always have, and I think the day was always going to come when you needed to know exactly how destructive she's been, so you could stand up to her if it ever came to that.'

Mike had smiled softly, then. 'You know, I remember when you first arrived here, bewildered, and broken-hearted. I never want you to feel those things again because of her. I want to strip that power away from her and arm you instead.'

He'd drained his glass and looked at Gavin squarely.

'If you think I've done the wrong thing by telling you, I'm sorry. But I do stand by it, Gavin. And another thing. As a gay man, I was never destined to have kids of my own. You're the closest thing I've ever had to a son, and I want to carry on loving you and treating you as if you were mine, because to all intents and purposes you are. I promised Martin I'd do that, if you'll let me, and I really hope you will. It's just that my way of loving and protecting you isn't to mend or shield you, like Martin's way was. My way is to enable you. I want you to be able to protect *yourself*, and you have to know what you're really up against, to

29

do that properly. Because she might try to wheedle her way back into your life, mate, now that it's changed.'

Maybe now that she can smell money around you.

Mike hadn't voiced that final thought, but it had hung in the air as if he had. The two men had sat in silence for a long time, until Gavin had cleared his throat and spoken. His voice had been husky with unshed tears.

'I'm so glad he had you, Mike. He had proper love in his life, the kind he really deserved. I'll always be thankful for that. Thank you for loving him, for being his rock. Thank you for loving me too. And yes please, since I've been luckier than most to have two great dads and I've now lost one, it's more important than ever that we stay close. I do want that. I need it. And I know the inheritance is a big one, even after all the taxes, so I wouldn't be at all surprised if she does come knocking. Thanks too, for preparing me for that.'

Over the ensuing days and weeks, Gavin's grief and profound sense of loss had jostled for prime position with a deep simmering anger and resentment towards his mother. For his whole life, he'd grappled with his feelings for Carla, and it was no easier now than it had ever been. Part of him wanted to show up at Nanny and Bampa's house, kick the front door off its hinges, and pin that deranged mess of a mother to the wall by her throat. He wisely sat on that emotion until it passed, and he waited until his brain bounced back towards some semblance of rationality, where he could at least try to be semi-objective about the woman's warped motives, and hopefully get her out of his head.

Gavin's life was musical, meaningful and happy, with the potential to become something truly remarkable and special. He wasn't willing to risk disrupting all of that by allowing the kind of toxicity that seemed to seep through every one of his mother's pores to tarnish or perhaps even destroy any of what he'd so carefully started working towards. He didn't need to be belittled or 'diminished' anymore.

No. Life with her back in it would be hell.

That decision was helped a lot, he mused now, by the fact that she'd moved back up here to the Lake District, years ago, to be closer to her ageing parents. He didn't know what kind of life she'd managed to make for herself when she'd come back to her childhood home, and he didn't much care. His relationship with her was non-existent, and he'd have been more than happy for it to have stayed that way, if a sticky situation hadn't cropped up that had left him compelled to contact her.

After Martin's funeral, a letter had arrived from one of his dad's old school mates. It was a very touching letter, offering condolences and apologising for only just having learned about Martin's passing, and expressing the most profound regret at having missed his chance to pay his respects at his old friend's funeral. In that letter, he shared a couple of his own lovely memories of Martin, which Gavin appreciated very much. It made him smile to think of his father as a young, carefree, bike-riding boy, playing hide and seek with his childhood pal in woodlands long-since bulldozed and covered with shops and houses.

But, in his letter, the friend had also asked if he could have a copy of a certain photograph that he knew Martin had, of a particular school-year class they'd shared.

Gavin had no knowledge of such a photo, and after painstakingly going through Martin's things, he drew a blank. He asked Mike what he might know about it, and was dismayed to learn that there had been a box of Martin's personal effects, including things like letters he'd received from his grandfather, photographs, and mementoes of different kinds. Mike was pretty sure there were at least two of Martin's grandfather's medals in the box, along with his grandmother's wedding ring and lace wedding handkerchief.

That box of treasured keepsakes had meant the world to Martin, but Carla had kept it. She had hidden it somewhere, and refused point blank to let him have it when she threw him out. It was just another weapon she had at her disposal, to hold over him. Mike said he even went round to her house once himself, to try and talk her into giving it back, but she'd screamed a barrage of homophobic obscenities in his face and he'd beaten a hasty retreat.

He confessed that the incident had occurred many years ago, and he'd long-since forgotten about it. He wondered if maybe the old photographs in that box would include the one Martin's old friend had asked about, and suggested that maybe Gavin should try to get the box back. 'Supposing she still has it,' he'd added.

The prospect was deeply unpalatable, but Martin's little family heirlooms now rightfully belonged to him, and he'd found himself in a difficult position. As unhappy as he was about the prospect of contacting Carla, he knew he had the right to Martin's box of treasured keepsakes. It was something he found himself badly wanting, knowing he would also treasure what was in there himself; important links to his paternal ancestry.

Carla choosing to withhold such important sentimental things proved how ruthless and selfish she was. She was clearly devoid of any empathy or compassion at all, and the thought of going up against her, to try and get his father's box back, made Gavin's stomach churn.

But what was more important? Being too much of a coward to face his foul mother and run the risk of having her trying to worm her way back into his life, or being able to have and cherish what had been important to his dad? Gavin already knew the answer.

So he'd called her. He still had her number stored in his phone; not so he could ever call her but so he could ignore her if she ever called him. She'd answered on the fourth ring, just as he was dreading having to leave a message. Her greeting was curt, wary.

'Gavin, is that you?' So she still had his number stored too!

'Hello, Mum. Yeah, long time no speak.'

There was silence at Carla's end. He took a deep breath.

'Mum, I wondered if I could see you, sometime soon?'

'Why?' Her question was guarded.

'I just want to have a chat with you about a few things, mostly related to Dad. I know you probably won't want to, but it's nothing too heavy, and I'd really appreciate it.'

'Would you, indeed?' she'd said silkily. 'And why now? If you're looking to kiss and make up, it's a bit late for that, don't you think? You made a choice, and I've had to live with it. Having trouble living with it yourself now, are you?'

Gavin was literally unable to find anything to say, to that.

Carla's tone had then become scathing. 'And you're right about one thing. There's nothing I want to say to you or anybody else about that scumbag. I'm glad he'd dead, and that's *all* I've got to say about it.'

Gavin had closed his eyes and counted to five, before playing the only card he had. 'I know, Mum, and I appreciate your position. I really do. I know it's asking you to open a can of worms, but I've just got some questions, and I wouldn't ask you if it wasn't important. He was my dad, and once upon a time you at least liked him enough to have sex with him and create me. Help me, Mum. Please? Meet me for coffee or something, just an hour or so. It would be good to see you,' he'd added, feeling desperate.

'Oh, would it, Gavin? Now I've got something you want, information you want - or at least you think I do, you decide it would be good to see me? Tell me. If you didn't think I could do you a bloody favour, would you even be ringing me?'

Gavin had stayed silent.

'That's what I thought. Either you've no answer at all or you don't want to say it. Either way, it means I'm just convenient for you right now. And once you've got what you want, assuming I can provide it, that will be the end of it, right? You'll just fade back into the brickwork, yes?'

To give her credit, she hadn't yelled, like she always used to. But her tone had been cold and uncompromising. Clearly, that much hadn't changed.

'So, tell me. Why should I help you? Come on, Gavin. Explain to me why I should suddenly step up for you now, when you haven't given me the time of day for a decade. I don't even know what you look like, these days, do I?' Her laugh had been hollow, humourless.

'Well, I dunno, Mum. Maybe you could help me because you're the only person who can? Maybe there's a chance that we can at least be friends or something now, after all this time?' Gavin had sighed. 'And maybe the reality of being an only child disconnected from everyone left in my family is finally taking its toll, Mum.'

The silence on the end of the phone had lengthened until he'd felt like crying with frustration. Then, his mother had spoken again.

'Well, alright. You've managed to convince me. But if you want to see me, you'll have to come up here. You're very much mistaken if you think I care enough to waste my time traipsing back to bloody London just for you.'

'That's fine Mum. I don't mind at all, coming up to you. It would be lovely to see Nanny and Bampa, after all this time.'

After making arrangements with his mother, Gavin had hung up feeling faintly sick, and determined to focus on seeing his beloved grandparents again as the only real advantage of an encounter he wasn't looking forward to one bit. It had felt incredibly unfair, that Carla living with Nanny and Bampa had precluded him for far too long, from spending precious time with them. There had been letters, cards, and even the occasional phone call from Bampa, to see how he was, and update him, but he hadn't actually seen them in the flesh since he was about twelve, and his memory of that wasn't as clear as he wanted it to be.

Dragging his focus back to the present now, he drained his mug of tea and looked out to the panoramic view of Torley valley as the sun hung low across it. Like a rogue wave, the image of the beautiful, tiny woman he'd seen in Carlisle came crashing back into his head.

Where is that utterly gorgeous creature now?

Suddenly, he was inexplicably bereft again, and restless. Unable to separate his constantly colliding thoughts about his despicable mother, the eviscerating loss of his father, and an ethereally beautiful little woman who had turned him inside out before disappearing off the face of the earth, he decided he couldn't just sit here with his head like a blender. He made up his mind to drive back into Torley town and see if he could at least find a shop that sold decent coffee. He would need some, first thing in the morning. He was starving too, but not really in the mood for eggs and bacon. A good-sized ready meal wouldn't go amiss, he decided. He could at least trust that old red Aga with something as basic as reheating.

Chapter Three

'Great!' Carla muttered to herself, through tightly clenched teeth, as she stared out through her bedroom window. For once, the tranquil, typically soul-restoring view of the lush rolling fields lying west of Fellyn Ridge couldn't calm her jagged nerves. 'Just bloody brilliant. This is all I need.'

After nearly ten years of no contact with her son Gavin, she could hardly believe he'd had the audacity to just ring out of the blue and ask if they could meet. Talk about bare-faced bloody cheek! He'd talked her into saying yes, too, a lot more easily than she'd have liked. She felt irritated, and decidedly wrongfooted.

Seeing that traitorous little toerag again is something I can do without. Why the hell have I agreed to it? What does he think I am, a pushover?

But that particular thought, so typical of her normal pattern, felt quite incongruous now, which wrong-footed her even more. With every fibre of her being, she wanted to be highly indignant and resentful at having been 'press-ganged' into agreeing to see her estranged son. She tried to summon up a level of outrage that would put her back on familiar mental ground but somehow, maddeningly, she couldn't seem to pull that off. Her 'righteous indignation,' which was usually bubbling and seething fairly close to the surface, stubbornly refused to fully materialise. It hovered around her instead, as a persistently unobliging bubble of thought that really didn't seem to know where to put itself.

Carla was confused and deeply uncomfortable about the prospect of meeting Gavin, especially as she knew how hard she'd struggle just to look him in the eye.

What she really felt now wasn't anger. It was fear, and - frustratingly - it wasn't the kind that could make her mad. Instead of rearing up and fighting her corner like she usually did, with all guns blazing and her emerald eyes flashing with fire, Carla just wanted to *close* her eyes and run; as fast and as far away as possible.

35

Martin Black had told her, as a parting shot, that she could only ever run away from herself for so long before she smacked into herself coming around a corner. Her psychotherapist, Dawn Mott, had repeatedly alluded to something similar - that people suffering from towering levels of guilt and shame could never fully escape from them. There wasn't a safe place to run to and hide. For the anguished, confronting and conquering their demons was really the only option if they wanted to be free of them, and go on to live some semblance of a happy life.

Carla had understood that, and she'd agreed with Dawn in principle, but she hadn't yet got to the point where she felt ready to stop playing hide and seek with the hellions in her own head. They might be monsters, but they were *familiar* ones. Sometimes there was a reassurance, even a comfort, in a discomfort you'd learned to live with. Sometimes, it was easier to keep things as they were, than poke a stick at them and watch or feel all hell break loose.

Better the devil you know.

She closed her eyes as her gut clenched. Meeting her son again and dealing with whatever he planned to throw at her was probably part of the horrible process Dawn kept wittering on about, that she thought Carla needed to undertake. Confronting herself, meeting her internal gremlins head-on, all that damn nonsense. Did Gavin's call mean that the hand of fate was forcing her to do that now, whether she liked it or not? Dawn would probably say, in her irritatingly relentless quest to drag everything out into the open; that the time had clearly come, to deal to some of her demons. To Carla, it felt like the devil himself showing up at the door, as an unwanted guest at a party.

Of course it *did* make sense, and it probably *was* time to grab this particular bull by the horns. But Carla knew that while meeting up with Gavin again might be a simple thing to do on the one hand, it was as complicated as hell on the other. It meant turning the corner Martin had talked about, when all she wanted was to stay on her safe straight road, going forward.

Could she finally find the courage now, to stop and turn, and look back?

Before today, she hadn't had a civil conversation with Gavin in ten years. Their relationship had more or less ended when he'd left home in a colossal huff, vowing to never come back, and she'd muttered 'good riddance' under her breath as he'd slammed the front door on his way out. She'd told herself that it was probably for the best; that she could do without having an acne-infested, lank-haired, grunting little Neanderthal, all moody and continually fed up and sulking, hanging around the house.

She'd found out straight away that he'd gone to his father's. Martin had messaged her himself, to let her know Gavin was safe. She'd been grateful for that at least, even though her gut had lurched in panic as she'd wondered how quickly he'd discover what had really happened in her and Martin's relationship. But when no angry young man had turned up back on her doorstep, demanding answers, kicking the door and shouting the odds, she'd started to relax a little. If Gavin knew the truth, he'd kept quiet about it. Carla figured if that was the case, he'd probably long-since decided she wasn't worth his effort. He'd be so disgusted with her that she'd probably just never hear from him again.

She'd got away with telling herself for ten years now that the persistent silence coming from Traitor's Gate was better than being confronted with realities that were far too uncomfortable to explain. As she'd kept insisting to herself, it was great to only have to think about her own wants and needs, and if her son had wanted her in his life he'd have found space and time for her. He'd kept his distance instead and she told herself, enough times to be *almost* convinced, that it suited her just fine.

She wasn't in the best place to argue about Gavin preferring to be with his father anyway, even if the truth hadn't come out. If she was being honest with herself (and it seemed that she was now being unwittingly dragged to a place where she had to at least start *trying* to be), she hadn't blamed him for absconding. She knew she'd been bitter and insufferable. Having to take his desertion on the chin was, she supposed, a fair enough punishment for the lies she'd told for so long she'd literally begun to believe them herself, to the point where it hadn't been hard to convince an impressionable young boy.

The psychotherapy she'd started a year ago was helping her to make some sense of herself, but it wasn't easy. Recognising the darkest side of oneself was a hard thing for anyone to do, especially when - as in Carla's case - it involved being spiteful enough to have committed a crime of unspeakable cruelty.

Last year, a woman called Adie Bostock had gone to house sit at a cottage at the edge of Ravensdown Farm, and had caught the attention of the farm's owner, Mark Raven, who Carla had been casually dating at the time. After what Carla saw as the other woman swiping her last chance at romance right from under her nose, she'd been hell-bent on revenge.

Destroying the house-owners' lawn with her father's four-wheel drive had felt harmless enough, but she'd taken her attempts to get Adie Bostock run out of town a step too far, by sneaking up to Teapot Cottage and poisoning the dog she was looking after. The police had got involved, and Carla had been charged with criminal damage. She'd ended up being hauled through the county court and collecting a criminal record. She'd then been directed by the judge to complete her community service at the local vet, where she came to appreciate how important cherished pets really were to their owners. As a result, she'd finally found enough insight and self-loathing to admit that she was out of control and needed professional help.

Quite simply, jealousy had taken hold and made her monstrous, and the crazy thing was, she'd already *known* that Mark Raven hadn't wanted a serious thing! He'd been tactful, and he'd acted like a gentleman every time he'd rebuffed her advances, but she'd consistently chosen to ignore him.

Her cheeks burned with embarrassment now as she recalled, with cringing clarity, how she'd hurled herself so shamelessly at a man who had already made it clear, more than once, that he didn't really want her.

Where the hell was my pride?

Dawn had offered insight and encouragement to Carla, to explore that part of herself, the 'desperate' part, and work out why hooking up with a thoroughly incompatible man had mattered so much at the time.

It was a true revelation, that it came down her inability to like herself until she thought someone else liked her first. Talking that through had left her with the inescapable fact that the reverse was far more true. On some level at least, she had to begin to like *herself* before anyone else would have a hope, and learning to

38

like herself had to start with being accountable and honest about who she really was, and what had *made* her who she was.

But she still wasn't ready to go there.

She turned her thoughts back to Gavin again, and wondered what sort of man he'd turned into.

He was pretty pathetic when he left. Wouldn't say boo to a goose. He reminded me of Martin, I suppose, and I guess that's why I treated him the same way. He sounded like he had a bit more about him on the phone though. It'll be interesting to see what Martin's made of him.

Martin Black had been one of the good guys. Carla had long ago stopped pretending to herself that he hadn't been, but she still wasn't able to comfortably admit that she'd despised him for the strengths she'd chosen to see as weaknesses. He was quiet, nurturing, patient, gentle and sweet, and she'd savaged him for it. Eventually, overcome with disgust at his inability to really stand up to her, she'd found the only weapon she felt she could use. She'd dragged him through the courts and had him thoroughly condemned, and she'd prevented him from seeing their son.

It was so ironic, that Gavin had ended up with him anyway. She had no choice but to hope that her ex would shape him well. It went without saying, that Gavin had a better shot at being a decent human being living with his father, than he'd have had if he'd stayed with her. There was a weird sort of solace in that, at least.

In the beginning, though, it seemed as if Martin had swallowed her little boy whole. Her initial attempts to communicate had fallen on deaf ears. Her overtures had been hostile and antagonistic, because that was all she'd known how to be for far too long, but the penny had only recently dropped, after Dawn asked a critical question;

'If your communications are hostile, how can you expect a positive response?'

The whole miserable, vicious cycle was suddenly crystal clear to her then; that the more she was ignored, the more frustrated and angry she got, the more she lashed out at the person who'd 'caused' it, and the more that person withdrew. In a painful process of self-examination that had still barely even started after a full year of dithering, Carla came to see that she'd hoisted herself with her own petard. It was her *own* antipathy that had prevented her from being able to mend any fences with Gavin. It wasn't something she could carry on blaming *him* for!

Back in the day, she'd still hated Martin with a vengeance, so going to the flat hadn't been an option. Neither was arranging to see Gavin somewhere neutral, because he'd probably have been expecting some kind of apology, and although she'd kept telling herself she had nothing to be sorry for, she'd known deep down that it wasn't the truth. Gavin *did* deserve an explanation, and the biggest apology imaginable. She had more to make up to him for than she could ever realistically hope to, but she also knew that eating humble pie on a scale that big was more than she could face.

No; she'd decided, a long time ago, that it was far better to leave the past where it was. Deep down, she loved Gavin as much as any mother could love her own child, and she only wanted what was best for him. Letting a sleeping dog lie was the right choice for them both. At least, that's what she'd always tried to tell herself, especially on those nights where being in the house alone felt a little more wretched than usual, when the feel of her own heartbeat - as proof that she even existed - simply nauseated her, and when the longing to see him was so strong that it almost robbed her of her breath.

Now, she faced the very real prospect of being confronted by that grown-up boy, and having to admit her own destructive, devastating, life-changing lies to him. The thought made her stomach clench with fear.

Knowing what a bitch you've been is one thing. Having the guts to admit it to the person who matters most to you, who probably already hates you, is something else again.

What could she tell him, if he asked her? There were no half-decent excuses, and no good reasons she could yet admit to, for what she'd done and said, all those years ago. He must know that too, so what else could he possibly want, after all this time? Did he still want to hold her accountable? Or was he simply feeling the loss of his father so keenly that even an embittered, 'monstrous' mother was still a better prospect than no parent at all?

40

Maybe he does know the truth, and maybe he does want to get in front of me and condemn me to my face.

But it really hadn't sounded like it, which only fuelled her confusion. He'd seemed far more reasonable than she deserved for him to be, on the phone. There was no anger or coldness in his voice, no animosity, no bitterness or censure. He hadn't implied that he was about to accuse her of anything. He wanted to see her, simply, briefly, and that was all he'd said. Something to do with Martin, yes, but she didn't know what.

People said it was being on the wrong side of fifty that made women in midlife as irritable, anxious and confused as Carla was feeling now. In all fairness, her oestrogen levels *were* still a little in free-fall, after the 'change' that had started early for her. Premature menopause, her doctor had confirmed, when she'd been barely forty.

She had already more or less accepted, at the time, that Gavin would probably never have a brother or a sister, and at the point of diagnosis she was already sliding quietly past the age where she might comfortably consider having another child even if an opportunity presented itself. But the door slamming shut so early was still a colossal shock. It was one thing, to not want to have another child, but having the choice completely ripped away was another thing altogether.

It hadn't yet occurred to Carla that so much of her enduring anger was grounded in grief. She wasn't even aware that she even had a list of 'things' to grieve for. And she certainly hadn't considered the fact that the death-knell for her fertility might be on it.

The menopause had been a feature of her life for nearly ten years now, but the symptoms were slowly tapering off. Crippling hormonal headaches had been a bitch to be managed, but they only came occasionally now. All things considered, her change of life was nowhere near as bad as what some of the women she knew were going through. Her process was long, and uncomfortable at times, but it wasn't crucifying. By comparison, she'd had an easy ride. It was great to have an end to a lifetime of painful periods too. She clung to that, as the upside.

But the plain truth was that the problem of her readiness to fly off the handle went much deeper than anything that could be blamed on helter-skelter hormones. She'd been angry and unhappy for as long as she could remember – for a long time prior to anything that could be explained away as menopause. She couldn't remember a time when she *hadn't* been bitter and enraged about *something*, even when she didn't know exactly what it was, and even after a full year of therapy, she was still trying to figure out how to be less caustic when she was hurting. That ongoing, age-old reluctance to meet herself coming around a corner wasn't helping. Dawn kept asking Carla to stop wasting her own time and money, and start talking 'properly,' and it was getting to the point where continuing to ignore her request was becoming even *more* of a chore and a bore than the sessions were themselves. Carla couldn't even answer her own question as to why she kept showing up there every week.

Damn that bloody boy! Why couldn't he have just left me alone? I've a good mind to ring him back and tell him to sling his hook. I don't need him waltzing in here, dragging up the past for everyone to get upset about. I'm doing just fine without all that, thanks very much.

But something deep within Carla wouldn't let her ring Gavin back. As much as she dreaded seeing him, and having to confront some potentially hellish consequences that might mean she'd *neve*r have another good night's sleep, the desire to see what sort of man he'd become was far too tempting to ignore.

She would meet him, as agreed. But she was astonished now, in that decision, to be fighting back an avalanche of grief and pain. And, in her age-old habit of needing to be 'as strong as steel,' even when there was nobody there to witness her turmoil, it didn't even occur to her that it might be okay - just for once - to let her tears fall.

Chapter Four

A Spell to Quell a Confused and Aching Heart

You will need:
Four heads of lavender flowers
A large, fresh maple leaf
An oil burner and tealight candle
Two drops of rose oil
White cotton
A tablespoon of distilled water

Place the water in the top of the oil burner,
add the two drops of rose oil, and lay the maple leaf on top.
Tie the four heads of lavender flowers in a cross-formation with
the white cotton and lay them on top of the maple leaf.
Place the lighted candle inside the burner to heat the
concoction. Allow the water to heat the leaves and flowers,
but do not allow the 'brew' to become too hot.
Place the middle finger of each hand against your temples and
let your thumbs touch, under your chin,
and inhale the aroma gently. Incantation (once):
'The path to acceptance is full of thorns,
allow me the space and time to mourn.
But if what is lost is meant to be,
return it please, with my heart, to me'

Feen looked up from her book and frowned as her stepmother Adie came running into the living room at full speed, clearly in a bit of a panic.

'Aren't you supposed to be at your yoga class, Adie? I thought it started at seven?'

'It does!' Adie wailed, looking at the little carriage clock on the mantlepiece. 'But I can't get my bloody car started! I don't know what's wrong with the stupid thing. It's such an old wreck. I do keep meaning to replace it, and Mark badgers me about it from time to time, but somehow I just never get around to doing anything.' She shook her head, as if to clear it.

'I'll have to, soon though, I guess. It'll break down on me one day when I'm a million miles from anywhere and I'll kick myself to Kingdom come. I don't suppose you could give me a lift, could you? I can probably get Trudie or Sheila, or another friend, to drop me home again.'

'Sure, just let me get my keys.' Feen grabbed her handbag and rummaged around in it. She ushered Adie out the door and into her own car, and as they set off down the driveway, her stepmother exclaimed again.

'Honestly! Where did this afternoon go? I've been so busy helping your dad with the seed delivery since I finished getting Teapot Cottage ready, I haven't even had time to check on the new tenant, to see if he's settled in or needs anything.' She nodded towards the sleek black Porsche Cayenne parked in front of Teapot Cottage. 'His car is there, look. I think he arrived about an hour ago. Would you mind just checking in with him on your way back?'

Adie rifled through her yoga bag. 'Could you also please give him this pack of ground coffee, and my apologies for forgetting to take it down with me earlier? I'd really appreciate it. I'm sure he will too. His name is Mr Black. I don't know much about him, but I think he's here alone.'

Feen nodded. 'Sure thing, although you always make everything so lovely, people never usually want anything more, do they?'

'Not usually, no. But it's nice just to touch base, to make sure people feel welcomed, and let them know they can come on up to the farmhouse if they do need something or have any

44

questions. And I did forget to supply coffee, which is critically important to most guests.'

Adie peered at Feen and frowned. 'Are you ok, darling? You look a little peaky, and you've been a bit quiet since you got back from town.'

Feen considered telling Adie about having fallen hopelessly and irretrievably in love with a random stranger she'd never even spoken to, and would probably never see again, and decided it would take too much explaining even if she *didn't* disintegrate into a full-blown blubbering mess while she tried. Besides, even if Adie understood (and Feen suspected that she might), there just wasn't time to get into it right now. Adie would only just make it to her yoga class on time as it was. Feen didn't want her to end up being properly late after feeling obliged to sit in the car acting as counsellor to her distraught and semi-hysterical stepdaughter. She shrugged, sighed, and gave a small, self-deprecating smile.

'Yeah, I'm fine, Adie. Just a bit out of sorts, an off-day, you know? Just stuff, messing with my head. I'm sure I'll be fine tomorrow.' Even as she said the words, she knew she wouldn't be.

Adie smiled sympathetically. 'Well, we're all entitled to an off-day. Take it easy tonight, darling. Have a hot bath with lots of bubbles, eat some chocolate, have a couple of glasses of wine, and watch some brainless rom-com on telly.'

Feen inwardly cringed. *Oh, God! Watch a movie where some unfeasibly gorgeous young woman falls in love with a ridiculously handsome Mr Nice-guy and gets to marry him? No way. That happily-ever-after crap would be the worst form of torture, tonight.*

She didn't say as much, merely nodded, and dropped Adie off at the community centre.

'Have fun, and call me if you do need a ride home.'

Minutes later, she pulled up at Teapot Cottage, behind the gorgeous, gleaming black Porsche. She got out of her car and was about to walk towards the front door when it suddenly opened and she looked up. In the instant that she did so, the breath was once again sucked straight out of her lungs, as the cottage's tenant came striding purposefully towards her.

This time, there was nowhere to run. Even if there was, Feen's feet would not have complied. She was rooted to the spot.

She put out a hand to steady herself against her car as he came forward and stopped just inches away from her. He had the most gorgeous green eyes she'd ever seen. They were like emeralds, bright and glittering, and full of life and fire. She knew those eyes were real. They weren't some coloured contact lenses designed for dazzling effect. He had long, thick black lashes to die for too, and the overall effect was utterly mesmerizing.

His gaze was intense, before he blinked hard, twice.

'You! You're actually here! Thank *God!*'

He looked up to the heavens and threw up his hands. 'Thank you, God, for answering my prayer.'

Thank you Spirit, for answering mine!

'Why did you run away?' he demanded. 'You left me panicking, thinking I'd never see you again. I must have run for bloody miles chasing after you. More to the point, how the hell did you know where to find me? This place isn't exactly on the beaten track to anywhere, as far as I can see.'

His voice was low, articulate, quite deep, and almost musical. The accent was Home Counties, and the pitch was both energising and soporific at the same time. It was a storyteller's voice, the kind that could either keep you completely enthralled or send you to sleep, depending on the circumstances. It was one hell of a sexy voice too, and she knew she would never tire of hearing it. Something inside her shuddered deliciously as she wondered what that voice might murmur in her ear, in an intimate moment.

'You remember me from Carlisle.' She spoke, rather than asked.

His eyes looked deep into hers, and her heart fell. Again.

'Of course I do', he said softly. 'What was I supposed to do - just somehow forget that you'd totally stolen my heart and my rational brain, and run off with them both? Try and think about something, *anything* else, for more than a nanosecond? Sweetheart, I did try that. Sadly, it didn't work. Nor, I suspect, will it ever.'

She simply started back at him, lost for words. He blinked hard again, as if to shake himself, and put out his hand.

'I'm Gavin Black, by the way, and even though I've just got here, I'm going out again, in search of life-sustaining provisions like coffee, crisps, cookies, and some coke for my Jack Daniels. All the important C's, in fact. I also think I might be headed for the nearest pub, since I could slay a pint of real ale. Will you come with me? Let me buy you a drink, please? Then, if you decide I'm something to be scraped off the pop of a tond or the shottom of a boo, you can run away again, and I won't follow you or try to change your mind.'

He had the grace, Feen noted, to look a little self-conscious. And, oh, God! What was his gorgeous voice doing to her heart, her stomach, and other parts of her anatomy, right now?

'I promise I'm not a stalker, and for what it's worth, this bizarre dact of esperation not to lose you again isn't my normal *modus operandi*. I normally don't care, to be honest, if women come or go. And I know it probably sounds like a load of bollocks, but somehow this feels very different.'

Feen could read him enough already, to know that he wasn't just hitting on her for amusement. It wasn't just her own thoughts that were bouncing in all directions. His were a hot mess too. And they had Spoonerism in common!

Well of *course* they did!

Mesmerized, she shook his warm hand. He lifted hers to his lips and kissed it very briefly, then let it go.

Refusing would be impossible, she knew. How could she say no to this glorious god of a man, and then be faced with the inevitable consequence; spending the rest of her life grieving the loss of him? Well, quite simply, she couldn't. It wasn't an option. Like her mother had decreed, earlier in the day from the other side of their portal, he had already become the other half of her.

'Erm, well let's see.' She nervously chewed her bottom lip for a moment, trying to ignore her wildly fluttering stomach.

Could I even keep a drink down, right now, if I had one?

'There's a little supermarket in the town that can offer what you need and as for pubs, well, there's the Feathers? That's about a minute's walk from the supermarket car park, or there's the Bull and Royal, which is on the edge of the town. The Bull's a bit nicer, a proper old coaching inn' she added, as an afterthought. 'It's about a minute as well, but more in this direction. There are others but they're all a fair way out of town.'

'The Bull it is, then. He turned and looked around. 'My car, or yours?'

'We can take mine. It will only take us a few minutes to drive down there.'

'Well, that makes a change from London, where you typically have to drive for an hour or more to find an honest country pub!'

Feen's heart momentarily plunged with dismay.

So, he's from London. Oh well, I guess that doesn't matter much, I suppose, since I'd still follow him home if he lived in a roofless mud hut in the bowels of rural Africa!

She gestured for him to get into her car, which he did.

'I actually came to see if you'd settled into the cottage okay. My stepmother Adie - you'll know her as Adrienne Raven - wanted to come and welcome you herself, She usually does that for guests, but she ran out of time tonight, and asked me to do it instead. Oh, and I have some coffee for you. She forgot to bring it with her when she set everything up for you in there.'

'Well I'm very glad you rocked up, maiden fair, and not just because you come bearing the all-important prize of caffeine. Whatever the reason we've collided twice, perhaps it's the universe conspiring in our favour. Maybe this is destiny, unfolding before us.'

Feen's spine suddenly tingled, as she drove. She glanced at him sideways. 'D'you really believe that?'

'Well, I believe there's no such thing as coincidence. I'm not religious, at least not to the point where I think there's a big guy in the sky with a grey beard sitting in an armchair, who somehow knows everything and disapproves of most of it. But... do I think there's something bigger out there than just us, and our own free will? Yeah. Actually, I do.'

Dumbfounded, Feen blinked and stayed silent, digesting what he'd just said, as she drove to the supermarket and found a parking spot. She watched him as he went to make his purchases, and then quickly ran a comb through her hair and swept a swathe of pink-tinted gloss across her lips. Luckily, she had a small bottle of her favourite perfume, nestled in the bottom of her bag. She sprayed a little behind her ears, just enough to be noticeable (she hoped) but not overpowering (she hoped again). She then straightened the bodice of her dress, rearranged its lace underlay nicely, and took a few good long deep breaths. She'd managed to calm herself down quite a lot, by the time Gavin came striding back with a small carrier bag, and put it on the back seat of her car.

'Tiny supermarket! Doesn't take long to find what you want and get served. I like that.'

They walked along the High Street, towards the cheeky sign for the Bull and Royal that was clearly visible on the next block down.

Inside, the pub was fairly quiet. At just gone seven in the evening, it had long-since lost its after-work 'happy-hour' crowd that hung around the bar from four until six, and the evening diners were only just starting to trickle in. Gavin picked a table, pulled out a chair, and gestured for her to sit.

'Welcome to the Rull and Boyal' Feen grinned. 'Finest coaching inn this side of the bancashire lorder. There's a pub with the same name in Preston, actually, but I don't think it's as nice as this one.'

Gavin grinned back at her. 'I'll take your word for it. What's your poison, milady?'

Feen thought for a moment. 'Gin and tonic please - but don't ask me which gin! There's so many, it makes my head spin. Just pick one for me, and I'd like some emon and lice in it, if you don't mind.'

'Would you like a packet of valt and sinegar crisps to go with that?' Or would you prefer eese and chonion?' Gavin's grin was infectious.

'Ooh, let's live dangerously and have an acket of peach!' Feen giggled and his face creased in silent laughter.

He bowed before her. 'I like the way you think, maiden fair.'

He swept off his coat and threw it carelessly along the back of the opposite chair. As he strode towards the bar, Feen was treated to the delectable sight of his rear end, perfectly encased in black jeans. She ran a hand over the leather of his coat. Even that felt sexy-soft and supple, like butter beneath her fingers. The rising urge to feel him touch her again, even just to shake or kiss

49

her hand like he already had, was overwhelming and she fought it back.

When he returned, he set the most beautiful drink in front of her. It was a purple gin-fizz in an outrageously elegant long-stemmed, generous, grooved goblet, with a slice of lemon, a cocktail umbrella, and a couple of cubes of ice.

'I only got a bit of ice. I hope you don't mind, but in my host mumble opinion, there's nothing worse than watery gin. Oh, and they didn't have any sparklers. The best they could do was a paper brolly.'

'What, no plastic pink flamingo?'

'Nope. I'm afraid not. Rubbish establishment. No class.'

They sipped their drinks. Gavin sat back in his chair, threw an arm across the back of the seat, crossed his right ankle over his left knee, and gazed at her.

'What's your name?'

'I'm Seraphine Raven, daughter of Mark Raven, who owns Ravensdown, the farm Teapot Cottage sits at the edge of. But close friends and family call me Feen. You can call me Feen if you want.'

'I do want, most definitely, so thank you Feen. I don't shorten my name; I'm just Gavin. As beautiful as you are, and as much of a slave as I'll be to you all my life if you'll let me, please don't ever call me Gav. I can't stand it. '

Gavin went on to tell Feen about himself, his education and his plans for the future. She was fascinated to learn that he was twenty-six, an emerging musician and songwriter, and had just finished his final full-time year of a Music Business & Innovation degree at the Academy of Contemporary Music in London.

'Music's my life, Feen. I got that passion from my father. He was a muso. A rocker. I grew up listening to all the old classic rock songs from his past, and he opened my mind to so much more besides; cabaret, classical, opera, jazz. Music's a wonderful form of self-expression.' He pulled a self-deprecating face, and continued.

'Sometimes I find it easier to say something as a written song, than to actually have a conversation, if you get what I mean. There's so much power in a song, or a piece of music. It can bring joy, comfort, and hope, too. Inspiration. Energy. All kinds of positive things. I feel really driven, to put more good vibrations into the world, and I think I can do that through music.'

Feen agreed. 'Yeah. Music evokes so many memories too, doesn't it? There's so much emotion tied in with some of it. There are songs I still can't listen to without crying, or at least wanting to, especially stuff that was around when my mother was dying, and from when I was at school and having a hard time being bullied. Some of the music from back then is still too tough for me to hear. But other music brings back *fantastic* memories, and makes me so happy. I do have to draw the line at country and western though, I'm afraid to say,' she confessed.

'The rest is good, or at least bearable, but that 'oh my wife has left me with fifteen kids and the mortgage and now my truck won't start' malarkey? No. I can't listen to that. Country and western tales of woe, even with a good meat or belody, just make me want to run away screaming!'

'Not a Garth Brooks fan, then? Not interested in hearing about achy breaky hearts?' Gavin was smirking, and Feen could see that he was struggling not to laugh out loud.

She grimaced. 'I'm afraid not. I do get it, that lots of people like country music, but it's really not my thing.' She cocked her head on one side and smiled at him. 'But it takes all sorts to make a world. Do you sing?'

He did laugh out loud then, and she welcomed the flare of warmth that ran through her, at the sound of it. He shook his head. 'You know, I once believed I could. Teenage boy, I thought I was amazing. I was convinced I'd singlehandedly set the world alight, until my dad knocked my self-delusion straight out of the park by telling me I actually sounded like two tomcats being stapled together. We both decided, quite a while ago now, that it's probably safer and kinder for everybody if I just stick to playing instruments. Drums and keyboards mostly, with a bit of bass guitar when the mood takes me. And I do all that reasonably well, even if I do say so myself,' he added with a smile that made him look quite shy.

'Ah well, nobody's perfect!' Feen responded, with a grin. 'You'll just have to settle for only being brilliant at *most* things!'

She learned that Gavin was an only child too, like her. His father had died a couple of months ago, and he was here in the Lake District visiting his estranged mother.

'We don't get along, sadly,' he admitted. 'Haven't for years. She and my dad separated when I was a toddler. I haven't seen or talked to her for a decade now, but there's a few loose ends around Dad's death that need to be tied up, so I kind of have to see her.'

He didn't elaborate further, but Feen could feel his frustration. That vibe was coming from him loud and clear. He was a real seething hodgepodge of turbulent, complex and interconnected emotions, in fact, but it didn't put her off. Instead, she found him most intriguing.

'I'm sorry about your dad,' she said simply, and he inclined his head in thanks.

He then explained that he lived full-time in London, and hadn't ventured this far north for years; a fact, he hastened to add, that had changed this very afternoon. 'I'll be spending a lot more time up here from now on', he said, reaching over and squeezing her hand. 'And eventually I'll be moving away from London, probably for at least half of my time.'

'Where will you live, then?' Feen enquired, as lightly as she could, although she already suspected what the answer might be.

He just looked at her, nonplussed. Then he shrugged. 'Well, wherever you want, really.'

Feen raised her eyebrows at him but said nothing. He leaned forward, his face serious.

'I'm going to marry you, Seraphine Raven, and very soon. Forgive me for sounding presumptuous and arrogant, and I really don't mean to be, but I'm assuming you do know I won't take no for an answer?'

Feen was drowning in those beautiful green eyes, in the silky warmth of his voice, and in the raw, intense honesty in his face. She was drowning, and she didn't mind a bit.

'I do,' she murmured, holding his gaze.

'And those are the two most important words I'll ever need to hear in my whole life. Say them again on our wedding day, and I'll be the happiest man that ever walked the earth.'

'You're not of this earth,' Feen observed quietly. 'You're ethereal,' she said to him. *Like me*, she thought to herself.

He nodded. 'Ethereal. Like you.'

She slurped her gin and tonic in its fabulous glass and tried not to poke herself in the eye with the paper umbrella. On some level, she felt as if she was teetering on the edge of a precipice, but it was one she didn't mind tumbling over. On a profound level, she already understood that her life was about to change beyond recognition, and she realised that never in her whole life had she felt as excited as she did right now.

Gavin interrupted her thoughts and brought her back to the present. 'D'you fancy another drink? And have you eaten?'

'Yes to a drink, and no I haven't eaten,' she responded. 'We usually have dinner about half past six, but on Adie's yoga nights Daddy and I generally fend for ourselves. He's gone to the local Indian for a meal with his friend Kevin, because Kevin's wife Trudie goes to the yame soga class. Daddy's probably got curry sauce all over his face as we speak. I hadn't got around to fixing myself anything. I'm starving, if you want the truth.'

Gavin picked up a menu from the table and scanned it. He nodded decisively. 'I am too. I bought a ready meal to put in that funny little Aga, but shall we just get some food here? It sounds good. My treat?'

Feen nodded. She definitely did want another drink, because her nerves were still all over the place, but sitting here with the man of her dreams meant she had to stay focussed. There would be nothing worse than forgetting some important detail later, thanks to a gin-soaked brain made worse by an empty stomach. Food was being served around them now, and the smells were causing her tummy to rumble.

The Bull and Royal served good traditional pub food, and she decided on a chicken and asparagus pie with chips and gravy. Gavin chose lasagne, and a starter of cheesy garlic bread for them to share. He went to the bar to order, and brought back another round of drinks.

He reached across the table, grabbed hold of her hand, and gave it a gentle, reassuring squeeze. 'So, I think I've rambled on enough about myself. Tell me everything I need to know about *you*, faiden mair.'

'Well, as you know already, I live at Ravensdown Farm with my dad Mark, and my step-mum Adie. My real mum died from bowel cancer, nine years ago now, and my nan used to live with us, but then she started getting a bit too forgetful for us to manage, and she had to go into a hare comb over in Keswick. So it was just me and Dad for a while, until he got married again last summer. And there's an assortment of critters; pigs, a Jersey cow, a bunch of sheep, and various dats and cogs of course, that are all classed as family, even the working ones.'

'So, you have a wicked stepmother?'

'Oh no!' Feen hastened to reassure him. 'Adie's lovely. She's an absolute sweetheart. I adore her. I did right from the beginning in fact, even before she and Daddy got together.

'And I'm an only child too, like you. But I've inherited quite a step-family! They're an interesting bunch with a slightly scandalous history, and I'm still figuring some of them out, which I do have to say is more of a challenge for me than it is with most of the people I meet.'

Their garlic bread arrived just then, so she took the opportunity to change the subject before she ended up feeling compelled to say more about her inherited family than was probably fair to them, to a man who was, after all, still a complete stranger to them!

'So your mother then, Gavin. You're not looking forward to seeing her, are you?'

He pulled a face. 'Not at all. I shut her out of my life a long time ago. Its more than ten years since we last said a civil word to one another, until last week. She's pretty hard work, to be honest. My life was certainly a lot happier without her in it'

'So why do you want to see her now? I get the feeling it's more a case of having to than wanting to.' Feen wondered at the faintly queasy feeling that suddenly came over her, and tried to ignore it.

Gavin grimaced again.

'Sadly, yeah. I'd rather not, but I think she has some stuff that belonged to my dad. Personal things that were important to him. I dunno if she still has them or not, but I've had to come up and find out. It's Dad's memories. Important family heirlooms. She has agreed to see me, so that's a start, and I'm going pick her up in Carlisle tomorrow when she finishes work.'

He looked downright miserable at the prospect. She felt compelled to try and reassure him, even though she couldn't - for once - see the result of his quest.

'You know, I'm sure she has what you're after. I think you'll get lucky. Truly, I do.'

They tucked into their meals quietly, too hungry to try to talk while they ate, but they never took their eyes off each other for more than a few seconds, and there were plenty of winks and smiles exchanged, as they polished off their food.

A short time later, Gavin looked at his watch and rolled his eyes.

'Feen, I'm so sorry. I hate to eat and run, but I do need to get back. I've got to make a couple of really important calls tonight. It's work stuff, phone calls to people in the USA. But I need your number, please, so I can call you later to say goodnight?'

Feen reached for his phone and quickly keyed her contact details into it, as he was draining the last of his pint.

As they left the pub, Gavin took her hand, and they wandered down the main street back towards the car park. Quietly, he let go and slid his arm gently around her waist. Feen responded by doing the same to him. Even though he was a full foot taller than Feen's neat four-feet-ten, it didn't feel awkward at all. In fact, it felt like the most natural thing in the world, like they'd already been together for years and years.

Every few steps, Gavin leaned down and dropped a kiss or two on the top of her head. It amused and excited her, how the two of them just instinctively knew that they would be together. Gavin hadn't bothered to ask her if she was already in a relationship with anyone else, and yet there was no arrogance about him. He wasn't in the least bit assuming. It was as if he just somehow already knew she wasn't seeing anybody else. And somehow, in a similar way, Feen just knew that he was single, or at least not involved with anyone he felt any loyalty or obligation to.

So many things are said when boy meets girl. So many questions are asked and answered, in that getting-to-know-you process; the mating ritual that establishes the expectations, the boundaries and the way forward, or if there should even be one. Here, with this man, none of that applied. There *were* no questions, no required answers. It was as if they already knew all they needed to, for now at least, and the way forward was crystal clear. Uncanny, unconventional, and indescribably illogical by most people's standards. Some would have simply said stark raving bonkers. But not in this case. Not for Feen Raven and not, as it clearly seemed, for Gavin Black.

When she dropped him back at Teapot Cottage, he took her face in his hands. 'Reen Faven, I seriously want to kiss you. The only problem I have is that once I start, I won't want to stop, even to the point of drowning, but right now I have stuff to do, so I can't start.' He pulled her hand to his mouth and quickly kissed it five times without lifting his lips in between.

'Please forgive me, faiden mair. I'll call you later. In the meantime, I hope it's enough for you to know that you truly have just become the love of my life.'

Feen clasped his hand in both of hers, pushing back the longing for that promised kiss, the one where they'd *both* drown. 'And you truly have just become the love of mine.'

*   *   *   *   *

At eleven o'clock that night, when Feen's phone rang, she pounced on it.

'Good evening, o' prandsome hince. How are you?'

'Fatigued, faiden meen, and ready for sleep, but alas it will not come until I know when I can see you again.'

She giggled, forcing back the impulse to jump out of bed, drag a coat on, bolt down the driveway, and hammer on the back door of Teapot Cottage. Instead, she thought quickly.

'What about tomorrow? Let's breet for munch at eleven? Can you make that? I'll already be in town, doing stuff. There's a great little cafe in Amble Walk, just off the High Street. It's called Ye Olde Torley Tea Shoppe. It's owned by a family friend. Let's meet there.'

Gavin agreed and she asked him if he was feeling any better about his upcoming meeting with his mother.

'Well, I'm sure I'd have more of a giggle getting all my back teeth ripped out with a pair of bull-nose pliers and no anaesthetic,' he admitted. 'But I'm hoping we can keep things civil, at least.'

'Will you tell her about me?'

'What?' Gavin exclaimed. 'Good God, no! I'm not going to tell her anything at all, about *anything*. No point in giving someone with a gun the bullets they need to shoot you, is there?'

His mother did sound truly horrendous. Feen had a very strong feeling of foreboding about the woman, but she couldn't identify exactly what was unsettling her so much. She told herself the bleak, black pall that settled over her whenever she thought about Gavin's mother was simply her reaction to his own reluctance to see her, which he clearly struggled to keep under control.

It must be a soulmate thing. That has to be it. There's no other reason why I should feel this sense of impending doom around someone I haven't even met. But since I've never had a soulmate before, how would I really know?

She knew Gavin would tell her when he was ready, about the bad blood between him and his mother. There was no rush. Whatever 'baggage' he might be carrying, it was part of who he was, and the time to unpack it all would come when it was meant to.

Chapter Five

A Spell to Create Calm Within the Self

You will need:
Two drops each of chamomile (German)
and geranium essential oil
An oil burner and a tealight candle
Distilled water for the top of the burner
A plain white cotton handkerchief

Place the water in the top of the oil burner,
add the essential oils, and place the lighted candle inside the
burner to gently warm the blend but do not let it get too hot to
place on the skin . Soak the handkerchief in the water.
Wring it out and fold it lengthwise, three times.
Place it across the forehead while
lying supine with closed eyes.
Incantation (once):
'Keep me centred, collected and calm,
the intention my one true love to charm'

The next morning, after being too excited to really get much
sleep, Feen tried on virtually every stitch in her wardrobe in an
effort to look like she hadn't made an effort at all. She finally
decided on a simple pair of dark denim skinny jeans, her black
buttoned boots (now polished and no longer caked in mud), and
a genuine Victorian black silk blouse with puffed sleeves and a

lace panel across the chest that swept up to a high neckline. It had been a rare find at an antiques fair and was one of her favourite pieces.

She swept a smattering of mascara across her lashes and applied some pale pink lip gloss, then pulled her hair up into an artfully messy bun and secured it with an old-fashioned jewelled clasp, and shrugged her way into a short pink velvet antique bed jacket to complete her outfit. She looked beautiful, not that she ever saw herself that way. It was one of Feen Raven's most endearing qualities that she had absolutely no idea how gorgeous she was and never took anyone seriously who ever tried to tell her.

Feen's mind drifted to the beautiful wedding gown that was currently hanging in one of her wardrobes in its heavy protective cover. After squirrelling it away to the back of her mind as well as the back of the wardrobe, she'd been quite content in the knowledge that one day in the distant future she would have cause to take it out, try it on again, and allow herself to get truly excited.

She went to the wardrobe now, and drew it out. A small thrill washed through her as she unzipped its protective cover and ran her hand over the top half of it. She'd found it quite by accident a couple of years ago on a trip to Whitby with her father and her uncle and aunt, Bob and Sheila Shalloe. While Mark and Bob had been attending a one-day agricultural conference, Feen and Sheila had spent the day pottering about in the charming little seaside town. They had each indulged in a lovely facial and manicure, and had shared a very nice lunch with a full bottle of bubbly, followed by a wander around the town and a mooch in its charity shops. 'Op-shopping' was a pastime both women always enjoyed, both separately and together, and many of Feen's quirky outfits came from a combination of lucky finds in such places.

That day in Whitby, despite having no idea when or even whom she might one day marry, Feen had unexpectedly discovered the gown she knew she wanted to wear on her wedding day. It was in a slightly dusty, musty-smelling charity shop, hanging among a rack of vaguely shopsoiled and dishevelled wedding and ball gowns. She had literally screamed with joy.

The creamy, dreamy satin dress, in her most perfect size six, was comprised of a finely boned, strapless corset laced at the back and both sides with ribbons. It had a small, delicate, crystal-encrusted crumb-catcher panel across the top of the corset's subtle sweetheart neckline and small crystals down it's slender front bones. The waist gave way to an A-line satin skirt that was studded here and there with small, exquisite clusters of crystals, all in the shape of little leaves. Every tiny stone sparkled like fire when it caught the light.

It was the most beautiful dress Feen had ever set eyes on and she'd known, instantly, that it was *her* dress. It didn't matter to her one bit, that it was second hand. She'd stepped excitedly into it, with Sheila's help to lace her up, in the fitting room at the back of the shop.

Sheila had initially protested that her niece deserved a brand new, lavish frock to get married in when the time came, instead of someone else's second-hand cast-off, but she had to hold back her tears at how stunning Feen had looked, dressed as a bride, in that incomparably beautiful dress. It would need no alteration at all. The size and length were utterly perfect, and Feen had said, as she stood and looked in the mirror, that she could actually feel the happiness of the woman who'd first worn it.

'It's still imbued with her spirit, Sheila! I can feel her joy in this dress as she wore it! It's like a cloak all around me; a warm, loving cloak. This is it! This is my dress!' Feen had been beyond excited. Her aunt had shook her head in disbelief.

'Well, ignoring the fact that there's currently no 'usband in the offing; not even so much as a sniff of a boyfriend, I might add, and buying a wedding dress under such circumstances is bloody peculiar at best, if it's what you want you must 'ave it, love, and it's my treat.'

Sheila's Lancashire accent wasn't quite as heavy as Feen's Dad's, but it still made the conversation slightly hilarious, and the shop assistant hadn't been able to stop giggling as she'd watched how they were getting on.

Sheila had been adamant, in spite of Feen's protests, that she would pay for the dress. 'It's what your mum would've wanted to do for you, and I'm the closest thing you've got, to a mum. And without a daughter of me own to indulge anymore, I'm afraid you're it, lass.'

Feen grinned now, remembering. She knew how maternal and protective her aunt was of her. Sheila had tragically lost her own daughter Amanda, Feen's little cousin, to meningitis many years ago. Feen's wedding, whenever it might happen, would be the closest Sheila would ever get to being the mother of a bride. Besides, when it came to planning and preparing for a wedding, an inexperienced girl definitely needed help from someone older and wiser. Feen wanted Sheila to be her close ally and confidante even at the earliest stages of a wedding that hadn't had a groom, or even the faintest prospect of one, waiting in the wings. That being the case, she was profoundly grateful that her aunt understood her overriding need - notwithstanding - to have *that* dress!

'It needs dry cleaning, and it'll need to be taken it to a specialist that cleans embellished wedding gowns,' Sheila had proclaimed. 'There used to be a place in Carlisle, but I don't know if it closed. If it 'as, you'll probably 'ave to take it to Preston. But I think it'll be worth every penny.'

'I do too, Aunty! I've never seen anything so gorgeous!'

Even second-hand, the gown had been expensive. But it was hundreds of pounds, rather than the thousands it would have cost originally, and Feen was profoundly grateful for her aunt's acceptance that they couldn't have left the shop without it.

The tiny, elegant dress really was stunning, and perfect in its proportions, almost as if it had been made just for her. She had no idea how it had ended up in a charity shop, of all places, instead of being sold elsewhere for closer to what it was really worth, but you couldn't argue with serendipity. Some things in life were simply meant to be, and that dress, that day in that shop, had been one of them.

Feen's father Mark had roared with laughter in the car on the way home, when Sheila told him what had happened. 'Daft buggers. Yer bloody crackers,' was all he had to say about it. He'd shaken his head and laughed again, when Feen brought it back from the dry cleaners a fortnight later, so she refused his request to see it.

'No, Daddy,' she'd said, through clenched teeth. 'Laughing hyena, since you think it's all so bloody funny, you can wait. Just like he will have to.'

'Who's 'e?' Mark had asked, before chuckling 'Oh, that's right. Yer don't know yet, d'yer?' And off he went again, guffawing to himself.

Feen really didn't see what was so bloody hilarious. Ok, yes; it was slightly unconventional, buying a wedding gown before even meeting the man who she'd one day walk down the aisle to, but for heaven's sake, nobody could describe her as conventional anyway, could they? A lot of descriptive words applied to Feen Raven, but 'conventional' certainly wasn't one of them! So why was her dad so surprised?

Feen had bought her beautiful gown purely because she couldn't *not* buy it, and she was quite content to bide her time until 'he' showed up - whoever 'he' happened to be!

She zipped up the gown's protective cover again now, and put it back in her wardrobe. As she got into her car and started driving towards Torley town, she remembered that she still had her mother's wedding veil too, wrapped up in soft, creased, age-old tissue paper. It was lying neatly rolled in an upholstered hatbox at the top of the same wardrobe, along with a couple of satin and lace horseshoes hanging from ribbons, which Beth Raven had been given by friends on her big day. One of the horseshoes had tiny blue bows all over it. So that took care of the 'old, borrowed and blue.' Feen now just needed the 'new', and she reasoned that a lovely pair of shoes would tick that particular box. The veil was very plain but she thought it would go perfectly with the stunning dress, without detracting from it.

Sheila had suggested sewing a few nice crystals to the edge of the veil to bring the outfit together. Feen knew her mother wouldn't have minded her making a few changes or enhancements to the beautiful vintage piece that had actually been Beth's mother, Anny Gralice's, before she had worn it. Feen had always known that as the third-generation daughter, she would wear that veil too, and since she truly believed she would eventually have a daughter herself, who would also one day wear it on her own wedding day, it would endure as a real family heirloom.

Gavin was already waiting for her in the cafe, when she arrived, and he stood up when she came in. He pulled out a chair for her, and she was quietly thrilled to see that he had good, old-fashioned manners - a rare thing in most men of his age. Feen was of the opinion that a man opening a door for a woman - while perhaps no longer *expected* - should certainly still be valued as a simple act of kindness, with no more read into it than that, and always acknowledged with thanks. Her own parents had known a thing or two about manners.

Gavin grinned and hugged her tightly. It felt fantastic, like she'd come home.

'You're here! And you look amazing! Like a delectable liquorice all-sort. Speaking of which, I'm starving again, are you? I've decided on the full English. D'you fancy the same? And how about sharing a big cot of poffee?'

Feen laughed. 'A full English! Well, sure! I'll give it my best shot, and yes please, to cots of loffee, since there's no such thing as too much.'

Peg, the owner of the shop, wandered over with her order pad, her eyebrows raised. Clearly, she'd already given Gavin the once-over and, if her expression was anything to go by, she approved of what she saw. She smirked and winked at Feen, but was wise enough not to make any comment. She took their order and gave Feen a quick squeeze on the shoulder as she left their table. Gavin smiled his thanks at her as she left, which Feen appreciated.

Gavin turned back to her.

'So, is that your friend? The owner?'

Feen nodded. 'Yes, that's Peg Tripper. We all call her Egg, because she has a husband called Eric. They only got married a couple of months ago. She's a really good friend of the family, one of Adie's closest friends. Adie's my step-mum', she added, in case Gavin had forgotten.

He nodded back at her, trying not to laugh. 'Let me guess; he's Peric? So, Egg and Peric, right? That's funny. And your stepmum's my landlady, with all the scamily fandal.'

Feen giggled. 'Well, yeah. But you mustn't judge her badly for that. Most of it was nothing to do with her. It was two of my step-siblings, Matty and Ruth, who were involved in it all. And

63

you definitely mustn't mention it to Adie when you meet her. She'd be mortified that I'd been discussing her.'

'That goes without saying, sweetheart. I'll be the soul of discretion. I'm looking forward to meeting your family,' he added. 'It can't happen soon enough.'

'Well, let's see if Adie's about. I know she was due to come into town at some point today. I'll find out where she is.' Feen dug into her bag for her phone, and quickly made a call. It went to voicemail, so she left a message on it.

'Adie, it's Feen. I'm at Egg's cafe with someone you should meet. I imagine we'll be here for another half hour or so. If you're about, I'd love it if you could call in.' She turned back to Gavin. 'It's a waiting game now, but I hope she does come. I really want you to meet her.'

Gavin grinned nervously. 'If she likes me, she could perhaps wave the pay for me to meet your father.'

Feen was amused, and touched, that he was nervous. Her family were an easy bunch, at least Adie and her Dad were, and uncle Bob and Aunt Sheila liked almost everybody they met until occasional people proved they didn't deserve it. She couldn't really speak for how any of her stepfamily might find Gavin, not that it mattered much what they thought. They all lived at the opposite end of the country and Feen could count on one hand, with fingers to spare, the number of times she might see them in a year. She shook her head.

'Don't worry about Daddy. He's a good sort. He likes most people. You'd have to really piss him off, for him to decide he didn't like you. He's very down-to-earth. What you see is what you get. He's as fit as a dutcher's bog, too, which is amazing really. He had a very bad accident last year, and he nearly died. It was the scariest thing that's ever happened in my whole life.'

'Bloody hell! What happened?'

'He fell through rotten mezzanine floorboards in the barn. He went straight through, fell twenty feet, and landed on the flone stoor. Broke his neck and ripped his liver. He was lucky to survive.'

Feen went on to describe how she had found Mark unconscious and bleeding, and feared he was dead. 'I was beside myself,' she admitted. 'I really wasn't sure he'd pull through. My mum had already died, don't forget, and as I sat there on that flone stoor with him, I really thought he was going to die too, right there in my arms.'

Gavin reached across, took her hand and gave it a quick squeeze. 'That must have been terrifying.' She just nodded, and at that moment their breakfast arrived - two heaving plates of fry-up, with full rack of toast. A large pot of coffee accompanied it all, with two good-sized mugs. Feen was relieved at the timing. It meant she didn't have to elaborate any further on what was still a traumatic event for her, more than a year after it had happened.

She wolfed down her breakfast, hoping Gavin didn't mind a woman with an appetite. It took a lot to put Feen off her food and, as tiny as she was, she regularly polished off the same sized meal as her father, which continually baffled the entire family as to where she put it all and how she never gained an ounce of weight. Aunt Sheila always said she had hollow legs.

They were finishing up the last of their coffee and mopping their plates with what was left of the toast when Adie came into the cafe. Feen waved, and her stepmother grinned at them.

'Hi guys. What a nice surprise! Thanks for the invitation, Feen.' She shot an enquiring look at her stepdaughter.

Peg caught Adie's eye and lifted her eyebrows and a teacup. Adie nodded, and Peg set about providing a pot of tea. She also brought over another rack of toast, which Feen and Gavin both instantly fell upon like starving vultures. Adie laughed.

'Gosh, you two look like nobody's fed you for a month!'

'Adie, this is Gavin Black, your tenant at Teapot Cottage. I went to see him last night, like you asked, and we've decided to get married.'

Adie had just taken a large gulp of her hot tea, and she struggled now, not to spit it out or choke on it. Gavin extended his hand.

Nice to meet you properly Adie. I've heard a lot about you.'

'Whereas, I've heard nothing at all about *you,*' Adie volleyed back, shaking his hand and still trying to get her coughing fit under control. Her eyes were watering. She looked intently at Feen, who just couldn't stop herself from beaming from ear to ear, and then she turned back to Gavin, confused. 'What an incredible surprise. I wasn't aware you two even knew one another!'

'We didn't, until yesterday.' Feen chipped in. Adie slowly blinked, in disbelief.

'Sorry?' she spluttered, clearly bewildered. 'Have I missed something?'

Gavin pulled an apologetic face.

'No, you haven't. I know this all sounds totally bonkers, and I'm the one who's sorry. It must be the last thing you'd expect to hear, out of the blue like this. I'm from London, but I'm up here visiting my mother. As Feen says, we met yesterday, and we've both been badly hit with Cupid's arrow. To be fair, it wasn't what I expected either, nor Feen. It's hit us both like a ton of bricks, but in a good way.'

Adie's face was a picture of confusion, so Feen felt compelled to explain. She described seeing Gavin in Carlisle the previous day, and the effect it had had on her. Gavin confirmed that it had been exactly the same way for him. She quickly grabbed Adie's hand.

'It's happened for us just like it did for Mum and Daddy. Love at first sight. I know you'll think I'm even more mad than usual, Adie, but Gavin is my destiny. I knew it as soon as I clapped eyes on him yesterday in Carlisle. I ran away then, in the absolute worst state of panic, but it seems we were destined to meet. Properly, at Teapot Cottage.'

Adie still looked incredulous. Gavin reached across, picked up Feen's other hand, and quickly kissed it.

'I would never have believed in love at first sight either, before yesterday. But when I saw this woman, I suddenly saw my whole life, what I wanted it to be. I know it probably doesn't make much sense, but I dunno what else we can tell you.'

Poor Adie was gobsmacked, Feen could tell.

'Adie, I just know. *We. We* just know. It's impossible to explain, I know that, but I do hope you'll try to understand how this feels.'

Adie nodded and gave her a wobbly smile. 'Feen I *am* trying to understand. Your dad's told me a lot about how he met your mum, and you're so very much her daughter. I'd never describe you as irresponsible, darling, and you're both fully-grown adults capable of making considered decisions. If you're sure it's happened for you too, if you're both *absolutely* certain, then I'm very happy for you, of course. But you must appreciate the suddenness of all this, for the rest of us. I know I speak for Mark too, when I say that you need to take a little time, before you go galloping up the aisle. He will want to get to know your lovely young man, Feen. You must allow him time for that.'

Her face was serious as she looked back at Gavin. 'It'll be a lot for him, all at once, his only daughter with a new man on the scene *and* already planning a wedding. You'll need to break this to him gently, and you'll need to give him real time, to digest it all. Will you do that?'

Feen reached over and squeezed Adie's hand with her own. 'Of *course* we will! There's doads to loo before we get to the altar anyway, but this is my world, right here, in this glorious man! It's the world I was born to step into, Adie; the world I've been waiting for all my life! Gavin is the missing piece of my puzzle, just like Daddy was for Mum.' Feen could hear the excitement in her own voice. She hadn't felt this sure of anything for years.

Gavin explained briefly about his need to see his mother. He wanted to sort everything out quickly with her and get back out of her orbit, but he no longer felt the urge to rush back to London.

'I don't suppose Teapot Cottage is available for longer, is it, Adie? No problem if not, but I will need to find somewhere else to stay after this week. I don't have to be back in the city for around a month, and I want to spend as much time as I can with Feen before I have to go back to work.'

'Well, I think you might be in luck,' Adie responded, after chewing her bottom lip for a second or two. 'I can probably make it available for another three weeks, actually. The people who have reserved it for a fortnight from next week keep putting off paying the deposit to firm up the booking, and I've already emailed to remind them twice. It's currently still vacant for the week after that too, so it's yours for a full month if you want it. You'd need to pay the lot up front though, I'm afraid. I'm sorry, but I have to insist on that, because I've been messed around enough already over it. If you're happy to do that, I'll just cancel those dithering idiots. I'm fed up with them.'

'Thank you very much, and paying up front is no problem. If I brought a few things from home, would you mind me using the cottage to work? It's just a couple of keyboards, a delectronic rum set and some sound stuff. Would that be okay?'

Adie couldn't hide her laughter. 'Oh, Lord! More Spoonerism for me to wrap my head around, as if I wasn't already permanently on the hop with this one.' Smiling gently, she inclined her head towards Feen.

'Maybe you two really *are* made for each other. As to your kit, you'd have to set everything up in the living room, as there's no real room upstairs. If you can live with it all around you and it won't be noisy for us up at the farm, then sure. No problem.'

'It'll be quiet, I promise. Thank you, Adie. That would be a big help.'

Adie gave another unsteady smile, finished her cup of tea, checked her watch, and stood up.

'Well, I'm on a dedicated bill-paying rampage today, so I'll leave you lovebirds to it. Gavin, I think it's important for you to meet Mark, Feen's dad, sooner rather than later. So, if you're free, would you like to come up and have dinner with us tonight? I'll probably just be throwing a fairly basic chicken stew with home-made bread onto the table, but you're welcome to join us.'

Gavin also stood, and gave Adie a quick hug.

'That would be amazing, thank you. What can I bring? And what time do you want me?'

Adie considered for a moment. 'Six thirty? Mark's usually in by six to get cleaned up for dinner at around half past. You don't need to bring anything. Just your 'A' game. That'll be pretty important tonight, I should think.'

She leaned across the table and hugged Feen, whispering quietly in her ear; 'He does seem very lovely, darling.' She then left the cafe, waving to Peg as she went.

Feen resolved to have another chat, very soon, with Adie. Her stepmother would be worried, despite putting on a brave face at the table. She was caring and sensitive, and Feen knew how anxious she'd be at having an impending wedding sprung at her by her stepdaughter, to someone she hadn't even met before, and to whom Feen had known for less than twenty-four hours, herself!

She also knew she'd need to have a grateful word with her guides and spirits later too, in a quiet moment. After viciously berating them yesterday, she figured they could probably do with a decent apology. They hadn't thrown her to the wolves after all, and she should have known they wouldn't.

A hefty wedge of humble pie, coming right up.

Gavin broke the silence. 'D'you think she's ok? She looked like you'd brit her with a hick.'

Feen nodded emphatically. 'Yeah, she'll be fine. She knows me. She'll get her head around this. She just needs a bit more time with you, I guess, to get more used to the idea. Tonight will help.'

Gavin looked nervous. 'What if your dad doesn't like me? What then?'

'Why wouldn't he like you?'

'Erm, because I'm a complete stranger, he doesn't know me from Adam, I dress like a bed-hanger, and I've already laid claim to his only child?'

Feen laughed out loud. 'Oh sweetie! Honestly, there's nothing not to like! He's been here himself, you know. He and my mother fell in love at first sight too. He'll understand, probably better than Adie does. You'll just have to promise to let him break your neck if you mess me around, because he *will* tell you that, and he absolutely *will* mean it.'

'Well, that does precisely nothing to make me want to shit myself any less, thank you very much.'

'Oh, come on!' Feen laughed again. 'It will only be a problem if you do mess me around, and you're not going to do that, are you?'

Gavin shook his head. His face was serious. 'I would rather die than do that.'

She reached over and grabbed his hand and kissed it. Mollified, he kissed hers back, just as Peg came over to clear the table.

'Egg, this is Gavin, my intended.'

Peg looked as incredulous as Adie had, but she quickly recovered herself, wiped her hand on her apron and stuck it out at Gavin.

69

'Pleased to meet you, Gavin Intended, and congratulations to you both. Feen never mentioned she was seeing anyone, but I can understand why she's kept you under wraps. You're quite a catch, young man. If I was forty years younger I'd be trying to get your attention myself!'

Gavin smiled broadly at Peg's light-hearted flirting. 'Thank you, Egg. Am I allowed to call you that? I'm the lucky one, but I agree, she could probably do a lot worse.'

Feen punched him playfully on the arm. 'Right, you, Bister Mighead. What are your plans for today?'

'I'm going to spend it with my lovely old grandparents, while the dragon's at work. Then I have to pick said dragon up at five o'clock, probably have a row or two, scrape the blood and guts off the walls, bury the body, clean myself up a bit, and be at yours for half past six. I'll be on the wire.'

Feen ignored a brief flash of disappointment. She'd been hoping to spend the day with him, herself.

But of course he wants to spend time with his grandies! He probably hasn't seen them since forever! I couldn't begrudge him that! It's interesting that he's staying in Torley, when his family are over in Carlisle, but I guess he has his reasons. I'm certainly not going to question whatever circumstances conspired for us to meet!

'I do think we were definitely meant to meet, one way or the other,' she mused aloud. 'And I do find it hilarious that fate's got you sleeping virtually under my bedroom window.'

Gavin grinned. 'I know, right? It's all a bit bonkers. But I can be your Romeo, serenading you with a set of delectronic rums, and you can be my Juliet, hanging halfway out the window imploring me to shut up and piss off before I wake up all the sheep and have them partying all night. I feel like the hand of fate's all over this.'

Feen laughed, knowing Gavin was right. The hand of fate *was* all over this. She also knew that he was in exactly the right place, at Teapot Cottage. The charming little house had its own vibrational energy; a rare, unusually calm aura of peace and healing, and it somehow seemed to attract people who had major problems they needed to resolve. It didn't surprise her in the slightest that Gavin, with his grief over losing his dad and with all the issues surrounding his relationship with his mother, had ended up there.

It also wasn't surprising that Adie had been able to clear the diary for him to be able to stay longer than he'd originally intended. It was funny how that happened. Time just seemed to open up at the cottage, somehow, for those who really needed it. The stunning, sweeping views of Torley valley invited contemplation, reflection and healing, even without the magic the cottage was infused with, that unfailingly triggered the process.

Feen knew that Gavin would be happy there, and more comfortably able to reconcile a lot of the trauma of his past. She looked forward to sharing some quiet time there with him too. It would be their private place, where they could get to know each other better, away from curious, prying eyes. She was already looking forward to the time when she could be more intimate with him.

To her immense surprise, as soon as they reached the car park, Gavin abruptly gathered her into his arms and passionately kissed her, right there in the street.

She melted into him as he pulled her closer, at the same time as he guided her backwards to lean against his car. Every inch of her body was suddenly pressed against every inch of his. The kiss was deep, knowing and gentle, yet full of longing and passion, full of the promise of so much more, of desire that came dangerously close to spilling uncontrollably over. She had waited all her life for this kiss. Nothing mattered, right here, right now, except this.

But, as abruptly as he'd kissed her, Gavin let her go.

'Damn. I wish I hadn't done that! Now I won't be able to think about anything else, until I can do it again.'

With a smirk, Feen pulled him back to her and kissed *him*. He surrendered to her, this time, dragging his fingers through her hair and pulling it gently. Then he gently pushed her back.

'Feen! I'm smouldering,' he said roughly. 'Please don't set me alight. Not here.'

She let him go. He took her hand and kissed it. Then he grinned.

71

'Right. Well, my head is completely scrambled now, thanks very much, and I'm not even going to *try* to explain what's happening to certain delicate parts of my anatomy, other than to call it a spontaneous and extremely localised form of rigor mortis. Now, God help me, I've got to somehow compose myself enough to go have tea and cake with a couple of crusty old codgers who probably haven't had sex in twenty years!'

As he got into his car, Feen slapped his backside playfully.

'Nice bum!'

He looked at her, smiling, then dragged his teeth across his bottom lip. Feen felt a quick, deep stab of lust, and closed her eyes.

He started his car. 'See you later, gorgeous.'

Then he put his Porsche quickly into gear and roared away. Weakly, Feen made her way to her own car, and sat there for a while before starting it up. The full-on, firework-laden promise of intimacy with Gavin had literally left her trembling at the knees.

The thought of losing him, of never having found him, was too awful to contemplate. A life without that kind of passion, now that she knew it, would be intolerable. She *had* to marry him now. He'd made sure of it. With just one kiss he'd spoiled her forever, for anybody else. As she started her own car and headed for home, she knew couldn't wait much longer to be alone with him.

Chapter Six

A Song for Love

Been lookin' for you, feels like forever.
Only been existin' with the dream of you
Findin' this love, I'd asked would I ever?
And yeah, the dream, it did come true.
Now you're here, with the love you give,
and finally I know what it means to live.
Those deep-blue eyes! I'm mesmerized.
I'm hypnotized by your beautiful eyes.

Driving towards his Grandparents' house, Gavin forced his feelings for Feen back into a box inside himself. It took some doing.

Women had flung themselves at him often enough, and he was well aware of how appealing he was to them. He'd dabbled, of course. Nobody could have described him as anything other than a red-blooded man, but he'd never been much into casual sex or one-night stands. He'd had a handful of girlfriends but he'd never felt serious about any of them. Since he'd made a full commitment to getting his Business and Music degree, he hadn't felt inclined to commit to anything else. He'd been content enough to 'window-shop,' as his dad had often described being able to appreciate a pretty woman without feeling the need to have her. He didn't need the complications that went with that.

The truth was, he hadn't been in the market for a long-term anything with *anyone*, certainly nothing that would have got in the way of what he was wanting to achieve in life before settling down with a wife and a family. Like most men, he wanted that -

but not yet. Until yesterday it had been the last thing on his list. But everything had changed without warning, and all of the plans Gavin had so carefully constructed were toppling faster than he could catch them. Everything he thought he wanted in a particular order had somehow just been turned upside down.

The weird thing was, he didn't mind. If someone had told him a week ago, that he was about to fall hopelessly in love, and be making marriage and relocation plans to a one-horse town at the other end of the country within an hour of first meeting the woman his life had just become meaningless without, he'd have thought they were clinically insane. What's more, he'd have fought like hell to avoid it.

He certainly hadn't been prepared for finding Feen. Or had she found him? It was a question he figured they'd always struggle to answer - who found whom first. The origins of their first encounter, that first flash of knowing, were fairly obscure, but she'd seen him first. That much had been clear, in Carlisle, when he'd looked up to find the most exquisitely beautiful woman staring at him, open-mouthed, like she'd had some kind of electric shock.

He'd been thunderstruck. The charge that had passed between them when he'd looked into her eyes was something he suspected nobody could *ever* be prepared for. It was the kind of thing you probably read about in low-rate romance novels or saw in soppy movies. You didn't really believe it existed, until it suddenly rocked up and stalled your own heart. Gavin's heart had simply stopped beating, for a few seconds at least. He'd had some sort of momentary cardiac arrest, he was certain of it.

He hadn't been able to believe his luck when just a few hours later she'd driven up to the door of his rental cottage. He'd known it was her in an instant. She had a face he'd never have forgotten, even if he had never seen her again.

And here they were, not twenty-four hours later, joyfully planning their wedding! Gavin smirked at the thought of what his mother would say, if she knew. She'd call him impulsive, irrational and completely irresponsible. But all Gavin could say about it, which sounded pathetic but was literally *all* he could say, was that it all made perfect sense. He'd found 'The One,' pure and simple. And when you know you've found The One, what was the point of waiting?

Of course, Feen's family would probably try to delay things for a while at least. Adie Raven's reaction had been clear proof of that. Nobody who loved Feen would want her to make any rash mistakes, but Gavin wasn't toying with her, and he needed her family to know that. He intended to cherish her, and he wanted them to know that too. Tonight, he'd get the chance to tell them, and he was determined not to blow it.

He pulled into his grandparents' driveway and got out of his car, unable to think of a better way to steady his irregular heartbeat than to spend the day with the other two people he loved best in the entire world.

His Nanny and Bampa, Hazel and Stan Walton, were the quintessential grandparents. You couldn't have sat down and designed a pair more perfect. Gavin's heart swelled at the thought of them. Although they were well into their seventies, they were both still strong and vibrant, keeping fit at the local oldies' exercise classes and still doing the odd bit of fell walking, when the weather was nice. It was only a couple of years since Bampa had given up his daily early-morning swim in the local lake, something he'd been doing all his life, rain or shine, summer or winter. A bad cramp and a near miss with serious hypothermia one winter's morning had forced him to accept that his body was no longer robust enough to cope with that gruelling ice-water swimming routine, even with a heavy wetsuit on. He also accepted that poor Nanny didn't deserve to be rigid with fear about his safety, every time he went. He still did swim occasionally though, on summer mornings when it was warm enough, and when Nanny or someone else could go along to keep a beady eye on him.

Bampa opened the door, gave an excited yelp, and exclaimed at how tall Gavin had got, before enveloping him in an almighty bear hug. Nanny virtually whizzed across the kitchen floor to throw her arms around him too. It was lovely to see them both, after so very long, and just have real quality time to properly hear one another's news without his peevish, irascible mother throwing vicious verbal barbs and sounding like a gas-powered chainsaw that didn't have an off-switch.

Carla hadn't been the worst mother, in fairness. She'd never hurt him, at least not physically, and he never wanted for much materially. He'd gone to a good school, and she'd paid for different clubs and hobbies. She'd made sure he always had what he needed. But she was emotionally detached and ice-cold, and Gavin couldn't see how she could possibly have got that from her parents. Nanny and Bampa were the warmest, most generous-hearted and funny people he'd ever known. They treated everybody they met with real warmth, and he idolised them both. He still had every letter they'd ever written him, and every Christmas and birthday card they'd ever sent. He'd always made sure too that whenever they sent money, he'd spent it on something meaningful, like a new cd or a good pen and a nice notebook for recording thoughts and ideas about music. He still had everything he'd ever bought with their money, along with the beautiful vintage six-string acoustic guitar they'd sent him for his twenty-first birthday, and he would never part with any of it.

Nanny plied him with tea. Bampa was the baker though, and to Gavin's amazement his grandfather had remember that his favourite biscuit from childhood was ginger crunch. A loaded plate appeared, and Nanny buzzed around him, making sure he ate most of the biscuits that were on it. He had no choice but to laugh and do his best. They'd have both been heartbroken if he'd confessed that not only was his matured palate railing against the sugary crunch and its heavy icing, but he was also already full to bursting point thanks to his massive brunch at Egg's café. He was struggling to fit another thing in.

Stan and Hazel Walton obviously knew about the rift between their daughter and grandson, but they chose to say nothing about it. It must have hurt them, but they didn't talk about it. The last thing they'd want, Gavin knew, was for him to feel like he had to explain himself. They both knew what Carla was like.

They were devout Christians, and they never failed to do whatever they could for anyone who needed help or support. And they loved straight from their hearts. Gavin liked to think his ability to do the same was a gift he'd inherited from them. To be as mean-spirited as his embittered mother? He couldn't imagine himself like that and he wondered, not for the first or the hundredth time, what sort of man he'd have turned out to be, if he hadn't got away from her influence when he did.

Mid-afternoon, Bampa made yet more food - soup and cheese toasties - and Nanny dragged out the family photo albums. Gavin grinned at the faded, yellowing pictures of his grandparents when they were young, with Nanny sporting mini-skirts and beehive hairdos. Bampa was equally hilarious with his silly hats, and shorts down to his cartoon-like knees. He'd owned some pretty impressive cars too, in his day. One of them had been an E-Type Jag that Gavin would cheerfully have surrendered every last one of his teeth for.

He was also astonished to find that throughout the years, Carla had sent them many photographs of *him* as he was growing up. He recognised some of the captured moments, like the day he'd finally mastered his first bicycle, and his tenth birthday party with its 'Star Wars' theme. They still had all her letters too, tied in a neat bundle, that described Gavin's childhood antics. He read a few of them, and was surprised at the level of love on the pages; his mother's love and pride in him as he was growing up.

He was even more amazed, a while later, when he checked the time and saw that it was already four o'clock. The day had just evaporated. Regretfully, he said goodbye to Nanny and Bampa and set off for Carlisle, to collect his mother. As they waved him off, after making him promise to see them again soon, he grinned to himself, wondering when he'd last been expected to eat so much food in one day. And of course there was still dinner at the Raven's to get through, later. He felt like he'd been fed to within an inch of his life already. He hoped he could do some justice to yet another meal.

Chapter Seven

Carla impatiently looked at her watch, for the hundredth time. She'd managed to get an early finish from work, and quickly get some food shopping done before Gavin picked her up. As she waited at their meeting point, outside the cathedral, her stomach was churning with nerves and exhaustion. She hadn't slept properly for days now, ever since he'd rung out of the blue. She'd more or less resigned herself to having to deal with whatever might happen when they met again, too, but she still hadn't been prepared for how nervous and sick she felt as she waited and watched the minutes count down.

She assumed Gavin would be staying for his tea, so she'd bought some fresh fish, remembering how much he used to enjoy it as a kid. Cod and cheesy mash, with peas and parsley sauce. It used to be a firm favourite, and she hoped it still was. Her parents would probably be expecting to have their tea with their grandson too, and they liked fish. She'd even splurged on a bottle of halfway decent pinot grigio, to go with it.

Ever since she'd agreed to meet Gavin, Carla had thought of a hundred different ways to try and explain her lies and deceit. She'd even booked an emergency appointment with Dawn, her therapist, to try and get some help to make sense of everything she was feeling and dreading.

Together, and somewhat reluctantly on Carla's part, they'd decided that honesty was the only way forward. It was no longer a realistic choice, to hide from the truth, or to let her son stay in the dark about what had really happened between his parents. He deserved to know, if he didn't already. And, if he did know, he had every right to drag her to hell over it. If he decided to do that, she'd just have to go there, and try not to choke on the crow she'd have to force down her own throat, in giving him the apology he deserved.

Even if she couldn't adequately explain herself, and even if whatever she did or said wouldn't be enough to repair her shattered relationship with him, the time for running was over.

Dawn had helped Carla to prepare for and accept the real possibility that her only child might never speak to her again for the rest of her life. But she decided, in the end, that if she did put the terrifying big girl pants on and admit that everything she'd said about his father had been a lie, at least that meant there would be nothing left to run from. She wouldn't have to be scared anymore. Ashamed, yes; maybe to the point of paralysis, but the cards of brutal honesty would stand or fall, and if the worst happened, she would pick up whatever pieces were left of herself and figure out how to put herself back together.

It was time to make a start, at least, towards laying some of her demons to rest. Maybe she would finally find some peace, either with or without Gavin in her life. But being resolved to deal with whatever he might throw at her didn't diminish the dread that had settled in her stomach.

She heard a short horn blast and looked up to see a beautiful black Porsche Cayenne SUV pull up at the kerb. The man inside was wearing a black rock concert t-shirt. He had long, dark hair that fell past his shoulders. Her green eyes locked on his identical ones, and she knew without a doubt that this was her boy. And he was beautiful beyond belief. She allowed herself a small surge of pride.

Holy shit, he's good-looking! Didn't I do well?

She got into the car, determined not to show any emotion. It wouldn't do for him to see her rattled, and she certainly didn't want him to think he was going to get an easy ride from her. He gave her a brief smile and said 'Hi,' but he didn't say anything else as he put the car in gear and pulled back out from the kerb. It was rush hour now, and he was concentrating as he swung out into the traffic.

Apart from the usual superficial pleasantries, mostly related to the weather, neither of them said much at all on the way back to Torley. Neither made reference to the fact that this was their first meeting in more than ten years. The atmosphere in the car was very subdued. It felt surreal to Carla, and almost bizarre, that they were driving together after a decade of no contact, and acting as if they'd already done it so many times, there wasn't a need for chat. Eventually she decided to break the silence, in as bored a voice as she could manage.

'So, you got here alright then. Nice car, by the way. Leather upholstery, very swanky. It's a bit big though, isn't it? What do you need something this size for?'

'It was Dad's', Gavin responded. 'It's got big boot space. He needed to cart all his music stuff around in it. I'd never bothered

79

buying a car myself, living in central London, but it's handy to have one occasionally, and I might need this myself for my own music stuff if I start moving it about. That's quite likely, as it turns out, so I'm hanging onto it for now.'

He kept his eyes on the road ahead, but Carla could tell that he was every bit as apprehensive as she was. He was chewing the inside of his cheek, and she remembered that he used to do that when he was little, when he was nervous or unsure. She tried again.

'Did you spend some time with Mum and Dad today?'

He nodded, and grinned slightly, clearly relieved to be offered a semi-safe topic.

'Yeah, I did. It was pretty cool, actually. They dragged the family albums out, which was really funny, and they made me eat shedloads of ginger crunch.'

Carla snorted. 'Dad made a double batch of that horrible stuff last night, in your honour.'

'He hasn't lost his touch, it's as good as I remember it from all those years ago. I'd forgotten how sweet it was, though. I couldn't eat as much as they wanted me to.'

'I've bought some fish for tea. I thought I'd cook us all a meal. Then we can talk properly and you can start, by telling me what you've come all this way for.'

Carla caught Gavin's quick, here-and-gone grimace as he checked his rear-view mirror. 'I can't do dinner tonight, Mum. Sorry, but I'm committed to other plans. Can we do it tomorrow night instead?'

'No we bloody can't,' she retorted, suddenly swamped with irritation and disappointment. 'If there's any left, it'll go in the bin. You can come and drag it out tomorrow, by all means, but I'm not dancing to your tune. You're the one who wants something from me, remember, not the other way around. *Tea* will happen like it always does. If you're not here for it, it's your loss.' Her voice, even to her own ears, was hard and uncompromising.

She felt mildly ashamed of her own attitude, but she had no real idea how to do a u-turn from it. She turned to look out the window, cringing, as Gavin tried to placate her.

'I'm sorry, Mum. If I'd known about it earlier I'd have made a different plan for tonight. It would've been nice to have had a family meal. It was a good idea, though. Maybe I can cook for us all, tomorrow night? Would you like that? I've just got to see someone tonight, and I've been invited to stay for dinner. I said yes because it felt a bit rude to refuse.'

'Dinner? You used to call it what it was – *tea*. Gone all snobby nowadays, have you?'

Gavin smiled faintly at that, but he didn't rise to the bait. Carla conceded that he was probably right to be polite to someone who'd got in first with an invitation, but she was still awash with annoyance. She turned back from the window.

'How long are you staying up here for?' she demanded.

Gavin stretched his neck from side to side as he drove, keeping his eyes on the road. 'I plan to be here for a few weeks, actually. I have to see some people back in London about writing the music for an indie movie they want to make, but that's not for a while. I thought I could use a bit of space from the flat, get creative again after all those months plodding away at uni. I've kind of stalled a bit, since Dad died, too, so I think it might be good to take a break, up here. Change of scene and all that.'

He looked sideways at her. 'You don't mind, do you?'

'Why would I mind?' she responded coolly, shrugging her shoulders and staring determinedly out of the window. 'It's nothing to do with me, what you choose to do. Just don't make any trouble for me while you're here.'

He shook his head. 'Not my intention.'

'Then you'd better tell me what your intention actually is, what you really want from me, and sooner rather than later, because I'm not playing games with you, Gavin. Nanny and Bampa might be over the moon that you're here, but I can't say the same for myself. All you being here does is remind me of a really shitty time in my life that I'd rather not remember.'

'Gee, Mum, you're a real sweetheart. Thanks for the warmth. I'll cook *dinner* for us all tomorrow night, and I'll tell you. I'll be out of your hair after that, I promise.'

Carla snorted again as her son checked his watch. He was clearly in a hurry to be wherever it was he'd promised to be. *Dinner*, indeed!

His sarcasm rankled, and so did the fact that he'd probably got that trait from her. If he was meeting her at her own point of intolerance, though, it probably served her right.

'You didn't have to pick me up, you know,' she said testily. 'You should have just said, if it was too much trouble. I could have got the bus, like I always do.'

'Mum, I was happy to pick you up. I said that and I meant it. I say what I mean and I mean what I say, and in one respect I'm just like you. I can't be bothered playing games either. I just have plans tonight, that's all, and to be fair, they were made before I knew you wanted to make us all a meal. But I'm all yours tomorrow night, if that suits. Or not. Let me know. You've got my number.'

Gavin shrugged as he glanced over at her, and she was again struck by how beautiful he was. Her son. Twenty-six, and a red-hot mess of drop-dead gorgeousness! She allowed herself another gentle surge of satisfaction.

Oh, my God! Flesh of my flesh! I created him!

He drew the car up in Bampa's driveway and she found herself unable to stop herself from sighing theatrically, as she got out of the car, heaving her bag of shopping. Gavin smiled again, apologetically, and once more offered to pick her up again tomorrow night and stay to cook a family meal.

'Whatever,' she mumbled curtly, and then decided to own the small surge of dismay at how unwilling she was still determined to be, to concede anything. Old habits die hard, even when they're mean ones. Carla knew she needed to make more of an effort, but why was that so hard? Trying to ignore how weak at the knees she'd gone, at her son's million-megawatt Walton smile, she took a deep, steadying breath, and gave him a curt nod.

'Tomorrow night will be fine, Gavin, if you want to cook. I'll let Mum and Dad know.'

'Okay. I'll pick you up from work again. Same time, same place.'

She managed another short nod. As she headed for the front door, determined not to look back, she heard him spin his car around and tear back down the driveway. She tried not to let her indignation get the better of her.

Deep breaths, Carla! Stay on top of this.

Whatever Gavin wanted, whatever he'd come all this way for, she clearly wasn't going to find out tonight. She'd need to have a bit more patience - a virtue that all too often escaped her when she needed it most.

Chapter Eight

A Song of Reflection

Was harder than I thought, to leave her.
But I couldn't do anythin' else.
The child that I was, I believed her.
But I just couldn't live in the hell.
I had to go find who I needed to be,
and I never had much regret
But love's what it is, and whatever you do,
you find that you can't forget.
U-turns, backtracks, revisitations,
it's not what we ever expected
In spite of the fire, I want to go back,
to find what we should have protected.

As he drove back towards Teapot Cottage, Gavin felt even more unsettled than he'd expected to feel, after reconnecting with Carla. They'd just completed the most inane and superficial conversation imaginable. On some level, after she'd got into his car and they'd made the initial, half-hearted attempt at small talk (about the weather, of all stupid things), it was almost as if they'd never been apart, and never fallen out; like they spent so much time together there wasn't any need for talking. On another level, it was like they'd never met at all, and were effectively two thrown-together strangers making meaningless conversation in preference to suffering an awkward silence.

Decidedly weird.

He hadn't been anticipating a full-blown row (even though on some level he was prepared for it), but he *had* been expecting at least some acknowledgment about the decade gone by. He'd expected her to at least have said something like 'Hey, Gavin, how are you? Long time, no see. Sorry about your dad.' But there'd been nothing. Zip. She hadn't said a single thing about the past. He couldn't decide whether he was frustrated or relieved that they'd both managed to completely avoid the 'elephant in the car' - the fact that they'd parted ten years ago on the very worst of terms, and that he'd gone to live with his father - the man she truly hated.

He was also still more disturbed than he wanted to admit, by the discovery of how committed Carla had been to keeping Nanny and Bampa updated about him as he was growing up. Her letters, and the photos she'd sent to them, showed a proud mother who adored her little boy, and who'd taken every opportunity to show him off to her own parents. That was completely at odds with her cool, dispassionate attitude towards him. Most people would be forgiven for thinking she didn't give a rat's arse!

He found himself baffled yet again at how, with such stalwart, upbeat, positive parents as role models, Carla could have become as viperish as she was. Nanny and Bampa had always loved her. There was no doubt about that. Even now, they still had her old school photos, smiling with braces and pigtails, proudly on show on the sideboard.

It was a complete mystery, how or why she'd become so caustic and bitter, lying without shame about really important things, holding everyone at arm's length, and blaming anyone else but herself for whatever had gone wrong in her life.

He glanced at his watched, and grimaced. Time had vanished, today. He remembered with relief that his bag had a clean shirt in it, although it would probably be hopelessly creased. He didn't have a chance now, of finding time to iron it, but he could certainly have a hot shower. That way, even if he *looked* like a rumpled homeless tramp, at least he wouldn't smell like one.

The evening was chilly. Despite being officially the first month of summer, June never guaranteed warm weather, no matter where you were in England. The Lake District was notorious for rain, too. A coat or a jacket was nearly always needed this far north, whatever the season, especially after the sun went down. But as much as Gavin loved the sun, this cooler climate was preferable to the all-too-often sweltering, oppressive London summer nights, where the smog mingled with the baking heat from the pavements and the sour smell of the Thames. He liked the city; it was home to him, but sometimes it felt like being in a grubby, polluted pressure cooker he often longed to escape from.

He'd just climbed back into his jeans and shrugged his way into the crumpled shirt (which wasn't quite as bad as he'd feared), when Adie Raven knocked on the back door.

'Ah Gavin! How are you settling in? I know Feen's already checked, but I wanted to just recap with you myself, that everything's ok for you in here.'

Gavin grinned at her. 'Adie, this place is gorgeous! It's perfect. It has such a special, cosy feel to it, almost like it's giving me a cuddle! That sounds mad, doesn't it? And those views! If this place doesn't inspire me to write amazing songs, nothing will!'

Adie laughed, delighted. 'It doesn't sound mad at all. The cottage is definitely special. It has its own unique, very special kind of energy. Feen can tell you a lot more about that, but let me just say that buying this place was the best decision I ever made.'

She looked fondly around the cottage. 'I rebuilt my life in here. The best bits for me were that lovely open fire, and waking up to the sound of birds.'

He nodded and laughed too. 'Nature's the best alarm clock. I probably won't even shut the curtains!'

'No, you won't need to. I did through the winter of course, when I was living here, but only to keep the heat in. Someone would need a pretty high-powered set of binoculars to spy on you up here!'

'Or a drone,' Gavin responded.

Adie smirked. 'Well, let's hope most people have better things to do. Oh, I have good news, by the way. Teapot Cottage is yours for a month, if you want it. I went ahead and cancelled the pencil booking. So you can move your music stuff in whenever you want. I've emailed you the invoice.'

She looked around the kitchen, then looked back at him.

'Well, now that's all taken care of and you have everything you need, I know someone who's champing madly at the bit to see you. So let's go.

'Welcome to Ravensdown House,' she announced, as they approached a rambling, elegant old stone farmhouse with mullioned bay windows and leadlight panes. Gavin stopped and stared. 'Whoa! What a stunning place! It's amazing, Adie.'

'Yes, it was beautifully restored by my husband and Feen's mother, thirty years ago, give or take. We do like that it can't be seen from the road. It's nice and private up here.' She gestured to a door down the hall.

'Go and make yourself at home in the kitchen. I'm not sure what Feen's cooking. I had planned to make dinner for us all myself, but she shooed me out of there at lightning speed.'

Gavin heard the front door open then close with a bang. Adie craned her neck.

'Ah, looks like Mark's in, a bit later than usual. He'll be getting in the shower, so maybe you could ask Feen to make a pot of tea for us all? And don't look so worried', she added. 'He's not going to make things difficult. I've done what I could to ease the way, and he's a sweet man really, nowhere near as gruff as he sounds. You'll find him very approachable and very nice, I promise.'

She turned on her heel and left Gavin facing the kitchen door. He pushed it open and saw Feen leaning over the kitchen table with a small blowtorch. From the concentration on her face, he could see she was too absorbed to notice he'd come in. Realising he'd startle her if he spoke, he decided to wait until her crème brulees were crunch-perfect, and she had put out the torch, before clearing his throat.

'Good evening, faiden mair! Whatever it is you're cooking smells delicious.'

Feen beamed and came around the table with her arms outstretched. He swept her into his own, burying his face in hair that smelled like sweet oranges.

'It's an oven-baked Bolognese with mozzarella, and a Mediterranean salad. Are you hungry? I've seen how much you eat, so I've made masses.' He voice was breathless against his ear.

86

'Oh yes, absolutely! I am *definitely* hungry.' *And not just for food,* he added to himself.

Feen released hm with a gentle smirk, and looked at him for a long time. Neither said a word but each knew what the other was thinking. Feen nodded almost imperceptibly. *Then I may have to follow you home tonight, o prandsome hince.* He heard the words in his head as if they'd come from Feen's own lips, although she hadn't said a thing. And that's when he understood the true depth of what they had.

Indeed tonight, maiden fair, should the notion please you.

And a small, knowing smile played around the edges of her mouth.

Well yes, sir. I mink perhaps it thight.

The kettle whistled on the huge dark blue Aga that dominated the kitchen, and Feen poured its steaming contents into a battered old cream enamel teapot. It was quite large, with various chips and dents in it, and although it had some character, it could really only be described as a bit of a wreck.

'I know what it looks like,' Feen giggled as she noted him staring at it. 'But it makes really good tea. We've tried loads of others, but we always end up going back to this one. It's like the tagic meapot.'

'Maybe it should live at Ceapot Tottage then!' Gavin joked.

'It did, originally! Funny you should say that. It was found half buried in the ground, by the Robinsons, the people who bought what used to be an old shepherds' hut and turned it into the place it is now, before Adie bought it. It's what gave Teapot Cottage its name! The Robinsons displayed it on the top shelf in the kitchen,' she explained. 'They were never game enough to clean it up and use it, but we gave it a whirl on the off-chance, because I just had a funny feeling it'd make a brilliant pot of tea, and it does. I'm afraid you'll have to prise this old hulk from my cold dead fingers. In fact, I shall insist on it coming into the grave with me.'

'It looks like it's been used as a football' Gavin observed.

'Ah, judge ye not, wait until you taste the tea. But I'm warning you. Slag off my teapot again and I might feel inclined to wrap it around your head.'

'I have no doubt whatsoever, that you'd do that. I am suitably a 'feared, milady. Consider me silenced!'

At that moment, a burly middle-aged man wandered into the room; undeniably Feen's father, with the same piercing blue eyes, and dark hair in the places where it hadn't yet gone grey. He looked at Gavin and held out his hand.

'Mark Raven. I take it yer Gavin Black.'

*   *   *   *   *

'Well, as interrogations go, that wasn't too bad,' Gavin murmured as they left Ravensdown House. 'He didn't run me through with the corkscrew or try to scoop my eye out with a pudding spoon. In fact, I think I was more at risk from you and that knackered old teapot than I was from anything your dad might've done.'

'See? I told you. He's a pussycat. And I will continue to ignore your relentless insistence on belittling my beautiful teapot.'

'Hmm... dunno if I 'd go so far as to call him a pussycat, but I think you're a winner if he likes you. Not sure how things would go if he didn't.'

'Don't worry. He likes you.'

'Good, because I really like *him*! And the way he talks, well, that's a bloody gem, right there. He's hilarious, Feen! I could listen to him for hours.'

'I know. He's one out of the box, that's for sure. Few men of his generation still speak that broadly anymore. He took after his own Dad, for that. He just loves the fact that the way he talks makes certain people naturally avoid him. He says they're the very type he'd have no time for anyway.'

As they got to the cottage door, Gavin realised he hadn't brought his key. But Feen managed to produce one from under a brick in the garden wall, so they managed to get inside.

He turned on the light and as he did so, Feen pulled him towards the big sofa. He fell on top of her, and immediately the floodgates opened. He started kissing her, and she responded with such passion he could think of nothing but making love to her right there on the sofa. After a few moments he managed to rein himself in enough to stand and lift her and carry her up the stairs. He placed her gently on the bed and she pulled him down to her again.

'I'm sorry, sweetheart,' he whispered gently into her hair, a good while later. 'I was quite overcome. I hope it was good for you.'

'It was perfect. So much better than my hopes and dreams. Very 'Mills-and-Boon' in fact! Earth moving, heart racing, and all that. Being gently pushed up and up a hill, to fly off the cledge of the iff at the top of it. How glorious that was!' She grinned, then became thoughtful, biting her bottom lip.

'It's always been a bit awkward, before,' she confessed. 'I never really got what all the fuss was about, to be honest. I was seeing a boy for about a year, and we did have sex a few times, but it never felt like something I'd ever yearn for if it never happened again.'

'Ah! You weren't with the right man then, were you?'

'No. I really wasn't. I liked him and everything, but I don't think that was enough for me to … well, you know, to get up the hill, so to speak.'

Gavin understood completely. 'Well, for what it's worth, I've had my fair share of women. But over the years I've learned that sex by itself means nothing much at all. Unless you have real feelings for someone, it's no different than just shacking off in the jower, to put it crudely. It's purely physical, which is ok if that's all you want, and I did now and then, back when I was a much younger and far more inquisitive slave to my teeming testosterone! But I always knew I'd want more than that, when the time came.'

Feen nestled closer into him. 'So, have there been women you've had feelings for?'

'Yeah, at least I thought I did, at the time. I've had a couple of really nice girlfriends actually, but they wanted more. Marriage, house, kids; the whole kit and caboodle. I just didn't have it to give, at the time. Wasn't ready to commit. They accused me of being a flake, and I suppose I was, because as much as I tried to put my heart into it, I really couldn't. Looking back, I guess they weren't the right ones either. I must've known that, because the last one was only last year, and I never got the big revelation, even after she dumped me, that I wanted a wife and a family. Before I met you, it wasn't even on the radar.'

'Just goes to show, when you know, you just know.'

'Yep. Your dad, he knew with your mum, didn't he? I think that's helped us a bit, because I can imagine what I'd be like myself, if our daughter came waltzing home with some motley swain she'd known for exactly one and a half days, and then said she was going to marry him. I'd be a basket case.'

Feen laughed. 'Well, you're not exactly motley! And you won't be like that. You know you won't. Our daughter may just find love at first sight too, and you'll be exactly like Daddy about it, because you'll get it.'

Our daughter.

'So, you're sure we'll be having a daughter, are you? What about a son? Or two? Maybe half a dozen? Rugby team?'

She giggled at the merry twinkle in his gorgeous green eyes, and shook her head. 'You'll be lucky! I don't exactly have child-bearing hips, if you hadn't already noticed! We'll have two children. One of each, and that's it.'

'Well, love at first sight or not, whoever our girl drags home will have to pass everything including the inkblot test, to pass muster. I'll still be footing my put down and saying no, if he or she's an asshole.'

Feen twisted around in his arms and faced him, grinning. He kissed her nose and she pushed the hair back from across the front of his face.

'Well, you ravishingly handsome devil, I need a cup of tea. Want one?'

'Sure. Hey - Adie doesn't have any Mills and Boon paperbacks stashed under the bed that I can take a look at, by any chance, while you're taking the mea? You know, to give me few pointers?'

'You don't need any pointers!' Feen picked up a pillow and hit him with it, then got up and padded downstairs. Gavin lay back in the bed and listened to the comforting sound of her moving around in the kitchen, and realised he'd never known that this kind of bliss even existed. He felt *whole,* in a way he'd never felt before. There was no familiar urge to get up and dressed, and find any excuse that came to mind, to bolt for the horizon. Instead, he wanted to stay exactly where he was, with Feen in his arms, until the end of time.

She returned to him with a broad smile and a tray of tea and hot buttered toast. She was wearing his shirt, which swamped her tiny frame. Her lips were red, swollen and almost bruised. Her pupils were huge, and her hair was a glorious tangle. She had a new sparkle in her eye now too. There was a cheekiness about her smile, and her posture was more confident. Something within her that had previously been dormant was now fully awake. She was sensual now, in a way she hadn't been before.

Gavin quietly wondered how he was going to explain this latest, life-changing turn of events to his family and friends. Carla would hopefully be more indifferent than spiteful, which would make a lovely change. Nanny and Bampa would probably be initially confused but then delighted, Mike would be incredulous and fiercely protective, and Gavin's mates would no doubt laugh him out of the room. But he figured he could handle it all.

'What are you chiting your beek for?' Feen chided. 'What's eating you the most? That your stepdad might have a tartan fit, your mother might skin you alive with her sixty-grit sandpaper tongue, or your mates might blow you off for being a romantic sap?'

He stared at her, not knowing whether to laugh or cry. 'Oh, God. Tell me I haven't just said a permanent goodbye to the luxury of private thoughts from now on.'

She laughed and threw herself onto the bed, allowing him to catch her and roll her over. He gazed into her eyes.

'Please tell me you don't have access to my every last thought and dream?'

She put out a hand and smoothed his hair back from across his forehead.

'No, but I do have to tell you that I can't control it. Some stuff I pick up on, but never all of it. Just snandom ratches of people's thoughts, like wadio raves or something. You're pretty safe, as long as you don't think horrible stuff.' She grinned. 'But I can show you how to put a kind of guard around certain thoughts, like what sort of surprise you might plan for my birthday in a couple of weeks, or something like that.'

'Well, that would be useful. Thank you. There are certain things I really would like to keep to myself, if at all possible. A man needs at least a small amount of privacy, from time to time. But of course I am more than happy to talk about your upcoming birthday, maiden fair.'

'We certainly should, but before we get to that, kind sir, may I have another of those rather ravishing hill-climbs please? Perhaps a longer and slower one, with a good long flight at the end?'

That I can give you, milady, as many times as your beautiful heart desires.

Chapter Nine

A Spell to Heal an Estranged Relationship

You will need:
A Fountain pen with black ink
Two small pieces of parchment
A green ribbon (to represent hope)
A small chip of Amazonite crystal
A small clear jar and white wax to seal it
Enough raw honey to fill the jar

With the fountain pen, write the names of the people involved,
one on each piece of parchment, and place together with the
names facing inward. Wrap with the green ribbon so that no
paper is still showing. Roll and place in the bottle, with the chip
of Amazonite. Fill the jar with honey and seal with the wax.
Put the jar in a secret place where nobody else will find it.
Incantation (three times):
'Let love regrow, in a vial sealed,
for two souls disconnected, the rift to be healed,'

As Feen left to go back to Ravensdown, lingering hugs and kisses at the front door were more sweet than passionate, but she didn't mind. It wasn't like a one-night stand where she'd be left wondering if she'd ever see him again. Something had been cemented, life had profoundly shifted for them both. She hadn't minded leaving him tonight, in fact she loved the delicious promise of reconnecting, tomorrow.

As Gavin had held her in his arms tonight, he'd talked a bit about his grandparents, his Nanny and Bampa, and how much they meant to him. They sounded like nice people. Feen vaguely wondered who they were, but she didn't suppose she would know them anyway. Carlisle was far enough away for her to know only a small handful of people, mostly of her own age, who she'd gone to school with and who had moved to where there was a bit more employment not too far from home.

Gavin had apologised as she was leaving, saying that he'd promised to cook dinner for his family the following night. He'd be back quite late, probably just before eleven. He'd said he'd love to have invited her to the meal, certain that his grandparents would love her and make her welcome, but he didn't feel ready to subject her to the scrutiny of his bats-in-the-belfry mother quite yet.

Whenever he mentioned her, Feen kept getting the same slightly sick feeling in the pit of her stomach. Where the 'evil' Mrs Black was concerned, something dark consistently clawed at her. A black shadow seemed to hang above them both, whenever Gavin mentioned her, and Feen always felt a noticeable chill. Her intuition was definitely trying to tell her something, but she'd somehow lost her ability to interpret it. Her subconscious was tapping her on the shoulder, whispering gently; *something is wrong.*

That in itself wasn't particularly unsettling, as Feen was used to her sixth sense sometimes warning her of danger. What worried her more was the fact that this was her first-ever failure to understand why the thought of something - in this case a woman she'd never met - plunged her into such an opaque emotional void. It was a feeling she wasn't used to, and the lack of transparency was maddening.

As per usual, there's nobody to talk to about anything off-beat. Oh, Mum! I wish you were here. You'd understand, and maybe you could even explain what this 'black block' means. It is literally driving me to distraction!

Ravensdown House was in darkness as she let herself back in, to go to bed. As she tiptoed to the top of the stairs, she heard Adie call out.

'Feen, darling? Is that you?'

'Yes,' Feen replied, in a low voice. 'I'm sorry if I woke you Adie, I was trying to be quiet.'

Adie appeared in the doorway of her and Mark's bedroom. She spoke softly.

'You didn't wake me. I've been struggling to get to sleep tonight, I think it's my hormones again, still messing with my sleep. Insomnia goes hand in hand with menopause for me, unfortunately. I'll be so glad when I eventually get to the end of this God-awful process. It's nowhere near as bad as it used to be, but it does feel like a rollercoaster I've been on since forever. It's the randomness of it all that annoys me the most. Some nights I'm fine, others I'm all over the place.'

She pulled a face, then looked more closely at Feen. 'D'you fancy a cup of tea before you go to bed?'

Feen giggled, whispering back. 'No, I'm awash with tea, thanks. I've been drinking gallons of it. I wouldn't mind a Baileys, though?'

Adie thought for a moment, then nodded. 'That sounds like a great idea. Forget the tea. Let's go straight to the top shelf.'

Downstairs in the kitchen, Adie reached for the glasses while Feen fetched the Baileys from the drinks' cabinet in the living room. She poured two good measures and handed a glass to her stepmother, who tried to hide a smirk, and failed.

'What?' Feen demanded.

'You know!' Adie was openly grinning now. Mortified, Feen flushed crimson.

'Oh Feen! Don't be embarrassed, darling! It's wonderful! You're a grown woman. It's high time you had a man in your life, *and* great sex! This is life as it's *meant* to be for someone your age!'

Feen giggled in spite of her burning cheeks. 'How do you know it was great sex? It might have been disastrous!'

Adie shook her head, laughing. 'I know it was great sex because of how starry-eyed you look! And how inept you've been, at sorting out your messed-up hair! It looks like a sweet

94

little bird's nest, darling. But all this? It's a good thing, Feen. It's a really, *really* good thing. I'm so happy for you.'

Feen plonked herself on the sofa, with a sigh. She looked at her stepmother, holding her gaze for a few seconds.

'D'you think Daddy liked him? D'you think he's really ok with all this? It's all so sudden, I know. It feels absolutely a thousand percent right for us both, but I can see how it might be a massive shock to him.'

Adie reached across, took Feen's hand and squeezed it.

'Mark will be just fine. Yes, it's all a bit unexpected, but he adores you. It's what he's always longed for, that someone who really, truly *gets* you will come along and sweep you off your feet, and make you happy, and cherish you forevermore. I think he'd have liked a bit more notice, and a lot more of a courtship of course, but there'll be time between now and whenever your wedding takes place for him to get used to everything.'

'Does he *like* Gavin, though? I know he's happy that I'm happy, but we're so close. It's important to me that he does like my choice of husband. I couldn't bear it if he only put up with it.'

Adie squeezed her hand again. 'Yes, from what he's seen so far, he does like him. They do have to spend more time together of course, to form some kind of bond, but I do think that will happen. Mark was a bit concerned that Gavin didn't want to talk much about his family, though. He's wondering what the mystery is there, but I'm sure Gavin has good reasons for not divulging too much too soon, especially since his dad has just died. Nobody knows more than Mark and I do, about complicated families and the feelings around them!'

Feen nodded, suddenly reflective. 'I've been very lucky, to have had amazing parents. I miss Mum every day, and I long for her sometimes, even after all these years. Even just tonight, I wished I could talk to her. It's like an ache that never stops for very long, that she died the way she did, far too early, and right when I needed her most. It's so frustrating that bowel cancer can be so much more successfully managed or even cured now, if they get to it early enough. But I have Daddy, who's the biggest rock in my world. I have Aunt Sheila and Uncle Bob, and now I

95

have you too. So, compared with a lot of people who have ferrible tamilies, I'm very lucky. I know that.'

She paused, before carrying on. 'Gavin didn't tell you that his parents have been estranged since he was little. He's an only child, and he has a complicated relationship with his mother. They're estranged too. He doesn't want anything to do with her, really, but there's some kind of problem about some belongings she has that were his dad's. He's trying to get them back. That's why he came here.' Feen rubbed her eyes and yawned.

'Sorry, Adie, but I'm getting a bit sleepy now. I think I need to go to bed. All I can say is that Gavin hasn't even told *me* much about his family dynamics yet, and I don't want to push him. It seems painful for him. He'll rell me when he's teady, I suppose. But he has grandparents he adores, which is helpful. I think they all live in Carlisle.'

Adie nodded. 'Well, he seems very mature and solid, and I'm sure he's got a good handle on things. He doesn't seem to be the kind of man who'd be at the mercy of anyone, even his family. It will all settle down in time, one way or another.' She drained her glass, stood up, and stretched. 'I'm going back up to bed now too, to try and get some sleep.'

'Do you want a potion? I can make one up in about five minutes. It'll probably taste disgusting but it will work.'

Adie shook her head. 'Thanks darling, but I think the Baileys has done the trick. Not my usual sleeping aid of choice, but I think tonight it's just enough to take the edge off. I may just drop off now. I really envy your dad, you know. He can sleep on a clothesline. He's gone within seconds of his head hitting the pillow. Once he's asleep, you could drive a train through the house and it wouldn't wake him.'

Feen grinned and stood also, and gave her stepmother a hug. 'You do look tired. I'll make you an 'evil tonic', tomorrow, a bottle of something you can use for a week or so that will help.'

'Thank you, Feen. And I'm genuinely thrilled for you. I do like Gavin. He's clearly besotted with you, but he's down-to-earth, so you know where you are with him, and Mark likes that in a person too. I think those two might find a lot in common, as time goes by.'

'Adie you always know how to say just the right thing. Thank you. I hope I didn't offend you earlier, in saying how much I miss Mum.'

Her stepmother frowned and shook her head. 'I'd be surprised and sad if you didn't miss her, darling. I've never sought to replace her, of course, and you know that already. But we never had the talk, did we, you and I, about my role in your life? We just kind of slotted together as a new family, fairly seamlessly I think, and it never occurred to me that we might need to talk about any kind of boundaries.'

Adie yawned again, and continued. 'You just have this 'knowing', and I guess I always just assumed you'd know what I wanted us to be to one another.'

Feen hugged her again. 'And I do, Adie. I know you're here for me, and I hope you know I love you too. I did even before you darried maddy.' She laughed quietly. 'I'm still getting to grips with *your* complicated family, but so far I think we're all doing ok, don't you?'

'Yeah, I think we are. As for my lot, I know they all think the world of you, Feen. Despite their funny quirks and bangs, they'll be loyal siblings if you let them. And I'm truly sorry if you do end up inheriting another complex family, but me and your dad are here to support you, whatever happens. I hope you know that.'

'I do. Goodnight Adie. Sleep well.'

Adie waved tiredly and started heading upstairs. As Feen rinsed out the glasses and put away the Baileys bottle, she sent a thought into the ether to Gavin.

Goodnight darling one. I'm counting the hours.

A tiny voice popped into her head. *Me too. Twenty-two to go.*

* * * * *

Friday morning dawned bright and sunny, and Feen set to work early fulfilling the last of a jewellery samples order for her new stepsister-in-law, Gina. The commission work was starting to provide a modest but steady income now, and with a new catalogue being launched in the autumn, there was the prospect of a lot more. It was enough to keep Feen busy. Gina gave her a lot of creative licence, and was always pleased with what was sent, but she had asked specifically for certain styles and colour combinations to complement the next winter collection.

Absorbed in her work, she looked up only when Adie came in with a sandwich and a mug of tea, around midday. The next time she checked the clock, she realised that she had barely enough time to get the package wrapped, addressed and down to the post office before it closed. Scrambling, she pulled everything together and jumped into her car. Down in the village there were no parks close to the post office, so she had to park behind the supermarket, and run to get there in time. She made it with just five minutes to spare and her friend Josie, the teller, burst out laughing as Feen crashed through the door, puffing and panting.

'Oh, Josie! I've just had to sprint all the way from the bloody supermarket! All the parking spots near here are taken. Just let me get my breath back!' She handed her parcel to Josie who started producing the necessary labels. She peered short-sightedly over her glasses at Feen.

'I've missed you, Feen! I haven't seen you for ages. You got time for a quick drink when we close up here? I've got news!'

Feen already knew what Josie's news would be, but she didn't want to steal her friend's thunder. 'Of course! A quick one though, as I've doads to loo, tonight.'

'Yes! I don't have much time myself, but I really want to talk to you.'

With the parcel prepared and put into the mail sack behind the counter, Josie turned the lights out and started preparing to close the post office, Feen wondered how Gavin was getting on. She checked her watch. He'd be picking up his mother from work about now. She wondered what he was going to cook for everyone.

The fact that he knew what to do in a kitchen was a bonus. Feen enjoyed cooking, but she was always very appreciative when someone else stepped in. Mark hadn't been much cop in the kitchen after Beth had died. His best efforts hadn't run to much beyond beans on toast with a slice of cheese underneath them or a ham and cheese omelette, with a handful of dried herbs thrown on top if he was feeling particularly creative. He had, however, taught Feen how to use a light hunting rifle, and how to skin, gut and prepare a rabbit for a pot of stew. Shooting living creatures certainly didn't feature on her list of happy pastimes, and she'd far rather watch a group of rabbits playing in the fields than get rid of them, but she wasn't naïve. They were outright pests, on farms. They were classed as vermin; prolific breeders who were capable of doing enormous damage to crops, and they had to be culled. In late summer, when the numbers were starting to look they were out of control, Mark would have hunters come over and spend a weekend shooting them. They'd end up with hundreds.

By necessity, Feen had ended up cooking most of the meals for herself and her dad, including rabbit stew! Beth had initially shown her how to use the Aga, and Sheila had later been a big help with teaching her the finer points of cooking, so her food wouldn't be boring and bland. She suddenly had a clear vision of Gavin in the kitchen at Teapot Cottage, pulling a pie from the oven, and humming to himself as he cut into it and dished it up.

After setting the alarms, Josie hustled her through the front door and locked it. As they walked towards the Feathers pub, Feen remembered that it was almost a year since her friend had married her childhood sweetheart, Tony Valley. He was a nice man who'd trained as a domestic electrician. He was reliable, competent and very fairly priced on his services, and so he had plenty of ongoing work in the area.

The position of Postmistress suited Josie down to the ground. She hadn't been at all academic, and after starting at the post office as a junior teller she'd been surprised to be offered the job. Her and Tony's work meant that their lives would always be in Torley. With both sets of parents, various siblings and cousins, and a good handful of friends around, they were well-settled and happy in the little town. People often teased Josie, that she'd married Tony Valley from Torley Valley!

Once inside the Feathers, Feen got a gin and tonic for herself and an orange and lemonade for Josie, and they found a quiet booth. The pub was just starting to get busy with the after-work set streaming in. Josie took a sip of her drink, then looked up and grinned.

'Can I have a drum-roll please?'

Feen smiled and obligingly started drumming on the table.

Josie didn't even wait until the drum roll was finished. 'I'm pregnant! I'm due in early December! We've just passed the first trimester and I'm so glad to finally be able to tell everyone!'

Feen beamed, pretending to be surprised. 'Josie that's such fab news! Huge congratulations! I'm thrilled for you and Tony.'

Josie blushed gently, toying with her glass. 'We weren't planning to start a family so soon,' she confessed, 'but I guess Mother Nature had different ideas for us.'

'She often does!' Feen laughed. 'But it's good, right?'

Josie nodded. 'Yes, yes, it is. All good. Actually Feen, Tony and I wondered if you'd like to be a Godmother. No pressure, I don't need an answer today', she added quickly as Feen's face registered her surprise.

'Really? Why me? I mean, I'd be thrilled to bits, of course. But surely you have other people, like mamily fembers, who might be more suitable?'

'Feen, honestly, you'd be perfect. From the minute I found out I was pregnant, I knew I wanted you in the mix. Our baby deserves to have a very special person as a Godparent. There will be others, of course, but none of them are as unique, quirky, and interesting as you. Baby Valley will need a quirky woman in his or her life, and you're exactly who I want, to fulfil that role. You can teach him or her about nature and mad clothes, you'll be perfect. But only if you want to,' she added with an enquiring smile.

Feen reached across and hugged Josie tightly. 'I truly would be honoured. I can be the crazy woman in odd shoes and daft hats, who turns her into a sorceress!'

'Or him into a warlock! But whichever, that would be fab!' Josie was beaming.

Josie, it's a girl! You're having a little girl.

Josie pulled out a photo of a scan, which meant very little to Feen, but she was enthusiastic for her happy friend anyway. They had a good chat about baby names and how the littlest people always seem to get the cutest clothes, then Josie looked at her watch and rolled her eyes.

'Crikey! I'd better go. Tony's van is in for repairs and I said I'd pick him up from the new housing estate he's working at, at half past. I'm already late!'

Feen needed to get going too, so the two women drained their drinks and stepped outside. It was a pretty evening. The sun had started to dip a little now in the sky, casting shadows, but the air was warm and the birds were singing their hearts out. Josie suddenly looked crestfallen.

'Oh, Feen, I haven't even had the chance to ask you what's been going on in *your* world! I'm so wrapped up in myself right now with all this baby business. I think it's already screwing up my hormones. I'm a selfish cow, for just prattling away about my own stuff. Please forgive my nappy-brain!'

Feen gave Josie a quick hug. 'No problem. I have news too, but it can wait for another day. We need to do this more often.'

'And we will,' Josie nodded. 'In fact, let's meet next Wednesday, at one o'clock, if that works for you? Its half-day at the post office and I have no other plans for the afternoon, except maybe to visit GladRagz to see if Trude has any whale-sized maternity clothes! I have a feeling I'm going to need them. If she doesn't, we could maybe pop over to Carlisle? And let's have a bite of lunch here first, at the pub, so I can properly hear *your* news. I'm always hungry these days, probably since I'm eating for two!'

She rubbed her still-flat belly tenderly, and winked at Feen. 'I'm guessing you'd have known my news before I said it, but thank you for letting me announce it. We don't want to know the sex of the baby, by the way, so try not to drop any clangers!'

'I know! And I'll do my level best!'

Feen hugged Josie tightly as they said goodbye. She looked forward to having lunch and time for a bit of shopping with her friend. It had been too long since they'd spent any quality time together. As she waved Josie off and turned towards her own car, she wondered again how Gavin was getting on with his dinner preparations. She looked forward to the night he'd cook a romantic meal for her, and she knew she wouldn't have to wait long. Once he was settled into Teapot Cottage, there would be many romantic dinners; of that she was certain.

As she rounded the corner to the supermarket carpark, immersed in her happy thoughts, she was surprised to see Gavin's Porsche pull up. She was about to run over to him, when she realised that he wasn't alone. He had a woman with him. Feen shrank back against the wall as they both got out of the car and walked into the supermarket. Suddenly lightheaded, and struggling not to be sick, she found herself fighting to stop her legs from giving way beneath her. And her reaction wasn't because Gavin was with another woman.

It was about who that woman was.

Her new fiancé had walked into the supermarket with Carla Walton; the 'ice-maiden' who had once pitched her cap at Feen's father, and who had viciously torn up the lawn at Teapot Cottage in a fit of jealousy at the sight of Adie Bostock (as she then was) attracting attention from Mark at a Christmas party a couple of years back. The crazy bitch had then gone on to feed poisoned meat to the lovely little dog Adie was looking after, in an effort to have her driven out of Torley. Evil Carla Walton, who was still considered the local town pariah by many who hadn't forgotten her shameful criminal acts.

Is she Gavin's mother? It certainly looks like it. Oh, God! How cruel a twist of fate is this?

Feen instantly connected the likeness. It was blindingly obvious that they were related, now that she knew. Gavin had Carla's glittering green eyes, almost-black hair, and bow-shaped mouth. She now understood completely why he didn't get along with her, and refused to have her in his life. And of course, it answered the bothersome question about why she always felt so wretched when Gavin mentioned his mother. It was Feen's guides, protecting her love for her soulmate, while they figured everything out.

Feen had been the one to find the poor dog, foaming at the mouth and dying where he lay, inside the front door at Teapot Cottage. Adie, a stranger to the area at the time, had been house sitting and looking after him for the Robinsons, the couple who'd owned the cottage back then, while they were away visiting family in Australia. Adie had been down south for the weekend with Mark, and Feen had woken up, alone in the big house, with a feeling of dread invading her whole body. She'd felt sick and lethargic, with her head pounding, but she'd known it wasn't a physical illness. Something entirely different was happening, and Feen had known, instinctively, to run as fast as her feet could carry her to Teapot Cottage, where the sickening vibrations were coming from.

Sid, the little spaniel, had nearly died that morning. With no time to lose, Feen had flung him into Adie's car and driven him at break-neck speed to the vet, and screamed as she'd hammered on the door. There was no question that she'd saved Sid's life by doing that.

Carla Walton had been arrested on suspicion of causing criminal damage, and with clear evidence stacking up against her, she had quickly caved and confessed to poisoning the dog, and to destroying the cottage lawn in an earlier attack against Adie. She'd been formally charged with two counts of criminal damage, had appeared before a magistrate in Carlisle town, and had received a hefty fine and community service. Adie, Feen and Mark had been devastated.

The woman was unhinged, there was no two ways about it. Mark had gone to her house, before her court appearance, and although he never told Feen or Adie what he'd said to Carla, he assured them both that she would never bother either of them again. From then onwards, Carla Walton had been effectively ostracized by the local community, who had *all* felt wounded by what she had done. She'd more or less gone to ground, and Feen had never seen her since. She was surprised Carla was even still in the area. She apparently had a job in Carlisle.

Doing what? Something a criminal record doesn't matter for, clearly!

Again, she fought back the urge to throw up. Carla was Gavin's mother.

Suddenly everything fell neatly and horribly into place. She'd got it all wrong. The family wasn't from Carlisle. Carla Walton lived right here in Torley, which meant Gavin's 'Nanny and Bampa' did too.

They must be Stan and Hazel Walton, she realised, from the other side of the valley. They had a nice, rambling old turn-of-the-century bungalow with a spectacular rose garden. Beth and Mark had taken Feen over there once, on a village open day

103

where people with lovely gardens invited the general public to come and view them in exchange for a small donation to charity. Feen remembered a glorious big garden, which Stan and Hazel had created and tended with pride, and which some people said had once been featured in a national magazine. It also had a water feature, and a pretty little white wrought iron bandstand, but it was the fragrant, gloriously colourful riot of roses Feen remembered the most. Those, and the tea and cake handed out by a smiling, proud Hazel on the patio by the fountain.

In shock, Feen stumbled to her car, and sat perfectly still, while she tried to make sense of everything. Eventually, she drove home to Ravensdown House, but by the time she got there, the tears were pouring down her face.

Coming into the house, she was too distracted to watch where she was going, and she ended up colliding roughly with her father, who was coming down the stairs after his shower. He took one look at her and growled; 'I'm gonna snap 'is fuckin' neck!'

'Daddy no, please!' she wailed tearfully. 'It's not Gavin. He hasn't upset me. I haven't seen him. He's with his mother.' And on that note she dissolved into full-blown sobs. 'Daddy, please help me,' she wailed. 'I don't know what to do!'

Adie came running into the hallway and cried 'Feen! Whatever's the matter, darling?' She guided Feen into the kitchen and sat her down at the table, sitting also, along with Mark.

Stuttering through her tears, Feen managed to explain. After she did, Mark and Adie looked at each other in horror. Mark looked stunned.

'Well, talk about bloody bastard luck!' he roared at the top of his voice. 'What were't fuckin' chances o' that?'

Adie cleared her throat. 'You don't have to shout, Mark. We're all in the same house! Let's just take a step back, here, and think about what you told me last night, Feen. As I understand it, Gavin doesn't get on with his mother? He doesn't want her in his life? He's only here to see her because he has to? If that's all true, maybe there's no real cause to worry.' She tore off a piece of kitchen roll and silently handed it to Feen, who promptly blew her nose on it, and nodded her head.

'Yes, you're right, Adie. They don't have a relationship. It shouldn't be a problem. But why do I feel so wretched?'

'Because 'appen there'll be a lot bloody more, to all this.' Mark growled.

'I just feel sick to my stomach,' Feen sniffled. 'I knew something wasn't right. He hasn't told me who his mother is, but every time he's mentioned her, I've been feeling like I do right now. Only it's worse now, because I know.'

'The woman's a bloody cot case,' Mark muttered in response.

Adie quickly interjected, clearly trying to head him off at the pass before he could say anything that would have his daughter in an even worse state than she was already.

'It doesn't mean anything, Mark. Nothing at all.'

Mark shook his head. Clearly, he didn't see it that way. He scraped back his chair and headed for the door.

'Where are you going?' Feen demanded.

'I need to clear me 'ead.' He stormed out of the room, slamming the kitchen door behind him, hard enough to make the clock on the wall above it rattle.

'Daddy!'

Feen was literally unable to stop sobbing. Shock and dismay were taking their toll, and now her father was upset too. In fact, he was more livid than she'd seen him in a long time; since, in fact, the business with Sid the dog that had been caused by Carla Walton in the first place.

Adie sighed heavily. 'Feen, you can't blame your dad for feeling like he does. That awful woman has caused so much heartache for this family. This is a big shock for us all. And while it's Gavin you're planning to marry, and not his mother, there are implications for *both* families. So you do need to think about that.'

Feen was suddenly angry now too. 'So, don't marry him! Is that what you're saying? That if I marry him, *you're* all going to suffer?'

Immediately, she regretted snapping at Adie. If she'd got this much of a shock herself, imagine how much worse the prospect of having Carla Walton as an in-law must be for her poor stepmother to contemplate, after being the undeserved target of the other woman's cruel intentions, and not so very long ago.

There *had* been a lot of suffering for Adie, to the point where she had even considered abandoning her house sit and leaving Torley early. Of course, Mark had been furious too, at the time. While he wasn't a man to hold a grudge, he certainly wouldn't find it easy to tolerate having Carla Walton as a part of his family, even if she never crossed the Ravensdown threshold. Her shadow would be across it, nonetheless. The fact that she was even still in the same town probably already annoyed him enough.

Feen sagged back in her chair, heavy with despair. Adie sat down again and grabbed hold of her hands.

'Of course I'm not suggesting you don't marry Gavin, Feen! I would never say such a thing, and you should know that by now. What I mean is that you need to consider how you'll manage the situation for your dad. Of *course* he hates the thought of Carla Walton joining this family, even as a person nobody's willing to engage with, including her own son! But it's not just that, Feen. This isn't really about him being pissed off for me, or for himself. He'll be worried sick about *you*, and how having Carla as a mother-in-law will impact on *you*, in this marriage. You mark my words, it's the kind of thing that can literally eat a worried dad alive!'

'And what about you, Adie? What about the prospect for you, of being related to her by marriage?'

Adie shrugged. 'You don't need to worry about me. I'm a big girl. I can take care of myself.'

At that moment, Mark came back into the kitchen. He pulled out his chair and sat back down at the table. He nodded at Adie. 'Put kettle on will yer, love?'

'Of course. Oh, and that door *is* still on its hinges, by the way, no thanks to you being so heavy-handed.'

He inclined his head, by way of apology, and turned to Feen. She was surprised to see how sad he looked. She hadn't seen him look that way since Beth had died. Like someone had reached inside him and switched something off, and it broke her heart.

'Daddy...' She got no further, as he raised his hand to stop her from speaking.

'You get yer bloke back up 'ere quick-smart. I need a few words with 'im, man to man, like.'

As Feen opened her mouth to speak he held up his hand again. He spoke slowly and deliberately.

'Now I'm not sayin' I'll stand in't way of yer marryin' 'im, if it's still what yer really want. But I need to be clear about a few things, includin' whether 'e's got the spine to stop 'er from interferin' in yer marriage, or givin' you an 'ard time. Because if I get even the slightest bloody idea that 'e might not be up to't job o' protecting yer from that fuckin' lunatic, I won't be givin' yer me blessin', and yer'd 'ave to get wed wi'out it. So get 'im back up 'ere. And sooner rather than later, lass.'

And with that, he left the room again, this time with less drama, closing the door - quietly this time - behind him.

Adie pulled a face. 'Well, it's a fair enough request, I suppose. He's going to give poor Gavin a grilling though, Feen. You'll need to prepare him for that, I think. Can you get him up here tonight?'

Feen shook her head. 'He won't be back at Teapot Cottage until very late tonight. Close to midnight, maybe. He's cooking dinner for his grandparents. Stan and Hazel Walton are his grandparents, I suppose. You probably don't know them but Daddy does. They live on the other vide of the salley. Carla lives with them.'

'Well, you'd better make sure he's here first thing in the morning, then. The longer this goes on, the more upset your dad's going to be. We need to get this situation cleared up quickly.'

Feen nodded. Suddenly she was conflicted about Gavin. She hated the feeling. He was her soul mate! As much as she adored him, and as much as she could no longer contemplate life without him, the cruel twist of fate that threw his mad mother into the mix would certainly complicate everything.

Feen knew Carla Walton didn't like her. The woman had made no bones about it, back in the day, when she was trying to snare Mark for herself. Feen was clearly an unwanted obstacle to be batted aside, like an annoying fly; an inconvenience to be ignored or derided rather than embraced as part of the package that came with Mark. Feen knew what Carla said about her, behind her back. She also knew it wouldn't help Gavin's

107

fractured relationship with his mother one bit, whether he wanted to mend it or not, to have Feen on the scene as a daughter-in-law.

What a mess! If she were ruthless enough, she would have said 'Sod it. Mad bitch or not, I'm marrying her son and that's that.' But Feen wasn't ruthless. She cared very much about whether her actions caused pain to someone else, and it was clear (and fair) that both Adie and her Dad were distressed by the prospect of having Carla Walton as part of their extended family.

With a heavy heart, Feen decided that since her head was a scrambled, unhappy mess, there would be no point in seeing Gavin tonight as planned. She was gutted about it, but common sense had to prevail. She needed time. She sent him a text message, to tell him she was unwell. He responded with a crying face emoji, and told her to get some sleep and feel better quickly.

She had never felt so miserable, and she really did have a horrible headache, now. Under different circumstances she wouldn't have let that stop her from being with the man she loved, but these were far from normal circumstances. Bewildered, with her happiness hanging in the balance, she had no choice but to trust whatever her father intended to do. After hugging him and Adie, who was trying valiantly to keep positive, she dragged herself off to bed, condemned to being awake all night, to toss and turn with worry, sadness, confusion and despair.

Suddenly, she realised she couldn't let Gavin walk straight into an ambush. She sent another text, telling him to wait for her to come down and get him in the morning.

She didn't get an immediate response. He must be busy with his family. It was the last thought she had before falling into a restless, fitful sleep. She didn't hear his car as it pulled into the driveway in front of Teapot Cottage, later that night.

Chapter Ten

A Song for Two Beautiful People

Two warm prisms of light, so bright I can barely see
Blending, and mending a heart that was broken
Even without a word being spoken
You light brings me back, brings me back,
Brings me back to me.
Without your love and your wisdom, where would this man be?
Just by being who you are, you bring me back to me.

Gavin drove away from Nanny and Bampa's, again with a full stomach, but also with an even fuller heart. Spending time with them was delightful and special, and it was always a wrench to leave. He wished he could scoop them both up and take them back to London with him, when the time came. Now that they'd reconnected, he had no intention of ever leaving it so long again, to visit and spend time with them, no matter how things might pan out with Carla.

Dinner had gone fairly well, all things considered. They'd been their usual warm and incredibly upbeat selves and, for once, his brittle mother had been almost teetering towards the friendly side of the fence. She'd even smiled at a couple of his lame jokes, and that was progress. When they'd stopped at the supermarket on the way home to pick up the ingredients he needed to make dinner, Carla had even bought a couple of bottles of wine to go with the meal, after asking him what the best choice might be. Gavin already had some wine in the car, but he wasn't about to refuse his mother's measure of generosity, especially when to do so was likely to instantly refreeze the layers of ice that were slowly, almost imperceptibly beginning to thaw in the space between them both.

He'd made his signature dish - nachos. It was a simple but firm favourite, because he didn't want to try anything too complicated or 'posh' (as Bampa would have called it) in his grandparents' fairly basic kitchen. They didn't go in much for kitchen gadgetry or labour-saving appliances. The best they could offer was an ageing bread maker, which they'd been given by friends for their 50th wedding anniversary. Gavin thought they'd probably used it twice.

They'd all enjoyed the nachos and the wine had poured freely, although he'd only had a couple of glasses himself, conscious that he was going to drive to Teapot Cottage at the end of the night. He was desperate to see Feen. Her text, telling him he wouldn't see her tonight after all, had all but disembowelled him, but the poor girl could hardly be expected to sit up and wait for him if she wasn't well.

He'd mentioned, over dinner, that he'd rented a holiday house locally. Bampa had asked him where it was but Gavin had been deliberately vague, gesturing across the valley, determined to keep some real distance between himself and his mother. Originally, it had been his plan to tell them tonight about Feen, but somehow the evening didn't lend itself to divulging the very special news. The timing wasn't right, and although he couldn't put his finger on exactly why he felt that way, he just knew there would be a better time. The last thing he wanted was his mother turning up, for whatever reason, and causing disruption by invading his space and casting a shadow over his joy. He wasn't ready for that yet.

Carla tended to cause chaos and frustration wherever she went, although he now sensed a slight mellowing. She'd managed to hold down a job, as a filing clerk in a factory, for a full year now, even though she said she didn't like it much. She also appeared to have a pretty relaxed relationship with Nanny and Bampa. All things considered, she had a fair measure of stability, and maybe that had helped chill her out a bit.

Gavin knew that the last thing Stan and Hazel would ever have expected, at their age, was to have their fifty-year-old daughter living with them. But they never turned away a friend in need, so however difficult a relationship might be, they were never going to slam the door on family. He knew he could have stayed with them himself, if he'd wanted. But their spare bedroom was full of junk, and sleeping on their ancient, lumpy sofa wasn't a prospect he relished. Being under the same roof as his mother made the prospect even less appealing. For the first time in a decade, he and Carla had managed to be civil, which was already more than he could have hoped for, but he didn't want to push his luck with her.

He still hadn't found the right moment to ask her about Martin's keepsake box, either, and she hadn't openly asked him again what he'd come for. She was waiting for him to be the one to ask but, since he was going to be around for a lot longer than his originally predicted few days, he reasoned there would be another, more appropriate time to talk to her about a lot of things, including his father and the possessions he'd held dear. As soon as he had what he'd come for (or not), Carla could fade from the picture of his life again. Like ripples in a pond, the water would return to its calm state, and life would carry on pretty much as it had before.

Nanny and Bampa had done their best with her. The way she was had nothing to do with bad parenting, because her elder brother, his Uncle Tristan, had by all accounts turned out absolutely fine. Gavin had never met him. As far as he knew, Uncle Tristan was a doctor who lived somewhere near Oxford. He was a bachelor, and busy with his work. He didn't get home much, according to Bampa, but he did get on well with his parents. He phoned home often, came home whenever he could, and there were smiling pictures of him on the sideboard in the living room; an old one in his cap and gown, clutching his medical degree aloft, and a more recent one, in a BMW convertible. Appearances suggested he was a happy sort - unlike his sister.

Uncle Tristan must have pissed her off too at some point, because she never talked about him, even while Gavin was living with her. He remembered a rocket-shaped money box arriving once for a birthday when he was quite young. Carla had made him write painstakingly to Uncle Tristan, in his childish scrawl, to say thank you. But that was it. There was no more contact after that. As a kid, Gavin hadn't wondered too much about it. But he thought about it now. Uncle Tristan was family too; maybe it wouldn't hurt to look him up.

As he was preparing to leave, Carla came out and leaned against the bonnet. She watched him load a fresh bag of the ginger crunch cookies Bampa had made for him, without saying anything. When he was ready to go, she stepped forward, smirking to herself.

'Well, if you're staying in town for a while, I guess I'll see you around. I suppose in time you'll tell me what you want.'

Gavin did his best to smile. He nodded. 'Yep. I'm here for a month or so. Maybe we could go for a drink.'

He wasn't expecting a positive response, and was astonished when he got one.

'Yeah, maybe we could. Thanks again for *tea* Gavin, it was nice. Not sure how Mum will deal with the spicy Mexican food. She'll probably need antacids as she goes to bed to avoid being up all night, but it was a nice gesture. We all appreciate it.'

Gavin chose to ignore the underlying accusation that he had compromised his grandmother's comfort with a meal she'd struggle to digest. Carla just couldn't help herself.

'It felt like a small thing to do, but I'm glad you all enjoyed it.'

Nanny and Bampa came wandering out. Both were in their pyjamas now, ready for bed. Bampa stepped forward and hugged Gavin.

'Don't be a stranger. Visit us lots before you head back to London.'

Nanny also hugged him tight. 'Thank you for that lovely Mexican meal, clever young man. You make sure you take care of yourself, and come and see us again soon. If you need anything at all, you know where we are.'

Carla merely nodded to him as he got into his car. He lowered his window.

'Thanks for having me. See you soon.' And with that, he was on the road again.

He checked the time. It was nearly quarter past ten. Nanny had brushed aside his offer to do the washing up before leaving. She said it would give her something to do in the morning, although he suspected she wouldn't go to bed until her kitchen was sparkling clean. They didn't even have a dishwasher.

Having got away earlier than planned, Gavin was hopeful of being able to catch Feen before she fell asleep, but Ravensdown House was all in darkness. He let himself in through the front door of Teapot Cottage and set Bampa's bag of biscuits on the kitchen bench.

He decided that since there was nothing to stay up for, he'd hit the hay himself. He shrugged off his disappointment, only for it to return as soon as he got into bed. The sheets smelled of Feen. The pillows carried the same rain-soft, orange fragrance of her hair. Reasoning that the sooner he fell asleep, the sooner it would be morning and he would see her, he nestled down and willed sleep to come.

The following morning, at quarter to eight, there was a short knock at the door, and Feen darted in. He could tell by the look on her face that something was badly wrong. She looked like she hadn't slept, and she seemed jittery and anxious. She didn't move to kiss him, as expected, and there was a sadness in her eyes that he just couldn't bear. His bowels loosened, just a little.

'Feen, what is it? What's wrong?'

She wasted no time in telling him. 'I saw you yesterday while I was in town. You were going into the supermarket with Carla Walton. She's your mother, isn't she?'

Gavin nodded, and spoke slowly. 'Erm… yeah. So, you already know her then?'

Feen laughed shortly, but there was no mirth in it. She motioned for him to sit, and she explained everything, at lightning speed, making it hard for him to keep up. She told him about Carla originally having her sights set on Mark, how she'd always treated Feen during that time, then the criminal damage she had inflicted on the lawn at Teapot Cottage, what she'd done to little Sid the spaniel, the court case, her community service, and how it had affected the Raven family and left the rest of the townsfolk reeling. She ended by telling Gavin that her father was beside himself and demanding to speak to him, and that was why she'd asked him to breakfast at the farm.

Gavin was horrified, and embarrassed beyond belief. Once again he found himself fighting to control the fury he felt towards

113

his mother. He literally couldn't speak. He also realised something else - that thanks to Carla's actions his relationship with Feen might be hanging in the balance and about to blow apart.

He couldn't even begin to imagine what Mark and Adie must be feeling about him right now, as the son of a woman who had put them through so much pain. It would be virtually impossible to continue a relationship with Feen if her family didn't want it to happen, and he could clearly see why they wouldn't. Although his first meeting with Mark Raven was friendly and positive, the man was already worried that his daughter was about to rush into a marriage with someone she hardly knew.

These latest revelations certainly wouldn't improve his fears for her happiness. And as for poor lovely Adie, who'd borne the brunt of Carla's viciousness, Mark would probably want to kill anyone who tried to hurt her, and Adie would want to protect Feen, just as much as Mark would. They seemed like a pretty tight, 'kick-one-and-we-all-scream' unit. No wonder everyone was so upset!

Gavin knew that the only thing he could do was be honest. All he could do was tell them everything, about his childhood, about how his mother had always treated him, and why he'd cut off relations with her. All he could do was explain that he was only in contact with her now because she had something that belonged to his father which was now Gavin's by right, and that he had no intention of keeping any contact with her after he'd got his father's box back.

Whether or not they believed him would be up to themselves. They were reasonable people, but protective of their own, like any good family. He fought back the nausea that threatened to swamp him.

Poor Feen! She hadn't got a lot of sleep, that much was clear.

'Are you ok, sweetheart?'

She nodded. 'I am, kind of, but I've had a pretty restless night so I'm feeling a bit 'spacey' this morning. It was such a huge shock, Gavin, and I have to say I reacted badly. I came home in a sobbing heap and Daddy was the first person to see me. He was furious. He thought *you'd* upset me, so I had to tell him and Adie what I'd seen before I'd even had chance to fully process it

114

myself, and I needed real time to get my head around it. I just couldn't see you last night. Please understand.' She looked thoroughly miserable.

Gavin felt a sudden swell of love for her. 'Of course I understand! I'd have done the exact same thing. I'm just sorry you were so upset and I had no idea!' His heart ached to see her so unhappy. Looking at her, across the table, he felt at a complete loss for what else to say.

She glanced up at the clock above the Aga. 'We need to go. I wanted to warn you about Daddy before you got there. I didn't want you to feel ambushed.'

'Feen. Tell me the truth. Given what you know now, and what's happened, do you still want me?'

She finally burst into the tears he knew she'd been struggling to hold in. 'Oh God, yes! More than *anything*! But I don't know how we're going to manage this, Gavin. I really don't. It's horrible. It's a potential nightmare for every last one of us.'

He got up from the table, walked around to her chair, and wrapped her in his arms. He hugged her tight. She was shaking.

'No, it's not. Feen, listen to me. Your dad, he can ask me anything he wants, and I'll tell him the truth. It's all I can do. I'll tell him everything he wants to know about my family, warts and all, no holds barred. I'll be straight with him about my mad mother, about my whole bloody life, and we'll see where are after that.'

He sounded a lot more confident than he really felt, but Feen needed reassurance. He picked up his jacket from across the back of the chair, and held his hand out to her.

'Right,' he said grimly. 'Let's get this row on the shoad.'

Adie was in the kitchen when they walked into Ravensdown House. The smell of freshly baked bread filled the room, thanks to a gently steaming new loaf on the bench beside the bread maker. She was getting something of a feast together. On the kitchen table, a dish of bacon strips sat alongside a bowl of mushrooms. Sausages lay in another shallow dish and halved tomatoes nestled in another bowl, alongside a pot of baked beans. She hadn't started cooking yet. Gavin's mouth watered and his stomach rumbled.

115

I wonder if I'll be invited to stay for this, or whether I'll just be slung out on my ear.

He didn't know what to say when Adie beamed at him, as if nothing was wrong. 'Good morning Gavin! I hope you've slept well at the cottage? There's a few creaks and bangs about the place at night, I forgot to say, but it's just the old bones settling down. It's like the house goes to bed too. And I do hope you're hungry,' she added. 'Saturday morning breakfast is always a big deal around here, to kick start a busy day. It's the only day I let Mark have bacon. Someone has to protect the idiot's arteries. He's never going to do it himself!' Her eyes twinkled with humour.

Her warmth overwhelmed him. Considering what his mother had put her through, he was amazed at her capacity to treat him as if it didn't matter. He stepped forward, flushed with shame.

'Adie... I...'

She shook her head and held up her hand. 'Gavin, it's fine. I'm fine. You and I can have a bit of a chat later. Right now, it's Mark you need to speak to.'

Mark entered the kitchen at that moment. 'Aye, I thought I could 'ear voices.' He reached out and shook Gavin's hand. ''Ow do?' He didn't wait for an answer.

'Come wi' me for a minute, lad. I've to see to't pigs, and you can give me an 'and.' He looked over at Adie. 'We'll not be long.'

As they made their way up towards the barn, Gavin held his breath. He'd been slightly wrong-footed by Adie being so nice to him. He'd expected her to be tearful, outraged, angry, he didn't know what. But he certainly hadn't expected to feel welcomed.

Mark was another matter. And he didn't have to wait long for the man to start speaking. They reached the barn door and Mark gestured to him to sit on the crude wooden bench that sat outside it. He pulled up a battered old green plastic chair, long faded from its time in the sun, and sat down opposite. He looked Gavin clear in the eye, and Gavin felt his bowels loosen again, just a little.

At least he hasn't swung for me! Not yet, anyway.

Mark cleared his throat. 'Has Feen told yer why I wanted to see yer?'

Gavin just nodded, unsure of what to say.

'Is it true, lad? Is Carla Walton yer mother?'

Gavin bit his lip, and nodded again.

Mark looked at him speculatively, for a good few seconds, before continuing.

'Families are a complicated business Gavin, I do know that. And I'd sooner not judge a man by 'is family, not until I know 'im better, because Adie's family are a bloody strange lot, an' if I'd let that get in the way o' marryin' the woman, I wouldn't 'ave the 'appiness I 'ave now. So I know that you can't rightly judge anyone just by who they've come from. But I do 'ave to say, that the 'eartache caused by your mother to my wife an' daughter is summat they've 'ad to work bloody 'ard to come to terms with.'

Gavin was starting to feel like a nodding donkey, but he knew it was important not to interrupt Mark until he'd finished saying his piece. He was straight up, no frills, and he had a big point to make, so Gavin needed to let him make it. He'd get chance to say his own piece at the end of it. Mark took a deep breath.

'Now I gather there's no love lost between you an' yer mother, and the reasons why are nowt to do wi' me. But Feen 'as *everythin'* to do wi' me. She 'as 'er own special vulnerabilities, shall we say, an' I'll not see that lass 'urt anymore by that woman. An' if that 'as to mean denyin' me blessin' for you two to get wed, so be it.'

He closed his eyes for a beat or two, and then opened them and looked Gavin squarely in the eye.

'So what I'm sayin' lad, is that I need you to convince me you can make sure that doesn't 'appen. I do not want that woman anywhere near my daughter *or* my wife. *Ever.* An' you need to be very clear about that, because if you do mend yer fences wi' yer mother at some stage, an' she does come back into yer life, that's one thing. But if she 'urts Feen in any way at all, make no mistake, man - I'll break her fuckin' neck as well as yours.'

He fell silent. Gavin realised it was his cue to speak. He felt shaky, but he spoke up.

'Well first of all, Mark, thanks for not judging me by my parentage. Because, of course, I can't help where I came from, any more than anyone else can. All I can tell you is that my relationship with my mother has been fractured since I was sixteen. Well, it was no great shakes before then, to be honest, but I left home at sixteen because I got to the point where I just couldn't live with her anymore and stay sane.' He ran a hand through his hair and ploughed on.

'I searched, and I found my father. I went to live with him, until he died two months ago. I haven't spoken properly with Carla for ten years, and nothing of any real note had been said for a long time even before that. The only reason I'm back in touch with her now is because she has possessions that were very important to my dad, and I want to get them back.'

He took a deep breath and continued. 'And unless I'm nice to her, that's not going to happen. I feel like I owe it to Dad to get his treasures back, things that meant the world to him. Things she deliberately withheld from him, to try and hurt him for leaving her.

'I know what she is, Mark. I'm more ashamed of her than I can say, and I wish to God she wasn't my mother. I wish I had a happier back-story, or came from saner stock, for want of a better term. But I don't.' He shrugged.

'It is what it is, for me. I can't change the past. All I can do is keep trying to be the best man I can be, now and in the future. I'm determined, I really am, to be a good man in spite of the past, not a bad one because of it.'

It was Mark's turn to nod. 'I'm sorry for yer loss. Losin' yer dad. Can't 'ave been easy.'

'It's been the worst nightmare, mostly because it was all really sudden. I didn't have much time to prepare. It was less than two months, in the end, from start to finish. And I miss him so much! I have everything in the world to thank him for, but I can't tell him. I miss him so much it actually hurts me physically, every day. I really feel like part of me went with him.'

Gavin felt self-conscious for confessing his innermost turmoil to a man he barely knew, and he struggled with the lump in his throat. It still hurt so much, to talk about his father. But it felt important to be real, and honest.

'Again, Mark, it is what it is. I just keep reminding myself that I had the amazing privilege of ten years with him. That's a gift I could so easily have missed out on, but I didn't.

'Look, I don't have the words to express how mortified I am at what Carla did to your family, and that's pretty ironic really, because I'm a songwriter! Words are my business. But this?' He shook his head and sighed deeply.

'Hellfire. I don't have the right words at *all*, for this. It's been a horrifying thing to learn, on top of everything else I've learned about her lately that's already caused me more upset that I thought I could ever feel. That's all related to my father really, and how she treated him. I'm still getting to grips with all that, and now this!'

He leaned forward. 'I can't imagine how devastating it must have been for all of you. Feen finding that poor dog, Adie feeling like she was being terrorized and hounded out of town, and you having to deal with it all.'

He looked Mark squarely in the eye. 'I'm not interested in having any kind of relationship with my mother, Mark, and I don't see that changing. And I would protect Feen to my last breath. On that you have my word. I can't explain Carla's actions, and I'm sure I'll never understand them. But I'm my father's son too, not just hers. I'm who I am *because* of *him* and in *spite* of her. Not the other way around.'

The other man remained silent but was watching him keenly.

Gavin took another deep breath. 'I didn't deliberately conceal anything from you, the other night, when I was here. I've just been trying to work out for *myself*, how I really feel, seeing her again after so long.' He shook his head, frustrated.

'I'm really not great at talking about emotional stuff, Mark, especially when it isn't clear in my own head. And I do want to explain everything about my life to you. I really do, because I don't want there to be any great mystery around me. I want you all to know exactly who I am, and where I've come from, what my journey's been. I've nothing to hide. But can I explain to *all* of you please, maybe over breakfast, so I only have to do it once? Those sausages do look bloody good,' he added, hoping his attempt at lightening the mood would work. It did.

Mark nodded in agreement. He put out his hand and Gavin shook it.

'Aye, lad. That's fair enough. Go on down and tell Adie she can start cookin'. The woman does make a mean brekkie, and yer welcome to join us. I'll see to't pigs, an' I'll be down in ten minutes.'

Back in the kitchen, Feen and Adie were sitting at the table with mugs of fresh coffee. Gavin gave them a tentative smile.

'I'm still in one piece. Un-dismembered. Mark says can you please start breakfast, he'll be back in ten.'

Feen rose and came over to him. She slipped her arms around his waist and he leaned into her, hugging her in return, and inhaling the sweet smell of her hair. Nothing had ever felt as good as this. He never wanted to let her go.

She spoke in a low voice. 'I knew it would be fine. He's not an ogre. Far from it. He's as soft as butter really. He just wants me to be happy.'

Gavin decided he could never write Mark Raven off as being as soft as *anything*. He also resisted saying that he had no idea whether it really would be 'fine.' Instead, he kissed the top of Feen's head lightly. 'As do I, milady. As do I.'

Adie handed him a steaming mug of dark, muddy coffee, which he was desperately in need of. He told her so, and she smiled and turned towards the Aga, busying herself with breakfast.

'Adie, from the bottom of my heart, I'm sorry for what my mother did to you. It's inexcusable. I've never been so horrified or embarrassed in my whole life. I'm truly, deeply sorry. I dunno what else to say.'

Adie turned back towards him. 'You have nothing to apologise for, Gavin. None of what happened was down to you. You can't be responsible for it, and I'd never suggest you were, so please don't feel bad.'

'Well, I'm not going to ask you to forgive her. And if you never do, that's fine by me.'

Adie grinned. 'I'm working on it. Bitterness does shorten the life-span.'

Not long after that, Mark came back in and poured himself a cup of coffee. The smell of sizzling bacon began to take over the kitchen, and even though it felt like he'd done nothing but stuff his face with food from the moment he'd arrived in Torley, Gavin was suddenly famished again.

Feen piped up. 'How are the new piglets doing, Daddy?'

'Yeah, they're a'right. Feedin' well and lookin' good, all ten. Pinky's 'appy, t'sow. Best we could've 'oped for.'

He raised his eyes and spoke loudly to the ceiling. 'Since the buggers were given monikers by someone standin' by't cooker, who shall remain nameless, we've 'ad to bloody keep 'em. But at least they've made their daft selves useful and done a bit o' procreatin'.' He then glowered pointedly at Adie, who studiously ignored him. He winked at Gavin.

'Well, sit yerself down, lad. Yer'll need to learn fast to fend for yerself around 'ere. Nobody waits on no bugger else.'

In spite of himself, Gavin laughed. Mark's broad Lancashire accent was both comical and endearing. He was as rough around the edges as you'd ever find, but he had a good heart, and it was clear how protective he was of his family. Gavin liked him very much. You always knew exactly where you were with a man like Mark Raven. He was solid. But anyone with an ounce of common sense would try to stay on the right side of him. There was little doubt that he'd make good on his word to break Gavin's neck, or Carla's, if either of them ever hurt Feen.

And, he concluded, a more unsuitable match for his mother would be pretty hard to find. Carla Walton appreciated the finer things in life. Gavin was fairly sure her erstwhile attempts to woo Mark Raven were more connected to his assets than to the man himself. He was certainly good looking for his age, and well-built, and most women would probably find him physically appealing in a rough-and-ready kind of way. But, under different circumstances than gold-digging, Carla would have simply looked down her nose at him and written him off as a poorly educated hillbilly, from the minute he opened his mouth.

And as for Feen, what would Carla have made of the idea of having a stepdaughter at *all*, let alone one so sensitive and sweet? She'd have walked all over Feen, there was no question. She'd have been bored rigid with being a farmer's wife too, in no time at all, and would probably have found a way to get a fairly quick divorce with a big chunk of cash attached to it. Gavin struggled, once again, to overcome his shame.

Over breakfast, which was huge and excellent, he did unload to the Raven family about what his life had been like with his mother. He told them everything, including what his father's partner Mike had told him about the way things had really been between his parents when he was a baby. As mortifying as it was, to lay it all bare before strangers, it was kind of cathartic too. And it was nice to know that these were decent people who he felt would understand and not judge him. Nice, not to have to keep it all to himself anymore. When he finally turned to look at Feen, her smile was gentle.

Adie said nothing but looked at him kindly. She picked up the coffee pot and waved it at him, and he gratefully accepted another cup. Gavin was amazed that none of the Ravens had made any derogatory comment about Carla at all. If they'd sat there calling her an evil, vindictive bitch, he wouldn't have blamed them one bit, and he wouldn't have defended her against it. But they didn't say a word. They chose, instead, to keep their judgements to themselves. This was a gracious family. However wounded they might be, they still knew plenty about dignity and respect.

Everyone ate in silence, relishing the food. Gavin was baffled once again, at how much Feen managed to polish off. She was tiny but she ate as much as her father.

He cleared his throat. 'Guys, I hope I haven't put too much of a downer on things. For what it's worth, I don't feel sorry for myself. I never have, and I don't want anyone else to, either. It's just not a pretty picture, unfortunately, so there's no way of dressing it up to sound any better.'

Mark snorted. 'Nay, lad. No point in puttin' a tutu on a pig.'

Adie smirked in spite of herself, then cleared her throat and interjected swiftly, clearly trying to deflect the insult, although it was all Gavin could do not to burst out laughing.

'I'm sure I speak for us all, Gavin, in saying how grateful we are for your honesty. It can't have been easy, telling all that to virtual strangers. But you're in safe company here. One day soon I'll tell you about *my* family. That'll be enough to curl your hair. It's a proper story too - one for a Saturday night with a takeaway and plenty of wine.'

She winked cheekily at him. 'We've got scandals galore, lurking in the shadows. I had a hand in some of it myself, and I hurt a lot of people in the midst of it all, so I couldn't in all conscience sit in judgement of *anyone*. Not with that lot behind me! And if Mark could take me on, with my own cupboards straining under the weight of all those skeletons, I think we can take one slightly deranged mother in our stride.'

Mark rolled his eyes and sighed.

'Well lass, as I've said before, I don't really feel I've married yer family. Only you. They come wi't territory in some form o' course, but we do 'ave choices, don't we?' He looked pointedly at Gavin and Feen.

'An' so do you pair. So, think on. Yer life together will be what yer make it. The choice is there; an 'appy life, or a world o' pain. It's up to you to decide.'

He then got up from the table. 'Right. Time to get on wi't day. Farms don't run their selves.' He nodded at Gavin, who nodded back. Then he was gone.

Adie got up also. 'I need to get going as well. The Farmer's Market doors need to open in fifteen minutes! I'll have to abandon the washing up - unless you two would do it? What are your plans for today?'

Gavin looked at Feen. 'Well, milady needs a fing for her ringer, and I somehow think what the local district has to offer might fall a little short. Maybe we could find a bigger town that might have something that bits the fill?'

Feen thought for a minute. 'Ok, well, what about Preston? That's a decent city, and its less than two hours away. We could spend the day down there, have a bit of lunch?'

'Sounds perfect. Let's get the dishwasher stacked and the rest of the washing up sorted, and then jump in the car and go and look at what they've got.'

He laughed as Feen happily clapped her hands. 'Ooh, yes please, sir! Shake me topping!'

Preston would be a good diversion today. Relieved to have something else to focus on for a while, Gavin now felt a million miles away from being even *vaguely* ready to tell his vindictive, miserable mother that he was engaged to be married, and to whom.

Chapter Eleven

Well, Carla thought to herself, yawning as she wandered through to the kitchen and started brewing her first pot of coffee. *It didn't go too badly, last night, for a first proper meeting.*

She didn't count the first night, when Gavin had collected her from Carlisle, as a 'meeting.' That had just been an awkward (and slightly surreal) first encounter. With neither of them knowing what to say, it had been a bit like sitting on a bus, talking briefly and superficially to a total stranger about things you both knew something about, but feeling no connection you'd want to try and build on. You'd get off the bus and never give them a second thought.

Even when he'd picked her up again last night, and they'd gone to the supermarket together to get what he needed for the meal he was making, they'd been wary around one another; still unsure of what to say, to bridge the chasm.

But Gavin's 'dinner' had been okay. Her son seemed to know his way around a kitchen, and clearly knew how to make a halfway decent meal. She suspected that the nachos he'd presented would have been a bit too spicy for her mother, but Hazel would never have let Gavin know that. Carla still wasn't sure why she'd felt compelled to score a point on it herself but, she supposed, at least she was aware that she'd done it. In the past, before having gained some self-insight, she would have been oblivious to that particular fault - and she would have torn a blistering strip off anyone who might have been reckless enough to have pointed it out to her.

The family had chatted amiably enough throughout the meal, about different things, but it was all fairly superficial stuff. Gavin still hadn't said why he'd come all the way up here to see her. She was starting to feel more than a bit impatient about it now, but she hadn't let it get the better of her. Not yet, anyway. For now, she decided, she could let him take his time. If what he said was true, that he was going to be in town for a while, he'd get around to saying what he needed to before he left again.

Maybe he was working up to a certain level of courage, about whatever it was. A long time apart, and the direct influence of his father in making him who he was today, had left Carla with no idea how to predict much about him anymore. She'd spent enough time wracking her brains about whatever it was he might be wanting, but she kept drawing blanks every time.

At least he wasn't hostile, as she'd been expecting from the start, but she wondered now if that would actually have been easier to deal with. She had no trouble meeting anger with anger. Having a temper on tap had served her well at different times, when anyone had stepped on her toes or tried to have a go at her about something. Taking prisoners wasn't a habit she'd ever felt compelled to fall into.

But her son's cordiality was unnerving, and she still didn't know what was behind it. Being civil was never too much of a problem for her (well, most of the time) when the situation required it, but a bridge to actual friendliness seemed to be appearing in front of her now, and she wasn't sure whether she was being invited to cross it or not. She wasn't even sure she'd even want to, if she was. The fear of being ambushed was still very real, which she fully admitted was directly connected to her guilty conscience. What to do about it all? Well that was a different conundrum entirely, and before her first decent caffeine hit, she wasn't even willing to consider it.

It didn't surprise her that Gavin had taken after Martin musically, and it reassured her a lot that he was so self-confident. He called himself Gavin Black now, after changing his name by deed poll, and she wasn't at all sure how to feel about that, but he'd turned into a man who knew exactly who he was, what he wanted, and where he was going in life. That was admirable. It was more than she'd ever managed to say about herself!

The gene pool had been generous with him too. He'd ended up with the best of both parents. He had Carla's emerald green eyes and near-black hair, but while her hair was shorter, ramrod straight and cut into an almost brutal bob, Gavin had inherited Martin's cascading waves. He was built like his father too, well-proportioned and solid, with a strong jaw; what any woman with half an eye would call a 'catch.'

Martin Black had been a catch too, but sadly not for Carla. It was the death of everything she'd ever hoped for when he'd finally admitted that the only people he wanted to be caught by anymore were other men. It had taken her a very long time to accept the fact that there was nothing in the world she could ever do to keep the interest of the only man she'd ever loved, mostly because she wasn't a man herself.

She'd touched on all that in therapy, but only superficially. She and Dawn hadn't 'deep-dived' it yet. She wasn't ready for that, nor could she guess when she might be. Martin Black was an abscess deep within her that needed to be drained, but the prospect was still too terrifying. Maybe it always would be. Dawn had suggested otherwise, but that of course meant 'going there,' and everything in Carla screamed that she couldn't. Nobody in the world had ever known how she truly felt about *anything* and that was exactly how she wanted to keep it, even from her therapist - the one person who could help her make sense of it all.

They can't hurt you as much, if they don't know your business.

Did she regret getting together with Martin in the first place? For a long time, if anyone had asked her, she'd have said with real conviction that she did. But looking across the table at her beautiful son last night, as she ate the meal he had made, she'd felt forced to think again.

Gavin was pretty much a perfect specimen of manhood, as far as she could tell. He was affable, sincere, intelligent, and gentle and considerate towards his elders. He was clever too, and already well on his way to being successful. The fact that he was also completely gorgeous was also inescapable. The greasy-haired, grunting, pimply adolescent she'd been 'glad to see the back of' had morphed into a truly magnificent man, and half of the genes that made him that way were down to her. He wouldn't exist if she hadn't got together with Martin, and what would the world have been robbed of?

So finally, there was Carla's answer. She could no longer say, with *any* conviction, that she regretted her relationship with her son's father. What she did regret was far more complex and difficult to describe. Somehow, along the way to coming to terms with losing the only relationship she'd ever had that had meant anything real to her, she'd done some morphing of her own, but it wasn't into anything good.

Something had been bugging Gavin last night, though. Part way through the evening he'd got a text on his phone, and his face had changed when he'd read it. She remembered how he used to look, as a little boy, whenever he was disappointed. She saw that look on his face again last night. It was fleeting, but it still made her chest go tight. Her very first thought was '*who's done what to him?*' That faint flare of worry had taken her completely by surprise.

But whatever it was, he'd shrugged it off almost immediately, and reverted to being his charming and attentive self. Whatever it was, he'd put it in a box, just like Martin always did; compartmentalising something so he could continue with what needed his attention at the time, then going back to deal with it later. It was a handy trait to have. Carla envied anyone who could so effectively squirrel away for later something that would straight-away get the better of people with less self-control; people like *her*.

She didn't know why it felt important to her, that someone had let Gavin down. She didn't know why she even cared.

Maybe I actually don't. Maybe it's just my stupid bloody hormones, messing with me like they still occasionally do. My moods are about as predictable right now as the next shower of rain, and I'm sure I've got them - and him - to thank for that.

But if she didn't care, why was she allowing herself to be so irritated by his reluctance to say why he'd wanted to see her in the first place? That, she couldn't answer.

When he'd left after tea, she'd reminded him that she was still waiting for him to tell her. He'd smiled gently and pulled a bit of an 'easy-osey' face, showing that he hadn't forgotten, but he wasn't about to start a discussion there and then. She'd had no choice but to let it go - again. She didn't have the sense that he was toying with her, but it *was* frustrating that she had no idea what was going on in his head. It would be up to him and not her, when he decided to own up to what he came for, whatever it might be.

But it bugged the hell out of Carla, that for the first time in a long time, *she* wasn't calling the shots.

127

Chapter Twelve

An Affirmation to Attract What Makes the Heart Sing

You will need:
Faith, belief and vision
A quiet moment alone, in a dark room with a candle, lighted,
and a small saucer of distilled water.
Incantation (twice):
'Find what is blessed and bring it to me,
in ways both the heart and the eye can see.
Allow me to know what is perfect and right
and true where the mind and the heart unite'

After the snap decision to head to Preston to shop for an engagement ring, Gavin and Feen managed to find a park behind the shopping mall next to the railway station. Typically for a Saturday, the city was heaving. They weaved their way through the crowds towards the main street, Fishergate, and the nearby mall, where most of the jewellery shops were concentrated.

Feen had remembered a tiny place she'd once walked past, down a side street, and recalled that as well as brand new jewellery, it also sold a few antique pieces, such as lockets and pocket-watches. She talked about it on the way down, in the car, and said she thought they might have rings. Gavin looked at her thoughtfully, chewing the inside of his cheek. She was coming to recognise it as a habit that indicated he was worried or unsure about something.

'What, a second-hand ring, Feen? Really? Are you sure you'd want someone else's cast-off?'

She smirked at him. 'No, not sure at all, but it might be a possibility. When I get compulsive feelings, I usually find that it helps to act on them, even if it's only to rule something out', she explained. 'I know I can be a bit of a pain, with things like that, but trust me, I'm a lot harder to live with if I *can't* act on my gut instincts!'

Gavin just shook his head and shrugged.

'Whatever you wish, milady, although let me point out that you are certainly not a pain, and let me also say that no decision of this magnitude should be driven purely by price, since money's no object at all. You can have whatever you want, as long as I don't have to fell my London slat to pay for it.'

She laughed heartily.

'Well good! I'm had to glear it!'

As they approached the start of the lane, Gavin spied a charity shop on the corner. He stopped and looked at her, and suddenly looked a bit sheepish, and fidgety.

'Actually, Feen - would you mind much, if I went in there? Sorry if you find it a bit naff, but charity shops are a bit of a magnet for me. I find them impossible to resist, if I'm honest. It's like a treasure-hunt thing.' He looked embarrassed, but Feen yelped with delight.

'Oh God! Yes, let's! I absolutely *live* for these places! What do you look for?'

He laughed out loud, as she all but dragged him across the road.

'Vinyl mostly, or rare CDs, old sheet music, that sort of thing. Musical stuff, mostly. I once found a saxophone in a charity shop. It cost me two hundred and fifty quid, but it's worth a thousand. I've got it hanging on the wall in the flasement of the bat.'

'Wow! A sax! D'you know how to play it?'

'Yeah, a bit. Something I would like to learn properly though, when I find the time.'

'I think the saxophone is really sexy when it's played well,' Feen confessed. Gavin leaned down and kissed the top of her head.

'Then that's all the incentive I need. Lessons will start as soon as I can get my hands on it again. The very day.'

Feen was over the moon that Gavin liked charity shops. Her hunt was usually for whacky, vintage or unusual clothes, antique jewellery, and other quirky accessories, but she had occasionally found other things that inspired her work, like old nature books, or paintings or prints of flowers in unusual or blended colours. It was quite normal for her to spend an entire day trawling the thrift shops or antique fairs of a city or large town, and now she had a soulmate who loved them just as much. It was almost too good to be true.

They arrived at the little jewellers Feen had remembered, but she was acutely disappointed to see that while some of the new rings on display were absolutely gorgeous, none of them appealed to her. She wondered what the pull had been about, to come here.

'See anything you like the look of?' Gavin asked.

'Let's go in,' she said decisively.

The jeweller greeted them politely. 'Good afternoon, madam, sir. How can I help?'

'We're looking for an engagement ring, but something a little different or unusual.'

The jeweller peered at her over the top of his glasses, one lens of which had a black contraption attached to it that appeared to be some kind of magnifying glass.

'All our current stock is on display, and you're welcome to try on whatever you wish.'

Feen tried on at a handful of rings, including two from the shop's one tray of antique ones, but one of them instantly flooded her with sadness, before it was even fully on her finger, and the other one left her feeling very neutral. She wasn't in the habit of misreading her own intuition but it did happen occasionally, and she decided that her pull to the shop might have just been a bit of wishful thinking. As she picked up her bag again, and prepared to leave, the jeweller cleared his throat.

'I do have one other ring. I wouldn't normally mention it, since most brides-to-be tend to reject the thought of a second-hand engagement ring. Many see them as unlucky. But since you've tried a couple on, I take it you're a little more open-minded?'

Feen nodded, holding her breath.

'It's out the back. It only came in a few days ago and it's not on display because I'm intending to remodel it. It's very old-fashioned, but you're welcome to take a look at it, if you like?'

Feen felt a familiar buzzing sensation at the base of her spine. She nodded, eagerly and glanced up at Gavin. *I think we might be onto something here!*

The jeweller disappeared for a minute and reappeared with an old, heart-shaped, dusty-green velvet ring box that had clearly seen better days. He set it on the counter. Next to all the sparkle of the bling-encrusted rings in the cabinet, the battered little box looked faded and forlorn, almost like it had no right to be there. However, the ring inside it was anything but inferior. In fact, it was spectacular.

It was a cluster ring with a central diamond, set into a small delicate flute-edged circle of filigree flower petals, that flashed under the LED lights in the shop. It was stunning. Six smaller diamonds were each set as the centrepieces in a cluster of identical but smaller gold filigree petals beneath the central one. The overall effect was that of a central daisy held up gently by six smaller ones, all with glittering little diamonds at their centres. Feen gasped.

'Oh my God! Gavin! I've never seen anything like this! It's utterly perfect!' Her throat felt constricted. She quickly slipped it on.

It was far too big for her. It spun around on her finger, with no hope of staying on. But when she held it in place it looked incredible. As tiny as her fingers were, as huge as the ring had seemed to be in its box, it didn't overwhelm her hand. The best bit was the feeling she got as she was wearing it. A happy, glowing, gentle hug to the heart was the best way of describing how she felt, wearing this ring; spiritual proof that it had seen a happy life. This was a million miles from the wretched feeling she'd experienced when trying on a different antique ring just moments before.

'Can you tell us anything about it?' Gavin asked.

The jeweller nodded. 'Yes, it was part of a deceased estate that had been inherited a long time ago by an elderly lady who brought it in for valuation last week. It had been her grandmother's. I valued it and she offered to sell it to me. Items of this quality very rarely come in, and it is beautiful, but most people would only want it as a dress ring.

'The diamonds are top quality, but the setting is very old-fashioned. As I said, my plan is to dismantle it and reset the diamonds into something a bit more modern.'

'Oh, no! It's beautiful, just as it is! I wouldn't want to change a single thing!' Feen cried, turning her hand in every direction, admiring how the perfect little diamonds glittered and flashed as the changing light bounced off them.

She looked at Gavin, her eyes shining as brightly as the stones. She felt truly alive, like her hair was standing on end. He laughed openly at her delight. He turned to the jeweller.

'How much would you be asking for the ring in its current state?'

The jeweller thought for a moment. 'Well, that's a good question. To be honest, I couldn't in all conscience sell it as seen. It needs a lot of work. It's an old ring, and very worn. As you can see, the band is wafer thin underneath, and needs to be built up and strengthened. It's old, soft eighteen carat gold, so I would recommend reinforcing it with something more robust, like nine carat, or even platinum.' The jeweller went on to explain that the claws holding the diamonds were platinum, but all very weak, and would have to be replaced.

'It would be a tragedy to lose one of the stones, and I couldn't guarantee anything if you left the shop with it in its current state. It's too much of a risk to wear it like it is. It would also benefit from being thoroughly cleaned and of course it would need to be resized to fit your tiny finger, madam.'

Nobody spoke. An expectant silence prevailed for what felt like forever to Feen. The chaotic sound of several mismatched ticking clocks filled the air as the anticipation grew. At last, the jeweller spoke again.

'If you wanted the ring just strengthened, reinforced as I've described, which doesn't interfere at all with the integrity of the design, I could do it in, say, ten working days. The cost of all that would bring the total to nine thousand pounds. And I'd give you a valuation for half as much again, for insurance purposes, because getting a ring like this made from scratch would cost that much at least, if it were possible at all. Jewellers don't want to take the time involved in making this kind of thing anymore, since there's no real demand for it.'

Feen's heart plunged. Nine thousand pounds! She looked at the floor, feeling torn beyond belief. She adored the ring and desperately wanted it, but the price was bonkers. She could buy an excellent second-hand car for that, and she did need one - a lot more than she needed a ring of equivalent value, however gorgeous it might be!

Gavin reached out his hand and lifted her chin. He looked into her eyes, and never said a word.

Do you love it? Honestly?

Honestly? More than anything. It's everything I ever dreamed of.

He turned to the jeweller. 'Right. Let's agree on that. I guess you accept credit cards?'

The jeweller nodded. 'Of course. And for what it's worth, I think it's an excellent choice. Madam and the ring are perfect together. Another perfect match.' He smiled gently at them both.

Once the details were agreed, which included getting the ring officially sized for Feen's finger, Gavin threw an arm around her shoulders.

'Right, milady. That's you sorted. We can come back in ten days and collect it. I vote we find a pub now and have a bit of lunch and celebratory bubbly. But before we do, I need to take a photo of this big bauble, so we've at least got something to show people until you've got the real fing on your thinger.'

As they left the shop, Feen was speechless. Nine thousand pounds! She noted that Gavin had paid for the ring without batting an eyelid, and with a black Amex credit card to boot. They were only issued by invitation, and only to the seriously wealthy. But still...

He stopped abruptly in the street, turned to her, and put his hands on her shoulders.

'Now look! Just stop, okay? I don't think that's too much money at all. In fact, I think it's an absolute bargain, for what it is. You heard the man. It's valued at over thirteen grand. And you're worth millions, to me. So stop worrying. It's my money and I'm happy to spend it. I'd have paid ten times that, to see you as excited as you were, back there, all fizzing and popping. I could never put *any* kind of price on seeing that in you.'

So Feen resolved to let it go and be joyous about her ring. Gavin was right. It was his choice. And the ring was more beautiful than anything she could ever have imagined. The second-hand car could wait a bit longer.

They found a quietish pub and had a delicious lunch, swilled down with a half-bottle of champagne. Feen then showed Gavin the rest of the charity shops dotted around Preston. He was thrilled to find a leather-bound Motorhead album in good condition, and a T-shirt with one of the same band's other album pictures printed on the front of it. Feen found a white, pure silk, flared 1950's skirt with black, brush- sketched pictures all around it of a woman holding an umbrella with the Eiffel Tower behind her. The skirt was a bona-fide retro piece. It was little loose on her tiny frame, but she could take it in, and once she'd put a stiff petticoat underneath it would be a lovely statement skirt. It needed a very plain black top, to be shown off for the best effect, but Feen had several that would do.

Gavin sent his picture of Feen's ring to her phone, so she was able to forward it to Adie, who fired a message back straight away, declaring how beautiful and perfect she thought it was.

'I'd better get on the blower soon, and let everyone on my side know I'm about to walk the plank,' Gavin declared.

'Some of my friends will be gobsmacked. And when you meet them, they'll all tell you the same thing; that I'm the least expected of any of us to be tying the knot, as a tender, unworldly lad with no life experience which, believe it or not, is how some of them see me. Don't believe a word of it, though. It's bollocks.'

Feen giggled. 'Oh, believe me, I *know* it's bollocks!'

'Oh yeah? And why is that? Are you suggesting I'm some kind of love 'em and leave 'em Lothario?'

Feen giggled again. 'Not at all. But let's just say that you know your way rather too well around certain parts of the female anatomy to be classed as unworldly and having no life experience.' She smirked and continued. 'I think your mates would be surprised at just how worldly you really are.'

Gavin pulled a face and rolled his shoulders back. 'My best mate Stewart; he'll be the one that gives me the hardest time. He's only twenty-seven, and he's already been married and divorced twice. He'll roast me, because it's not that long since I told him to save himself the bother trying for a third. I said he should just speed up the process of losing his shirt again by finding some woman he hates and giving her a house, a car, his dog, an exotic holiday, and whatever he has in the bank, instead.'

Feen laughed. 'Well that's not likely to make him beel any fetter, is it?'

'Oh, he can handle it. He's the first to admit that he knew the last one was a mistake, even before he went into it. She had about four brain cells, as far as we could tell, on the day of the wedding. But she somehow managed to find around four hundred billion more just after it, and took him to the cleaners good and proper, within two years. He's as broke as a dropped egg. No real prospects to offer any woman, which I happen to think is no bad thing, for now. The poor bastard needs a break from being plundered.'

'I will never clake you to the teaners. I promise.'

'I'll hold you to that.'

And as Feen looked across at Gavin's gorgeous profile as he drove them home from Preston, she had to concede that being with him was as perfect as anything could realistically be, with the ugly spectre of Carla Walton hanging over it.

* * * * *

Unfortunately, Feen couldn't escape the fact that her family still had a lot of questions about Gavin's relationship with his mother. Adie collared her later that evening, to try and clarify a few things that were clearly weighing heavily on her and Mark's minds.

'What if Carla decides she does want to be part of your lives, Feen? And what kind of havoc could she wreak if she does? More to the point, how might she be, if either of you freeze her out? Gavin has said he doesn't want anything to do with her, but I know his emotions might be quite complicated about her, darling; particularly as he's just lost his father, who's been the rock of his life.'

How strong was Gavin really, she wanted to know, in his conviction to keep Carla out of the way?

'I know he's not the sort of man who would deliberately hurt someone, Feen. I'm sure enough of that. But does he really know how manipulative Carla can be, over something she really wants, and how vindictive she's capable of being if she's been told she can't have it?'

Feen bit her bottom lip, reluctant to divulge too much about what she already suspected might happen with Gavin and his mother. She chose her words as carefully as she could.

'It's really complicated between them, Adie. For what it's worth, no matter what happens, I don't think he'd let her bet the getter of him and somehow wangle her way into our lives if neither of us wanted her there. Yes, she's horrible, and she does have the potential to create complete and utter mayhem, but Gavin's a smart guy, and I'm no slouch either, remember, when it comes to sussing people out!'

Her stepmother laughed a little. 'There's no disputing that, of course, Feen. But I worry about the amount of conflict she might cause. I also worry about what Mark might do if it started to impact on your happiness.'

Feen grinned, in spite of herself. 'Visions of shovels and hiding bodies in the woods late at night keep hovering around in my mind, and I have to keep pushing them away.'

'Me too!' Adie admitted, but her eyes danced with humour.

'Adie, I'm certain that as a family, we can handle Carla. The woman has little shame, and even less conscience, but she was found guilty of crimes against you, and has very publicly paid the penalty. She's been jarshly hudged, and virtually ostracised, by everyone in the local community. I do think that's more than enough to make her reluctant to try and inflict any more damage on us all, don't you?'

'Yeah, fair point. I guess it's a tough situation for her,' Adie mused. 'Albeit one she's brought upon herself.'

Feen felt compelled to remind her stepmother that even the most brazen of women would probably think twice about rocking the boat with a local family of note who had such good reason to despise her, particularly when they stood with the full weight of the town behind them. 'Carla might be brazen,' she concluded, 'but she does know a bit about self-preservation.'

Adie nodded. 'You're right, of course. I just worry about when you guys are *not* here. When you're living in London, which presumably you intend to do for at least part of the time, with Gavin's work being mostly down there?'

Feen grimaced. 'I think the distance might work in our favour. And we haven't talked much yet, about where we want to live. I guess there will be some kind of split. Gavin's open to that, and so am I. We'll figure it out as we go along, I expect.'

She sighed heavily. *Why does everything have to be so bloody complicated?*

Mark glanced over at her. 'That were an 'eavy sigh, lass?'

Feen grinned ruefully. 'Yeah. All this stuff with Gavin's mother, Daddy. Its stressful. I can't deny that.'

Her father lifted his eyebrows and closed his eyes. 'Aye, lass. I know. You couldn't make it up, could yer? I just want everythin' to be right for yer; you know, 'ow it *should* be, newly married an' all. I can't stand't thought of yer 'appiness being stained or even destroyed because of that crazy bloody bitch. She's a mean-spirited, spiteful woman, Feen.'

Adie piped up, 'I just can't shake this nagging feeling I have, that you two might struggle, after the wedding, if she tries to interfere.'

'If they get that far' Mark observed sagely, looking intently now at Feen. 'It's not that I don't want yer to be 'appy, pet. O' course I bloody do. But if that lad breaks 'is promise, an' 'e lets yer down before't weddin,' there won't bloody be one. I'll see to that. An' if there is, an' 'e breaks yer 'eart after, I'll put 'im six feet in't bloody ground.'

Adie sighed. 'Alright, Mark, that's enough.'

Feen shook her head. Already there were threats being made, and knowing her father as she did, they weren't empty ones. All hell would break loose if Gavin put a foot wrong in protecting their marriage against Carla. There were choppy seas ahead; she had no doubt about that. She just had to hope that her and Gavin's love and commitment had created sturdy sails.

Adie stood up. 'Sorry, guys. I feel wiped out after the farmer's market. It was unusually busy today. I'm off to bed.'

Feen knew Adie's menopause was still knocking her around from time to time, and messing with her sleep was part of it. But she also knew that the situation with Carla Walton, hovering like a hornet around the edge of the family, wasn't helping her to relax.

Her dad nodded off more or less immediately after Adie left the room. He was snoring softly now, in his battered old armchair. Feen's heart swelled at the sight of him.

He was still a good-looking man, a solid, dependable, heart-of-gold rock to his family, and she adored him. And never a day went by that she didn't thank everyone's lucky stars that he and Adie had managed to find one another, at this time of life. A second chance at love was something neither one of them had sought or expected to find, in their fifties, after devastating losses; Adie's marriage falling apart and Mark being widowed too young. Feen knew that they both cherished their lovely relationship all the more for that.

It also made her realise how lucky she was to have found a soulmate of her own. She couldn't blame Mark and Adie for their grave misgivings for her and Gavin, but they already had their big love, didn't they? In spite the challenges that stood in *their* way, they'd managed to get together. Feen hoped they would understand how real – and how important – Gavin's love truly was to her very existence; every bit as much as theirs was to each other. She needed their support more than ever, now.

As much as she hated to wake him, Feen knew that if Mark stayed asleep in his chair, his back would be giving him hell come the morning. It hadn't been the same since the accident that had all but finished him off last year, when he'd fallen through the upstairs floor in the barn. He was as tough as nine-inch-nails; that's what had kept him alive, but he had residual back pain now, and it plagued him a lot more if he slept upright instead of supine like he was supposed to.

She shook him gently. 'Wake up, sleepyhead. It's time to go to bed.'

Mark startled awake and yawned, expansively, without covering his mouth.

'Bloody hell, Daddy! I nearly fell into that! Come on, you can't keep cheeping in you slair. You'll be crippled by morning.'

'A'reet, yer can stop yer bloody mytherin',' he mumbled good-naturedly, as he got up and shuffled out of the room, blinking and rubbing his eyes.

'Goodnight,' Feen called after him, and he waved a hand at her. She switched off the lamps and followed him out. She watched him climb the stairs, then shrugged her way into her coat to head down to Teapot Cottage, to Gavin. As she left the house, she sent a silent prayer into the ether that somehow, as a family, they would all get through this turbulent time with their hearts and minds intact.

Chapter Thirteen

A Song To Soothe

Thoughts runnin' through my mind
like crazy kids on rollerblades
Who won't stop speedin' down the hallways in my head
Crashin' into everything, joltin' me and shakin' me
Put the brakes on, slow it down, I need some peace instead
Takin' time to breathe, and takin' time for calm,
Away from thoughts I need to leave because they do me harm.
So come on, peace, roll over me, and let the worry fade,
About the life I'm chooosin' and the promises I've made.

Gavin turned over in bed and dragged his thoughts reluctantly to his latest mental challenge. He desperately wanted to tell his grandparents about his intended marriage to Feen, but he wasn't sure how Carla would react to the news. Today was the day he planned to go over there and fess up, so it wasn't going to take long, to find out.

To hell with the consequences. It's my life, and I have to get on with it. People can either like it or lump it, but I can't keep dragging my feet.

Nanny and Bampa would be happy about his engagement, he knew, once they'd got over the shock of how quickly it had happened. As for Carla? Well, it would make life a lot easier for everybody if she was only indifferent, instead of being upset. Was he going to get that lucky? Mentally he braced himself, in case he wasn't. He was still agonising over how to pick his moment to ask about his father's box, too. That would go one of two ways, as well.

He glanced over at Feen, to find her awake, propped up on one elbow, and smiling at him in her usual enigmatic way.

'Don't worry about your mother, Gavin. She'll react in whichever way the mood takes her, and then it will all settle down again. Pipples in a rond, my love. She'll accept the reality eventually, even if she doesn't like it. That I can promise you. It might take a while, but that can be managed, can't it?'

He shrugged, accepting the fact once again that she'd picked up his thoughts. He knew it was something he'd just have to get used to.

'Maybe. But in all honesty Feen, it doesn't really matter if it doesn't settle down. She's irrelevant, in the bigger picture. It's just a whole lot easier if there aren't any tantrums to have to deal with, that's all. She does throw a spectacular tantrum.'

Feen stretched, yawned, and shrugged. 'I know, but she doesn't like me, or my family, so I guess that probably means she won't have much to say to us. Believe me, we can certainly live with that.'

Gavin felt a pang of sympathy for Feen. She didn't deserve to be disliked by anyone. She certainly didn't deserve to have to manage an eternally belligerent and thoroughly unpleasant mother-in-law.

Again, he strengthened his resolve to keep Carla as far away from his fiancée and her family as he possibly could. It would be easier if they were down in London, of course, but they hadn't actually discussed yet where they would live. He knew it was something they'd need to talk about soon, as neither wanted a long engagement, and they had to live *somewhere* once they were married.

Still, there would be enough time to figure all that out. They hadn't set a date for the wedding yet either, although he wanted that settled soon too, and he knew Feen felt the same way. He couldn't wait to start married life with her. *What's the point of waiting, when you know you've found the one?*

Feen leaned over and kissed him. 'I know you have to go and talk to your family. But maybe you could be back for lunday sunch at the farm? You'd be more than welcome. There's usually enough food to feed the whole of Torley town. We normally have it around one o'clock.'

Gavin kissed her forehead. 'I'd rather you came with me.'

'I know you would, but I do think the big talk with your mother is something you need to have by yourself. Me being there would only make her worse. It seems unfair to ambush her. Give her a bit of time to get used to the idea before she has to set eyes on me again.'

He grabbed her hand and kissed it. 'Alright, maiden fair. I'll venture into the lion's den alone. I shall be lack in time for bunch. Minus my head perhaps, but it would take a lot more than a missing or crooked noggin to keep me from Adie's glorious table. That woman could cook for England!'

Feen grinned and nodded. 'She's certainly a mean cook, but in the beginning she was a quivering wreck with the Aga. You should have seen her. It scared her to death! Aunt Sheila came over and showed her how to use this one here at Teapot Cottage, because that's all there was, when she was staying here looking after the place. The little bench top oven in here now was her own addition when she bought the cottage and started renting it out.

'But she mastered the Aga, and with Sheila's help she slowly worked her way up to taking on the big one in the main house. Since she got the hang of it she's never looked back. Says she wouldn't go back to a conventional oven now if you paid her.'

'Yeah, that hulk in the farmhouse kitchen is a monster and a half. I'm always half waiting for it to start hissing or growling, or something. I'm assuming you've tamed it too, milady?'

'Oh yes! I grew up with it. I've been using it since I was about twelve. Mum showed me how to work it. That old beast will never bet the getter of me!'

It was Gavin's turn to laugh.

'Right then, if you're too much of a chicken to face *my* old beast, you'll have to love me and leave me, at least for now.'

Feen poked her tongue out at him, then kissed him again, a long, lingering, gentle, sweet kiss, and then promptly got out of bed and got dressed.

'I do love you. Totally. Good luck!' she shouted over her shoulder as she raced down the stairs.

I'm gonna need it, Gavin thought grimly, as he got up too. He glanced at his watch. He had two hours. He decided it was plenty.

Who knew, he might be out on his ear after five minutes, with no hope of getting Martin's cherished box. He certainly had no intention of spending two hours arguing with his miserable mother.

He really had no idea what to expect. Carla might go completely hysterical, or she might simply respond with a cold-as-ice shrug, and a dismissive remark along the lines of not giving a monkey's *what* he did. Either way, it wasn't going to be the most comfortable of conversations, but he was hanging his hopes on indifference.

He parked in Bampa's driveway, took a few deep, steadying breaths, and got out of the car. He didn't even have to knock on the door. As he got to it, Nanny flung it wide open and enveloped him in a huge hug.

'Gavin! What a lovely surprise! We've not long had breakfast, but I can make you an omelette or some scrambled egg, if you like. I don't know what we've got left in the biscuit tin, since Stanley keeps sneaking all the best ones when I'm not looking, but I'll get the kettle on!'

She shepherded Gavin through to the kitchen and called to Bampa, who came clattering down the hallway and also gave Gavin a hug.

'I'm just out in the back bedroom, messing with the model village. D'you want to come through?' He looked shrewdly at his grandson. 'Or d'you have something on your mind?'

Gavin nodded. As he turned, his mother came into the kitchen. Their eyes locked, for a brief moment, and Gavin thought he saw something akin to pleasure flare slightly in hers. Strangely, it gave him an unexpected surge of hope. But the look was so fleeting, and so quickly gone, he wondered if he'd imagined it. Maybe he had. Maybe it was just wishful thinking, although at this point a relationship with his mother was the last thing he wanted. That fleeting flare, of wanting her to be glad he was there, confused him; especially after he'd told himself it didn't matter one way or the other what her reaction to his news might be. He pushed those thoughts to the back of his mind

Carla quickly assumed her usual air of disdain and looked him up and down, neutrally, like she'd look at a passing car.

'Good morning. To what do we owe the honour?' she enquired lazily.

Gavin was acutely aware that all three of them were now looking expectantly at him.

'Can you all sit down please? I've got something to tell you.'

Carla smirked and raised her eyebrows, but obediently sat at the kitchen table, as did Bampa. Nanny bustled around, making a pot of tea, and she sat it down with the various accompaniments. She finally sat herself down too, muttering an apology at only having plain digestive biscuits to offer them all, since Bampa had scoffed the last of the chocolate ones. They all focussed their attention squarely on Gavin. He cleared his throat.

'Right. I've had a development. It's very sudden, and completely unexpected. In fact, it's the last thing I ever thought would happen, at least not for a long time yet, but it's the *best* thing that's ever happened to me.'

All three stayed expectantly silent. Carla's eyebrows were at hairline level, but she didn't encourage him to continue. He ploughed on, his words coming out in a rush.

'I've just got engaged, to the most beautiful girl on the planet. She's agreed to marry me, and I can't believe my luck. I'm head over heels in love like I thought I could never be, and I've never been happier, or more certain of anything, in my whole life. So, I hope you'll all be happy for me.'

There. It was out. Well, partly, at least.

Bampa was the first to react. He scraped back his chair, came bounding around the table, more like an energetic adolescent than the septuagenarian he was, and hugged his grandson like his life depended on it.

'Congratulations, boy! Engaged! That's wonderful news, isn't it, Hazel?' He looked over at Nanny who was nodding vigorously and beaming from ear to ear. 'I hope you'll both be as happy as Hazel and I have been together. Fifty-nine years at the end of this year, and I've never regretted a single day of it. Marriage can be hard, but if you get the right girl you'll have a wonderful life together.'

Nanny clapped her hands and beamed at Gavin. Carla never moved, never changed her facial expression. Then she leaned forward.

Here it comes.

'Who's the girl?'

Gavin's stomach roiled. He spoke quietly. 'Her name's Seraphine Raven. I believe you already know her, Carla.'

His mother blinked and half-smirked. Then her expression froze.

Bampa's mouth formed a perfect 'O.'

'What, you mean Mark and Beth Raven's girl from across the valley? Little Feen Raven? Bloody hell, boy! We *all* know her!' Bampa glanced furtively at Carla but said nothing more.

Nanny didn't look at Carla at all, but nodded at her grandson. 'Yes, I remember her. She came here with her parents when her poor mother was still alive, to see the garden, after it had been in the magazine. She died of cancer didn't she, Beth Raven? Terrible thing, that poor child losing her mum like that.' Nanny shook her head and smiled wistfully.

'Anyway. Charming little dot of a thing, she was. A bit self-contained, a little aloof, didn't talk much, but I remember how enchanted she was with the wrought iron bandstand. D'you remember that, Stan? She said it made her think of angels. I still see her about in the village, off and on, usually charging about with a basket of something. She's still very slight, not much meat on her bones, and she's only five foot tall, if that. What a small world! I didn't know you knew her.'

There was silence for a few heartbeats. Then his mother spoke up.

'He doesn't. He doesn't know her, do you Gavin?' She looked squarely at him, her green eyes boring into his.

He stood his ground and spoke softly. 'I know enough, Mum. More than you think.'

Carla had the grace to blush crimson, but she shrugged off her embarrassment. 'When *did* you meet her?' she demanded.

'Not long ago, but it's enough. When you meet the right one, you just know. And we both do. We just know.'

Bampa looked confused. 'What? You've only just met?' His voice was incredulous. Nanny also looked a bit baffled, but only fleetingly. She quickly composed her expression and said nothing. She just kept staring intently at her grandson.

Gavin nodded emphatically. 'Yeah, Bampa, we've only just met. But I feel like I've known her all my life. Something just clicked into place. I can't explain it any better than that.'

'Old souls?' Nanny enquired softly.

He thought for a moment, then inclined his head and spoke equally softly. 'Something like that Nanny, yes. Something completely profound and indescribable really, but 'old souls' isn't a bad term.'

Carla's harsh laugh sounded like nails being dragged down a blackboard.

'Well, lucky me! I get to inherit the most insane member of the ridiculous Raven family as a fucking daughter-in-law. That girl is a raving lunatic, dancing naked in the woods at full moon, howling at the owls and snogging badgers. Everyone calls her a mad witch, and maybe it's the truth. She's certainly put a stupidity spell on *you*!'

Gavin couldn't stop himself from biting a retort.

'Mum, this isn't about you. Not everything is, you know. And you're not 'inheriting' anyone! Feen's not some kind of chattel, to be *acquired*. She's a human being, and a beautiful one at that. And considering what you did to them, I doubt any of the Raven family really want to come within a country mile of you anyway, so don't worry. You'll be perfectly safe, and none of us will mind at all if you choose to keep your distance!'

Flushing beet red again, Carla glared at him, but said nothing further.

Bampa sat back down. He looked astonished. 'Well, I don't know what to say, boy. I *could* say 'marry in haste, repent at leisure', but you're a man now, and you have the right to decide for yourself what you want. As it goes, I think the Ravens are a nice family. Beth - God rest her - was a real cracker. I think I was a little bit in love with that girl, to be honest. I think most men around here were, to some degree. And I've always had a lot of time for Mark. Salt of the earth, he is! The hardest worker I know, always has a kind word for whoever he meets in the town. Feen's a perfectly pleasant little lass, from the bit I know about her, and if you think she'll make you happy, then we're happy for you - aren't we, Hazel?'

Gavin's grandmother hadn't taken her eyes off Gavin for all the time he'd been talking. She stood up herself, now, and came around the table to embrace him. Then she held his face in her hands and looked into his eyes. She spoke slowly and deliberately.

'It's there, young man. I can see it shining out of you. It's no flash in the pan, is it, Gavin? It's real and wonderful to you. And if it's real and wonderful to her too, then it is as real and wonderful as anything could be.'

Gavin was amazed to see tears in his grandmother's eyes. She grabbed him by the shoulders then, and shook him gently.

'I'm thrilled for you, Gavin! It's all incredibly sudden, bordering on barmy in fact, and of course we're going to worry about that. We wouldn't be halfway decent grandparents if we didn't! But all we want is for you to be happy. Maybe take some time planning a wedding, give yourselves a bit more time, but when two old souls meet, they do just somehow know.'

She looked fondly across the table at Bampa. '*I* knew. It took Stanley a bit longer to catch on, mind, but in the first moment I met him, I knew. I went home from our first date with banged-up feet, because the silly sod had stomped all over my toes while we were dancing. He was a *rubbish* dancer! He was the only man I knew who could butcher someone else's feet doing the bloody twist, of all things! But I hobbled home from that dance half crippled, with one foot bleeding and the other battered and bruised, and I told my mother I'd met the man I was going to marry.'

Nanny chuckled, softly. 'She thought *I* was barmy, and we were only kids. Stan was eighteen and I was sixteen, and everyone said we were far too young, but we got wed, and we've never looked back, have we Stan? Fifty-nine years, two kids and a grandson later, and here we are, still going strong!'

'We were married within a year' Bampa declared. 'So maybe give it a year, boy, if you don't mind? Just be sure, before you take the plunge. Do that for me, will you?

Gavin grinned at the old man. 'Nope. Sorry. We don't want to wait a year. But I'll do a couple of months, Bamps. How's that?'

Bampa shrugged, clearly worried, but he tempered it with a brave smile. 'Ah well, I suppose it will take that long to plan the wedding anyway.'

Gavin looked at his mother, who hadn't said another word. 'So? Anything to say, Mum?'

She snorted. 'Not really. What do you *want* me to say?'

He shook his head, resigned yet again to her lack of warmth. 'Nothing, I guess.'

She looked at him levelly, almost dispassionately.

'Well, you're either going to be happy or you're not. It'll only go one of two ways, won't it? I think I know which way it'll go with that silly scrap of nonsense, but if you want to marry her, go ahead, and find out for yourself how terminally crazy she is. I want nothing to do with it, or her, or *you*.'

Nanny, who usually kept well out of other people's problems, suddenly picked up a large wooden spoon and banged it very hard on the table twice. Everyone jumped and stared at her, completely shocked. Ignoring the reactions, she stood up and pushed her chair back so hard that it hit the sideboard, with another big bang. She glared at her daughter.

'My God! You can be a shameful creature at times, Carla,' she thundered. 'You're my daughter and I love you dearly, but I do have to say that I don't *like* you much, especially not right now.'

She shook her head, wildly. 'I don't know where we went wrong, raising you. Your father and I, we gave you and Tristan the best of everything, the best we had, and we have *always* loved you completely, without restraint.'

Bampa opened his mouth to speak but Nanny held up her hand at him. Her mouth was set in a grim line, and she was more furious than Gavin could ever remember seeing *anyone*. He was astonished. Nanny's capacity for fury outstripped his mother's and that was saying something! She glared at Carla, with real ferocity in her eyes.

'How you've turned into such a cold, mean-spirited, unfeeling wretch of a woman, I'll never know! I've wracked my brains for years over it, since well before you ended up in court for poisoning that poor dog and everything, but I can't weigh it up.'

147

The silence around the table was charged. But Nanny still had a ways to go. With a determination seldom seen, she ploughed on, almost shouting.

'I really can't fathom you at all. But what I *do* know is that you didn't learn such disgusting behaviour from either me or your father, and your actions back then were uncalled for, just as your comments are now. If you can't say anything nice to your own son at my table, I'd rather you didn't sit at it. Just get up and pee off, you miserable cow, if you really can't be good to this lovely young man while you're living under my roof.'

Abruptly, Carla scraped back her chair, stood up, and bolted from the room.

Silence settled as Nanny pulled her chair back towards the table. She sat back down abruptly, blinking, in clear disbelief at her own incredible outburst. Gavin was literally lost for words, knowing nothing he could have said would have helped, anyway. Bampa cleared his throat, reached out, and patted her shaking hand.

'Now, Hazel, calm down love. There's no point in being this upset! It won't help your dodgy ticker, old duck.'

He looked at Gavin, sighed deeply, and sadly shook his head. 'Well, I guess your mum hasn't changed much, has she, boy? I'm sorry she's disappointed you again. But look here, you've done fine without her, all these years, haven't you? It can't have been easy, but you've made a jolly good go of it, and you're a credit to your dad, God rest him.' He pushed his glasses up onto his forehead and rubbed his eyes. He looked tired.

'We know what Carla can be like, Gavin, and I'm sure you've heard about what she did to that family and that poor little dog. The shame we went through here, after; well, it was hard. Really hard, for a long time, and we certainly found out who our friends were.'

'And who they weren't,' Nanny muttered.

Stan's mouth turned down. 'Torley's a small town, and people can be very opinionated, even when they don't know all the facts,' he explained. 'Some of the people we've known all our lives stopped speaking to us, and a few never started again. But Hazel's right. Although Carla's our flesh and blood and we love her, and we have to stand by her as best we can, please don't

148

think we condone or agree with her behaviour, because we don't.'

He took off his glasses and polished them with the tea towel that was lying on the table. He looked unhappy, and Gavin's heart went out to him. Poor Bampa.

Nanny had composed herself, and she spoke up. 'We met your dad, many years ago, Gavin. You probably won't remember. It was when we went down for a weekend to see you. You were very small, only just walking, I think, and he was still living at the house with you. He seemed like a nice man, to us.

'We have to believe that we were right to think that, despite what your mother might say or think about him, because he's turned you into a very fine man, one we're proud to call our grandson. And we're both deeply sorry for your loss, Gavin. Losing Martin like you did, so suddenly, it must've been hard.' She sighed, and suddenly looked tired and old. Gavin's heart swelled with love for her.

Bampa growled; 'Your mother has some big issues, Gavin, even demons maybe, but we both hope that one day you two will manage to reconcile. Maybe you will, maybe you won't, but for as long as we're alive, we'll be here for you, and whatever you do with your life, whatever choices you make, we're behind you every step of the way.'

Gavin felt a lump in his throat. Nanny and Bampa. They were amazing.

He got up to leave, explaining that he was expected at the Raven's for Sunday lunch. He asked his grandparents if they might like to have a meal with him and Feen later in the week. They seemed excited at the idea, and he knew how thrilled Feen would be to meet them. His mother, she could and *should* do without, but he suspected she would adore his grandparents and they would love her too. A meal at one of the local pubs might be a good idea. It was a neutral space, away from Carla, and it meant Nanny wouldn't have to cook or clean up. She could just relax and enjoy herself for a change.

Promising to get back to them with a day and time, Gavin picked up his car keys. He could see his mother out in the garden, sitting on the steps of the wrought iron bandstand, looking out over the valley. The old structure was a spectacular, intricate, hand-wrought work of art, but it was looking a bit rusted and shabby, and in need of new coat of paint. He walked towards Carla. She didn't see him, and he was surprised to find that she was crying.

'Mum? Are you ok?'

Carla sniffed and hastily wiped her tears away with the back of her hand. She didn't answer, or look at him.

'Mum, this is happening, whether you like it or not. I love Feen, and I'm going to marry her. It's my life and I'm going to live it how I choose. I'm sorry if my decisions make you unhappy, because despite everything, you being angry or upset over it is never what I'd want. Whether you believe that or not is up to you, but it's the truth.'

As he stood looking at her profile, she shook her head and stared off into the middle distance.

'Fuck off, Gavin.'

Shocked, he took a couple of steadying breaths and then spoke quietly.

'No problem.'

And he turned on his heel and left.

*　　*　　*　　*　　*

Back at Teapot Cottage, Gavin sat on a window seat with a very strong cup of coffee, and allowed himself time to process his mother's hostile reaction. It had been much worse than he'd feared. As he struggled to loosen the lump in his throat, he realised a deeply uncomfortable fact. It *did* matter to him, what she thought. He'd tried to convince himself that whatever she felt about the choices he'd made, and how he was living his life, was of no real concern to him. But he was wrong.

Seeing Carla crying tonight, he'd been surprised to feel a peculiar mix of mesh and disconnection that was impossible to explain. He struggled to like or respect her, but she was still his mother; his flesh and blood.

He couldn't work out why she'd been crying. He was fairly sure they weren't crocodile tears. She seemed to be genuinely upset, but he didn't have the faintest idea why. Was it humiliation, at her own mother berating her like a child in front

150

of her own son? Was it a feeling of having no control over events that were going to force her to be a part of a justifiably hostile family who she'd wronged so horribly? Was she angry? Scared? Guilty? What?

He had no idea how she really, truly felt about *anything*. To say she was an enigma, was the understatement of the century.

Why should I even care? She's made her feelings plain enough. She doesn't want me in her life.

And yet ... that spark, that initial flare of pleasure he'd seen in her eyes when he'd arrived at Nanny and Bampa's, *had* he imagined it? And if so, why? Deep down, maybe he did want her to be happy to see him, but what did that even mean?

She'd been embarrassed that he'd discovered her weeping, that much was clear. She hadn't minced her words in pushing him away, and she'd refused to look at him.

The fact that he even *wanted* to understand was a surprise to him, and it was far from a comfortable one, given the strenuous and heartfelt assurances he'd given to Mark and Adie Raven, just twenty-four hours ago.

What a difference a day makes.

Gavin had never seen his mother cry before, and he couldn't remember the last time *he'd* shed a tear over *her*. But he couldn't help asking himself now, if they were as 'done and dusted' as he'd always thought?

A kernel of doubt started forming in his gut. The Raven's observations, that things were perhaps not quite as clearly squared away as Gavin wanted or believed them to be, had proved remarkably astute.

He hadn't lied to them, he reminded himself. He'd told them the truth about his feelings as he believed them to be at the time, but he was acutely aware of how it would it look if he went back on his word to them now. Assuming Carla even wanted to have a relationship with him (and right now he had no sense of that), it was impossible to see how he'd manage it without a complete collapse of the trust he'd worked so hard to earn from the Raven family.

Coming back here had certainly opened old wounds, and clearly not just for Gavin. Mike had warned him about that, and he'd also cautioned him against allowing his mother to manipulate him. But, if he was honest, nothing felt manipulative, here. He didn't feel like his mother was messing with his head, as Mike had been so afraid of. So far at least, she wasn't trying to be a part of his life again. She hadn't tried to influence his choices, either. She'd simply said her piece, poisonous as it was, but only after he'd invited her to comment. He was certain she wouldn't have told him how she felt if he hadn't asked her. And what was that? Indifference? Incredulity? Respect?

And why was she still living back at home, up here in the back of beyond? She was a middle-aged woman, and although Nanny and Bampa seemed happy enough to have her there, it wasn't as if she was needed. They were still fit and healthy enough not to need any kind of care or home support.

It occurred to Gavin that they probably just wanted to be by themselves now, at this time of life, to enjoy each other as much as they could before old age and dependency started settling in, which was quite possibly only a few years away now, with them both in their seventies. They hadn't said as much, but they wouldn't. The last thing they'd want would be to upset their daughter or make her feel she wasn't wanted. Was Carla so insensitive that she didn't see that, though? She had a job, and presumably some savings, since her rent would be low, if she paid anything at all. It was a mystery to Gavin, why she didn't seem to want her independence. She didn't even have her own car!

Lunch at Ravensdown House was huge, delicious, and funny. Mark's sister and brother-in-law, Sheila and Bob Shalloe, were there too, and it was great to meet them. Feen had already told him a lot about them, and he was humbled by how readily they congratulated him and Feen, and welcomed him into the family. They were fun. Sheila's own Lancashire accent was less coarse than Mark's, and Bob spoke like an educated man. They bounced well off one another, with great affection and humour, and Gavin enjoyed their family stories.

As Adie piled everyone's plates with roast chicken, home-made stuffing, rich gravy and a vast array of vegetables, Mark made everyone roar with laughter over farm tales from the previous week, including one of the hens getting its beak stuck in a lump of stale pudding that had gone out with the rest of the scraps for their feed.

'Yer should o' sint bloody bird! Runnin' around in circles wi' it's wings flappin' fifteen to't dozen. Its beak were so tightly jammed, daft bugger couldn't even squawk.'

It wasn't just the tales themselves – it was the way Mark told them, that had everyone in stitches. Gavin already had quite a soft spot for his future father-in-law, he decided, with his down to earth, Northern humour and his funny way of talking.

After lunch, as Feen walked back with him to Teapot Cottage, she lightly took his hand and swung it a little as they went.

'So? I think I know how it went, with your family, but how do you feel about it all?'

He took off his jacket, slung it over the back of the armchair, and threw himself down on the sofa.

'Well, if you saw, or sensed, Nanny and Bampa doing a happy-dance and mum being a bitch, it did go more or less as you'd think,' he shrugged. 'After establishing that I really do know what I'm doing, and after a few half-hearted mumblings about marrying in haste and repenting at leisure, the grampies were thrilled. Mum was less so, but she said she didn't give a damn one way or the other. She did tell me to fuck off though,' he added, more or less as an afterthought.

'Ouch!' Feen responded, trying not to laugh. She kept her eyes on him, as she went through the mechanics of making a pot of coffee, and then inclined her head. She became more serious now. 'And you were hoping for something different. A more positive reaction?'

He nodded, sighing heavily. She was, as usual, unnervingly correct. He knew he'd never get much past her.

'Yeah. I guess I was. Hoping for a blessing, or something like that. As it stands, I don't know what her next move might be, if any.'

Feen pulled a face. 'And your dad's box? You haven't had chance yet to ask her about that, have you?'

'Nope. It really wasn't the right time. Not after she kicked off like she did, after my nan threw some rather explosive and unexpected fire at her. I wish you could've seen that, Feen! It was bloody spectacular. Go, Nanny! But something, I dunno what, is telling me to wait for the right moment to ask about the box.'

She nodded at that, then came to hug him. He buried his face in her hair. She smelled earthy and sweet, like he imagined baby spring ferns would, after a rainstorm. She spoke gently.

'You're right. It's something you do need to pick your time over. But, for what it's worth, if you do that, I think you'll get what you want. I'm positive now, that she has the box. And I know you're confused about her. It's understandable. You had very big, thrilling, life-changing news, today; the kind where it matters what your thamily fink. And whether you like each other or not, she *is* your family.'

Gavin shook his head. 'I dunno *why* it matters, Feen. I really don't. It *shouldn't* matter, what she thinks.'

'But somehow it does?'

He looked at her and nodded. He told her how he'd felt when he'd walked into his grandparents' house and thought Carla had been momentarily glad to see him. He didn't know what to think or feel about it, but he owed it to Feen to say so, and to try and explain. He couldn't imagine being anything other than totally honest with her, even about things she might not want to hear.

She smiled back at him thoughtfully. 'There's a really big block in front of your mother, Gavin, and it's not possible for me to see through it. She has put it there herself, and she is the only one who can remove it, to let anyone in. I don't have the answers, but even if I did, I'd still have to hold back and let you find them for yourself, because whatever happens has to be driven by you, under whatever terms you can manage, without any influence from anywhere else.'

She took hold of his hands and kissed his knuckles. 'But what I do know is that you can't help how you feel about someone. I also know that feelings change. Family does matter. I've been lucky that there's never been anyone in my family who I haven't liked. But if there was someone, I think I'd always have the *hope* that it would change. It takes real energy to daintain a mislike for someone, and I don't know how long I could keep that up. I'd want to find something to like, and I'd work hard at that.' She stretched and yawned.

154

Gavin chuckled humourlessly. 'Carla must be bloody exhausted then, since she hates everyone. Personally, I think she's missed her calling. Forget being a filing clerk! She should have got a job on a building site. She's as cold and hard as a diamond drill-bit, she's usually got a face like a slate-hanger's nail-bag, and she possesses all the personal charm of a concrete slab.'

Feen laughed and threw up her hands in mock horror. 'Oh my God! She really *is* the small, cheerless, windowless building - the one that built itself! It's true! Ha! But maybe you shouldn't be so unkind. I think that all this frustration you've got originates from your disappointment, that she was never what you needed, and still isn't. Not that I'm judging you, of course.'

She added, almost as an afterthought; 'you know, the opposite of love isn't hate; it's indifference. But you're a long way from that, aren't you?'

Gavin blew air through pursed lips. 'Am I, though? So much of me really doesn't care.'

'Ah, but there's still a big part of you that hasn't given up yet. It's normal, by the way - it really is - to be this confused. And I should say that if she did come back into your life, I'd try to forgive her. I can't speak for Daddy and Adie, of course. I think it's safe to say Daddy would be a hard nut to crack. But Carla's your mum, Gavin, and I think even he would try to understand, especially since he had to raise me without my mother. He understands how important mothers are. Adie does too. She's had to overcome estrangement too, remember, from her children.

'They *would* try, and if you want to have a relationship with Carla, if it's what she wants too, and if you can work it out with her, well, we'll just have to manage it as best we can.'

Gavin just stared at her in disbelief. She shook her head again, and let out a long, deep breath and shrugged helplessly at him. 'Look. You have to try and see it from my perspective too. I don't want to be the bad guy in all this. I'm never going to stand here and tell you that you can't have your own Mother. It would never be *anyone's* place to do that. Nor would I ever ask you to choose between us, because that would be unfair.

'If she is going to be back in your life again, so be it, and if the best we can ever muster is that you see her separately, away

155

from our home, and she doesn't interfere in our lives, then so be that too. If we could achieve that, I wouldn't stand in the way of you having a relationship with her. I couldn't imagine not getting on with my own Mum. I adored her, and she loved me to pieces. Of *course* I want you to have that if you can. A mother's love is everything.'

A mother's love.

Feen's readiness to stand behind him was humbling. Gavin didn't know how long he'd suffer the shame of what his mother had done to her family. Even if some kind of reconciliation was on the cards, those stumbling blocks were huge, alongside all the years of anguish and abuse that had gone before.

Gavin suddenly remembered his invitation to Nanny and Bampa to meet for dinner. Feen was excited about meeting his grandparents and made him promise to tell them yes; dinner as soon as they wanted would be lovely, and forget the pub; she would happily do the cooking herself here at Teapot Cottage. She told him he had to find out what their favourite dishes were, in plenty of time, so she could prepare the feast of their lives, for them.

They talked about taking a walk, but when they looked out down the valley, they could see black clouds rolling in. The sun had gone, and a storm was brewing. As thunder gently rolled and grumbled in the distance, Gavin decided to light the fire. It wasn't cold, but in the midst of a thunderstorm, a living flame was always comforting. He turned on the lamps and pulled Feen down on to the floor where they lay, arms entwined, watching the fire and drifting gently into sleep, as the storm turned the afternoon black.

Chapter Fourteen

A Spell For Personal Strength

You will need:
Faith, belief and vision
A quiet moment alone, in a room full of light,
with three cones of smouldering incense;
any fragrance will do.
Incantation (twice):
'From power thine, grant fortitude mine,
Protect and shield, bring strength to wield '

At some point in the evening, they went upstairs to bed, as the storm continued to rage around them, with its tooth-jarring cracks of thunder and violent flashes of forked lightning.

Gavin was sleeping soundly, and lightly snoring. A flash lit up the bedroom for a split-second, throwing his profile into view. Feen had been fully asleep for a little while, and had latterly been just dozing, but she was now fully awake and alert.

What had woken her? It wasn't the storm. Although most people she knew were agitated by storms, Feen found them comforting. She normally slept like a rock through a storm, somehow completely in tune with its vibrational force. But something had woken her tonight. As the rain flung itself relentlessly against the bedroom window it managed to drown out most other noise, but *something* had jolted her awake.

She got up, padded to the window and peered around the edge of the curtain. Outside in the blackness, nothing was visible, until another bolt of lightning momentarily lit up the night. To Feen's astonishment, a car was parked outside the front of Teapot Cottage, directly behind Gavin's. She didn't know whose it was, and as the lightning flash was so short, she couldn't see if anyone was inside it. To most people, it would feel more than a tad creepy, that someone had driven up to the cottage in the middle of an electrical storm, in the dead of night, and just parked there without coming to the door. But Feen had an idea of who she thought it might be.

She peered at Gavin's bedside clock and was surprised to see that it was only eleven o'clock. Hardly the 'dead of night,' but still far too late for anyone to be visiting unannounced. She debated waking Gavin and decided against it. Instead, she tiptoed downstairs, shrugging her way into her dress as she did so. She decided not to put any lights on, for now at least. At the bottom of the stairs, another bolt of lightning lit up the living room, and she noticed that the embers of their fire were still gently glowing in the dark. She craned her neck at the side of the window nearest the door, to see if anyone was sitting in the car, but it was just out of her line of vision.

There was nothing for it but to open the front door and take a decent look. As it silently swung open on its well-oiled hinges, another lightning flash revealed that there was indeed someone sitting in the car parked directly behind Gavin's. It was Carla Walton, in Stan Walton's Shogun.

Of course it's her. Who else would it be?

Carla hadn't noticed the front door opening, and she wasn't aware she'd been seen, sitting out there in the dark. Feen could feel the woman's debate with herself about whether to make her presence known. She sensed a wavering in Carla, an uncertainty, probably because the house was in darkness, but also because she wasn't sure she was doing the right thing, either for herself or for her son.

Standing in the doorway Feen considered her two choices. She could quietly close the door, allowing the other woman to either come to it of her own accord or leave without knowing she'd been seen. Or she could go out there and invite her in. With

158

a heavy sigh, she stepped out into the rain, and instantly regretted her decision to remain barefooted. The ground was soaking wet and freezing cold. She found herself immediately up to her ankles in an inky puddle.

Rather than give Carla a huge fright by knocking on the window, Feen called to her instead, as she got alongside the car. The other woman still jumped out of her skin anyway, which Feen conceded was probably unavoidable, considering the elements. Carla glared at her, clearly angry that she'd been noticed, and by Feen instead of Gavin. She stared forward into the blackness. Feen rapped on the window.

'Carla! Come inside. Don't sit out here in the rain, in the dark. Please, come into the cottage!'

Carla's window came down two inches. 'Save your breath. It's not you I've come to see.'

'I know that. But I can tell you right now, Gavin won't come out here in this, and he'll just tell me I'm stupid for doing it. You need to come inside. Please, Carla. It's a filthy night.' Feen could feel the rain soaking her to the skin, but she ploughed on.

'Just come in. I can make some tea, and then I'll make myself scarce while you talk to him. You *do* need to talk to him. I don't know if he wants to talk, but I'm sure he wants to listen. Please, just come inside. Don't stay out here in this.'

Carla looked at her again. Feen started shivering.

I must look like a drowned rat by now!

Suddenly she ran out of patience, and decided to call Carla's bluff. 'Look, either come in or go home. You can't sit out here all night. It's as cold as the depths of bloody winter, and it's as creepy as fuck.'

Her teeth were chattering now, and she turned away. As she did so, she heard Carla's car door open. Sighing with relief, she kept walking towards the front door and stepped inside. Without looking back to see if Carla was following, she switched on the two lamps and hastily tidied up the throw and cushions from the floor. As she threw a couple of small pieces of wood onto the fire and blew on them to get it restarted, Carla came through the door and closed it behind her.

Well, at least she did that!

Carla offered no preamble. 'Where is he?'

'Upstairs asleep. I'll get him, but let me at least get the kettle on first, you look frozen.'

Carla snorted. 'Like you really care!'

Feen retorted, firmly but quietly 'I'd provide the same welcome for anyone who showed up here late at night in the stiddle of a morm. Please don't think you're anything special, Ms Walton.'

Carla's mouth twitched, and she rolled her eyes. 'Don't you ever get sick of speaking utter nonsense?' she snapped.

Feen decided to ignore the jibe. Instead, she turned away and filled the kettle, then set it on the Aga. She took three cups and a teapot down from the shelf and set about putting some teabags into the pot. She cleared her throat.

'Righto. While that's underway I'll go and wake your son.'

'Wait. Don't wake him yet.'

Feen spun around. 'Why not?'

Carla just shrugged, then looked at the floor. Feen could sense that she wanted to say something but wasn't sure what, so she prompted her.

'Do you have something you want to ask me, Carla?'

The other woman thought for a moment. 'I suppose I do.'

'Well, spit it out then.'

'Gavin tells me you two are getting married.'

Feen stood her ground and folded her arms across her chest. Her voice was as even and as cordial as she could muster. She wasn't going to let Carla Walton intimidate her on her family's own property. She mentally prepared herself for a fight, even as the thought made her stomach seethe.

'Yes, that's right.'

Carla nodded. 'Well, I'm not going to bother telling you what I think about that, but you can probably guess. All I'll say is that if you mess him about or hurt him, I will personally wring your stupid, scrawny little neck.'

Feen stared. 'Like _you_ really care!' she snapped.

Carla stepped back. She looked at Feen, dumbfounded.

'What? What kind of comment is *that*? He's my son, for Christ's sake! Of *course* I fucking care!'

'Well, he thinks you don't. He thinks you couldn't give a damn about him. You've spent years showing him that.'

160

Carla cast her eyes downward. Feen continued. Her voice was quiet, but she made her words hit home.

'I'll tell you what, Carla. Let's ignore the fact that you've shown up here at stupid o'clock at night, and insulted and threatened me in my family's home. Let's put your pathetic cheap shots to one side and talk about the *real* reason you're here. All those years you ignored your son? Told him *ad nauseum* what a disappointment he was to you for choosing to live with his father instead of you? Then cut him out of your life without a single word that wasn't laced with enough vitriol to make paint peel? All the vicious lies you told him about his father for all the time before he left you? That's what you're here to talk about, isn't it?'

Feen took a breath and ploughed on. 'Yes, you can stop wondering. He *does* know, about *all* of it. His dad adored him! The man never laid a hand on either of you. *You* were the abuser. If you cared about Gavin like you say you do, you'd never have let him grow up believing you don't care whether he exists or not, and wondering why you told him such licious vies; letting him falsely believe for more than half his life that his dad was an abusive bully.'

Galvanised by her own convictions, Feen found herself on a roll. She took a step towards Carla. 'You know, it's significant, don't you think, that in spite of the lies you'd fed him about his dad, he still preferred to take his chances there than stay with you? Is that what's stuck in your craw? The fact that he'd prefer to live with a so-called violent thug, than with a miserable wretch like you?'

Carla looked like she'd been slapped. Feen suddenly felt a wave of the woman's pain and confusion, and a rush of compassion flooded her. Her shoulders sagged.

'Look, Carla. Maybe you really don't appreciate how much you messed him up; how much he is *still* messed up, over you. But trust me, he is. He doesn't know whether he's coming or going with you. If you really do love him, it's important that you tell him that. Neither of you gets it, how critically important those words are to both of you, if you mean them.'

Carla lowered herself to sit at the kitchen table. She still said nothing.

Feen sat also. 'I lost my own mother, as you probably already know, at the most critical time of my life. I was just a teenager too; not much younger than Gavin was when he chose to leave home. I'd give anything in the entire world to have my mum back, even now, but I can't. I have to live with that, and I dight to foo it, every single day. There isn't a moment in my life when I don't wish she was here. Mothers are important, no matter how old you are. Your mother's important to you, right? Hazel, that's her name, isn't it?'

Carla nodded briefly. 'Yes. Of course she is.'

'So why would you imagine you wouldn't be as important to your son, as Hazel is to you?' Feen sighed heavily, exasperated.

'Don't you get it, Carla? Just because he didn't want to live with you, just because he needed to leave to make sense of his life in his own way, that didn't mean he didn't love or need you!'

She looked levelly at Carla. 'He *still* loves you. It doesn't matter how horrible you were to him, still are to him. It should, but it doesn't! In really important ways, he is still what he was; a wounded and confused young boy. He was hurting, back then, and he wanted it to stop. He needed to figure things out, and finding his dad was part of that, but you've punished him so hard for it!

'You've been unable to forgive him, because you've only ever seen how wounded *you* were in that process! You couldn't focus on anyone's pain but your own. You harangued him for months after he left, with bitchy texts, then you abandoned all contact completely. What was he supposed to think? He was in pain too, Carla. He still is.'

'Selfish.' The one word came so quietly that Feen wondered at first if she'd imagined it. Then she nodded.

'Yeah.' She couldn't resist a subtle twist of the knife. 'If you like. Let's agree on that, then. You're his mother, yet you threw him to the lions! I just tell myself you didn't understand; that you didn't know what damage you were doing.' Feen shook her head, as if to clear it.

'I can't tell myself you were deliberately cruel and mean, because that would just be too hard to accept. He has to come from something better than that, and you can't be so wretched as to get pleasure from hurting your own child like that. Not your own flesh and blood.'

Carla glared at her. 'It's none of your damn business, is it? You don't understand anything about our lives,' she snapped.

'Maybe not,' Feen said softly. 'But I'd like to, and since I'm going to marry him, his pain is my business, whether you like it or not, Carla.'

The kettle chose that moment to start whistling, so Feen quickly pulled it off the Aga and filled the teapot. When she looked up, she was astonished to see that Carla was weeping. She reached up to the shelf and pulled down a roll of kitchen towels. Silently, she handed it to her.

At that moment, Gavin came down the stairs. He opened his mouth to speak but abruptly froze at the sight of his mother sitting, as large as life, crying at his kitchen table.

'What the f...?' He looked at Feen, confusion written across his face.

Feen shrugged. Gavin looked at each woman, saw that his mother was crying but Feen was not, saw that Feen was wet through and his mother was not, and his face was a picture of confusion.

Feen stood up. 'Carla's here to talk to you. There's tea in the pot. I'm going up to the main house to get some dry clothes. I'll see you later.'

Gavin moved towards her, but she brushed past him. She was shivering hard now, and still soaking wet. Her teeth were chattering. He grabbed her by the shoulders.

'I'll walk you up to the house, I don't want you going up there alone in the pitch dark in the pouring rain. You're wet through.'

Feen opened her mouth to protest, as she dragged her boots onto her still-wet feet, but Gavin held up his hand. 'It's not negotiable. I'll see you to the house, then I'll come straight back.'

He shot a dark look at his mother. 'I'll be five minutes.'

Carla nodded grimly back, then stared at the table.

Gavin frowned at Feen. She shrugged again and shook her head. As they left the cottage, he grabbed an umbrella and put it over her head. She thought of saying that it was a bit like shutting the stable door after the horse had bolted, since she was already soaked to the skin, but she held her tongue and allowed him to

163

be protective. He slipped an arm around her waist as they made their way up the drive towards Ravensdown House.

She snuggled close to him, appreciating his warmth. She explained, distractedly. 'I woke up to find her sitting outside in her car. Just sitting there, in the dark, in the pouring rain. So, I invited her in. I'm sorry, but it seemed like the right thing to do.'

Gavin gave her waist a squeeze. 'Has she been nasty to you? Did she say anything mean?'

Feen chuckled. 'Nothing I didn't fire straight back at her. No, it was fine. Honestly.'

Clearly, he didn't know what else to say, so she continued. 'She cares about you. And I think she's had her head so far up her own arse, she doesn't realise how hurtful she's been to you. You guys really need to talk. I think there's a lot to be said, on both sides.'

Gavin didn't respond. As they reached the front door of Ravensdown House, Feen spoke again.

'I'm going to stay here tonight. I need a hot bath or shower, to warm up, and I think you need space with her.'

Gavin shook his head. 'No. Please come back. I mean it. I need you back there with me. Take all the time you need here now, but please say you'll come back. Whether she's gone or not. I want you with me tonight. I *need* you. Please, Feen. This isn't just about me anymore, it's about both of us.'

'Tonight it's about you and her, Gavin.'

He shook his head at her again, more vehemently this time. 'Please Feen. Come back. Whatever this is, we face it as a united front. That's what we are now.'

Reluctantly Feen agreed. 'Ok, I'll come back. Whether she's there or not, I'll just walk in, and take it as it comes.'

Gavin hugged her. She was wet and shivering, but his warmth helped. He kissed her gently on the lips. 'I love you. But your teeth are chattering. Go inside and get warmed up'

She kissed him back. 'I love you too. See you in a bit.'

Surprisingly, Adie and her dad were still up. Adie peered over the top of her glasses and raised her eyebrows at her, as she came into the house. Reluctant to fully explain and cause unnecessary panic, she just gestured to herself and smiled sheepishly, saying she'd forgotten a few things and the storm wouldn't let up, so she simply had to brave it and come up anyway.

Adie frowned slightly but seemed to accept her explanation and had then smiled and gone straight back to reading her book. Mark was sound asleep and snoring in his chair, as per usual for a Sunday night. Feen felt comforted by the family routine. For her, it would all be very different, soon enough.

As she stood in the shower and let the hot water sluice and heat her body, she thought back to Carla Walton's face as she'd tried to absorb Feen's home truths. It was a risk, stepping in and speaking for Gavin while he wasn't there, and she hoped he wouldn't mind too much.

No grown man wants someone else bighting his fattles!

But Feen knew they were things that had to be said, and she was very protective of her brand new, sensitive husband-to-be.

She knew why Carla had come to Teapot Cottage. She'd come because she couldn't have *not* come. She was drawn to the place, just like so many other people who arrived there in a state of turmoil, trying to make sense of whatever was in their messed-up heads and find a way forward. Most of the people who turned up at Teapot Cottage had no idea what had pulled them there, but Feen understood perfectly.

Most people didn't understand that unseen frequencies were everywhere, influencing people in different ways, or that healing energy tended to be concentrated in specific places. There were special pockets of it all over the world. People who were tuned into them never found them hard to find, and even people who weren't consciously tuned in sometimes just got pulled in anyway. The universe knew what they needed and pushed or pulled them in that direction. It really was as simple as that. It was crystal clear to Feen that if Gavin and his mother were to heal their fractured relationship, Teapot Cottage was where they would do it.

She fully understood that while she had to take a backseat, at least for now, she did have a role in trying to help mother and son bridge the chasm that had opened up between them. She'd tried to make Carla fully aware of how things were between them. It was all she could do. It was no small thing that Carla had admitted her selfishness. That in itself was big progress; the cottage at work, again.

Feen instinctively knew that by the time she did go back to Teapot Cottage, Gavin and his mother would still be sitting right where she'd left them, and the atmosphere would be very subdued, like it so often is after a big argument when the two people involved have both run out of steam and there isn't much left to be said. Mother and son would have gone back into their respective corners to regroup, like a couple of heavyweight boxers, but Feen knew that by the time she returned, the verbal punches would all have been thrown, and Carla and Gavin would both be spent.

The storm had moved away a little now, but it was still raining hard, and thunder still growled and grumbled. Feen found a long raincoat and heavier boots that would keep her completely dry, and she grabbed a nice bottle of wine from the rack beneath the stairs to take with her. Maybe a peace-offering would help. She put everything by the front door, ready for when she could feel that the business between Gavin and his mother had gone as far as it could tonight. Then she went into the kitchen to make a cup of tea for herself and Adie.

She also resolved to do a spiritual cleanse of Teapot Cottage too, as soon as the opportunity came, to restore its rare and special healing aura of serenity and peace. It was a place that gently supported and nurtured whoever entered. It wouldn't be fair to Adie, or to anyone else who needed that sacred energy, if it wasn't quickly rebalanced.

Chapter Fifteen

A Song About Allegiance

You an' me, we're in this together.
Can't do it without you, can't let you do it without me.
The pain of losin' and the glory of winnin'
None of it means nothin' if we don't share it all
We're in this together, in it together
Together, you an' me.

By the time Gavin had jogged back to Teapot Cottage, he was
soaked and shivering too. He hoped against all hope that his
mother had seen sense and left, but his heart sank to see that
Bampas' Shogun was still in the driveway, and Carla was exactly
where he'd left her, sitting at the kitchen table with her eyes
downcast.

He threw another log onto the fire, walked into the kitchen,
and got straight to the point.

'Why are you here, Mum? Is it Nanny or Bampa? Has
something happened?'

His mother shook her head but said nothing. Gavin didn't sit
down. He was furious that she'd just turned up here uninvited,
late at night, disturbing Feen, and expecting her to have to deal
with whatever it was she'd come for.

'Then why the hell have you come here at this bloody hour,
in this weather?' he demanded.

She turned to him, stony faced. 'We need to talk.'

He stared at her in disbelief. 'What, right now? Can't it wait
until morning? It's the middle of the bloody night.'

The clock above the Aga showed him it was in fact only a quarter past eleven - but still way too late to be making an uninvited house call. Fair play to Feen for even opening the door!

'Well you'd better start then,' he said shortly, remembering how painfully her parting shot had stung him, earlier in the evening. He wasn't going to take any more abuse from her, and she'd soon find out how mistaken she was, if she thought she could waltz in and start throwing her weight around.

'And if you've threatened Feen or been a bitch to her in any way at all, I'll bodily throw you out of here. Don't be stupid enough to make the mistake of thinking I don't mean it.'

Carla closed her eyes and sighed. 'I haven't been mean to her. I did mention that she spoke like a simpleton, but that's nothing more than the truth, is it?'

He stared hard at her as she sat at the table staring mutely at its surface.

'So you *were* a bitch to her. Well I suppose you just can't help yourself, can you? Afflicted as you are, with a mind-bending lack of kindness in the face of someone's hospitality. She didn't have to invite you in. It's more than I would have done. Maybe you should fuck off yourself, Carla. You don't get to come in here and insult the woman I love.'

His mother flinched briefly, as if his words had landed like a punch, then she stared at the table again, like it was the most fascinating thing she'd ever seen.

'So?' Gavin prompted, fighting his own turmoil. 'If you're going to keep sitting there, like a half-sucked acid-drop, you'd better offer something, because right now you're pissing me off to the point where I'm an inch away from doing you some serious harm.

'I'm surprised you've had the nerve to show up at this time of night, at this house, of all places. But yeah, let's not forget that you do know your way here in the dark, don't you, Mum? Got any poison in the truck, by any chance? Or do we only have to worry about the kind that haemorrhages from your mouth, tonight?'

To credit her with something, his mother showed some shame, but Gavin wasn't in the mood to cut her any slack. He did manage to sound a lot calmer than he felt, which was no small thing.

'You know, you turning up here is actually breath-taking; especially since it was *you* who told *me* to fuck off just a few hours ago.'

Carla looked up and met his eyes.

'I know. I've come to apologise for that. It was uncalled for, and so was what I said about your engagement. It's up to you what you do. Considering what the past ten years has been like, it's hardly my place to interfere, is it?'

'No, it's not. Even if we'd been in touch in all that time, even if we had a good relationship, you wouldn't have the right to tell me who I should or shouldn't fall in love with or marry. Nobody has that right, and anyone who thinks they *do* can fuck off. And that includes you. So now you know what it feels like to be told that too, by your own flesh and blood.'

Carla turned to face him. 'I didn't mean to hurt you by what I said. I don't even know why I said it.'

Gavin shrugged as nonchalantly as he could, even as his thoughts were boiling. 'It's water under the bridge, Mum. It doesn't matter.'

'Yes, it bloody does.' Carla's tone was vehement enough to make him step back from the table. 'It matters to me. My *own* mother wounded me today, for the first time ever. In all my life, she's never gone for me like that. She's put up with all sorts of shit from me, and God knows why, but she's never complained, at least not to my face.

'I never imagined she'd ever attack me like that, let alone do it in front of anybody else.' Carla laughed, harshly. 'I can imagine what she probably says to Dad when I'm not around, but she's never openly criticised me for my behaviour. Until today. She was really pissed off, and she berated me like a naughty child in front of my own son. And do you know what? It hurt like hell.'

Gavin stared at her, at a total loss for what to say to such a stark and unexpected confession. Nothing would be the right thing anyway; he was sure of that. He stayed silent and let her carry on.

'So, when I said that to you, I didn't mean it. When I'd calmed down, I realised how much that must have hurt, so I came to say I'm sorry.'

'It could have waited, Mum. You didn't have to come up here in the dead of night, in the middle of a bloody electrical storm and drag my fiancée out of bed, to say it.'

'Yes, I did. Because there are things I have to say that can't wait. I'm enlightened enough nowadays to know what I am, Gavin. Yes, I'm an embittered, irrational woman, on the tail-end of menopause and a midlife crisis that feels like it's been going on for ever and doesn't seem to want to stop. But after learning today how it feels to be attacked by your own parent, I decided that even if this messed-up relationship of ours never gets any better, I don't want it to get any worse, even overnight.'

'Do you want it to get better, Mum? Do you? As usual you're making everything about *you*. How hurt *you* are. What *you* want. How about having some empathy for poor Nanny, and how distraught *she* must have been, to have said what she did, so completely out of character like that?'

Gavin sighed, pulled out a chair, and sat down abruptly, opposite his quietly weeping mother.

'Nanny didn't attack you, Mum. She just told you how she felt, and how she expected you to behave in her house. Personally, I thought it was fair enough. Quite heroic, actually.'

He decided against voicing the observation that he could see where Carla got her temper from, but he decided to plough on.

'And this 'messed-up relationship' we have, as you so eloquently put it? That's yours to own. I never asked or wanted to be cut out of your life completely. Who the hell has diplomatic skills at sixteen? Not me! I was just a messed-up *kid,* who needed to put some distance between us to figure things out. The only thing I was guilty of was not wanting to live with you anymore. It was your choice to turn your back on me. Months of blistering hostility, telling me more times than I could count that I was - among various things – 'the biggest disappointment of your life'! Then radio silence. Total white noise.

'Think about that. Why would I have tried to contact you? You'd turned your back on me! All those texts and emails? I got the message Mum, but you weren't the only one with a choice. I chose too; to turn *my* back on it all.'

'So, if it's not a messed-up relationship, how *would* you describe it?' Carla demanded, pointedly choosing to ignore the rest of what he'd said.

'I'd describe it as complicated.' Gavin conceded. 'Complicated and difficult.' Tears unexpectedly pricked his eyes, to his horror, but he blinked them away before his mother could see them. He was damned if he was going to give her the satisfaction of seeing him cry.

But is it beyond salvage?

The words came into his head, as clearly as if they'd been spoken aloud. He knew they hadn't been, but what *was* that? Was it Feen, from up at the house? Gavin had the distinct feeling that it was the house itself that had spoken, but in his voice. That did seem more than a little insane, he had to admit. He shook his head.

I must be going mad, myself!

'I've always loved you, Gavin. But you've never believed that, have you?' Carla's voice was quiet now.

'I tried, Mum. But it was pretty bloody hard. Your love has so many strings attached. I didn't want to be your puppet, and you're not the easiest person to love, yourself, by the way!'

Carla laughed shortly. 'That's been said before.'

Gavin shrugged. 'Well, what do you expect? Most people don't tell vicious, damaging lies to their loved ones, or shut them out. Most people take responsibility for their own shortcomings and somehow manage to stop short of blaming everyone else for them instead. Most people don't go out into the world and trash someone else's reputation in their own self-interest! You just don't do those things to the people you're supposed to care about, Mum! You messed with Dad's head for bloody years, and mine, over us, over him, over *everything!*'

'Well, you seem to have turned out alright, from what I can see, even if your ludicrous choice of bride does throw your soundness of mind into question.'

Gavin felt a savage spark of anger at that, but he refused to let his mother's snide remark at Feen get the better of him. Rising to the bait wouldn't help matters, but it really pissed him off that after coming here, ostensibly to apologise, she still managed to make a sarcastic remark at someone else's expense when they weren't around to defend themselves. Carla really was a piece of work. He was still only a hair's breadth away from throwing her out of the cottage, to land on her arse in the rain.

'If I've turned out halfway decent, it's because of Martin and Mike. Not because of you, Mum. If I've turned out alright, it's in *spite* of you.'

'What do you really want, Gavin?' she demanded. 'What is it you want from me? You came all this way, because you said you needed to discuss something with me. Whatever it is, it's important enough for you to break cover and drag your backside all the way to the other end of the country – to *me*! But it's been a few days now, and you haven't said a word. I'm still none the wiser, am I?'

She ran a hand through her hair, and he noted it as one of his own habits. She looked up at him. 'If all you wanted to do was tell me you were getting married, well, you've done that. Congratulations, and I hope you'll be very happy, blah-de-blah-de-blah, against all reasonable odds. But that's not it, is it? Because that wasn't even on the bloody cards before you got here.'

Gavin stayed silent, glaring at Carla, as she continued. 'You hadn't even met that feather-brained fool when you first arrived. That means you came up here for another reason, and I don't buy that crap about just wanting to reconnect. There's more to the story, isn't there Gavin?'

A short silence ensued, before she spoke again, quietly.

'So, *you'd* better stop messing with *my* head, and tell me what it is.'

He looked at her levelly and took a deep breath.

Ok, here goes nothing and everything.

'I believe you had a box of Dad's things, Mum; birth certificates, old photos, his father's medals, his grandmother's wedding ring, and other bits and pieces that meant a lot to him. I'm wondering if you still have it, and whether I could have it, please.'

She stared at him for a few beats. 'How did you know about that?'

172

'Mike told me about it, after the funeral. An old friend of Dad's was asking about a photo. He wanted a copy so I had to ask Mike where I might find it, because there was nothing at the flat that resembled what the guy was asking about. It all just came out in conversation, about the box.'

Carla looked down again at the kitchen table but said nothing. Obviously, she had originally kept the box. Gavin resisted uttering judgement of the fact that she had more or less stolen what had rightfully belonged to someone else. It would have been a huge mistake to do that, but he still had to battle with himself not to say it.

'Mum? D'you still have the box?'

He held his breath and waited. The atmosphere was delicate, to say the least. He dared not prompt her again. He felt like he was walking a tightrope, almost too afraid to breathe in case that somehow jinxed his balance, sending him crashing to the ground with his hopes forever dashed.

She cleared her throat and looked at him wearily.

'That's it? That's what you came all this way for? An old box of mouldy pictures and papers?'

'Yes Mum. They were important things to Dad, so that's important to me, and since what I've inherited includes it, I'd like to see what's in it. I think there's some stuff from his side of the family, which probably isn't relevant to you, but it is to me, of course.'

Carla nodded slowly but didn't speak again. She just kept staring at the damn table.

Hellfire! It's like trying to get blood out of a stone!

Gavin prompted her again, but more gently now. 'D'you remember that box at all, Mum? D'you still have it?'

She nodded again, and hope soared in his chest.

'I'd forgotten all about it. I think it's in the loft at Mum and Dad's.'

'May I have it please, Mum?' He asked her as gently as he could.

Carla gnawed at her knuckle for a moment but still, infuriatingly, said nothing.

'Mum? What's in that box doesn't mean anything to you, does it? I don't know why it would, but if it does, just tell me why, because it means a lot to *me* and I need to understand. But I need *you* to understand too! He was my father, and however meaningless he might have been to you, he was everything to me, and I've lost him. Those things in there, whatever they are, were precious to *him*, so by default, they're precious to me too.'

Carla still refused to speak. Gavin struggled to control his anger, and forced himself not to show it. Instead, he phrased his next question carefully.

'If you found out that Bampa - your dad that you really loved - had treasured keepsakes hidden away somewhere after he died, you'd want them, wouldn't you? You wouldn't want anyone who didn't have a right to have them to refuse to give them back, would you?'

His mother continued to stare mutely at the table. He couldn't read her at all.

What is she thinking right now? What's going through that crazy bloody head of hers?

To his astonishment, she started to cry again, quite earnestly now, and he had no idea how to react. Tantrums, rages, blistering sarcasm and ruthlessly caustic comments; he was used to all that from her, but all these tears? This was something different. It signalled a completely different state of mind that he simply couldn't fathom. He really didn't know her at all.

He gritted his teeth. 'Mum, talk to me. I want to understand what's going on with you. I *need* to! Can't you see that? Help me out here, please?'

Carla looked up at him with tear-filled eyes. Her face was so raw with pain and anguish, it made him catch his breath. This was no act. Her agony was real, and he didn't have a clue how to respond to it.

She quickly ran the back of her hand across her eyes, trying to wipe her tears away.

'Your dad was never meaningless to me, Gavin. I loved him. I never stopped loving him, in spite of what he did.'

Something inside Gavin snapped at that point. Box or no box, he couldn't just accept her words – not after everything she'd said and done. He looked at her squarely. He was furious, and no longer made any effort to hide it.

174

'What?' he roared. 'Seriously? In spite of what *he* did? How can you say that? How can you sit there and tell me you loved him? You crucified him! You set him up as a villain to the world, and to your own son! You cast so much doubt over his character he had to move away to the other side of the city and start his life from scratch! That's not love! That's ... that's ..., well, I dunno what it is. Twisted? Sick? Downright fucking insane? Whatever you want to call it Carla, there's no good word for it, and it sure as hell wasn't the kind of love he needed. It's not the kind *anyone* needs!'

And that was it. He realised that in one enraged outburst, he'd pretty much burned his chances of getting Martin's box back. He'd insulted his mother at the highest level, and she wasn't likely to take a blow like that lying down. She would punish him for his candour by denying him the one thing that really mattered to him about his father's past, why he'd come here in the first place, and she'd take great delight in it.

But he hadn't been able to stop himself from speaking up. For her to sit there and declare her love for his father, after everything she'd put him through, just felt too rich. He couldn't square that one away, not yet. Not without a really good explanation of what was actually going on in her irrational, twisted head. It was all he could do, not to cry.

She then spoke up properly, and he was surprised at the strength in her voice.

'I did love your father. I loved him more than anything in the world, except for you. I loved him so much that I've never been able to love anyone since. There's never been anyone else, after him. I've been on my own since he left, nearly twenty-five years ago. But he left me emotionally, long before that, Gavin. Right from the start, I only ever had a tiny piece of who he was, and even *that* wasn't authentic!

'He was living a complete lie with me, and with you. But I was so naive, back then, fresh out of the Lake District with no real experience of the world. I thought I knew everything, but I knew jack shit! I certainly didn't know anything about gay men, or the fact that so many of them had kids with women as well! I didn't have a *hope* of knowing what Martin's failure to fully commit to us really meant.'

She laughed, without a trace of humour. 'I found out eventually, of course, didn't I, when he ultimately fell in love with Mike Drew? How could I ever have competed with that? There was no way! I never stood a bloody chance, right from the start of my life with him, and he never bothered to give me the head's up.'

She was dabbing almost savagely at her eyes now, with a soggy, bunched-up piece of kitchen roll.

'Oh, he did want to stay, but only for your sake. He wanted to keep living with us, because he wanted to carry on being a father to you, but he also wanted to live his life openly as a gay man, and I was just expected to swallow that!' Her breath hitched as she ploughed on.

'At first I couldn't believe he'd expect me - us - to live like that. But he'd made up his mind, and he just expected me to tolerate it. He told me, if I wanted to meet someone else myself, that was fine, all that. Said we could still be a family of a kind. Open relationship sort of thing. But he was all I wanted, Gavin; him, and you, and some brothers or sisters for you. He didn't understand that doing what *he* wanted wasn't just humiliating to me. It shattered every dream I had. It broke my heart in such a way that I've never known how to put it back together.

'He didn't love me! He pretended to, for a long time. But he never saw how much that hurt, when it all came out that he'd been hankering after someone else, for a different kind of relationship, for *years*.' Carla's voice became nasal and heavy, as her nose completely blocked up from crying.

'He was such a hypocrite, Gavin. He wouldn't live one sort of lie anymore, but he was clearly prepared to live another and expect me to as well. And you, too! I just couldn't put you through that. I didn't know how to manage it for *myself*, let alone how to deal with the impact it might have on you, growing up. There was still more stigma than there should have been back then, even at the end of the nineties, about people living openly gay lives.'

Carla blew her nose again, and carried on. 'You might've been persecuted at school because of it, or damaged in some other way. I didn't know! I was a small-town girl with no experience of the world, and I was frightened for you – for *us*.

For what *our* lives would be like. I told him it would never work, living two separate lives rolled into one and expecting us to do the same. It just wasn't fair to expect that. It wasn't realistic. So I couldn't help myself. I started hating him.'

Her voice then dropped almost to a ragged whisper. 'It wasn't because Martin was gay, Gavin. I just wanted him to love *me*. It was pathetic, I know. But I adored him! I didn't want to lose him, so I did try for a little while to live with him the way he wanted, always with the hope that he'd change his mind and want me again. That's how totally naïve I was! But a little bit more of me was dying every day, and I finally had to face the fact that he wanted to belong to another man instead of me!

'I was so hurt, and angry. The need to punish him, destroy him as much as he'd destroyed me, overtook everything else. I'm not proud of it, but it's true. Then, all of a sudden, you were all I had left. I was literally on my own, and trying to make sense of everything.'

Carla sniffed hard, and wiped her tears with the back of her hand. 'I couldn't have explained it to Mum and Dad. They'd never have understood. I didn't think *anyone* would have. I was ashamed, and embarrassed, confused, alone, and *so* hurt. Decimated. Bleeding out. I couldn't have come home with you, and tried to explain all that! Mum and Dad would never have got their heads around it.

'I did okay with you I think, for a bit, but then I had an early menopause that clashed with your adolescence. I don't think that helped us much. I lost my way, with you and everything else, and I couldn't work out how to find my way back. I went crazy! I'm sure I did!'

As he looked at his mother, in a crumpled sobbing heap, Gavin had felt the first pang of pity for her. It *must* have been hellish, to be so much in love with someone who didn't love you back, when you'd already had a child together, and you still had so much hope for a love-filled future. Without much warning at all, Carla's world had literally come crashing down around her ears. God alone knew what that must have felt like. Who was *anyone*, to sit in judgement of how someone else coped with that?

Loving Feen the way he did, how would he react to her coming home and telling him she was in love with another woman, and wanted to pursue a different relationship but wanted him to live a lie with her? It would send him mad with rage and grief, he was certain of that. And how would he protect a child against it?

For the first time, he found himself starting to see from a different perspective. There were always two sides to every story, he'd always understood that, but he'd only really heard Mike's interpretation of this one, since his father had chosen never to cast aspersions on Gavin's mother. All else that he'd ever had to judge by was Carla's treatment of him, which was connected of course to how poorly she'd handled the end of her relationship with Martin.

Has she had any counselling or other support, to process what happened? Has anyone, anywhere, in all this time, helped her work through the trauma? Or did shame and pride prevent her from even asking? Has she really tried to deal with everything all by herself?

He suspected he knew the answers.

Was Carla really the monster everyone assumed her to be? Maybe she was just a woman in the worst way scorned; an abandoned, devastated, wounded young mother, who had lashed out like any injured animal and let her venom loose. It was fair to say that she hadn't coped well at all, turning her attention obsessively inwards, virtually smothering the young Gavin as the only worthwhile person she had left. When he started maturing, the knowledge that he would one day leave must have terrified her; the notion that she'd then be truly on her own, with no one to love or be loved by.

Martin Black was no saint. He was a human being, as flawed and self-righteous as any other, and Gavin wasn't naïve enough to think otherwise. But it dawned on him now, that while Martin had never openly badmouthed Gavin's mother to him, which was commendable, he had never acknowledged his responsibility for her pain either, which must have been unimaginable. Maybe his silence on that, for the ten years Gavin had lived with him, was tied up in some kind of guilt. Maybe he had even tried to help her at the time, in some way. But she couldn't have accepted it, could she, wounded as she was?

Gavin didn't have a clue what to say to her but, with the first flash of understanding, he also felt the first glimmer of potential for forgiveness. There always *were* two sides to every story. He'd grown up knowing that. Why was he only able to admit now, that it applied here as much as anywhere else?

Feen came back into the cottage, not long after that, waving a bottle of wine. She offered a glass to Carla, who accepted with the kind of grace and humility Gavin had never seen in her before. But he couldn't accept one too. Even in the embryonic stages of understanding his screwed-up mother, he wasn't ready to sit at a table and drink with her. Feen though - bless her - did exactly that.

Not for the first time, he acknowledged how incredible his new fiancée was, in her capacity to be kind, when the more understandable thing would have been to break the bottle over Carla's head. And, to give Carla some well-deserved credit, she held her tongue impressively against saying anything else unkind, herself. The result was an unexpectedly impressive civility between the two most significant women in his life, who had polarised views about everything, and had absolutely nothing in common except him. He sat, feeling strangely detached from the conversation, like he was seeing it from another room, or watching it on video, as if it was happening to someone else.

'Are you getting any support, Carla?' Feen asked her, softly.

'Sort of. I'm having psychotherapy once a week, but mostly I'm enjoying the challenge of changing my freakishly horrible life, and overcoming my nightmares and wretchedness, all by myself, thanks.' The fight had gone from her voice now. She was subdued, and almost hard to hear, when she did speak.

'I'm sure the therapy will help you get to a much better place,' Gavin ventured.

'Well, it's a slow process. And thank you for insinuating that being miserable is never going to make me happy. Your insight is beyond extraordinary. How lucky I am to have such a wise old sage for a son.'

Gavin struggled mightily not to rise to her sarcasm, which she always resorted to using whenever she found herself in an awkward place. He suspected there was more to come, and there was. He steeled himself to ride it out.

'You know, Gavin, I was fine before you showed up. I was doing quite well actually, safely submerged in denial, in relative peace and quiet. Now you're here, I feel like I've been stripped bare, put under a bloody microscope then stuffed into a beaker and sat on a Bunsen burner. I feel like my arse is on fire.'

Gavin shrugged. 'How you feel is your own responsibility,' he countered evenly. 'If you feel like you're on fire, you've done that to *yourself*. All I want is a box, Mum.'

He was in no mood to take any prisoners. Not tonight. It wouldn't have helped his addled head, if he'd even made an attempt to go easy on his mother. He needed to stick to what he *could* control.

Feen smiled gently and tried again. 'So you have a job, Carla, over in Carlisle. What is it, that you do?'

'I'm a filing clerk. You'll understand, of course, that the criminal record put paid to my glittering career in retail. Carlisle's - quote; 'finest department store,' unquote - sacked me for gross misconduct after I failed to tell them about it. The place lurches along still, like the proverbial graveyard, with a few half-alive corpses rattling round in there in the form of rude staff and half-hearted customers.

'It had already turned into a retail desert before I got thrown out, to be fair, so I don't suppose they're missing me much, in my erstwhile 'position of responsibility.' Carla put her hands up in mock quotation marks.

Feen nodded. 'I know. That place is wretched nowadays, and it's a shame. It used to be a fantastic store. I stopped going in there a couple of years ago, because the atmosphere was always awful. There's a truly horrible woman in the shoe department. I once asked if they had any nice shoes for women with finy teet, and she actually sneered at me because I *dared* to be disappointed when she said they'd stopped stocking a certain brand I used to buy there.

'She was so snotty and belittling! And get this; I don't usually complain about stuff like that. I usually shrug it off and forget about it, but that day I'd had enough. I asked to speak to a manager, who turned out to be even *worse*! She was totally up-herself. She didn't give a toss, and she even sided with the bloody shoe woman! She more or less told me that they could do without my money. I couldn't believe that. It was outrageous!'

Gavin appreciated Feen's attempt at making a connection with his mother, and finding some common ground. She was very adept at deflecting tension, and talking about something so inane as a woeful department store - incredibly - seemed to be doing the trick.

'I'd shopped there for *years*,' Feen continued, 'and so had my mum before she died. She used to love that place. But I'll never fet soot in there again, and I'm not the only one around here who says that. They just don't seem to care anymore. Did you work there when it was doing well? What was it like back then? I'll bet it was amazing.'

Carla nodded. 'I did, yeah, and it was. I loved working there, at one time. It was quite prestigious, to have a job there, and it certainly was something, in its day. But it's *had* its day. It's gone to the dogs, and I guess I knew that when I kept the news of my conviction to myself. I knew they'd find out and let me go, but I really wasn't bothered, and I think it was because I'd stopped seeing it as a job worth fighting for, so I just let it happen.' Carla shrugged, took another sip of her wine, and continued.

'Just another damn thing that rolled me over. But I needed another job, and this was the one position the Jobcentre and my probation officer could come up with, that anyone thought I could be trusted with. It was either that or factory-floor work, packing stuff into boxes, and I'd have gone even more crazy than I already am, doing that. But, you know, I think I have a wildly successful future as a filing clerk. My way of setting the world on fire.'

Gavin cleared his throat. 'I think there's been enough talk, about fire.'

Carla narrowed her eyes and snapped at him, waspishly. 'Oh, sorry. Wasn't aware you had an agenda for how you wanted the conversation to run.'

'I didn't want the conversation at *all*, Mum. You came here. I didn't ask you. Neither of us did.'

'Well, you came here first! And I didn't ask *you!*'

Feen coughed lightly and reached out to cover Carla's hand with her own. To Gavin's amazement, his mother didn't snatch her hand away as he expected. He knew Feen was trying to head a potential slanging match off at the pass, bless her, but he'd sailed straight past the point of being able to control what happened next. He had no fight left in him, now, and barely a scrap of conversation. His head was a mess of colliding thoughts and feelings that he couldn't have put into words if his life depended on it.

Feen leaned forward, determined not to let the uncomfortable silence lengthen, which would soon become unbearable, with God knows what being said as a result.

'You know, talking about the criminal record, Carla, I was the one who found Sid, the little dog. I was the one who saved him. He would have died if I hadn't had that sixth sense to come down here and find him and get him to the vet.'

Gavin held his breath, waiting for his mother to erupt. But he was horrified when she burst into tears again, instead. Feen had pulled at a certain string, and the grief and remorse that had been held together by it now came tumbling out.

'I know. It was all in the report, what had happened after I'd done it. I can't tell you how sorry I am. It's another on my list of the horrible things I've done, that I'd take back if I could. But I can't, Feen. I can't take *anything* back, and all I can hope for is that one day everyone I've hurt will find a way to forgive me.

'As for ever being able to forgive myself, well, you can take great comfort in the knowledge that I probably never will. Feel free to pop a champagne cork and drink a happy toast to my torment.'

Feen shook her head. 'Carla, the idea that you'll never be able to forgive yourself gives me no joy at all! You have to try to find a way to be at peace with yourself. Keep going to therapy. If you let it, I'm sure it will help.'

Carla gave another of her trademark snorts. 'Well, maybe. You know how I just love to talk about my fascinating, scintillating self.'

She rose from the table. 'Thank you for the wine and the wisdom. I think it's time for me to go. By the way, Feen, I know who you were talking about in the store in Carlisle. The woman in the shoe department never gave a monkey's about much at all, and that manager you complained to? She's even more of a bitch than I am, and that's saying something, right?'

Feen grinned at her, and nodded gently. But all Gavin could do was sit staring at the table, in much the same way Carla had done while she'd sat there too. It was Feen who walked his mother to the door and saw her off. As a parting shot, she told Gavin he could have his father's box, as soon as she could get it down from the loft.

Afterwards, a strange sense of peace settled over the cottage. Feen again offered wine, and Gavin finally accepted. It was well after midnight now, but he was too tired to conduct any kind of post-mortem about the events of the evening, and far too wired to go back to bed.

Feen seemed to understand his muddled headspace completely, and didn't ask him a single thing, but suggested instead that they snuggle up by the fire again for a bit. It was quickly becoming their favourite place.

Curled up against him on the sofa, she'd mumbled something semi-coherent about honesty, fire, ley lines, and the healing energy within the cottage walls. But before he could ask her to explain what she meant, she'd fallen asleep completely, in the way the innocent of blame who've done their best can always do. He knew that sleep would be a long time coming for him. He hadn't done his best tonight, and he was acutely aware of the fact.

He gazed into the fire, taking comfort from the softly glowing flames that cast their gentle orange light across the otherwise darkened room, and feeling the ever-present, inexplicable feeling of being cocooned and perfectly safe within the house. He noticed that the thunder and lightning had stopped, almost as if his turbulent, stormy mother had hauled it here with her and dragged it away again when she left.

Was it finally time to put the past behind him and look forward, without bitterness and resentment? Within the shortest time imaginable, since arriving at Teapot Cottage, Gavin had quickly found himself with so much more to look forward to. Marriage (hopefully with children) to a beautiful, ethereal and endlessly compassionate woman, relocating up here to this stunning, tranquil environment for at least part of the time, and being closer to Nanny and Bampa to cherish and share whatever time they might have left.

Could his mother fit into that picture, somehow? Was there room in there for her? *And does she even want me to be in her life? She said she loves me, but is that the same thing as wanting me around her?*

Carla had come to Teapot Cottage of her own volition, and she'd said, among other things, that she'd always loved him. He now found himself more inclined to believe her, in whatever way she could mean that, after tonight. Her unexpected visit was significant, a seismic shift of some sort in their relationship, and she'd been the instigator.

Feen could probably articulate much better than he could himself what that meant in real terms but, in essence, the ravaged woman who'd sat at his table had been vulnerable and honest - a far cry from the one he remembered from long ago, whose words were always laced with spite and sarcasm; whose brittleness had become, in the end, more of a burden than he could bear.

She was still bitingly sarcastic and abrasive, but she seemed to have some insight now, about herself. He felt certain now, that his mother had been carrying a huge protective shield for most of her own life and probably all of his, and she had simply, finally, grown too weary of wielding it.

Whatever had prompted her to lay herself bare, she'd revealed an anguished reality. She was a woman whose lover had betrayed and hurt her so much that she couldn't bring herself to trust another man in a relationship, and she'd been so devastated after driving away her own son that she hadn't been capable for far too long, of understanding how much of it had been her own fault. It beggared belief, that she'd been on her own ever since Martin had broken her heart. It amounted to nearly a quarter of a century! Almost half of her life. It meant that she'd had so little love, in *all* her life. If anyone had asked him about that yesterday, he'd have said he wasn't surprised, and would probably have made some crack about no man having the human fortitude to take her on.

Now though, all the knowledge did was make him sad. He literally couldn't imagine how hurt he'd have to be by someone, to refuse to take another chance on love. Carla had been in her twenties when she'd met Martin, after moving to the big city because she wanted a 'bigger' life. Gavin knew all too well, how much seemed possible in your twenties, in place like London; how big your dreams could be, and how easily you could believe you'd find the happiness you wanted. It was all there for the taking. She'd been, then, where he was now. And she must have loved Martin so much, to have ended up so completely devastated.

She'd confessed to that here tonight, and with the other revelations as well, including the fact that she'd wanted Gavin to have siblings, and believed she would have that family with Martin, a crack had appeared that Gavin could at last see into. Carla felt like she'd been robbed of everything. It left him wondering, and even kind of hoping, that he might now have a chance to see and better understand his enigmatic, complicated mother.

The biggest fly in the ointment of course was how the Ravens would feel about it all. It had only been a few days since he'd given them the most heartfelt assurances that his mother would never be a blight on any of their lives. His stomach clenched at the thought of Mark and Adie's reaction to the latest developments, given how fast everything seemed to have changed.

In the blink of an eye, his life had become far more complicated than he'd once believed possible. Feeling the way he did about Feen, there was no question that he would give up on the idea of having any kind of relationship with his mother, if he had to. If forced to choose, he would, pure and simple. But it was hard to ignore that nagging, tiny, hopeful little voice that kept asking now, if it would have to come to that.

Chapter Sixteen

Carla switched the ignition off and glided the Shogun down the driveway towards the house, so the rattly old diesel engine wouldn't wake her parents.

Dad needs to get rid of this old tank. It's a gas-guzzler and he doesn't need anything this big anymore, now he and Mum have sold their caravan.

The house was in total darkness. Stan and Hazel had obviously gone to bed, but they hadn't bothered to leave a single light on for her. The'd even switched off the outside light she'd made a point of turning on, when she'd left the house on her way out. It was, she knew, their declaration of how much they disapproved of her behaviour towards Gavin. 'Fend for yourself,' was the clear message from the dark and silent house.

She couldn't blame them for how they felt, or the fact that her mother hadn't spoken a single word to her for the rest of the day. What's more, she'd banged Carla's tea onto the table so hard, half the peas had actually jumped off the plate. It was nothing more than she deserved, she supposed.

Although all the lights were off, the front door wasn't locked. *Great*, she thought. *Someone could've sneaked up to the house, walked straight in, and murdered those two silly old sods in their bed.*

She made a note to herself to remind Stan in the morning, to always check the doors before going to bed. The house might be located in the back of beyond, a long way further up Fellyn Ridge Road than most of the other houses out this way, but that didn't mean they were safe from unwanted intrusion. In fact, it could have been quite the opposite. Some people preyed on isolated houses as sitting targets for burglary, and they were often the kind of people who wouldn't think twice about hurting or even killing a homeowner who might try to get in their way. Isolated houses meant no witnesses.

It was a macabre train of thought, but it was happening to people ever-more often these days. You only had to switch on the news at night to hear about some poor fool who'd been randomly murdered at home while trying to confront an intruder, or sent to prison after an act of self-defence. Stan and Hazel weren't getting any younger. They could be seen as easy pickings by people with malicious intent. She doubted her father would even notice if someone he didn't know followed him home from town.

As she rubbed her tired eyes, Carla felt the crust of dried tears all around them. In the bathroom mirror she pulled a face at her blotched, puffy, red-eyed reflection.

Half-sucked acid-drop, huh? Well I've been called a lot worse, I suppose, and right now I look more like a deranged dish of Eton Mess.

She washed her face with a cool cloth and applied a rich night cream before brushing her hair and her teeth. As she climbed into bed and turned off the bedside lamp, she suspected that despite feeling deeply drained and utterly exhausted, she probably wouldn't sleep much.

She felt strangely unburdened though, after telling Gavin what her life had been like with his father. She'd kept it to herself, all these long years, never imagining she'd ever feel the need to talk about it. She'd buried it all, like a lot of other people who had complications in their lives that they simply had to find a way to live with.

But she hadn't managed to live with it, had she? At least, not very well. She'd found a place in her head to park the hurt that Martin had caused her, yes, but she hadn't managed to stop it from blighting her life. In fact, the shadow it cast over her was long and dark indeed. Is that what had driven her mean, self-centred actions and reactions so hard for so long? Had the bitterness it created overshadowed Gavin's life too? Carla already knew the uncomfortable answer to that question. Of course it had. How could it have been avoided?

'I've got no filter,' she'd said, by way of explanation for how scathing and abrasive she'd always been, and Gavin had been quick with his retort.

'You say that like it's something to be proud of! It's not, Mum. It's a poor excuse for being a bitch and nothing more.'

187

His comments had stung. He wasn't going to cut her much slack, she'd known that before she'd even turned up at Teapot Cottage, and from the minute he'd laid eyes on her he'd made it crystal clear that he was furious with her and wasn't going to tolerate any bullshit.

I wonder who he gets that from? And he's right to feel the way he does. Of course he is. But I love my son. I've always loved him, so why could I never show him that? I was a shit parent, especially after he left home. I could have been more help, but I washed my hands of him instead. I only have myself to blame for how he is with me now.

Carla found herself weeping again, quietly, into her pillow, finally facing what Dawn Mott had tried in vain for almost a year now, to get her to confront. Clearly, she had damaged Gavin. His father had gone a long way towards repairing that damage, but Carla still had a lot to answer for, and she knew it.

He needed me. All those long years, he needed me, and I wasn't there for him. Feen's right. I only thought about myself. Gavin needed to get to know his father. He had every right to do that, but all I could do was abuse him for it because I thought that meant he only wanted him and not me. So I abandoned him. When did it all become about my pain and no one else's?

Only now could she acknowledge that she'd made Martin's rejection of her the biggest issue of her life, and it had ultimately come to define her. She'd punished Gavin horribly, rejecting him so cruelly, for simply wanting the basic human right of being involved with his own father. And what was the result? Her son, the one true love of her life, her one true triumph, the one thing she'd 'done' that she could be proud of, had grown up believing she didn't love him. Of course he would believe that. What else could he have thought?

As she lay there, restless in the dark, another thought occurred to Carla. Poor Martin must have been *so* conflicted. As a gay man, he was programmed to want one kind of life, but Carla had tried to insist on him living a different one. Maybe it was as hard for him to live the life of pretence she'd demanded as it was for her to accept or agree to *his* terms. Only now could she actually appreciate that his willingness to live a lie with her was not to punish or torture her, but to stay close to the child he was so desperate to have in his life. She hadn't been willing to compromise so he could do it. She'd made it all about how wounded *she* was. It hadn't occurred to her, all these long, lonely years, that Martin had been in anguish too.

It was all coming home to roost now. Martin was dead, and when she'd heard that, her immediate reaction had been to shrug and say that it made no difference. 'Martin Black is dead, and yet - incredibly - the world keeps turning!'

But she'd felt an immense wave of sadness. Determined to keep that under wraps, she'd blocked it off and told herself it didn't matter. Good riddance, and all that. She'd rather have died than told anyone how she really felt. Exposing such a chink in her armour was unthinkable after all this time. But part of her was permanently broken now, by the knowledge that a chance to put things right had been lost forever. With Martin's passing, a door had slammed shut, never to be reopened.

So what were all these tears for, now? Was the effort of keeping that huge pain hidden finally starting to take its toll? Had she done the right thing by showing her vulnerability to Gavin? It had been a leap of faith, one she'd struggled to take, but it was driven by the newly-found conviction that no matter what the cost, it was time for the truth to come out.

It was hard to shed the armour, monumentally difficult to change from sticking to type and being abrasive and self-shielding in the face of pain. And it was hard to stay angry with a dead man, especially with one whose genes had helped to produce such a spectacular son. Despite all best intentions, Carla felt her heart softening. A thaw had started, but all the knowledge did was create more turmoil in her head.

At least now I know what he's here for, what he really wants from me. What a relief it is, that it's something I can easily give him.

She'd long since forgotten about Martin's box, squirreled away in a dark, cobweb-covered corner of Stan and Hazel's loft. It meant nothing to her now, and hadn't for years. She would certainly let Gavin have it but what would happen after that? Would that be the last communication she'd ever have with him?

Feen had told her she needed to tell him she loved him. Well, she'd done that tonight, and it hadn't been as hard as she'd imagined it would be. She'd laid herself wide open, but had it made a difference? She didn't know. Even after she'd poured her heart out, he'd sat there at the kitchen table impassively, like a lump of immovable granite.

She realised now that she *did* care. It did matter, what he thought of her. It did matter, if he chose never to speak to her again. It had *always* mattered. It was only now that she could accept the weight of her own responsibility for how their relationship had foundered, that she could finally admit it to herself. What she hadn't done, in such predictable Carla fashion, was admit it to *him*. It needed to be said, and it would be, but for tonight there was nothing more to be done.

She hadn't expected to sleep, but she found herself drifting off, as the last rumbles of distant thunder finally faded and a sense of calm returned to the fells that flanked the valley. The last thought that went through her overloaded head was that tomorrow, straight after work, she needed to get up into the loft, find Martin's blasted box, and take it to her son. The outcome would be whatever it was, but at least she would never have to hide from the fact *or* tell herself, ever again, that she'd stood in the way of what he needed.

*   *   *   *   *

The following evening, as soon as she got home, Carla changed into old jeans and a t-shirt, and tied a protective scarf around her hair. She opened up the manhole in the hallway ceiling, and dragged down the rickety aluminium ladder that gave access to the loft. It came down with a long, high-pitched, tooth-jangling screech that made the hairs prickle on the back of her neck. She fought back her fear of spiders, and flicked on the light, grateful that Stan had provided power up here. As she'd dreaded, the rafters were dusty and covered in grime-laden cobwebs, blackened with age and dust, drooping down from the rafters.

Urgh! Nobody's been up here for bloody years.

It was a roomy and dry space, with plenty of potential for a loft conversion. She was surprised that Stan had never thought about it, but she shrugged off the notion as she stood up straight, in the area where the roof peaked. It wasn't like they needed the space, and 'resale value' didn't matter. Stan and Hazel had long-ago decided that the only way they'd be leaving the home they'd lived in for their whole married life would be in a couple of wooden boxes with the lids nailed down.

The bare bulb that hung from the centre of the middle rafter shone a dim and dreary light that threw long shadows to the corners of the roof. Although the loft wasn't what Carla would have called spooky, it wasn't particularly inviting either. Keeping the cobwebs in mind, she resolved to find Martin's box as quickly as she could and get the hell out of there.

As she looked around she could just make out, piled into one corner, the remnants of her own and her brother Tristan's childhoods. Their old rocking horse lay on its side next to the living room chimney, alongside an old cardboard sea-trunk that Carla knew had her teddies and dolls stored in it. An old pink hula hoop with its paint peeling off was propped up next to the trunk, and there were various boxes labelled 'books', which she knew had been her and Tris' school-years reads.

They were both avid bookworms when they were little. Stan and Hazel had cottoned on early to the idea of giving them books to read, in the interest of bagging themselves a much-needed Sunday morning lie-in. Every Sunday, when Carla and Tris had woken up, they would each find a new book on the nightstand next to their bed, and they'd be so enthralled, they'd forget about bothering their parents for hours.

Carla remembered that the Narnia Chronicles would be in those boxes, along with all her Jinty, Bunty and Tammy annuals, the Moomintroll set, the Peter Rabbit books, Alice in Wonderland and her volumes of Little House on the Prairie, Anne of Green Gables, and Enid Blyton's Mallory Towers, Naughtiest Girl, and Famous Five. Tristan had liked the Arabian Nights. He'd enjoyed the Famous Five too, but had favoured the Secret Seven slightly more. He had also loved his Winnie the Pooh stories when he was smaller. His books would all be in there too. She wondered if some of them might be worth something, especially if they were first editions, but there'd only be a chance if the mice, moths or silverfish hadn't got to them all.

Why wasn't Gavin offered any of this stuff when he was little? I didn't even know Mum and Dad had kept it all! If I'd known, I'd have made sure he got all that.

Carla wondered if maybe any children Gavin might go on to have would one day want these things, when they were old enough. They were ancient, dusty, dogeared relics from the distant past, certainly, but they were family things that could still have a place in the world. They deserved to be handed down through the generations to be loved and treasured by new children. A simple lick of paint would sort the hula hoop out, and the rocking horse could definitely be restored. That could easily become a family heirloom. Maybe Gavin could restore that with Stan, his Bampa.

Steady on, woman! Best not get too far ahead of yourself here!

The loft full of faded, forgotten childhood memories was poignant. Maybe Stan and Hazel were hopeful that these things could one day again be loved, perhaps by grandchildren. But, more likely, they'd probably simply forgotten they were up here. Carla literally couldn't remember her father coming up into the loft, in all the years she'd been living back at home.

As she moved closer to the pile, she saw another box, marked 'photos.' She wasn't big on nostalgia, as a rule. Looking through old snaps was something she'd normally pass off as a chore that would bore her rigid. It was more her parents' thing, but on this occasion her curiosity got the better of her and she passed a hand across the top to move some of the dust away. She opened the box, which had just been closed by its own interlocking flaps, and not taped shut. She feared the worst, for the condition of everything, but a layer of ancient plastic bubble wrap had been tucked around the top, which offered a decent amount of protection.

She rummaged beneath the plastic and pulled out a small white photo album. It felt like leather, good quality, but it was slightly yellowed around the edges with age. It had a blue heart on the front of it. As she flicked through the pages, she could see they held pictures of her brother Tristan, as a baby. He looked so sweet, green-eyed and moon-faced, grinning at the camera in one particularly candid shot while being tightly held by someone that Carla presumed to be their mother. The resemblance between Tris and Gavin struck her immediately. She couldn't believe she wasn't looking at baby photos of her own son!

Since the light in the loft was poor, she decided to take the box downstairs and have a better look through it. Initially, she found it odd that there were no photos of her in the first album. Every picture taken was of Tristan. But then, when she put her hand into the box again, she pulled out another album, identical, but this time with a pink heart on the front of it. It wasn't so yellowed with age, probably having been protected by Tristan's album sitting on top.

Carla opened the pages. Sure enough, the album was full of more sweet baby photos - but this time they were all of *her*. She found herself struggling to swallow the lump in her throat, especially when she came across a picture of herself being held aloft by her father. Maybe she was about two years old here, with pudgy little legs sticking out of balloon-like nappy pants, and a mass of dark hair. Arms akimbo in the picture, she was grinning widely, and Stan was looking up at her with the biggest smile on his face. The love between the two of them was clear. It made her heart ache, to see that shot of her dad, so young, happy and vibrant, holding his baby daughter aloft like a prize he'd won and was showing off to the world. Again, his shock of lustrous black hair, long-since gone grey and sparse, reminded her of Gavin. The family resemblances were so clear. Gavin's face was soft, oval and open, like Nanny's, but his sharp green eyes and dark hair were definitely Stan's and Carla's. Thank God Gavin hadn't inherited Nanny's tight curls. He'd got gentle waves instead, courtesy of Martin.

He'd have hated curls.

Carla was amazed - and frustrated - to find herself crying again! She was quiet about it, lest Hazel or Stan might hear her and wonder what was going on. But, for a change, she simply sat back and let herself cry. She didn't battle it, like she usually did when a surge of emotion hit her. Uncharacteristically, she simply allowed the tears to fall. Her bout of weeping didn't last long. It was only a few minutes, but she was surprised at how much it helped.

I guess I needed to do that. But I have to get on with finding this bloody box. I can't just sit here snivelling all night!

Nostalgia was an interesting emotion. It felt like peeling back layers of something profoundly poignant and bittersweet; an acknowledgment of the past with its joys and sorrows, combined with the acceptance of getting older and having left childish things behind, at the same time as remembering what they'd meant to her once. And the tears were also about all the time in between; what had been said and done that shouldn't have been, or what had not been said and done that should have been, and what had been endured, and all that had been missed.

When she'd composed herself, Carla gathered herself together and went back up into the loft, to look for Martin's box. It took her a few minutes to find it. Most of what was up here was shrouded in shadow. The light barely reached to the edges. She finally located it at the far end, wedged behind an old ironing board whose padding was all hanging off, that was leaning against a tattered old chair with its upholstery half chewed away. She didn't want to think about what vermin might have munched its way through all that, as she pulled the ironing board off it.

But then she looked at the chair a little more closely. It was what some people might call an occasional chair, one that would just sit somewhere in a hallway or be used in a bedroom in front of a dressing table. It had arms and looked sturdy, despite the thin, elegant strips of wood that gave it shape, and the forlornly tattered fabric that made it look a mess.

That could look great with a lick of white paint and some bright floral fabric. I could put it in the bedroom. I might ask Dad if I can have it. I quite fancy this as a project!

She moved the chair off to one side, bent down, and gave a good tug on the handle of Martin's box. It slid towards her in a cloud of dust, with a small squeal, sounding almost resentful to have been disturbed.

The box was a wooden one with an arched lid. It resembled an old pirate's trunk, but it was about half the size. It had metal hinges, handles and catches, which may at one time have been brass, but the whole thing had been painted a dull, matt black. It didn't look at all inspiring. Carla debated whether or not to open it up here, to see what was in it, but in a rare moment of integrity she decided that she shouldn't open it at all, up here in the loft, or anywhere else. These were her son's things now, and since she never had a right to them in the first place, she certainly had no right to them now. It was up to Gavin to open the box and make what he would of its contents.

Carla hoped it would give him what he wanted, whatever that may have been. Closure? Answers? Trinkets? She shrugged and lifted the box. She rattled it slightly, relieved to see that the catches had remained tightly closed. No mice or moths would have got in there to feast on the contents.

There were certain things in the box that she did vaguely remember from the brief, uninterested glance she'd given it when she first decided not to give it back to Martin, but a cursory check had revealed nothing about why it had been so meaningful to him. Everything in there was ancient, but not in an interesting way, so delving into it properly had never really crossed her mind. There were documents in there, along with a few photographs, a postcard or two, a lace handkerchief and a couple of old medals on slightly moth-eaten ribbons. That was about it, as far as Carla could remember.

She blew a layer of dust off the box and carried it to the manhole, and called to her father to come and lift it down as she handed it to him. She asked him about the old chair and he looked at her blankly, before shrugging his shoulders.

'Chair? I don't remember an old chair, girl. Can't be terribly important then, so I suppose you can have it.'

Carla went over, got the chair and handed it down to her father.

'Ah, this old thing! Yes, I do remember it now. I don't even know where it came from, to be honest. We couldn't find a use for it, but it seemed too good to throw out, so we shoved it up there out of the way. It's an ugly old thing. Looks like it's been a bit nibbled at, too. What do you want with it?'

'I think I'll sand it down and paint it white, get some new fabric and sponge to reupholster it with, and put it in my bedroom.'

Stan surveyed the chair for a moment with his head on one side, chewing the inside of his cheek. Then he shrugged.

'Well, it's seen better days. It was probably reasonable, before the mice got to it. And I don't think it's ever going to be a statement piece. Too plain to be that, really. But why *not* give it a new lease of life? It's a good idea. I'll be interested to see how you get on with it.'

Carla found herself beaming. Stan laughed when he saw she'd found the baby albums.

'Ah yes, you kids should have those, of course. We should send Tris' to him, shouldn't we?'

'Yes, Dad. I really think we should.'

Carla wondered whether or not Tristan might be invited to Gavin and Feen's wedding. Gavin had never met his uncle, but he was family. Stan and Hazel would undoubtedly be included but she doubted whether she'd get an invite herself. She knew she really didn't deserve one. But at least she now had the one thing her son was truly interested in, to give him. That should make him happy, at least. Whatever happened after that, only time would tell.

She turned her attention to the battered old chair. She had no idea what era it was from, and her parents couldn't tell her much about it. Neither could remember how or when they'd got it.

She decided to get to work on it straight away. It didn't really matter whether or not it had any value. Carla somehow doubted it, but she felt determined to make the poor old thing a bit nicer. All it needed was a little TLC, she thought to herself as she carried it from the house over to her father's workshop. *I can give it that.*

Stan gave her a small pot of paint stripper and a brush and scraper tool, and she got to work. She tore off the old upholstery and was relieved to see that the chair didn't have any woodworm in it. In a couple of hours, she'd managed to get rid of the worst of the varnish, and finished sanding the chair with Stan's Dremel, which worked like a charm. There were a couple of deep gouges in the top of the chair, battle-scars from seeing something of life, but she managed to smooth them off without altering the line of the arch across the top. She felt a real sense of satisfaction at that.

She raided Stan's little paint cupboard, and was pleased to find a half-full tin of quick-dry undercoat, which she decided to use on the wood. She had never worked on a piece of furniture before and had only rudimentary knowledge of what to do. But it was all coming together quite nicely, and she was surprised when Hazel popped her head around the workshop door and asked her if she was ready yet, to come and have her dinner before it was burned beyond recognition in the oven. It was nearly nine o'clock! She'd been so absorbed in her little project that she'd lost all track of time.

It was getting a bit late now, to get Martin's box over to Gavin tonight. She'd already shown up once on his doorstep late at night and uninvited. She didn't want him to think she planned to make a habit of it. She could borrow her mum's car after work, on some other night this week, and take it to Teapot Cottage.

'I'll be right there, Mum. I'm just going to do a bit more on this chair, and I'll be in after that. Give me another fifteen minutes.'

Hazel nodded and left. Carla worked steadily to finish the first coat of paint on the chair, and then went in for her dinner. For the first time in as long as she could remember, she was actually ravenous. Hazel had made sausage and mash with her wonderful onion gravy, and Carla devoured it.

Stan watched in amusement. 'You must have been starving!'

Carla grinned. 'I was, Dad. I think having something different to focus on has made my appetite better!'

Stan chuckled. 'How's it coming along so far?'

'You can have a look for yourself tomorrow if you want, while I'm at work, and tell me what you think. I've used some of your grey undercoat, if that's okay?'

Stan nodded and told her it was fine to help herself to whatever was in the paint cupboard, with the simple request that she replaced whatever she ended up using the last of.

'I've got some white gloss in there, I think. And I've got a staple-gun you can use to fit the new upholstery when you're ready.'

Carla nodded. 'I might have it finished by the weekend. That'd be great.'

She vowed to herself that she definitely *would* have it finished. Two coats of gloss, she thought, let it dry, then whack the new fabric on. She made a mental note to stop at the soft furnishing store in the High Street in Carlisle, pick up some foam, and maybe choose some nice fabric for the chair.

The following evening after work, she stopped in at the store and bought a new foam pad, and a gorgeous metre of bright floral fabric, in shades of yellow and bright pink, with a small splash here and there of purple, and with lime green cacti running through it all. She suddenly had a radical thought to buy some purple gloss paint for her chair, deciding it would be a much nicer way to make it really 'pop' than plain old boring white.

A small independent hardware store on the edge of the city had exactly what she was looking for, and she was massively relieved, knowing how frustrated she would otherwise be if what she wanted hadn't been available there. There'd be nothing worse than being unable to complete her little project in the time she'd set herself, just because she couldn't find the one thing she'd set her heart on!

Happy with her choices, Carla got home, changed into her 'scruffies', and set about putting the first coat of the thick purple gloss onto the chair. It went on smoothly over the undercoat, which she was thrilled about. As it was drying, she found what was left of the old padding for the seat and cut her piece of foam to suit. The chair originally had quite a shallow seat pad, so she hadn't needed to buy much, but she did want to make it a little more padded than it looked to have been originally. It wasn't much more, just enough to be a little more inviting and comfortable. She'd fallen in love with the fabric instantly. It had been expensive, and she'd berated herself for grossly underestimating what she thought it should have cost.

Double it, then double it again!

But it was gorgeous fabric, and when the chair was finished it would look amazing. The irony of sitting on cactus wasn't lost on her; it made her laugh, and that in itself pulled her up short. When was the last time she'd actually laughed, with real, unbridled delight?

The seat pad had popped straight out of the chair. It really was the simplest of designs, and ridiculously easy to upgrade. Carla scraped away the last of the old foam that had been glued to the panel that fitted neatly into the seat of the chair, and carefully cut her fabric to fit over it. Instead of staples, she'd opted for silver-coloured upholstery studs, thinking that maybe a bit of old-world charm might enhance it a bit. Staples somehow seemed a bit modern, and a bit slap-dash. She felt she wanted to do the best job she could with the chair. There would be nothing worse than hating the end result because she'd cut corners on the finishing, and she knew that any obvious mistakes would end up being the only thing she'd see, once the chair was in her bedroom. There was only one thing for it - to do it to the best standard possible - so she did.

On Friday, she took a half day off work, just on a whim, wanting to get home as quickly as possible so she could finish the chair. The project really had taken hold of her, in a way she hadn't been expecting. She didn't yet recognise it as the beginning of a new passion for recycling and renovation; a hobby that would feed her famished soul.

Chapter Seventeen

A Spell To Bring Clarity

You will need:
A small mirror
A hagstone
A small piece of raw amethyst
A tealight candle
A Wind chime or a small bell
A small piece of silk
A goblet of Blackberry juice

Sit the mirror vertically and place the lighted the candle in front of it. Wrap the amethyst in the piece of silk and place it between the mirror and the candle. Ring the chime or the bell with your left hand, and drink the blackberry juice with the goblet in your right hand. Then hold the hagstone with your right hand and look through the eye, at the flickering candle.
Incantation (once):
'Pull back the veil that covers my eyes,
Define the future, make me wise.
Invoke the insight that helps me to know,
which is the way the wind should blow.'

When Feen awoke, Gavin was already up. She could hear him clattering around in the kitchen and, after a few minutes, she could smell the wonderful aroma of freshly brewed coffee. In her humble opinion, few other things could rival a good cup of coffee in a morning. Toasted crumpets with lashings of lovely salty butter was a close second, of course, and she thought that if she was very lucky some of those might be coming up the stairs too; hot and buttered with nothing else on them, just the way she liked them.

Gavin brought her coffee - and the longed-for crumpets - and sat in the chair beside the bed.

'Feen, I owe you an apology. I've been distracted, haven't I? You already know why, I guess. But this hodgepodge of emotions I haven't been able to separate; it's got me in a bit of a tailspin, if I'm honest.'

'Of course it has. I wouldn't have expected anything else. But you're hopeful, though? That you and Carla can establish something good?'

He stared at her. 'Why would you ask that?' he countered, clearly playing for time.

'Um, well let's see … because she's your mother, and in spite of everything, that does matter. And don't forget the weird window I can see straight into. So, you tell me!'

She didn't want to let him off the hook. He still needed to process everything properly, and that meant acknowledging and confronting *all* of the emotions it dragged up.

You don't get to be selective in what you deal with here.

He blinked at her. 'I guess I don't.' He was lost in thought for a few seconds, then he spoke up again.

'You didn't actually *say* what I just heard from you, did you?'

She shook her head, smiling.

'Bloody hell,' he said softly.

'Yup. We're working!'

'Maybe we are, but how do we really sort this, Feen?'

He recounted to her everything his mother had said at their stormy meeting, before Feen had come back to the cottage.

'Sorry I haven't laid it all out with you before. I know my silence has probably driven you crazy. I just needed time, that's all. It wasn't an attempt to keep you out.'

'I know. And it's understandable of course, because it's all been so unexpected and sudden. One minute you were sound asleep, then the next you were being turned upside down by the stuff you were hearing. You've been processing it, and trying to work out what it is you really want now. I get that.

'But, as to how we 'sort it,' to use your words, I think that once you've thought things through, you need to decide what you really want, and then tell her, but get yourself prepared for the fact that you might not get it. Or for the mact that you fight,' she added, half to herself.

Gavin nodded. 'I think, deep down, I do want *some* kind of relationship with her going forward. I'm just not quite sure how I want it to be. Anything better than hostility, I guess, as a starting point. But even if she wants that too, and even if we can agree on how it'll be between us, how will it sit with your folks, after all the promises I made?'

'Well, that's a very good question. But before you go ahead and say anything to anyone, you'll have to work out if an ongoing relationship *is* what you really want. It's easy to make a bad decision when there's so much emotion flying about.'

Feen chewed her bottom lip, and chose her words carefully.

'The other important question though, is whether she's even capable of that? And if so, under what terms? You'd have to set really firm expectations and boundaries with her, and then explain to Dad and Adie what they are. And you'd have to really commit to maintaining them, to expect *anyone* to have faith in you.'

'And what about you?'

'What *about* me?' Feen retorted. 'I'm not scared of your mother, Gavin. I'm not quite the delicate fragile flower my father seems to think I am, either. I do have some backbone, and I *can* hold my own here, but that's not to say I'm prepared to cope with ongoing conflict. It makes me physically and emotionally ill, people fickering and bighting.

'I can lay some boundaries of my own around her involvement with me, but she's your mother. It's up to you, how you manage any relationship you might end up having with her, but I can tell you now - having to deal with her as an ongoing lurdle in our hives because you can't or won't put some limits around what's tolerable from her? That will not be an option for me. I won't do that.'

201

She let out a long slow breath and continued. 'So, you have to be crystal clear about the expectations and limits on both sides, and somehow figure out how to manage it all. Assuming she does want to have a relationship with you of course. She may not, and you have to be prepared for that too.'

She watched Gavin as he gnawed the inside of his cheek and gazed out into the middle distance. 'I have to talk to her again,' he said slowly.

Feen nodded. 'Yeah. But only when you're clear about what you want. Don't waste her time, or your own, until you're absolutely sure this *is* what you want, because if you agree anything with her then have reason to change your mind, things could get a trot lickier than they already are.'

She knew his heart. He didn't have to explain how conflicted he was, how much he'd had to process about his mother in recent days. It was a lot for anyone to try and work through. One minute his mind was made up, that he didn't want to have anything to do with her anymore. The next, he heard something new that changed everything about how he felt about her. But she knew, deep down, that the damaged little boy inside Gavin needed to be healed, and that the other night's revelations had opened the door to that healing. He wanted it to continue, of course.

As much as Gavin wasn't anywhere near ready to admit it, she knew he still needed his mother to love him. And he wanted to love *her*. It was as normal a set of expectations as anyone could realistically have. Families were important, and Feen was already looking forward to having Stan and Hazel Walton, as part of her extended family. Would it be a mistake to assume that because of her past actions Carla couldn't be included too?

As an evolved, spiritual soul with a rare window into a different realm, Feen felt that she was already a long way towards forgiving Carla for what she'd done. The woman had already offered a tearful, heartfelt apology and the best explanation she could manage. If she could go a step further and treat Gavin and Feen with respect instead of the contempt she'd shown so far, they might all have a chance at making it work. It would certainly require some mediation with Mark and Adie, but they knew all too well how complicated family dynamics could be, and how important forgiveness was. Feen was quietly hopeful that if it was what Gavin really, really wanted, she could swing them both around.

She wouldn't tell Gavin that just yet though. He needed to appreciate the importance of strong boundaries, and what was - and wasn't - acceptable behaviour. Once he could prove that, Feen was confident that they'd all have a decent chance of making something work.

'And, if the worst happens, my love, and there turns out to be no further contact between you, I promise I'll do everything in my power to help you come to terms with it and move on.'

He reached across and ruffled her hair gently and grinned at her.

'You know what? That's the most sensible thing I've heard in all this. For now, I have a few other things to think about. I want to get my music stuff up here asap. How do you fancy a quick trip to the big smoke?'

They decided to head down to London later that afternoon, so that Gavin could pick up his music equipment and other personal items to bring back to Teapot Cottage for the month. They would stay a couple of nights at Gavin's flat, get some stuff packed up, and bring it up to Torley. Gavin got on the phone to Mike, to tell him he was coming down briefly, and bringing a very big surprise with him.

Feen was excited about meeting Gavin's step-dad. It was a terrible shame that she'd never get to meet his real one, who sounded amazing. But Mike was a huge part of Gavin's life, and far more genial than his permanently prickly mother. It would be good to see this other side of Gavin's life.

A trip to London, meeting Mike, and maybe even some of Gavin's London friends, getting reacquainted with Stan and Hazel, and a rare chance to catch up with Gina Giordano, if she was available; even without a wedding to plan there was so much to look forward to!

Gavin informed her that they'd be flying down to London from Carlisle and back again by private jet, as he didn't want to waste more than five hours each way driving.

'But isn't that really expensive?' she said, startled.

I'm not even going to touch on the issue of the carbon footprint!

Gavin smiled and shook his head.

'Sweetheart, let me be clear. Hiring private planes is not something I do willy-nilly, but occasionally it does make sense, and the cost isn't something I have to worry about.'

'Oh. Um, okay then. Sorry.' Suddenly Feen felt foolish. She hadn't even considered what Gavin's financial status might be. She'd supposed - clearly incorrectly - that since he was a student, he'd be as cash-strapped as the next one. But then she remembered his black Amex credit card, and how nonchalantly he'd paid for her engagement ring. Evidently he wasn't exactly destitute, and she wasn't sure what to say next.

He laughed at her. 'It's fine. I haven't really talked to you about my finances, have I? But I guess I probably should. Dad was quite well heeled. He was a very successful session musician, for many years, and he played and recorded with a lot of big bands. He also got a big lucky break financially when he started writing some really good songs for well-known artists here, and in the States.' Gavin ran a hand through his hair, and Feen was touched to see that he was slightly embarrassed.

' He was careful with his money, Feen, and he's left me pretty well set-up, with the flat, an interim trust fund, other stuff, and access to his capital when I'm 35. There's also a stupendously valuable collection of vintage motorbikes. It doesn't amount to *too* many millions but it does mean that unless I'm very stupid - and I don't plan to be - money's not something I'll ever have to worry about, and neither will you.'

Feen laughed, shakily. Wow! Now she understood why he'd paid for her engagement ring without so much as batting an eyelid.

'Well my dad's quite well-heeled too, as a matter of fact,' she responded. 'He owns Ravensdown, a couple of other farms that he leases, a few houses and commercial buildings that he rents out, he's got a ton tied up in stocks and shares, and he's in talks with a development company over a piece of his land between here and Carlisle that they want to have rezoned as residential for a housing estate to be built there. Most of it will come to me eventually, with Adie well provided-for too, of course. And she personally owns this cottage and the quarter-acre it sits on.'

It was Gavin's turn to be impressed. 'So, it seems your dad's no financial slouch either!'

She laughed. 'No, he most certainly is not. He might come from working class stock, and he might sound it, but believe me, his financial acumen is blade-sharp! And he gets a lot of good advice from his financial adviser, Kevin Sangster, who is also my godfather, by the way. You'll probably meet him soon, and his wife Trudie. She runs a dress shop called GladRagz, in town. They come up to the farm for dinner quite often.'

They drove to the airport and parked in the long-stay car park. The flight was straightforward, complete with a very attentive flight attendant who quickly produced a chilled bottle of bubbly and a cheeseboard with grapes and a lovely assortment of crackers, and they were at London City airport in just over an hour.

Gosh, I could get used to this!

'Mike's meeting us. He'll take us straight to a nice little Italian restaurant we go to quite a lot, then he'll drop us at the flat after that.'

Suddenly, Feen felt incredibly nervous, almost sick. She was about to meet one of the most important people in Gavin's life. She prayed that Mike would like her, that he wouldn't make them feel awkward about the shortness of their relationship. She had a strong feeling it would all be ok, but her nerves were running on high alert, nonetheless. Never before had it ever mattered this much, what someone thought of her. Now she understood how nervous Gavin had been, with the boot on the other foot just days ago, as he was gearing up to meet her father!

In the terminal, with no warning whatsoever, a bald, slim middle-aged man came rushing up, threw his arms around Gavin, and held him in a long hug. As they stepped away from one another, Feen immediately sensed a great love, and a certain relief, in both men. It was powerful.

Mike was the same height as Gavin, but that was where the similarities ended. While Gavin had long, dark hair that framed his face, Mike was completely shaven headed. He was as wiry and slight as Gavin was solid, and his clothes were a lot more conservative too - blue jeans, brown brogues, and a pale blue sweater over a blue and white checked shirt. He wore round, rimless glasses. His brown eyes were gentle, and his grin was infectious. Feen liked him straight away.

She felt a little self-conscious as he stepped back and appraised her with a wide smile.

'Well, who's this? Have you been holding out on me, mate?' Mike's educated but slightly Cockney twang made Feen laugh, thinking he should be on a very popular soap opera. For some reason she'd been expecting him to sound a bit posh, with a Home Counties cadence like Gavin's. She couldn't have been more wrong. Mike's voice was deep and almost gravelly, and definitely east London.

Gavin put an arm around Feen. 'This is Miss Seraphine Raven. My fiancée.'

Mike looked completely baffled, but in a good way. He stared, and when he realised Gavin wasn't joking, he just laughed and shook his head.

'Well, there's obviously a story 'ere, champ! Let's go get some grub, and you can fill me in.'

Mike drove expertly through the heaving London rush-hour traffic and eventually parked up a back-street before ushering Gavin and Feen to an ordinary-looking terraced house with an unassuming door, with only a business card in the front bay window to indicate it was a business at all. He rang the bell, and they waited to be let in.

Inside, the front room had been laid out with six tables, and all were full except one. As they were quickly ushered to it, Feen noted that it was only laid for two people. Mike spoke to the maître'd, who he seemed to know well, and who also gave Gavin a warm handshake before disappearing and returning to discreetly lay another place and produce another chair from under a set of stairs at the side of the room. A carafe each of red and white wine appeared, as did another of water, along with a sheaf of single-page menus with very little on them. You had to take what was on offer here, it seemed, in terms of food and drink, but everything sounded truly delicious. Feen noted that there were no prices listed.

She'd heard about places like this, where the clientele was regular enough for them to never need to advertise, where the food was of sublime quality, and nobody queried the cost. Such places were a well-kept gastronomic secret, with only a select few knowing exactly where or how good they were, and they absolutely never accepted walk-ins. It was bookings only, and nearly always made months in advance.

They all sat, and Gavin turned to Mike as he poured a glass of wine for Feen. 'You did well to get in here at such short notice.'

Mike laughed. 'Nah. It's you who's got lucky, mate. I was coming anyway tonight, but I was bringing a work colleague. I blew her out so I could share it with you instead.'

'At the last minute? Oh, you mean bastard.'

'It's fine. We've rescheduled for the end of next month. She had a plan B anyway. Tickets to some music thing at the Albert Hall with her old mum. I think I did 'er a favour.'

He yawned and stretched, as far out as he could in the confined space, then rolled his shoulders and looked squarely at Feen.

'So, Miss Seraphine Raven, with one of the loveliest names I've ever 'eard. Have you captured my son's heart good and proper, or is this just his idea of a wind-up?'

Feen giggled. 'I'm afraid it's real. I know it sounds mad, but it's true. I have literally lost my heart to him.'

Gavin looked stony-faced at Mike. 'The maiden has holen my start. It is, and shall remain, irretrievable.'

Mike smirked and rolled his eyes. 'Ah, bloody hell!'

Gavin continued to look serious. 'So, go and buy a hat and a posh frock, you old queen.'

Mike just gaped at him. Feen was struggling hard not to laugh. He looked so comical. She could feel the turbulence of his emotions as he sat there trying to make sense of what Gavin was telling him, still trying to decide if it was indeed a wind-up. She felt she had to come to the poor man's rescue.

'Mike, we met last week, and it was love at first sight. We both know it, and we're planning a wedding. That's it, in a nutshell. And please call me Feen. Seraphine's a bit too formal for family, which I hope you'll want to be.'

Poor Mike. He still thought they were joking. Neither of them said anything while they let him process what Feen had said. After a few beats he cleared his throat and took a deep breath.

'Right. Okay. Well, congratulations both, for a start. Forgive me if I'm a little shocked 'ere though, since this is so out of character from you, Gavin. Impulsive is the last word I'd ever use to describe you, so for this to have come out of nowhere for me is a tad strange.' He turned to Feen.

'This little toerag was a committed singleton for the foreseeable, just last week, when I waved 'im off for what I thought was a couple o' days. I thought at best he'd be coming back with a box. I didn't predict him bringing back a wife-to be! Nobody - and I mean *nobody* - would have seen that coming in a million years. But you're not besotted fifteen-year-olds, are ya? If you're both really sure about this, and I guess you are, then I s'pose we need some champagne, quick-smart.'

He gestured to the maître'd, who came swiftly over. Mike asked him for a bottle of their very best bubbly. When it arrived, the Maître'd expertly popped the cork and filled three exquisite crystal flutes. Mike was the first to raise his glass.

'A toast then! To love at first sight, to two of the luckiest buggers I've ever met, and to a lifetime of 'ealf and 'appiness.'

They placed their food orders, then Mike began to gently grill Feen about herself, her life and her family. She'd fully expected him to do his 'due diligence' in protecting Gavin, as any father would. But his questions were considered and kind, and asked with genuine interest in getting to know her. As they talked, she realised that this nice man would be a lovely addition to her family. She felt his approval of her steadily increasing, as the time passed. As they finished their gorgeous minestrone soup, Mike turned his attention directly to Gavin, asking how things had gone with Carla.

This was Gavin's floor now, so she sat back while he claimed Mike's attention. She listened almost absently to their conversation, and tucked into her linguine *all'astice*, which was easily the best she'd ever eaten.

Mike had no love for Carla Walton, that was plain to hear, but he did understand Gavin's dilemma. To his credit, he didn't try and steer Gavin away from his musings about having a relationship with his mother. In fact, he mostly echoed Feen's own thoughts on the matter. He made some interesting observations about Carla, after Gavin described the events of the previous week, including the woman's obvious need to heal from old wounds. Mike made it clear that whatever Gavin decided about her, he'd be there to support him and Feen.

Suddenly, an almighty crash came from the kitchen and all three of them jumped. Someone let loose with a volley of strident Italian, at the same time as another member of staff came running out of the kitchen, with his hands covering his head, followed by several dinner plates that flew through the air like frisbees and crashed on the wall and then onto the floor all around him. Mercifully, none had hit him, but the floor was now littered with broken china.

Mike grinned and rolled his eyes. 'Sounds like Stefano's chucked 'is toys out of 'is pram again.' He explained to Feen.

'The chef, Stefano. He does this. Every time a bloody coconut, whenever we come 'ere, there's some kind of kitchen drama. Usually it's just a bit o' shouting, but tonight it sounds like he's upended the whole bloody plate cart.'

Gavin too seemed unworried. 'He'll be all smiles again, in five minutes. That did sound like an expensive crash this time, though, didn't it? He gets through a lot of plates, but I suppose he's got insurance. Either that or he's worked for nothing, tonight.'

Stefano did come out a little later, to personally deliver their desserts. He was, as predicted, quite jovial again, and when Mike asked him if they needed to check their tiramisu for shards of china, he merely shrugged, with an unapologetic twinkle in his eye.

'No, amico mio! Non c'è niente nel cibo che ti possa rompere i denti.'

No, my friend! There is nothing in the food that will break your teeth.

As they were driving towards Gavin's flat, replete with the most amazing food that Feen thought had ever graced a table, Mike met her eyes in the rear-view mirror. 'What are your plans for the couple o' days you're down 'ere, doll? Sightseeing? Shopping?'

She giggled. 'An important meeting first thing, then mostly shopping, I think! I've got a little list.'

209

'And none of it be missed!' Mike quipped, and they all laughed.

All Monty Python fans, thought Feen, thrilled.

They pulled up in a seriously exclusive, quiet square in Mayfair. Mike got out of the car and opened the door for Feen, and as she stepped out, he enveloped her in a huge, warm hug. Surprised, she hugged him back, tightly.

'So glad to have met you, Mike! And thank you for tonight, it's been just wonderful.'

'Welcome to the family, such as it is, Feen. You're a beautiful girl, and you've clearly made a big impression on the boy, 'ere. Let me know when you've set a date for the wedding, and please do let me contribute in some way. Gavin's like a son to me, so I want to keep playing the Dad, if that's ok.'

She laughed. 'Of course it is! We wouldn't have it any other way, would we, Gavin?'

Mike hugged Gavin too, for a long time again, and then released him and waved at them both as he stepped back towards his car. In a moment, he'd swung away from the kerb and was gone, swallowed whole amid the still-dense London traffic.

Chapter Eighteen

A Song of Gratitude

Thank you, thank you, just two words,
but so much more in meaning
How do I really thank you for the rock you are to me?
You got me knowin' I can be much more than
I once thought I'd ever be
With my virtues intact and my faults redeeming
Thank you, thank you, for your love and faith in me

'Welcome to the flayfair mat, milady! Be it ever so humble, there's no place like home.' Gavin opened the front door, and bowed with a flourish.

By his own admission, the 'flat' was anything but humble. It nestled in a neat, elegant square of white pillar-fronted homes, with mostly black-painted doorways and wrought iron railings flanking the frontages, all facing a small and perfect patch of lush green, tree-covered park. Eye-wateringly expensive cars were parked outside most of the houses; at least three Bentleys, half a dozen top-of-the-range Mercedes, a handful of Aston Martins, and Range Rovers galore. The entire square silently screamed of affluence. The park itself was protected by wrought-iron railings too, with a tall gate standing at one end. It had a huge chain and padlock on it. Gavin saw Feen staring at it.

'Westminster council has to lock the park at night,' he explained. 'Otherwise it ends up being flooded with the homeless, and addicts of various kinds. Not what the Bentley drivers around here want to look at while they scoff their truffle-topped breakfasts!'

Feen pulled a face at him.

'It's terrible, Gavin. I know homelessness is a big problem in cities, but London especially seems to have more than its fair share. Even just on the way here tonight, I saw so many homeless people. They're everywhere!'

Gavin nodded. The sad shapes of huddled human misery, the city's displaced people who tried to sleep in shop doorways in filthy sleeping bags, with their meagre belongings tucked around them for extra warmth, made him feel sad too. So many people struggled these days, to put a decent roof over their own heads. It was a basic human right, to have a home; a warm and safe place to sleep at night. The fact that so many didn't would hardly be believable, if he didn't see it so often with his own eyes.

He stepped back to let Feen enter the flat. It was a welcoming place, and he hoped she would like it. He watched her as she gently smiled at the rows of gold music discs and photos in hammered-steel frames that ran the entire length of the long hallway. She was gazing at them with real interest. Most of the photos were of Gavin's father, Martin, playing, standing, or sitting happily with an assortment of famous musicians. She exclaimed in delight as she recognised a few of the rock and pop stars with him.

One black and white photo seemed to captivate her completely. It was an old shot, of a younger Martin in animated conversation with Bruce Springsteen. Clearly, neither was aware of the picture being taken. She ran her hand over another photo, of Martin laughing with a couple of members of the Rolling Stones.

She turned to him, her eyes shining. 'Oh my God! Your dad was famous!'

Gavin inclined his head briefly. 'Well, not so much famous by most people's standards. That was never what he wanted, really. He always said fame was a monster he didn't want to be eaten alive by, and he preferred to stay more in the background. Even when he was actually on stage, playing, you'd normally find him more towards the back. He was well respected in the industry, though, and connected to a lot of important people. I was amazed at who showed up at his funeral, and who sent tributes. He'd have been thrilled.'

212

His voice snagged a little in his throat, and he swallowed hard to dislodge the lump that had formed there.

Feen stepped forward and slid her arms around his waist. 'Where's the kitchen?' she asked gently. 'I think we could do with a cup of tea.'

He gave her a quick, grateful hug and indicated a door down the hallway to the left. 'Good idea. The milk should still be ok. If not, there's some long-life stuff in the cupboard above the kettle, that we always use in emergencies.'

Feen gave his shoulder a light squeeze, and left him where he was, for which he was grateful. He needed a moment or two, to collect himself.

He could hear her pottering about in the kitchen. It was strangely reassuring, having her here, going through the routine motions of making a simple cup of tea. He'd been dreading walking back in here tonight, and was grateful for Mike's distraction of dinner out, but a great sadness had washed over him as Mike had driven away. With Feen here, by his side, coming back into the flat was bearable - just.

It was hard to believe Martin had only been gone a couple of months. Gavin had somehow mostly managed to keep his grief at bay while he'd been up in Torley, while he and Feen were both revelling in the fact that they'd found one another, and dealing with the situation with his mother had taken the rest of his attention. But being back here in the flat, with the spirit of his dad all around him, it all came flooding back to him and once again he felt completely overwhelmed by what the loss of his father really meant.

He went into the kitchen, sat at the breakfast bar, and promptly burst into tears.

'Dad.' Was all he managed. Feen started weeping too, just gently, and she came and put her arms around him. He hugged her back as they both cried.

'You look so much like him, you know,' she said softly through her own tears, stroking his hair.

'Yeah, a lot of people say that.' His voice sounded muffled to himself, as he spoke into her shoulder. 'If I could be half the man he was, I'd be proud of myself. He was really something, you know?'

Feen shook him gently. 'You're really something, yourself. So much of him lives on in you, it and will through our children. And you can *already* be proud of who you are. You *should* be proud. How proud d'you think he is of you, right now? You're his finest composition, my love. His masterpiece.'

'He won't be here to see us get married.' Gavin's voice was cracked and hoarse with grief.

'Not in the way you want him to be, no,' Feen said gently. 'But he will be here, in his own way. He will, Gavin. I promise you that.'

Gavin wiped his eyes roughly with the back of his hand and stood up. Wallowing wasn't his style. He rolled his shoulders and moved his neck from side to side a couple of times.

'Well, I'd better give you the guided tour. You need to know where things are.'

As he showed Feen around, he could see that she really liked the airy, spacious flat. 'Oh, Gavin! I love the gentle, creative, lovely energy here! I can connect with it in every gorgeous room! Something is bothering me, though' She looked at him and frowned.

'You call this a flat. But it isn't really, is it? I mean, a flat is like a small place, maybe two bedrooms if you're lucky, all on one level and a bit cramped. This is actually a house, isn't it? It's pretty big. The rooms are enormous and the ceilings are really high, even in the kitchen, so why do you call it a flat?'

Gavin grinned. 'That's a good question. I dunno, really, to be honest. Maybe it's because it's very small, compared with the mansions all around here with eight-to-fifteen bedrooms, several reception rooms and spread across four storeys, with price tags upwards of fifty-six million quid. This place has four bedrooms, two bathrooms, only two above-ground levels, and it's sandwiched in between two very large houses.'

He shrugged. 'Dad always called it a flat, and I've just adopted the description. I suppose it is a house, really, but the estate agents around here would list it as a flat if it went on the market. It would only fetch around a quarter of what some of those mansion houses go for.'

She smiled at him. 'Well, that's still a ridiculous amount of money for a pile of bricks and mortar! But it's lovely. I can sense

Martin, particularly down here in the basement, where you've set your instruments up. His presence is so strong, in here. He was quite a gentle and laid-back man, wasn't he?'

Gavin nodded. He had no reason to doubt Feen, and he was pleased that she was picking up the vibe that he could feel himself, in the quiet spaces that still held so much of his father's spirit.

She cast her eye over Gavin's musical equipment. 'Wow! Good luck fitting all *that* into Teapot Cottage!'

Gavin chuckled, in spite of himself.

'Don't worry, it's not all coming. Just a couple of the keyboards, and the delectronic rums. And my computer.'

Feen wandered over to a shelf crammed with framed pictures and picked up a large front-on photo of Martin sitting on a vintage motorcycle. He had his arms folded across the handlebars and he was looking straight at the camera with the biggest, sunniest smile she'd ever seen on anyone. It was a brilliant photo. Joy just crackled and fizzed from it.

She held it out to him. 'I think we should take this one back with us. It's an absolute belter, isn't it?'

Gavin agreed. 'Yeah. It's my favourite photo of him ever. It's interesting you've picked that one up, actually. I took that. He'd just given me a camera for my 18th birthday and I was practising with it. That bike he's on? It's a 1936 Brough Superior; an incredibly rare machine, with the most amazing provenance. He bought it as a wreck and restored it. He'd just finished it after three years of work, and he was over the moon that it started up on the very first kick. I got him in a special moment, there.'

'All the more reason to bring this photo back with us. It's a rare and special moment that ties you both together.'

'They were all special moments, Feen, every last one,' he said softly, almost to himself. 'I just didn't know it, at the time.' He gently took the photo out of her hands and held onto it, cradling it close to his chest as if it were a new-born baby.

The following morning, he felt a little more readjusted, and as he and Feen sat having breakfast, a phone call came in from Mike. Gavin put it on speaker phone.

'Hello, mate. Just though you might want to know, Matt and Rich are in town for a few days. Here for some comic convention, by the sound of it, and they want to know if the three of us would like to meet them for dinner tonight. I know its short notice, and I hope you don't mind, but I filled them in about you and Feen, and they're well up for meeting 'er. They're staying at the Savoy. They suggested a meal there, at The Grill. Whaddya think?'

Gavin beamed at Feen. His eyes danced. 'How would you like to meet two of the coolest characters I've ever known in my whole entire life?'

'Well, when you put it like that, how can I cot be naptivated? Tell me more!'

'Matthew and Richard. Really good friends of my dad and Mike. Gay couple; native Bostonians. Dad met them when he was there on tour, years ago. They are *such* fun, Feen! So entertaining, with a million funny stories. They're really important to me, and I haven't seen them for a long time. Would you be interested in having dinner with them tonight?'

'I'd love to. But why don't we have it here? I can cook something?'

Gavin shook his head. Feen was so generous, but he just wanted her to have fun on this trip, and the Savoy would be a lovely experience for her. He told her so, and she pulled a face at him, then nodded. 'Okay. But if I'm going somewhere posh I'm going to need a frice nock, so I need to go shopping. Like, as soon as I'm finished my meeting with Gina - which starts in less than an hour, by the way! We need to get out skates on! But you'll need to point me in the right direction for dress-shopping, because I don't know where to start.'

Gavin confirmed the arrangements with Mike, then thought about the day ahead. He'd already decided to put Feen in a taxi bound for the offices of GinGio, in Kensington and get on with the task of packing his musical equipment ready for it to be taken to the plane tomorrow. But now he thought he should probably go with her, and wait, then take her to some upmarket stores he knew in London where she could find something nice to wear tonight. It wouldn't take long to pack up his drums, keyboards and computer.

He called a cab and decided that while he was waiting for Feen at the GinGio offices, he could fill in the time by phoning his best mate Stuart, to tell him how ridiculously excited he was, that he was going to marry the most beautiful woman on the planet.

*　　*　　*　　*　　*

Feen looked gorgeous tonight, and the sight of her made Gavin's heart swell. She'd been longer than expected in her meeting with Gina Giordano, this morning, but when she'd come out of it she'd been floating on cloud nine, because Gina had given her a dress!

It was a one-off commission piece, in hot-pink satin that had been meant for someone else, but it had been made slightly too small. Trying to make it bigger would apparently have destroyed the integrity of the design, and the team was still debating about what to do with it, when Feen had walked into the office and unwittingly provided the answer. The dress had still been too big for her, but Gina had arranged for a seamstress to fix it right away. It had taken half an hour to bring the seams in enough to fit Feen's tiny frame, and to drape a little romantic ruffled sash across the front of it, to make it truly unique and perfect for her.

She was so excited, she hadn't been able to sit still in the taxi, on the way back to the flat. On Gina's recommendation, they'd detoured to a shoe shop that specialised in footwear for women with tiny feet, and Feen had taken Gina's advice and chosen a pair of sparkly high-heeled silver sandals in her size two-and-a-half, and a matching clutch bag, to complement her gorgeous dress.

Gavin had then got the taxi to stop again, at a jewellery store, where he'd dashed in and bought a very pretty pair of tiny teardrop diamond earrings for her.

She'd been as nervous as a cat on a hot tin roof, before leaving the flat.

'I've never worn anything this bright before! Are you sure I don't look ridiculous? I feel like a Christmas bauble, or something. Don't let anyone trang me in a hee!'

Gavin had done his best to reassure her. 'Sweetheart, you look incredible. Stop worrying. That colour just explodes on you. It's gorgeous! And although I don't know Gina, this shows me she was right. Besides, I'd flet the bat that she'd never risk her reputation by putting anyone in something if she didn't think it suited them.'

217

'I know. I did tell her I'm not big on bright bold colours, but she said she would never dress a woman in something that wasn't right for her. She insisted that this was perfect for me, so I've chosen to believe her.'

In the car, she was happy, but pensive. 'You know, this gesture of Gina's is really important. It means real acceptance into Adie's family, because I've wondered about that. You know; whether they'd all just find me too weird to want to bother with? The business relationship is one thing, but this feels so much more personal, being given such a valuable gift. This dress is worth pousands of thounds, Gavin! All I did was mention that I was going shopping for a dinner dress, and I asked if she could recommend somewhere. She offered me this dress, out of the blue. She didn't have to do that.'

Gavin squeezed Feen's hand. He was thrilled that Gina Giordano had made such an amazing gesture but, to him, it was nothing more than Feen deserved. And Gina was right. She looked *amazing* The dress had already pumped up her confidence too, and the high heels she was wearing gave her a rather sexy 'swagger,' in his opinion.

Within minutes of arriving at the Savoy Grill, and meeting Matthew and Richard, it became clear to him that Feen adored them both. In no time at all, they'd veered off into an animated conversation of their own, leaving Gavin and Mike more or less to their own devices, and feeling vaguely 'dumped.'

He didn't mind much. It was great that they all liked each other. Matt and Rich were like family to him. They'd been in his life from the moment he'd gone to live with Martin. They'd been here in the UK at the time, on their way to a house they were renting for a few months somewhere in Europe. They travelled a lot and always tried to make time to touch down in London, if they could make it work, on their way to somewhere else. Rich owned a nightclub in Boston, and had a competent manager who took care of the place while he and Matt took time off, whenever it suited them, to see different parts of the world.

'Martin and the band came into the club one night after they'd done a gig,' Rich explained, when Feen had asked how they'd all met. 'Unusually - and lucky for me I think - I was workin' the bar that night 'cause we were short-handed. We got talkin', and kinda found a connection. Martin invited us to come see him in London so we thought, 'what the hell, why not?'

'And the rest is history,' Matt added, with a gentle smile. 'It's a friendship that goes back twenty years now. We've visited Mike and Martin, they've visited us. We'd all see each other somewhere, around once or twice a year, but we weren't able to get here for Martin's funeral, or even to see him after he found out he was dying, so this is the next best thing. There's also a huge comic book convention being held here in London at the weekend. Rich collects comic books, so we decided it was the perfect chance to spend a little time with Mike and Gavin too. Under the circumstances, it felt more important than ever, to touch base with them, so I'm glad we could make this happen.'

'I collect Beano annuals, actually,' Feen giggled. 'And I still have them all, boxed up and squirreled away somewhere. I used to be a member of the Beano Club.'

Rich nodded. 'I still am! I have an international subscription. Still get the Beano, every week! You know, early copies can sell for thousands of dollars. I keep all my comic books in plastic sleeves, to keep 'em in good condition. Eventually they'll be part of our retirement fund.'

Dinner was a jolly event. As predicted, Mike, Matt and Rich were on fine form, bouncing well off one another, and sharing stories of past antics and tongue-in-cheek political opinions with great humour. Their friendship was easy and close, and Gavin was thrilled to see how naturally Feen slotted into it all. It was like they'd *all* been friends for years.

As they left the restaurant at the end of the night, Feen threw her arms around everyone, declaring that she'd had one of the best nights of her life. 'Ratt, and Mich, *please* come up to Torley next time you're in England. Don't make me beg, you must promise! There's a fabulous family cottage you can fay in, on our starm. It's where Gavin is staying at the moment. I'd love to show you our beautiful Lake District too, and some real Northern hospitality. Whenever you can make it work, do come!'

In the back of the taxi on the way home, Gavin pulled Feen close and snuggled her against him. 'They loved you, you know. I think you've put one of your spells on them both. They hung off every word you said, all night. I can't believe you called them Ratt and

Mitch, though! Dunno whether to laugh or cry, at that, and I'm not sure I can ever think of them by their proper names anymore now.'

'Oh, I don't think they minded, in fact I know they didn't! And I love *them*! What amazing men they are. Such huge hearts and warm words, from both of them. I love their Bostonian accents, too. If all your friends are that lovely, I think I'm marrying rather well!'

'Erm… I thought you'd already decided that you were, anyway, milady? And it was nice of you to invite 'Ratt and Mich' to Teapot Cottage, by the way. Just don't be surprised if they spring up out of the blue one day and announce their imminent arrival. They will take you literally, you know, and when they told you they thought of you as family too now, they really meant it.'

'That would be amazing. I *absolutely* want them to come, and if the cottage isn't free when they want to, they can stay at Ravensdown. Daddy and Adie would love them, I'm sure. I do hope we can see them again soon.'

'Well, I may have to go to New York too, sometime soon, for work. If the conference calls I've been having with a band that's based there come to anything, it might mean a trip to the Big Apple. Boston's only a few hours north of New York city, so we can certainly make something work, if the guys are around. Hire a car and scoot up there for a day or three.'

'That would be amazing! And talking of amazing, that restaurant; the Savoy Grill! How fabulous was that?'

'See? That's why I didn't want you to cook! I wanted you to have the chance to see that place, with all its art deco, mirrors and stuff. It's iconic, and something you'll never forget.'

'I certainly won't! So beautiful, and with great food and the best company *ever*, it couldn't have been a better night. I'm so glad I got dressed up, and so happy we did that. Heading home tomorrow means we wouldn't have had another chance. But will I have a chance to wear this outfit again, d'you think? There isn't much call for fratin socks and sparkly high heels around the farm, or in Torley at all, come to that!'

Gavin gave her a squeeze. 'Don't worry about that. There'll be lots of chances to wear glad-rags in the future. If things go the way I plan, you might need to invest in a few more frosh pocks.'

'Ok, maybe. But for now, I am perfectly happy on cloud nine-and-a-half with this one, thank you very much. My very own

GinGio creation, tailored especially for me! I will be the envy of every woman who knows me, and most of the ones who don't! I'm sappy to havour this, for now, but I do need to go to the shops on my own tomorrow for a few hours, if that's okay, before we head home?'

'That's no problem. I'll stay at home because I've stuff to do and get ready, but I can pop you in a private car and get the driver to take you wherever you want to go, and stay with you. Our flight back leaves at five-thirty. As long as you're back here for about half past three, and can be packed and ready to go by quarter past four, that should work out perfect. We'll be back at Teapot Cottage in time for dinner.'

'Ooh! Let's grab some chish and fips with pushy meas and gravy on the way home! Can we do that?'

Her enthusiasm made him laugh. 'We can do anything your heart desires, faiden meen!'

On the plane the following afternoon, they talked about the initial plans for their wedding. They decided it would be in Torley, and Gavin was confident that his grandparents would cheerfully offer whatever help they could. He was hopeful that they'd say yes to having the wedding at their house. They had the most beautiful garden and, because he knew how much Feen loved it, their bandstand would be the perfect 'altar.' All it needed was a lick of fresh paint, and he could give it that himself. Feen mused that it would also still work out, with a few heavy lace panels ready to hang at short notice, if the Lake District weather decided to pull its common stunt of throwing wind and rain at everybody on what was meant to be a summer's day.

He was relieved that she didn't want a big church event. Neither of them was religious in the conventional sense, so a civil ceremony felt like the perfect solution. They decided they would keep things small, and just have family and close friends to their actual ceremony, then have a more informal, catered evening party for their wider network of friends and family. A marquee could be set up too, for mingling and dancing, just in case the weather let them down. It sounded about as perfect to Gavin as anything could. He was more excited about his wedding than he'd ever been about anything else, in his whole entire life.

221

Chapter Nineteen

By Friday tea-time, Carla's chair was finished, and although she wasn't usually one to blow her own trumpet, she was very proud of the result. She couldn't hide the smile of satisfaction as she looked at it, glistening with its glossy purple paint, with the most beautiful covering, held in by a border of small shiny studs around the now-amply upholstered seat. The hospital corners that she'd carefully hand-stitched into place were perfect. She'd also opted to put a small, upholstered back panel on the chair too, because there was enough space for it. As a little statement piece of furniture, it was quite beautiful.

She took it into the house and placed it carefully on the kitchen table. Stan and Hazel weren't at home. She figured that her parents had probably gone over to Carlisle for some groceries, as they normally did on a Friday afternoon. They'd probably stop at the Feathers pub in Torley for their tea on their way back, as usual, taking advantage of the early-bird two-for-one, two-course special that ran until six o'clock.

They might not be back for a couple of hours yet, which suited Carla because she really just wanted them to come in and see the chair, and hopefully be thrilled at how a battered, unloved relic had been so quickly and beautifully transformed. But she didn't want to be there to see their reaction. That felt like just a bit too much.

She decided to get cleaned up and take Gavin's box to him. It was a good reason, other than work, to get of the house for a while. Socially, invitations and opportunities had always been in very short supply, but they had more or less dried up completely since the court case last year. Even the people who'd once vaguely liked her would be a long time forgiving her for what she'd done, if they *ever* did.

It had been a grave mistake, going up against the Raven family. They had a lot of friends in Torley who'd made their loyalties plain. She didn't blame people, but she did wonder if there would ever be a time when she'd walk into a shop and be treated with anything more than stiff politeness. She wondered if there would ever be a chance, to show people there was more to her than the meanness, cruelty and selfishness she was now known for, far and wide.

She sent Gavin a text to ask him if he was home. He replied that he was, so she let him know she was on her way to Teapot Cottage with the box. She quickly showered, and skimmed a new razor across the 'Sherwood Forest' that had been sprouting for far too long on the lower half of her legs. She couldn't even remember last time she'd shaved them.

She dug into her wardrobe and found a halfway decent dress; a burnt-orange waterfall tunic with half-sleeves, that skimmed forgivingly over her various bumps, and she slipped on a pair of cream canvas rope-soled wedges and tried not to think about how shapeless and out of date her outfit might be. She always wore functional, perfectly presentable clothes for work (trousers, mostly, with an appropriate top), but most people would probably say - and fairly enough she supposed - that her social wardrobe left a lot to be desired.

She'd always had a good figure, before her oestrogen had headed for the hills. Tall and slim as she'd always been, she used to look good in almost anything. Now, since she'd lost her defined figure, and had put on an amount of extra weight that somehow made her look shorter, she had no idea what suited her anymore. Although she'd never suffered much from vanity, she had always taken her shape for granted. Now, she was dismayed at how lumpy and frumpy she'd allowed herself to get, squirreled away in the back of beyond with her ageing parents, and with nobody to think about looking nice for. The last time she'd gone shopping for anything other than work gear was well before the court case, and she hadn't had the heart, since then.

It's easy to get lazy and complacent, when you've nowhere special to go. But I'm not quite ready to morph into my mother. I guess it wouldn't hurt to go to the gym and tone up a bit. Not to join a class - too awkward for all concerned, really - but I could do some treadmill, weights, maybe get a personal trainer for a few sessions, if anyone was willing to work with me.

Carla was under no illusions about the people of Torley town. They tended to have long memories, and while they might not still be as hostile towards her now as they had been, that didn't mean they'd be queueing around a corner to help her. But, she reasoned, her money was as good an anyone else's, and a personal trainer might help her feel better about herself. She resolved to drop in later at The Beeches, the hotel on the road to Carlisle, and check out their health club. If she could pay for her membership monthly, she might still be able to manage it alongside the eye-watering cost of her therapy sessions.

I need to make more of those too. Instead of pitching up at Dawn's office once a week and sitting in virtual silence, like the 'half-sucked acid drop' my son thinks I am, and refusing to talk properly about anything, I may as well start getting my money's worth.

On her way out the door, with Gavin's box in her hands, Carla looked back at the chair, sitting on the table, smelling of new paint and glowing in the light from the range-hood, which Hazel always liked to leave on while she and Stan were out. The chair looked lovely, and she was proud of her work.

During the drive to Teapot Cottage, she wondered whether she might be able to find some other neglected pieces of furniture that she could upcycle. That was the new term everyone used, wasn't it? Upcycling? She'd enjoyed renovating the old chair immensely. It had been a short, easy and gratifying project. Could she do something like that again?

She found herself smiling. Maybe she could! Maybe it was worth heading back to Carlisle over the weekend to see what might be on offer in the charity and second-hand shops over there. She could check out nearby car-boot sales too, this Sunday, if the weather allowed. Maybe she could find another cheap chair, or a chest of drawers, an old bedding chest or something else that she could work some magic on. These thoughts, this idea that she could do another meaningful and transformational project - it all felt like the beginning of something quite new and exciting.

She decided she'd talk to her dad about it. Stan might be helpful with his Shogun, when it came to picking things up and helping her get them home and into the workshop. She wondered if up-cycling furniture would encroach much on his workspace, but in fairness he wasn't doing much project work himself these days. He seemed to be quite absorbed with playing with and expanding his little model village. Maybe he'd let her have free reign in the workshop for a while. She thought she might ask him to give her a crash course on how to use the various different tools he had. The little Dremel had been wonderful to use, after Stan had shown her what it could do. Its different attachments were remarkable, and it was the perfect tool for her small hands.

Carla felt a tiny spark of excitement. This could turn out to be a lot of fun, especially if there was a market for tastefully refurbished furniture.

As she pulled up at Teapot Cottage, Gavin opened the front door and came out to open the driver's door of Hazel's little Nissan for her. She pulled the box out from the back seat. Holding it by its dull black metal handles, she proffered it to Gavin, who took it without a word. He merely stared at it, with his lips compressed and his jaw working, as if he was trying not to cry. Neither of them really knew what to say.

'Sorry, Mum. I'm a bit overwhelmed. I wasn't sure you'd give this to me. I'm almost afraid to look inside it.'

'No problem. As you said, it's your property. It's time you had it.'

Gavin shook himself a little. 'I'm sorry, I've forgotten my manners. Please, come in for a coffee or a glass of wine. You look nice, by the way. That dark orange suits you.'

Carla felt herself blushing, and she started to think of an excuse to leave again straight away, but one look at her son's face, which was full of emotion, caused her to change her mind. He was doing his best with her. She recognised that. Maybe it was time she started behaving like the mother he might need. She shrugged at him.

'Okay, I'll come in for a quick coffee if you're making one. Best not have a wine, as tempting as it is. Dunno if I could stop at one, to be honest, and Mum needs her car in one piece. I also don't need to be done for drink-driving. The last thing I need is a growing rap sheet!'

Gavin grinned at that, and stepped back to allow her entry to the cottage. As soon as she walked in, she felt instantly warm and cocooned. The cottage somehow gave her the feeling of being almost shielded from the world, in some weird way.

225

This place definitely has an aura about it, Carla thought to herself, but she wasn't quite enlightened enough about such matters to have described it as anything distinct. There was just something gentle and nurturing here. She hadn't noticed it the first time she'd come, late at night in the middle of an electrical storm, with her thoughts no less unsettled. She'd been far too distracted then, to pay much attention to her surroundings.

She couldn't identify exactly what it was, in here, that made the place feel so special. No doubt the witchy Feen Raven could explain it, in fact Carla wondered whether the slight young woman might even be responsible for it; as mad as that sounded.

Gavin was ahead of her now and placing Martin's box on the kitchen table. He moved to the Aga and set the whistling kettle on one of its hotplates to boil. He reached up to retrieve the coffee pot from a shelf alongside, glancing at the box every few seconds. He was quite plainly going through the motions of doing something mundane at the same time as champing at the bit to focus on what was really important to him. Carla looked at his keyboards and drum set, stacked in one corner of the living room.

'I see you've brought some music stuff, to work with while you're here. Where's Feen?'

'Up at home, working on some jewellery. I suppose you've heard of Gina Giordano, the dress designer? She's Feen's step sister-in-law. She's commissioning Feen to provide a small exclusive jewellery line, to accessorize her winter collection.'

Carla was impressed. 'Wow! That's quite a coup. I wish I could afford something from GinGio. Maybe if I ever win the lottery. It's a very exclusive label. She never makes many of each design. They're like hen's teeth to get hold of, even if you can afford them.' She looked around the kitchen.

'You know, this place feels really nice, Gavin. Cosy. Why don't I make the coffee, while you open the box? Unless you'd rather wait until after I've gone?'

Gavin shook his head and she set about brewing the coffee She found everything easily in the compact kitchen, and when the kettle started to whistle she poured the hot water into the coffee pot and set it to stand. She turned around to find her son still staring at the box, as if too afraid to open it.

'Well, come on, you idiot! Stop messing about! You've made a big enough song and dance about getting your hands on the damn thing, just get it open!'

She sat at the table and Gavin did the same. He was still staring at the unopened box. His face was obscured by his hair. She had no idea what he was thinking.

She reached across and lifted his chin. She was surprised to find that he had tears in his eyes. His voice was husky.

'It's him, Mum. So much of him, in here. I dunno if I can bear it. I really miss him.'

Carla didn't allow her own pang of sorrow to show. Instead, she resolved to remain practical. 'C'mon, Gavin. He'd have wanted you to have this. I know it brings back memories. You're still grieving. I know that too. But what's in here might actually help.'

He looked up at her. 'Have you opened it?'

Carla shook her head. 'Not for very many years. I don't remember much of what's in it, to be truthful.'

Gavin nodded, took a deep breath, and lifted the lid on the box. Carla turned her attention to plunging and pouring the coffee, giving him a minute or two without scrutiny. When she turned back, he was reaching into the box with a shaking hand. He took out a small scrap of fabric, maybe four inches square, with about the same sized border of intricate, gossamer-like lace around it. It was clearly very old, but it was still white and beautiful.

'Jesus! What a bloody sacrilege, to wipe a snotty nose on that!'

Gavin nodded, and grinned in spite of himself. 'Yeah, it really would be, wouldn't it?'

The handkerchief had been folded up, and nestled inside it was a plain gold wedding ring. Carla cleared her throat.

'Well, as I said, I don't know all that much, but I do know that hankie was Martin's Grandma's. Your great-grandmother. He once told me she had it tucked into the sleeve of her dress, on her wedding day. The wedding ring must've been hers as well, I suppose, since it was wrapped in it.'

'Did you ever know her name?' Gavin asked hopefully.

227

Carla shook her head. 'I'm sorry. If I did, I've long since forgotten it. But there might be clues in there. I wouldn't be surprised.'

Gavin spoke softly. 'I wonder if Feen might like to wear this, up her sleeve or somewhere, on our wedding day.'

In spite of herself, Carla snorted. Then thinking again, she said carefully, 'I imagine she would accept such an honour. I dunno why anyone wouldn't.'

Gavin smiled gently. 'Well, if she doesn't want to, I will.'

'You could wear it instead of a buttonhole?' Carla offered.

Gavin had his hand in the box again and was drawing out a sheaf of papers. They appeared to be old birth, death and marriage certificates. It looked like Martin had spent a bit of time finding out about his family tree. Gavin sifted through them.

'Gwendolen,' he said, smiling. 'It looks like her name was Gwendolen. That's interesting. Gwendolen was one of the principal characters in George Eliot's Daniel Deronda. We studied that novel in school.'

'Gwendolen was also supposedly the wizard Merlin's wife, in Arthurian legend.' Carla responded. 'That should impress Feen, shouldn't it?'

Gavin openly laughed. 'Oh, I think so, yes indeed, Mum!'

'In that case maybe you wouldn't be able to *stop* her from wearing your great-grandmother's hankie at the wedding, even if you wanted to!'

Gavin's eyes danced. 'Maybe you're right. I can't wait to tell her, to show her all this.'

He glanced through the other certificates, and then picked up an envelope that was sealed. He opened it up and shook out a sheaf of photos. There were only a handful, but one of them was an old, faded, black and white wedding photo of a young, serious-looking couple. On the back was scrawled, simply, 'Charles and Gwendolen, 1936.'

'Look, Mum! Here they are, my great-grandparents!' Gavin set aside the photo carefully, clearly intending to go back to it later. He picked up another photo, this time of a woman who looked a lot like Martin. There was nothing on the back to say who it was, but Carla knew.

'That's Martin's mother, Margaret. She died of pneumonia when he was about nine, I think. He said she was never strong, health-wise. He remembered her always being poorly with something or other. He thought it was probably because she inhaled a lot of chemicals when she worked in a munitions factory somewhere in Lancashire, making bombs and stuff, when she was younger. He believed it destroyed her immune system.'

Gavin's eyebrows shot to his hairline.

'She made bombs? Why the hell would she have a job doing something like that?'

Carla shrugged. 'For the money? Apparently the wages were better than most so-called 'excellent paying jobs' for men, even tradesmen, around that time. It was danger money, I suppose. They were at constant risk of blowing themselves up, with all the nitro glycerine and other volatile stuff they were handling. They worked in individual cubicles so if they did cause an explosion it wouldn't kill anyone else, only them.'

'Bloody hell! Did that ever happen?'

'According to your dad it did, sadly, once or twice. Did he really never tell you anything about his mother?'

Gavin nodded slowly. 'Yeah, bits now and again, but never very much, and nothing like that! I'm remembering now that her family did come from Lancashire. That's so funny, because Feen's family all hail from there too!' Gavin ran a hand through his hair, and she noted it as one of her own habits. He nodded slowly.

'Yeah, that's right. Her dad was never able to go back to work after the war, so the family always struggled. I guess maybe she did that work to help out. Since Dad was quite young when she died, whatever memories he had would all have been his childhood ones anyway, or stuff he'd heard from his own dad. Did you ever meet *him*?'

Carla thought for a minute, then nodded slowly. 'Yes, I did actually, a couple of times. His name was Jack. He died not long before Martin left us, and I can't remember why but he was only in his fifties. I think it might've been a heart attack or something. I do know he'd been a heavy smoker. But you were still a baby. You never met him. I don't think you ever would have, to be honest. Jack wasn't a very nice man. He and Martin never got along, and he washed his hands of him completely when he found out he was gay. I don't know if he ever even knew about you.'

Gavin picked up another old photo, of a man in a soldier's uniform. He compared it to the wedding photo, and it was clearly the same man; Charles. Evidently, he had done active service in World War II.

'Looks like you've a bit to go through, there,' Carla observed. 'The death certificates will give you an idea of how old they all were, what they died of, and everything. It was good that Martin kept all that stuff. It tells you who your family were on that side. I don't know what he told you about his parents, but he never seemed to want to talk about them with me, so I couldn't have offered you much.'

'Well, as I say, he told me bits, here and there, but I never wanted to dig at him, you know? It never felt like a sore subject, *per se*, but I just think if he'd wanted to talk about them, or his early life, he would've.' Gavin shrugged.

Carla considered this for a minute, then agreed. 'Yeah. It was incredibly hard to be a gay man until relatively recently, Gavin. Your generation has grown up appreciating same-gender relationships as a normal way of life for many people. But the stigma was bad, back then. It's still bad now, sadly, in some circles where intolerance and misunderstanding still have too much influence. It must have been unimaginable back in those days, when Martin was a small child, trying to make sense of himself and his place in the world. The fact that he still tried to live like a heterosexual man with you and me shows how hard things still were, not so very long ago.'

'Mum... is this you?' Gavin was holding out a photograph of a young, attractive, dark-haired woman in a blue denim maternity dress. She was sitting next to Martin, who had an arm casually draped across her shoulders. They were sitting on a lime green sofa. The woman held one hand protectively over her bump, and her other palm was pointed at the camera, in a 'talk-to-the-hand' gesture. She was smiling faintly but was clearly camera shy. On the back of the photo was an inscription, written in handwriting that she immediately recognised as Martin's. 'Lots of love to my darling girl - me and you, and bumpy-doo!' There were three kisses beneath.

Tears sprang to Carla's eyes. She hadn't known about this picture. Clearly it had been intended for her, but she'd never received it, and she'd never rifled through the box to have found it. She struggled to remember who'd taken it. She recalled that they'd been at a party somewhere, but she no longer remembered whose, or where it had been. She remembered the lovely denim maternity dress she was wearing in the photo, though, and how tight it got when she was around seven months. It went into the bin around that time, after her last attempts to squeeze into it had left it ripped beyond repair. But there was nothing else. Her memory remained resolutely shut down.

'Lots of love to my darling girl - me and you, and bumpy-doo!' He did love me once, then, before he stopped being able to resist the call of who he truly was.

Gavin was clearly thinking the same thing. He was looking intently at her. She was struggling not to cry. Again! She found herself unable to speak. Again!

Gavin leaned forward and picked up her hand. 'He loved you, Mum. There it is, in black and white. Forgive him? Please try? He couldn't help who he was, any more than anyone else can. He loved you as best he could, and it wasn't enough because he couldn't love you the way you wanted him to - *needed* him to. He couldn't do that and be true to himself. But he did love you. He loved us both.'

'I destroyed his love.' Her voice was just a whisper.

'You behaved in the only way you knew how, at the time. I get that. It's pretty much all I've thought about since you told me everything, the other night. It wasn't right, what you did, or how you behaved, but you were in shock, Mum. You were in pain too, and young, and naïve, and bewildered, with a toddler to take care of by yourself, and you lashed out. Yes, you and Dad could have carried on and established a different kind of love; still supportive in some way, if you'd let it. But you didn't know how to, did you?'

Carla was crying openly now. The thought occurred to her that she'd cried more tears in the last few days than she'd cried in the last ten years!

Oh, God. What I've missed! Gavin's right. Martin still wanted to love me, in a way that he could manage, and maybe if I could

231

have found a way to settle for that we might have made something work. Maybe we wouldn't be where we are now, damaged, dead or broken.'

Through her tears, she looked over at her son. His image was blurred but solid, there in front of her.

And I really am broken. I know that. I just never knew how badly, until now.

She took the biggest breath of her life and plunged in. She was sobbing and her words were all running together, but she had to say it. She had to acknowledge it.

'Gavin, I wasn't right, was I? In the head, I mean. It's ok for you to say what you've probably always thought. I don't think I was alright, the way I should have been, you know? I think I must have been mentally ill. And I think, along the way, I somehow forgot how to try and get better. I just let everything roll me over. I fought back, but in the wrong way. I lost sight of what the right way was. I don't know if I could help it. Maybe I couldn't. Maybe I was ill.'

The last few words came out in a whisper.

Gavin took her hand across the table, and she let him. 'I think you were, Mum,' he said softly. 'I think you *were* ill, back then. I was far too young to see it, or understand it, and then later too angry to consider it even if I *had* seen it. I wouldn't have known what to do about it. But yes, looking back, I think you were suffering, in ways Dad and I couldn't imagine, and it pushed you over the edge. Please forgive me, Mum, if I let you down. Dad, he really *did* let you down, there were no two ways about it. But maybe you could forgive him too, in time.'

Gavin pushed his hair out of his eyes and finally let his own tears fall. 'You know what? I just think we all did the best we bloody could, back then. We coped badly, individually, and as a family, and none of that helped. We didn't even know how to talk, did we? We were just who we were, confused, hurt, with no real insight or capability to understand ourselves or each other. I think it really is as simple - and as sad - as that.'

Carla nodded, fighting and failing to stop her sobs. The sight of her grown son crying was almost more than she could bear. 'Maybe you're right,' she whispered.

232

They sat quietly, holding hands, for a minute or two. It seemed like a long time, that they just sat there, wordlessly, each lost in their own private thoughts. Finally, Gavin squeezed his mother's hand, let go of it, wiped his eyes, and looked at her. He raised his hands and let them fall into his lap.

'Mum, how about we leave the past where it is? Can we do that, d'you think? Can we just start now, and look forward, and see if we can get to know and like and respect one another? Can we let go of the resentment, the disappointment, and the hurt? I'd like to try, if you would too.'

Carla rolled her shoulders. Her neck hurt. She realised she'd been holding all her tension in her upper body.

'Yeah. We can try, Gavin. I'd like that too. But I still have a lot of things to resolve, in my own mind. It will take me time to get there, but I've been in therapy for a while now. It costs a bloody fortune, but it's helping, and it will help even more if I let myself be more open to it instead of resisting all Dawn's attempts to dig into the real stuff. Living cheaply with Mum and Dad is helping me to pay for it. It's why I'm there. I really want a place of my own, but I can't afford it yet. I'm only on low wages.'

But I'll see if I can work with Dawn now, on the things that are stopping me from throwing my arms around you and saying yes.

'I feel like I've got blocks,' she admitted. 'Really big barriers I can't explain or understand. I want to tear them all down but I'm scared, Gavin, because I don't know what will be left of myself at the end of all that. I need you to be patient with me. If you can, maybe I can work out how to bring some of them down and still feel like I'll have a life at the other side of them.'

It was all she could offer. But it was a start. It *felt* like a start, anyway. Whether Gavin saw it as that, she really couldn't tell, but he'd shown his willingness to move forward and, sitting here at the table in Teapot Cottage, it did feel like something significant had changed for him as well as for her. Carla wasn't able to explain exactly what, but she could feel *something* evolving and changing, and it didn't feel bad.

She sniffed hard and stood up. 'Well, I think you've got enough to get on with, looking through that lot.' She gestured at the box. 'I'm all tapped out of emotion, so if you don't mind I'll get myself home, and get off this rollercoaster. You'll have a lot to work through yourself, as you go through what's in there, I'm sure. You might want to treat yourself and splurge on another pack of kitchen towels too, since I've cried this lot off the bloody roll.'

Gavin gestured at the box. 'Thanks Mum, for being here while I opened all this, and for shedding a bit of light on a few mysteries. There might be more. There's a fair swag of stuff in there, but you've helped a lot just with what we've looked through together. I appreciate it. And this is yours, by the way.' He handed her the photo of herself. 'I'd like a copy of it though, if that's okay?'

Carla looked at him for a long moment. Then she put her hand to his cheek and felt an immediate surge of relief when he didn't brush it aside or move away from her.

'You've turned out really well. You're a credit to your dad, Gavin. He did a good job of raising you. I'll see you.'

He nodded, and gave her a brief smile. She turned and walked quickly out of the cottage. *Would* she see him again? He'd indicated he was open to it, to see if they could build on the shy truce they'd managed to declare here just now. Maybe they could.

But right now, I need a little distance.

A tad too much emotion had flung Carla squarely into unfamiliar territory. Yet again, she was floundering and unsure of herself. She didn't know where her confidence had gone, and that was feeling she didn't like. It was time to put some distance between herself and Gavin again so she could regroup. But this time it didn't feel like a hostile or frustrated silence. All things considered, that was a big achievement.

As she started up her mother's car to head home again, she had no idea what the future would hold. She had no idea, that the meeting she'd just had with her son had set a new direction for her life that would change it beyond recognition.

234

A Song of Celebration

You came into my life and you fired up my heart
And now it looks like you and me will never be apart
Everything is very, very sweet
And you know I'm never gonna walk away from you, baby
It's you and me, it was meant to be
We were meant to be.
Forever meant to be.

I'll be there ready, waiting when you walk up the aisle
Ready to greet you with the biggest ever smile
You're the one and only girl for me
And you know I'm never gonna let you down, pretty baby
It's you and me, it was meant to be
We were meant to be.
Forever meant to be.
(riff)
Some things we have to trust are written in the stars
And we both know the brightest-ever future will be ours
We were meant to be
And one long-time day, when we are old and grey, we'll be
sayin'
Hey, you and me, we were meant to be!
We were meant to be.
Forever meant to be.

Chapter Twenty

A Spell To Bless Your Own Marriage

You will need:
one sprig of fresh rosemary
one sprig of fresh lavender
five whole dried cloves
two velvet drawstring pouches
1one small chip of charcoal
A heat resistant plate
three drops each of rose/bergamot essential oil
two small pieces of rose quartz crystal (to represent two hearts)

At sunrise on the day of your marriage, grind the herbs in a
mortar and pestle. Blend with the drops of essential oils.
Light the charcoal in the dish, then place the mix on top.
Gently blow to keep it a-smoulder
and hold the crystals over the smoke.
Incantation; just once, directly over the smoking concoction:
'Bless and bind these hearts together.
Let love be true and hold forever.'
Place one crystal in each drawstring pouch and give to two
trusted loved ones who are joyfully wedded to one another,
to offer one each back to you and your spouse
as soon as your vows are taken.

The day of the wedding dawned bright and sunny. Although it had only been ten weeks since she'd met Gavin, Feen was never more sure of anything in her life than the fact that she wanted to marry him. The long wait (which had actually been a very short wait by most people's standards but frustratingly long for *her*) was over. Today she would walk down the aisle to her soulmate - the man of her dreams made real.

She looked at her engagement ring now, the thin gold band with its delicate filigree, diamond-centred flowers sitting on top of it. The ring was beyond beautiful. The jeweller in Preston had done a magnificent job of overhauling it and making it sound. It was perfect in Feen's eyes.

Gavin's great-grandmother Gwendolen's wedding ring, which she prayed was tucked safely into Mike's shirt pocket, had been slightly modified too, by the same jeweller. He'd put in a small curve in it, to fit neatly around the engagement ring, and embedded a small diamond at each side. Feen's wedding ring for Gavin was a plain platinum, bevel-edged band, engraved on the underside with two tiny hearts with their initials in them - S and G - with a tiny musical note in the middle, and inscribed on the other side with the date of their marriage.

Since her dad had now remarried, he'd gifted Feen his own and Beth's wedding rings to one another. She wore them now, threaded through a delicate gold chain around her neck. That felt perfect too.

Gwendolen's beautiful lace handkerchief was pinned inside the bodice of her dress, close to her heart. Her and the bridesmaids' flowers were all cascading bouquets that she had wrought with her own loving, excited hands, with ferns and forest flowers that she'd gathered herself, and interspersed with the most gorgeous white full-bloom roses that Fiona Frost at Heavenly Blooms had donated as a wedding gift. Feen had also created her own crown of ferns and flowers, to sit on top of her mother's wedding veil, which was now studded with small crystals across its delicate edge.

Her beautiful shoes had been a present from Adie - a pair of tiny, embossed satin kitten-heeled mules, in the same creamy shade as her wedding dress, with crystal flowers sewn across the vamp. She giggled to herself, remembering the evenings when they had sat down together, each with a large, fortifying glass of wine in hand, to shop for wedding shoes online. Adie had told her to choose anything she wanted, but it had proved rather more difficult than either of them could have imagined, until Adie had had the sudden brainwave of contacting Gina, to ask if she could help.

Gina readily pointed them in the direction of an Italian shoemaker who she often used as a supplier to complement her fashion collections. His website showed exquisite designs, all vastly different and superior to anything Feen and Adie had already managed to find. There weren't any wedding shoes on offer, but the designer did say he took bespoke orders. After seeing some shoes first in dark green pleated velvet with pink and purple silk crocus flowers sewn right across the vamps, Feen had fallen in love with the idea of having them made in the same cream satin as her gorgeous dress, and replacing the flowers with crystals. She had emailed the design team with her request.

The suggested design that quickly came back was stunning, exactly as she'd imagined it to look. The shoes were utterly perfect, and she had literally squealed with delight. They had been eye-wateringly expensive, more than the dress had cost in fact, but Adie batted Feen's protests away like she would bat away a buzzing bee, saying the cost was not for her to worry about; the shoes were Adie's pre-wedding gift.

Feen had also bitten the bullet herself, and bought a pair of the green floral ones, after receiving a 25% discount voucher for a second pair after the wedding shoes had been ordered. It seemed like too good a deal to pass up, for something so beautiful. Every time she wore them, they'd remind her of her wedding shoes and what she hoped would be the happiest day of her life.

Carla had stunned her with a pre-wedding gift too! She'd dropped by with a small parcel that was exquisitely wrapped in white and gold tissue paper, with half a dozen gold ribbons trailing from a white and gold rosette. She'd offered it almost tentatively. Feen had unwrapped the paper to find the most beautiful little handbag nestled within it; a little house in the shape of a toadstool. It had a red velvety top, with little white spots on, and the 'stalk' had sequins and lace butterflies all over it. There were roses, too, and a forest scene.

Everything Feen lived and breathed was right there, on that exquisite little bag. The front door had two panels, and tiny brass knockers. When Feen pulled at them, the little doors opened to reveal a cat and a woodland squirrel inside. She'd instantly fallen in love with the bag, but her smile had quickly faded when she'd seen the inscription on the back. It was a quote from Shakespeare's play, A Midsummer Night's Dream, which read; *'The Course of True Love Never Did Run Smooth.'* She'd struggled to know what to think or say about it, until Carla explained, with a half-defensive shrug.

'Well, it doesn't run smoothly at all. Not for long. And anyone who thinks it does is an imbecile.'

Well, nobody could call you anything but a straight-shooter, Carla!

Feen bit her lip, as her mother-in-law to-be continued.

'Of course you'll have your ups and downs. Every couple does, but that doesn't mean you won't be happy. You just have to remember - always, Feen - that whatever dramas turn up, and even the longest and happiest marriages have them, you and Gavin must face them together, to get through them. Don't go into this with some deluded notion that it'll all be romantic and lovely, twenty-four-seven, and you won't have any spade-work to do.

'There'll be days when he'll lose his patience with your mad-witch ways, and slam out of the house to go God knows where, and nights when you'll want to stuff one of his sweaty socks down his throat and happily watch while he chokes on it. I hope he keeps a bedroom cleaner than he used to,' she added, half to herself.

Feen had laughed at that. 'You're right, I know. And thank you for saying that, actually, because everyone else is all garry-eyed and stooey about all this, and nobody has said anything much about the tough times. I know there will be some. My own mother would have offered some version of what you've just said, I'm sure, but she's not here, of course. But oh, Carla! How bagical this little mag is! Wherever did you find it? I've never seen anything like it. It's just *gorgeous*!'

Carla had gone a bit shy at Feen's enthusiasm.

'Well, I'm a collector of a certain brand of handbag. They are all very special, and only made in small batches. This one was very limited edition, and it wasn't around for long. I'd never part with mine, but I decided to try to track one down for you. It took a while, but I eventually managed it. I thought you might like to have it on your arm, on your wedding day.'

She'd shrugged again, even more self-consciously. 'But no problem if not. You can use it somewhere else. I dunno; it just seemed perfect for you, and I know we've never been on good terms, but since you're joining the family I thought this would be a bit more use to you than a half dead olive branch, all jagged and full of bloody splinters, which is more my usual style.'

Feen had laughed again, thinking that in some weird way she might actually end up liking her abrasive, sarcastic mother-in-law a lot. That was no small thing. In fact, all things considered, it was monumental. But that's how life was, sometimes. With a little contrition and forgiveness; someone waving an olive branch (albeit with splinters) and someone else accepting it (albeit with a pair of protective gloves on), a person who had hurt you immeasurably could end up being a lifelong friend. Carla's gift brought tears to Feen's eyes.

'I *will* use it on my wedding day, absolutely. I can put a bit of touch-up makeup in it, and my phone.'

'Well I hope you'll have the damn thing switched off. None of us will want to hear *that* going off halfway up the aisle, even if it *is* the theme from Watership Down!'

'Well it's not, actually. It's just a rather boring time chone. But you've given me an idea.'

'Let me guess. The theme from the Twilight Zone?'

Feen had smirked at that. 'Well, it beats the hell out of The Exorcist!'

'Touché! But mine's not The Exorcist. It's the shower-scene music, from Psycho.'

Feen hadn't been able to stop a full-blown belly-laugh, at that. 'Of course it is, Carla!'

Abruptly, Gavin's mother had made her excuses and left, leaving Feen wondering what had changed so quickly. One minute they were getting on okay, and then without warning Carla had slammed the shutters down and run away.

The woman certainly was an enigma. Feen was frustrated that after many weeks of dedicated effort, she was still unable to fully read someone so close in her orbit. When it came to Carla, Feen's intuition persistently failed, but she knew that Gavin's mother was like an onion; she had many layers, and it would take a fair amount of time and tears to peel through them, to the more tender part that lay within. Feen knew it was there, but she knew just as well that Carla was never going to make it easy for anyone to find it. She could still slam the door on communication abruptly enough to topple someone's head, when she sensed that they wanted to get too close.

The little toadstool bag *was* indescribably beautiful, and as she'd turned it over, and looked at the intricate detail, she'd been humbled and incredulous, to have been given something so incredibly lovely, and *meaningful*, from a person who'd never had a scrap of time or tolerance for her until that moment. It was as if Carla had actually taken the time, to think about who Feen really was. Not only that, but she had also gone to great lengths to secure one of these rare little bags for her. It said a lot. There was plenty of hope, Feen decided, for her relationship with Carla to strengthen and become meaningful too, over time.

The bag was hanging on the back of the bedroom doorhandle now, ready for Feen to pick up, when she would leave Ravensdown House for the very last time as a single woman. She looked at it, and smiled.

Maybe I will have to become a collector of these gorgeous little handbags too. It would be nice to have something more than Gavin, and the avoidance of a horrible Carlisle department store, in common with Carla!

She checked her watch. Gavin was at his grandparents' house now, getting ready. His attendants were there also; Mike as his best man and his friend Stewart as his groomsman. 'Ratt and Mich' were there too, having flown in a few days before. They were staying with Mike, at Teapot Cottage. Feen was thrilled that they'd come back from the States, for the wedding.

Her matron of honour was Josie, with her baby bump on show, and Adie's elegant daughter Teresa was a bridesmaid.

Ruth and Gina's little girl Chiara was a flower girl, just like she'd been at Mark and Adie's nuptials a year or so before.

The wedding was to be a small, early afternoon event in Stan and Hazel's gorgeous garden, with the civil ceremony being conducted in the beautiful wrought-iron bandstand. A special early dinner would follow at the Beeches, the five-star hotel complex on the main road between Torley and Carlisle, and then a party would follow, back at Stan and Hazel's. A gorgeous vintage minibus, decked out to the nines with cream ribbons and roses, had been hired to transport the wedding party there and back.

Hazel and Stan had contributed that, along with the DJ and the constant drinks-and-canapé-catering that would see them all through until late into the night. Hazel had worked tirelessly in the garden to get it ready for the wedding, and Gavin himself had repainted the bandstand a pristine white. It really did look beautiful, with a riot of different coloured roses woven all through it, and Feen was looking forward to seeing it at night, with the delicate fairy lights Gavin had thoughtfully strung all across it. Initially anxious about the prospect of rain, after a week of grumbly weather all across the Lake District, she had been relieved to learn that the up-to-date forecast had promised a clear day and a warm and starlit night - perfect conditions for a wedding! There wouldn't be a moon, but she figured she could live with that. There was no point in being greedy, was there? A fine day and night in the Lake District - even in summertime - was never to be sneezed at.

Although Gavin and Feen had observed the tradition of not seeing each other right before the event, he had texted her lovingly, three times, which warmed her heart. The last text had come just a few minutes ago.

In a few more hours, you'll be my wife, the one and only love of my life. I'm so excited I can't sit still. I adore you today and I always will.

It would soon be time to start getting ready. The hairdresser would be here in half an hour. There was just enough time to grab a light bit of lunch - she needed to eat something if she wasn't going to pass out from hunger halfway down the aisle!

Feen wondered how her dad would be feeling, today.

I know how much he loves Adie, but I know he'll be sad that Mum's not here to see me get married. It'll be a strange day for him. I need to remember that, and be extra gentle with him today.

She took a quiet moment to have a whispered chat to her mother.

'I always wish you were here, Mum, but never more than today. Look at me! I'm metting garried! I wish you could help me into my dress and veil, and get me ready to marry my lovely man. Isn't he wonderful?'

She allowed a few poignant tears to fall. There was never a more important day for any woman to have her mother there for, than her wedding day. The loss of Beth was always hard to bear. Today it was more acute than she'd ever felt it before.

Later, as Sheila was putting the finishing touches to Feen's veil, Mark knocked lightly at the door. He coughed gently, and called;

'Cars are 'ere, lass. Don't keep poor bugger waitin'; 'e'll be a bag o' bloody nerves as it is.'

Sheila opened the door with a dramatic flourish, and Mark gasped. Tears sprang to his eyes as he looked Feen, dressed so exquisitely for her wedding day. He couldn't speak. Instead, he swallowed hard and just nodded, before turning on his heel and walking away. He was quite overcome. Sheila grabbed hold of Feen's hand and squeezed it.

'He's a bit emotional today, love, as you'd expect. You know, who's 'ere and who's not, what it means, an' all that. It's hard for 'im. On the realest level, 'e knows 'e's losing you to another man. As your dad, 'e knows how right and proper that is, but he's going to miss you so much when you've left 'ome.'

'I know, Sheila. I've thought about that a lot. He'll be missing Mum today too, more than usual, won't he?'

'We all will, love.' Sheila's own eyes were glistening. She was emotional too. 'It's a day she should have been 'ere for. She'd have wanted, more than anything in the world, to see you like this, and to watch you wed the man of your dreams.'

Feen felt the lump in her throat again. 'Don't say anymore. I don't want to start crying and ruin my make up!'

At that moment, Josie came limping up the stairs, good-naturedly cursing the low heels that were already pinching her slightly swollen feet. 'Come on, you! It's fashionable to be late, but not *this* bloody late!'

Feen jumped, and immediately refocussed on the imminent event. 'Oh, Josie, I don't want to be late for him at all! I want to be bang on time; let's cart as we mean to starry on!'

'Well hurry up, then! Get in the bloody car!' And with that, Josie turned and heaved her way back down the stairs.

Despite Josie's initial protests about not being a suitable Matron of Honour at five and a half months pregnant, Feen had been adamant that it was *entirely* appropriate, and refused to take no for an answer. Josie wore a deep purple, slub-silk maternity dress that had a fitted bodice and satin roses sewn across the front of its simple scooped neckline. It had a roomy skirt, which curved in an inverted U shape across the top of her surprisingly large belly and fell in folds around her knees, a bit like an upside-down tulip. It was a gorgeous dress, and the colour suited her pale, freckled skin and her wavy strawberry blonde hair, which was left loose around her shoulders and just pinned up at the sides with tiny cream roses. The flattering dress had been expertly sourced by Trudie Sangster at GladRagz boutique, and it somehow seemed to enhance Josie's bump beautifully, making her look sweet and wholesome.

Teresa's bridesmaid dress, also tracked down by Trudie, was in the same colour and fabric, but was more of a straight sheath dress with spaghetti straps. It was plain but stunning on Teresa, who was tall and slim.

Chiara's flower-girl dress was cream satin, very plain, but with a purple sash that matched Josie and Teresa's frocks. The little girl also had a tiny purple velvet evening purse with a chain handle that had been slipped over her arm. It had a clear lip-gloss in it, along with a pound coin and a tiny comb. It made her feel and act all grown up and serious. Josie and Teresa had been doing a great job of keeping her distracted so her nerves wouldn't get the better of her as the time drew nearer to get into the white '57 Chevrolet, decorated with purple ribbons, that was serving as the bridesmaids' car. Chiara's mothers, Ruth and Gina, were already at Stan and Hazel's.

Mark was waiting at an identical but gleaming black Chevrolet, resplendent with white ribbons, when Feen emerged from Ravensdown House. He held the door open for her, and Adie helped her into the car, rearranged her veil, and sat beside her. Mark went around the other side so Feen would be in the middle.

The hired V8 'Chevvies' were a gift from Mike, as his contribution to the wedding. He had gone over early with Matt and Rich in their hire car, to help Gavin get properly organized.

Feen leaned against her father as the car pulled away from the farm. She was nervous and excited, but nostalgic too, for the life she was leaving behind. Mark had got his emotions under control, and he reassuringly patted her hand.

'Yer mother would be so proud o' you right now, lass. You look as beautiful today as she did on *our* weddin' day. I saw 'er comin' up the aisle, and I didn't think I'd ever see summat that beautiful ever again. But I do get a second look, because 'ere you are, and I can't tell yer 'ow blindin' bloody gorgeous you are, and 'ow lucky Gavin is. An' you were right all that time ago about yer dress, by the way. It's as perfect as owt could ever be.'

He cleared his throat, clearly unable to say any more. Feen turned and straightened his purple tie.

'I'm sure Mum was as happy on your wedding day as I am today, Daddy. And I'm lucky too. Gavin's a good man.'

Mark coughed gently into his hand. 'Aye, I think 'e is, an' I know you've got yer 'eart set on 'im, but I do 'ave to ask the question, lass. You know I do.'

Feen grabbed his hand and squeezed it. 'Yes, I'm sure. I've never been more certain of anything.'

Mark chuckled. 'Well, that's alright then. Wasn't sure what we'd do wi' all't bloody caterin' if yer changed yer mind. It would be ok though, if yer did, lass. You know that, right?'

'I do, Daddy. I know it would.'

As the cars pulled up outside Stan and Hazel's, Feen could see their guests milling about. Gavin's Porsche was already parked up, so he was definitely here, she noted with relief. There hadn't been a single moment when she'd doubted he would be, but it was reassuring nonetheless to see the evidence that he was ready and waiting for her.

As the guests saw the cars approaching, they started scuttling into the garden, where white wooden foldaway chairs with purple bows on the back had been laid out in two groups, to form an aisle between. Everyone wanted to be in place before the bride made her entrance, and Uncle Bob appeared to be doing a fine job of shepherding everyone to a suitable seat.

Adie held the door open for Feen. She was wearing the most gorgeous lime green, sleeveless silk pencil dress with turquoise polka dots on it. It had a matching bolero jacket in the turquoise with lime green polka dots. Adie's hat was a plain, understated straw-coloured one with no adornments, but it was elegant and every bit as expensive as it looked. Her outfit was rounded off with a pair of towering nude heels. She looked glamorous and stunning.

Feen loved the whole idea of getting dressed up for something special. It was beyond wonderful to see everyone all dolled up like this, especially seeing the men dressed in suits and ties. That almost *never* happened, so when it did, it was a sight to behold. How handsome they all looked! Her heart swelled with excitement.

She stepped out of the car, holding her father's hand. Hazel Walton came forward, dressed in a beautiful fuchsia pink trouser suit with a cream camisole underneath it, and a short-brimmed cream hat. The old lady looked beautiful, and excited. She gave Feen a kiss on the cheek, told her how gorgeous she looked, and handed her a tiny white lace umbrella with a ribboned loop. Feen slipped it over her arm to hang with the satin and lace horseshoes she already had in place that had been her mother's, and the lovely little toadstool bag that she'd been given from Carla. Stanley gave her a cheeky wink, before steering Hazel towards the seats on the lawn.

Matt and Rich stepped forward too, to each give her a kiss on the cheek before going to takt their seats. They already felt like family to her, and she felt a small fizz of gratitude for how much richer her life was going to be, with such wonderful and interesting new people in it, who loved Gavin so much that they'd readily taken her to their hearts too; enough to fly all the way from Boston, just for the wedding.

Once everyone was in place, and the music started, Josie made a couple of small adjustments to Feen's veil, and they started walking forward. Rather than the traditional wedding march, Feen and Gavin had opted for the beautiful and more majestic Saint Saens Symphony No. 3 finale, with its first crescendo timed perfectly to coincide with Feen's arrival at the bandstand. On her way down, she locked eyes with Gavin, and he grinned at her and blew her a kiss. It was the single best moment of her life. She struggled not to let her tears fall.

He looked amazing in his suit. She'd never seen him dressed in anything but jeans. As she approached him, she murmured to him, under her breath,

'Well, you rub up squite nicely,' she whispered.

'As do you, milady,' he murmured back, and the ceremony began.

Feen held her breath through the heart-stopping moment when the celebrant had asked anyone who had objections to speak now or forever keep quiet. She'd half expected Carla to speak out against the wedding, despite having settled most of her differences with her son and with Feen herself, in recent weeks. Gavin also had a twinkle in his eye, as they waited, as if daring Carla or anyone else to speak, and he squeezed Feen's hand when the moment passed. It seemed like no time at all, that they had exchanged vows and been pronounced a married couple. Gavin didn't wait to be told he could kiss his bride. He swept her straight into his arms, lifted her off her feet, and kissed her passionately, right there in front of everyone, and they all clapped and cheered.

It had already been agreed that Carla would be included in the family wedding photos. The Ravens were as cordial towards her as could be expected, under the circumstances. For her part, Carla behaved very well, and she looked lovely today too. She wore a sky-blue silk trouser suit with huge white, yellow-centred camellias printed on it. Its flared pants and kimono-style top really flattered her. It was a very pretty outfit, completed with strappy white heels and a white straw hat with a feather in it that matched the blue of the suit. She wore dark, white-framed sunglasses for most of the time.

The effect was understated but glamorous - a far cry from the vulgar, too-tight dress she'd worn for the Raven's Christmas party, back when she was trying to catch Mark's attention. Feen was vastly relieved to see that today Carla looked like what she really was - a well-dressed mother on the most important day of her son's life. She hadn't let him down.

It was a magnificent day. The meal at the Beeches was lovely, complete with funny speeches and shared memories. Stewart had shared some hilarious hijinks that he and Gavin had got up to when they were younger. Mark had become a little choked up on giving his speech, making reference to how proud Beth Raven would be today of her beautiful daughter. He ended by saying how happy he and Adie were for their gorgeous girl, and how loved and deserving of happiness she was with her new husband, who they warmly welcomed into their family. Adie gave a short speech too, welcoming everyone, and inviting them to agree on how stunning the bridal couple looked. She rounded off by saying how thrilled she was, that they'd found one another.

Once everyone invited to the evening party had started arriving, the champagne started flowing, and the music started. Gavin and Feen's first dance took place in the bandstand.

As everyone started to join in, on the lawn outside, Uncle Bob asked Carla to dance. It was an incredibly kind gesture that nobody had prompted. He'd just decided, on his own, to make that overture to welcome the controversial woman into the family.

Peg came over to see them with Eric in tow. Feen hugged them both hard. She introduced Gavin to Eric Tripper, explaining that he'd acted as stand-in Farm Manager the previous year, after Mark had his accident. Eric had fallen for Peg over the Friday-night takeaways that everyone had come to regard as a sacred oasis during what had undeniably been a horrendously difficult time. Peg was a widow and Eric was divorced. Everyone who knew them was thrilled that they'd unexpectedly found a second chance at love in their later years.

Peg chided Feen gently for not letting her cater the canapes.

'Oh no, Egg! You always cater for everything you show up for, and it's always fab, but I hope you know we deliberately avoided asking you, because we wanted you and Peric to just relax for a change and be our guests today, without having to charge around, intent on feeding the five thousand!'

Kevin and Trudie Sangster also came over and introduced themselves to Gavin. 'We're Feen's godparents,' Kevin explained, with a grin. 'Welcome to the Raven family, Gavin. If you ever want financial advice, you can always give me a call. Family rates will apply.'

Feen grabbed Trudie's hands. 'Oh, my God, Trudie! The bridal party ladies look absolutely *stunning*! Thank you for working so hard, to make sure we've got the most well-dressed women on the planet here tonight!'

'It was fun!' Trudie confessed, with a grin. 'And you know who I had the *best* fun dressing? Carla Walton! How about that!'

Feen grinned back. 'She's not as bad as she wants everyone to think, is she? But don't tell anyone! She'd be livid if you did!'

Later in the evening, Gavin tapped her on the shoulder and whispered in her ear;

'I think it's time we got out of here.'

He'd booked the honeymoon suite back at the Beeches, and Feen had packed an overnight bag for them both, the day before, so everything they needed was already in the boot of Gavin's car. They debated whether to sneak away unnoticed, but decided instead to let people know, and say goodbye and properly thank everyone who had shared their special day.

Gavin looked over at his grandparents, smiling. 'We need to say goodbye to Han and Stazel first. They look knackered. They've been amazing though, haven't they?'

Feen laughed. Han and Stazel! That was a new one, and she was sure it would be used often within the family from now on, just like Egg and Peric.

'Yes, they have! They've done us bloody proud!'

They found the grandparents who were starting to show serious signs of fatigue, which didn't surprise Feen one bit, since they'd been on the go since dawn.

'Go to bed!' her new husband ordered, grinning as he embraced them both. 'We're heading off now, and the pair of you look worn out. Let Mark, Adie and Carla manage this lot until they're all ready to leave.'

Hazel shook her head. 'The DJ stops in another ten minutes anyway love, and once a few start trickling away, the rest generally follow. I think it'll all be over in another hour or so.'

Feen embraced them both. 'Thank you so much for everything, it's been the best day *ever*! It couldn't have been more perfect, and I can't wait to see the photos of us in the bandstand!'

Stan gathered her up in a surprisingly strong hug. 'We know how much you've always loved that bandstand! You were enchanted with it when you were a child, so it was only right that you got to use it on your wedding day. We're very glad you're part of our family, Feen!'

Mark and Adie came over too, and thanked Stan and Hazel for their hospitality. They confirmed that they'd also be leaving, as soon as the music stopped, and hoped that others would also take that as a cue to go, so poor Hazel and Stan could get to bed.

Mark roughly embraced Gavin. 'Welcome to't family, lad. Look after me girl, won't yer? It's not my job anymore.'

'I'll do my utmost. I'll make her as happy as I possibly can, Mark, I promise.'

'Good, 'cause I'll be watchin' yer. Think on!'

Carla also came forward.

'Congratulations to you both. You look gorgeous, and you seem very happy. It's all anyone could ask for.'

She stepped forward and gave Gavin a perfunctory hug. She seemed unsure and uncomfortable about whether to do the same to Feen, so Feen took the initiative instead and took hold of both of Carla's hands.

'Thank you for being here, Carla. I also want to thank you so much for the beautiful churple pair! We just *love* that, don't we Gavin? It's ridiculously lovely. As wedding gifts go, I think it has to be our absolute favourite – especially since you renovated it yourself! I love your trouser suit by the way. I've been admiring it all day. You do know about brunch tomorrow morning at the Beeches? Ten o'clock? Anyone who wants to come is very welcome to join us, and that includes you, of course.'

Carla gave a tight smile. 'Thanks. Maybe I will.'

'I mean it Carla, you'd be very welcome.'

Carla nodded, and then looked around at everyone.

'Mum, Dad, go to bed if you want. I'll watch this crowd until they leave. I'll round up the wedding presents in the morning too, first thing, and put them all in the living room. I presume you two will come and get them some time tomorrow? Most have been opened, but I've already made sure the cards are attached to everything so you know who's given you what.'

'Thanks Mum, that's a big help. We haven't had time to give them much more than a quick look, so far. Hopefully, we'll see you at the Beeches.'

As Feen and Gavin got into the car, everyone gave a cheer. They were waved off, and as the car pulled away, Feen was suddenly overcome by a heavy wave of fatigue.

'What a dorious glay! But I'm so exhausted. Are you?'

'Yep. Cream bloody crackered. But I can honestly say I've never had a better day in my entire life. It was absolutely perfect, wasn't it?'

Feen yawned and nodded. Suddenly she felt very sleepy. 'Yes it was. Absolutely perfect.'

Gavin grinned her, and yawned himself.

'Well, I'm going to let you off the hook tonight Mrs Black, since you're more or less asleep on your feet and you're not the only one. But tomorrow morning, we are going to consummate this marriage. I am going to devour you and leave you trembling and aching for more.'

'That had better be a promise, Mr Black.'

'Oh, trust me. It is.'

Chapter Twenty-One

Carla's feet were aching. It was years since she'd worn heels this high. After seeing Gavin and Feen off, she picked up a chair and took it to a quiet part of the garden while she waited for the music to finish. She could still see everything, but she needed to detach from it, at least a little, and slip off her killer shoes for a while. She let her hot, bare feet sink into the lush grass. It felt wonderful.

It had been a long day, and she still hadn't fully decided how she really felt, about the fact that her son had married into a family she had a horrible history with. She was still trying to figure it out when Adie Raven approached her, out of the blue, a few minutes later. She was carrying a chair of her own, and asked if she could sit. Carla's normal modus operandi, of refusing or responding with an unfriendly shrug, seemed churlish under the circumstances, so she sighed instead and gave Adie a quick nod.

Adie was precariously balancing two glasses of bubbly in one hand. She set her chair down and handed a glass over to Carla.

'I rescued these before the last of them went. I think we're almost drained out now. The finger-food's all but finished too, so if you wanted anything else to eat, now would be the time to get whatever scraps are left.'

Carla shook her head, but didn't say anything. She wasn't sure where to rest her eyes. Part of her wanted to get up and run away, but it seemed mean not to let her visitor have her moment, albeit uninvited.

'I hope you don't mind me crashing in on you Carla, but I thought that since we're now all related by marriage, I should take the bull by the horns and try to move things forward onto a more positive footing for us all, before we disperse for the night. If you're willing, that is. And I do need to sit down for a bit. My feet are bloody killing me.' She took a sip of her champagne, and kicked off her own shoes, while Carla stared pointedly into the middle distance.

'Gavin and Feen are planning to spend roughly half their time in London and the other half in Torley, so I guess that means we're all more likely to cross paths at different times than we were before, and even if the best we can achieve for those two lovebirds is some degree of civility, it would be nice to have that, don't you think? I didn't want us to all go our separate ways tonight without a conversation, because to me that would feel a bit weird.

'I very much like your parents, by the way, Stan and Hazel,' she added. 'They're lovely, and what a fantastic job they've done today! You must be so proud of them.'

Carla felt torn about indulging Adie in conversation. Mark Raven had resolutely ignored her from the start of proceedings, and she couldn't really blame him for that, even though it had really stung. But it seemed that Adie, at least, wanted to try and improve relations. That deserved a response, she decided, although she still couldn't make herself look her in the eye.

'Yeah. I am proud of Mum and Dad. They're in their seventies, but they seem to have had more stamina today than the rest of us put together. I guess it's the excitement. But they're starting to look a bit wiped out now. I've tried to herd them off to bed, but I doubt they'll call it quits until everyone's gone.'

Her parents really had done an amazing job of getting the house and garden ready for today. The flower beds were perfect, bushes and trees were neatly trimmed and pruned, and the grass had been freshly mowed. Then Stan and Hazel had welcomed everyone into their home, including those who were strangers to them, and worked their butts off to ensure every guest's needs were catered for.

Their house was a small and fairly modest three-bedroom bungalow, but with the marquee set up in the big back garden and a small row of hired posh porta-loos set up at one side, there hadn't been any pressure on the house itself to meet everyone's needs.

The bandstand looked truly beautiful and romantic, and it seemed to glow with an ethereal light, against the starlit sky. Carla could see why everyone thought it was a little bit magical, and she understood why Feen adored it and had wanted to get married in it.

'It would have been hard to have found a more perfect setting for a summer's wedding and evening party,' Adie offered, as if she'd read Carla's thoughts. 'It's been quite a day, hasn't it? Have *you* enjoyed it?'

Carla bit her bottom lip, unsure of how to respond. Nobody had asked her that, and it occurred to her now that she'd simply assumed that nobody would care whether or not she'd enjoyed her son's big day. She hesitated for a second, then spoke up. 'Yes. I suppose I have. They seem happy. I hope they stay that way.'

Adie smiled gently at her. 'Oh, I hope so too! But I'm sure they will. They seem made for each other.' She shifted in her seat. 'Look, Carla, I know you and Gavin have had a rocky relationship. He did tell us about it. But he's in a really good place. Feen adores him, and wants to make him happy, and he clearly loves her to pieces. I think we just have to accept what is and, as you say, hope it stays that way.'

Carla couldn't help a retort. 'He's had enough upheaval in his life already. If she messes him about, with her airy-fairy ways, she'll have me to answer to. I may not have been the best mother, in fact I was probably the worst, but that doesn't mean I'll stand by and see him hurt anymore, especially by her.'

To her surprise, Adie reached out and put her hand just briefly on her arm. 'I know,' she admitted. 'Mark feels the same way about *his* only child! He's made his feelings clear about all this too, and I do have a few misgivings of my own, so I know what you mean.' She shrugged, musing almost to herself; 'They've known each other such a short time, haven't they? We have to just trust the process, I guess. Personally, I think they'll be okay though, don't you?'

Carla considered this for a moment then nodded again, slowly. 'Yeah, maybe. Hopefully.'

Adie winked at her. 'Feen's an unusual woman, and we've always said that it would take someone very special to understand her and love her for her quirkiness, instead of being freaked out by it, but I do think Gavin does. He seems to 'get' her, if you know what I mean? That makes him incredibly special too, as far as we're concerned. We already like him very much. And as for *you* and us, well, I think we need to put the past behind us and leave it where it is. For all our sakes, I'd like for us to move on as well as we can, as a blended family. What do you think?'

Carla didn't answer. Instead, she took a deep breath and kept staring out into the middle distance. When she did speak, her voice was barely audible, even to herself. 'I've been in psychotherapy ever since the court case. What I did back then was hard even for *me* to understand. I knew I needed help. So I went and got it.'

Adie responded quietly. 'That was a brave thing to do. Is it helping?'

Carla nodded slowly. 'It's starting to, now that I'm more committed to it. I wasn't for a long time. It's pretty uncomfortable sometimes, when I confront my own actions, who I've hurt, how I've always been, when and why it started, all that.'

Her hand was shaking now, and she took a long gulp of her drink to steady her nerves and ploughed on. 'Look, Adie. I'm sorry, ok? I'm sorry for what I did to you and your family, and to that dog. I'm not proud of myself. I don't even have a decent reason, because there could never be one, could there, for what I did? I was pathetic and desperate, jealous, all the stuff I've been good at, all my life. I'm sorry. I'm in a place now where I'm learning to appreciate the hurt and the cruelty for what it was. I should never have done those things.'

She turned and finally looked squarely at Adie, her eyes brimming with the tears she fought to hold back. 'As out of control as I felt at the time, I still knew right from wrong. I know I had the choices, and I still went ahead and made the wrong ones. It's what I seem to do best. I seem to fuck up everything I touch. But I am trying to be a better person' she added, almost as an afterthought.

Adie drained her own drink in one long gulp. 'I accept your apology, Carla. And for what it's worth, I do get it, that whole feeling like you're out of control and making a monumental mess of everything, and you just can't stop yourself.' Adie nodded over to a stunning, willowy, mixed-race woman dancing with Chiara, the little flower girl, who was showing signs of tiredness now, and getting a little grizzly.

'See that woman in the blue dress? That's Ruth, my first daughter. I had her at fifteen and my parents forced me to give her up for adoption. I never told anyone, and I never would have, not even her. But I still bought a house and upended my happily settled family, and moved them to be closer to her anyway, in whatever way I could. Then something happened with my son Matthew that blew it all apart.' Adie gestured over to where a young man was sitting with his pretty partner, a toddler, and a very young baby.

'It's a long story, and I won't bore you with the ins and outs of it, but Matty was arrested on suspicion of murder. He was cleared, but not before his routine DNA sample was shown as a partial match to Ruth's. It turned out that the woman murdered was Ruth's adopted sister Rebekah. The police were taking everyone's DNA, to rule out who'd been at her flat, as part of their investigation. She was actually killed by their father, as it turned out. He'd abused her all her life, horribly, in different ways, and he'd never hidden it from Ruth. He was horrible to her too, for her whole life.'

Something stirred in Carla's memory, as Adie carried on.

'He was a vicar, of all people, and his terrible wife just turned a blind eye to what he was doing to both of those little girls. It broke my heart that I'd sent my baby, with every last hope in my heart for a better life for her, to a home where she wasn't just unloved but actually abused. It literally drove me mad, for a while. Everything came tumbling out after Matty's arrest, as the truth always does. I lost my marriage, and the trust of all my kids.'

Adie gave a short, forced laugh. 'Ironically, we all later found out that my husband had been cheating on me for years anyway. It was like someone had wandered in and thrown a hand grenade into the middle of my family. It's taking a while to piece everything back together, but I think we're getting there. Most of us anyway.'

She reached out a hand and squeezed Carla's, and Carla surprised herself by squeezing Adie's in return.

'So I know, Carla. I know how complicated families can be, and I know what it is to feel half mad with rage and grief and unable to understand or control what you're doing. I know how you were feeling, because I've been there myself. And you know, for what it's worth, I'm having a right old game with the menopause, and maybe you are too. Maybe that's part of all this. Most women our age are off their own heads for at least some of the time!'

Carla lowered her voice. 'I remember that case you were talking about. It was in the papers. She was a call-girl wasn't she, the murdered girl?'

Adie shook her head. 'No. She was a normal enough girl, from what I understand, just with very specific sexual needs. My son was involved with her through an agency that provided what women like her want, so they can have it discreetly.' She gave another short, humourless laugh.

'That rocked me to the core as well, him being capable of that kind of work. I really couldn't look at him for a long time. I wasn't the best mother for a while there either, you know, failing to tell one lost child she was mine, abandoning one of the others at a time when *he* was morally lost, and more or less ignoring the one who seemed functional.' She gestured over at Teresa, who was chatting to Ruth's wife Gina, at the edge of the dance floor.

'But they're a tough bunch, my lot. They're pulling together. We're finding our way forward.'

Carla snorted, but gently, without her usual derision. 'And now you've got a few grandkids, and Feen, and now Gavin, and probably more grandkids to follow. Here's to your ever-expanding family.' She hoped her words didn't sound unkind, as she raised her glass, and splashed a mouthful of her own bubbly into Adie's empty glass.

'And, with your movie star looks and that trouser suit to die for, here's to you one day being the most glamorous granny in Torley!' Adie responded.

Carla did snort with full disdain, at that. 'Well,' she observed. 'It will be interesting to see if that does happen, and if I'll be allowed to be part of it.'

'Oh, you will! Feen is a very wise old soul. She's a quirky girl, takes some getting to know. She baffled me a bit at first, but I'm well used to her now, and I love her very much. She has the most generous spirit of anyone I know. And Gavin clearly wants you in his life. I know he's wrestled with that. But you're his Mum, and when all is said and done, that's what it always comes back to. Flesh and blood.' Her smile was gentle.

257

'Give them time, Carla. They know what's important, like most grown up children do. They'll get to it. Right now, I'm sure they're not thinking about much except one another, and that's how it should be for a while now, as newlyweds.'

'Feen surprised me, you know,' Carla ventured. 'She offered to restyle me, a few weeks ago. At the time I didn't know whether to be grateful or insulted, because she always looks a bit off-the-wall, if you ask me. I mean, she looks nice and everything, but that vintage thing, it wouldn't have worked for me. I used to love all that stuff, but I'm the wrong shape nowadays for most of it, and I didn't want to end up looking like I was stuck in some tragic time-warp.

'But she dragged me off to GladRagz, and Trudie was surprisingly kind to me. I wasn't expecting that, but she gave me the same attention she gives everyone else, and that really mattered, because although I'm hard-enough faced, the humiliation of being politely told that my business wasn't welcomed was more than I could have stood.' Carla took a swig of her now-flat champagne and continued.

'And you're right about the menopause. I went through early, and I wasn't prepared for that at all. Almost overnight, nothing I had would fit me anymore, and I had no idea what *suited* me anymore. This trouser-suit came from Trudie's. It wasn't in stock but she ordered it in for me after showing it to me online. It was nice of her.'

Adie nodded in agreement. 'Yeah, Trudie's good like that. She dressed the bridesmaids too, and your mum, Hazel. They all look amazing today, don't they? She has an incredible eye. She got hold of *me* at my worst, and overhauled me too. I was a total basket-case when I arrived at Teapot Cottage, all hormonal and hysterical, overweight and shapeless, ostracized by my whole family, and genuinely believing I was going not-so-quietly mad!' She looked at Carla and rolled her eyes.

'You didn't see any of that, but trust me; I really was half insane. All I could do was cry, back then. I was so out of kilter I'd burst into tears if it rained! Trudie made me feel a lot better about myself. She helped me rebuild my confidence. You look fabulous today, though. Your hair looks lovely too, by the way.'

'Well, I've washed it, you know, with it being August, and all.' Carla felt a small flare of warmth, when Adie laughed at her joke.

'The trouser suit is a bit different, for me,' she admitted. 'First time I've ever worn one. I'm not very confident at showing my shape. I used to be, when I had one! I've started going to the health club, at the Beeches, and I've been on a bit of a diet, and that's helped. But before I lost a few pounds, I'd probably have gone for a small tent, for this bash today. They work wonders, you know, for hiding middle-aged spread. I just wasn't confident I'd find one that was fit for a wedding, that didn't look like I'd just landed by parachute after being spat out of a time machine from the nineteen-eighties.

'I've also officially given up being enslaved by strangulation pants and reinforced underwire bras,' she added. 'I might have arrived in Spread City, with a belly and a bum like a baker's castoffs, but at least I don't have to put up with being stabbed in the neck by renegade wires anymore, or risk being sliced in half whenever I try to sit down.'

Adie laughed again. 'I hear you. I gave up too. Those things drove me crazy. What the hell were we all thinking? I just wear the soft bras now, those tank-top things. And granny knickers. Nice ones, with a bit of lace, but I'm done with those silly little bikini pants and skimpy thongs that made me feel like I was straddling a razorblade, for God's sake! I *never* saw the attraction there!'

Carla pulled a face. 'Hazel horrifies me. She's at the opposite end of skimpy. She still wears those bloody old corsets with the bra attached, you know, like iron lungs? I dunno how the hell she walks or sits down in the damn things. When she pegs them out on the clothesline, I never know whether to laugh or cry. The really stupid part is that there's nothing of her. She's about seven stone wet through! I don't know why she thinks she even needs them.'

Adie nodded. 'My mum was the same, bless her. That generation were all trussed up for most of their lives, weren't they?' She shook her head.

'I'm glad things are easier for us, that we've been able to break free from feeling like we need to look perfect. I'm a bit spready and shapeless too, these days, but I do a lot of walking on the farm, and I go to the yoga class in town every week. It all helps. You could try the yoga, actually. You might enjoy it. It's a bit kinder on the ageing body than the gym. That's too brutal for me.'

'Yeah, maybe. It's worth thinking about, I guess.' Carla drained her glass and stood up, feeling like there'd been enough heart-to-heart for the time being.

'Thanks Adie. For what it's worth, I'm glad you found Mark. Everyone deserves to be happy.' She walked off, leaving Adie sitting on her own, but she made sure she left with a smile.

All things considered, and even though it had bizarrely featured the pros and cons of underwear, it had been a fairly nice conversation. Age and menopause supplied some commonality, and since the families had now blended, it felt right to make an effort. There was nothing to be gained by continuing to be hostile. If Adie Raven was prepared to make an overture, Carla decided she could meet her halfway and accept it in the spirit in which it had been offered. It no longer rankled, that Adie had ended up with Mark. Carla had meant it, when she said she was glad. Outrunning her humiliation at having thrown herself at him was still a work in progress, but she was getting there.

Her back was throbbing. The tension of the day was mostly gone, but the residue was a raft of aches and pains. God alone knew how exhausted her poor parents must be, particularly Hazel, who hadn't stopped since sunrise. Quite a few people had taken their cue from Feen and Gavin and had already left. The music had stopped now, and the DJ was packing his stuff away. Hazel was hugging guests as they came up to her and Stan, to give their thanks and say goodbye.

Mike Drew, Gavin's other Dad, was preparing to leave, with Mark and Adie and two American guys. Carla didn't know them, but they seemed to be very good friends with Mike and Gavin. Mike had ignored Carla for the entire day too, which was no more than she'd expected. She could see that he was quite a character, engaging with a lot of people and making them laugh, and the bond he shared with Gavin had been clear for all to see. Mike was staying at Teapot Cottage tonight, with the Americans, who were supposedly heading back to London tomorrow after the brunch at the Beeches, to catch a flight back to the States. Maybe she'd get to meet them, if she did decide to go to brunch herself. She still hadn't made up her mind about it.

She noticed that Adie looked tired now too, and she felt a sudden urge to speak to Mark before they left. After her conversation with Adie, she knew she could say what she needed to in front of her, so she braced herself and went over to them.

'Mark, I want to apologise again for the harm I caused to you and your family. I've been in a bad place for a long time, and I didn't want to acknowledge that, but I'm working on being a better person. I hope one day you'll be able to forgive me.'

Mark looked at her impassively. 'Well, that's big of yer, Carla. It takes guts to admit it, when yer wrong, an' I appreciate it. I'm not sure I can forgive yer, but I will try. For Feen and Gavin's sake, I will. It's better, I know, if we can all get on.'

Adie gave Carla a small smile, before they turned and walked away. Carla watched them go and shrugged to herself. Only time would tell, if they could all leave the past where it belonged, and be more united as in-laws, for their only children.

Well, it's a start. I didn't expect him to be all over me, and he's not letting me off the hook very easily. But as new beginnings go, I'll take it.

Chapter Twenty-Two

On Children … A Poem

'Your children are not your children.
They are the sons and daughters of Life's longing for itself.
They come through you but not from you.
And though they are with you, they belong not to you.
You may give them your love but not your thoughts.
For they have their own thoughts.
You may house their bodies but not their souls,
For their souls dwell in the house of tomorrow,
Which you cannot visit, not even in your dreams.
You may strive to be like them,
but seek not to make them like you.
For life goes not backward nor tarries with yesterday.
You are the bows from which your children
as living arrows are sent forth.
The archer sees the mark upon the path of the infinite.
And He bends you with His might that
His arrows may go swift and far.
Let your bending in the archer's hands be for happiness;
For even as He loves the arrow that flies,
So He loves the bow that is stable.'

KAHLIL GIBRAN

The months had flown by. Spring was well underway now, but nobody would be criticised for refusing to believe it. The weather had been consistently terrible, ever since Easter, which had been almost a month ago. Feen's first thought, as she left Ravensdown House in Gavin's Porsche Cayenne, was how heavy the rain was tonight. Her second thought, as she turned onto the main road that would take her into Torley town, was how bad the traffic was! This wasn't even an official holiday weekend, but the town seemed to be heaving. She couldn't understand where everyone had come from, or why they'd chosen to descend on Torley, of all places, on this particular Friday night. It was bucketing with rain and freezing cold, which wasn't even a surprise; it had been forecast well enough in advance.

It was mid-April, and while the Lake District was renowned for its lush green colours with the fells and valleys tempting hikers and ramblers who were keen to emerge from a long, cold winter, it was pretty hard to see why so many had braved shocking weather, to pile into the town this weekend.

Maybe there's something big going on in Carlisle, or somewhere else that's brought them all up here.

Feen knew that sometimes the city struggled to provide accommodation for enough people when something big was happening there. On those occasions, rare as they were, all of the nearby inns, B & B's and holiday homes that could accommodate the spill-over benefitted greatly. Adie had fielded several requests for Teapot Cottage for this weekend, but since she never usually let it for anything less than a full week, it was no bargain for anyone who only wanted it for two days. Still, it had been snapped up fairly quickly, and Adie had taken at least a dozen more calls enquiring about it since, even though the website had clearly shown it to be unavailable. For whatever reason, this far-flung little corner of the Lake District was the place everyone seemed to want to be right now, despite the howling gale and almost biblical rain.

Feen almost never wanted to go into the town in the early evenings, especially to the supermarket, since it was usually crowded out with people finishing work and frantically shopping for dinner, and the fight for a parking space or a trolley was all too often ridiculous. Tonight, it looked like the town would be chock-a-block with soggy strangers as well, raiding whatever might be left on the shelves.

She also hated driving in the rain and the dark. Normally, in this situation, she'd simply ask Gavin to take her. But he was up to his eyeballs, upstairs in their little living room at Ravensdown, putting a particularly sticky refrain together. He would have stopped without much complaint, to drive her into town for what she needed, but she didn't want to bother him. He felt he was finally on the verge of a breakthrough, and the last thing she wanted to do was interrupt his creative flow at a critical point, and potentially send him skittering back to square one. When a songwriter had the makings of a melody in his head, it really had to stay at the front of it until he'd got everything in some sort of order. That much, she had learned.

Having to go out was irritating, for just two of the ingredients they needed for their evening meal, but since Feen had already started making the chicken cacciatore before realising she didn't have tomato puree and parmesan, she thought she may as well just jump in the Porsche and take a quick run to the supermarket. If she was lucky, it would only be twenty minutes or so. She could be back before anyone even realised she was gone, and she'd still have dinner on the table for everyone at close to the usual time.

As she drove, she reflected on the past year. She and Gavin would soon be celebrating their first wedding anniversary. After spending their month-long honeymoon in the Caribbean, they had lived in the London flat for the first seven months. It had been a crazy, fun-filled, fascinating time that Feen had fully enjoyed. But she'd fallen pregnant less than two months into their marriage so they'd decided to come back to spend the spring and summer at Torley, to await the birth of their twins. The babies were due in early July.

They hadn't been actively trying to conceive, but they hadn't been avoiding it either. They were happy enough with the notion that Mother Nature would take her own intended course and give them children when she deemed fit. It had happened sooner than expected, and Feen and Gavin were both slightly stunned initially (especially at the prospect of twins), but they soon became excited about being parents.

264

Even though they'd married incredibly quickly, and a lot of their friends and family had been worried about it, most had come around now to the fact that Feen and Gavin were true soulmates, as well-suited as anyone could be. Now that the babies were on the way, with the expectant parents clearly over the moon about it, most of the running commentary about marrying in haste had died away. Friends and family were now just as thrilled and excited as they were themselves, about the impending new arrivals.

Matt and Rich had agreed to be distant but doting Godfathers, and Josie was set to become a Godmother, along with Gina Giordano, to whom Feen had got a lot closer over the past year. Mark and Adie were beyond excited, and even Carla, who was usually twice as prickly as the average porcupine, seemed happy enough to become a grandmother.

While they'd been in the city, they'd seen a few shows, and a lot of live bands. Gavin often got free tickets to gigs, and they'd even been to a few backstage parties, which were always fun. Feen had finally managed to overcome the paralysing effect of being almost permanently star-struck, after meeting a slew of famous people from the music world. Her confidence at being around people had grown a lot, in that time.

She'd travelled extensively by bus too, so she could soak up London's amazing atmosphere. She'd soon become familiar with routes that took her where she needed to go, and had often been content to just wander along the Thames, past the various monuments and iconic buildings.

London didn't overwhelm her as much as she and everyone else had initially feared it would. She actually took to the city like a duck to water, surprising even herself at how much - as a committed nature lover - she managed to enjoy it all. There were still many magnificent gardens and open spaces that offered a bit of peace and quiet amid the heaving city's hustle and bustle, and as a newcomer she was more than content with those.

The park opposite Gavin's flat was nice to visit, especially on a sunny day. There was a surprising range of trees, flowers and bushes planted in there, and it meant there were plenty of birds, hedgehogs and squirrels to listen and talk to, which Feen was very happy about. A pair of urban foxes trotted around in the evenings too, and she always made sure to leave any leftovers out for them.

But, right from the start, she'd known she'd eventually tire of the fast pace and the noise, pollution, rudeness, traffic jams, and host of other challenges that characterized London life. She knew she'd eventually start longing for home. As Gavin often joked, you can take the girl out of the Lake District, but you'll never take the Lake District out of the girl.

Feen was a 'country lass' through and through, and as the spring got underway the urge to go back to her roots became stronger. Gavin was a born-and-bred Londoner, but even he was becoming more and more keen to travel back to Torley. Throughout the summer months, London could get hot, sticky and uncomfortable, especially at nights. Being heavily pregnant and trying to cope with all that didn't appeal much to Feen, and they both decided that it made more sense to head back to Ravensdown in the spring, so they'd have plenty of support around them when the babies arrived. Feen had rearranged her pre-natal care with the family GP in Torley, and her midwifery appointments, scans and other related events would be done at Cumberland infirmary.

While they'd been away, Mark had made some minor renovations to Ravensdown House, putting in a temporary wall and door at the top of the stairs that effectively blocked part of the house off from the rest. It enabled Feen and Gavin to have their privacy. Mark had even installed a small kitchenette within the new alterations, so the couple could cook light meals for themselves if they didn't want to come down to the main kitchen.

All of the work had been designed to be reversed at some later stage, to bring the house back to its original state with only some light redecoration required, when Feen eventually inherited it, but for now it effectively created two separate dwellings within the house, to offer the most privacy to both couples. It had been a loving, sensitive thing for Mark to do, even though Feen suspected it had really been Adie who'd come up with the idea.

So they were settled back in Torley and wouldn't be going back to London until mid-September and they'd stay there until Christmas. Mike was using the flat himself from time to time, so it was being well taken care of in their absence and he assured

Feen that her herbs and pot plants were being watered and yes, even talked to, while she was away.

Feen was glad she'd come home. She was more than six months pregnant now, and starting to feel a little heavy and more frequently tired. Since she was only tiny herself, her belly (or her 'bumpy-double-do,' as Gavin had affectionately named it) was quite large. But, even carrying two babies, she hadn't put on a lot of extra weight. Her poor friend Josie had put on nearly three stone while pregnant with her first child, who'd burst into the world at a whopping nine pounds and five ounces. Josie had had a difficult birth, with a protracted labour and a few other complications, and she was having real trouble slimming back down after it.

Feen was grateful for her own small frame and the fact that she hadn't piled on quite as many pounds (well, not so far at least), and the babies were destined to be more like her, she felt, than like her strapping, stocky husband.

Having two babies at one time was a daunting prospect. The thought of having two huge ones was truly terrifying, especially since Josie had had such a difficult time just with her one. Feen had discussed her misgivings with her midwife, who assured her that all would be well. She wasn't to worry, everything looked absolutely fine, and there was no reason why she couldn't have her babies naturally, without complications, and the twins were expected to each be slightly smaller than one single baby.

Josie had joked with her about how lucky she was, having a ready-made family about to arrive with just the one pregnancy and birth to deal with. Feen had to acknowledge that it was indeed the ideal situation, along with the fact that if predictions were reliable, her twins would be sensitive little Cancerians, which aligned perfectly with her being the water sign of Cancer herself, and Gavin being the earth sign of Capricorn.

'The earth needs water to sustain it, and water needs the earth to contain it,' Anny Gralice had proclaimed while teaching Feen the rudiments of astrological compatibility, many moons ago.

Gavin had resisted finding out the sex of the twins. Feen already knew, but she didn't tell him, or anyone else. It was her secret, and hers alone, and she talked quietly to her unborn son and daughter all the time. She already knew their hearts and loved them totally. She also knew that Gavin was going to be a brilliant dad. She'd seen him with enough small children and noticed how well he understood and interacted with them, how patient and tender he was with them, to be a hundred percent sure of his heart too.

Mark had told her that when she had her first baby, he would give her the eternity ring he'd given to Beth when Feen was born. It had been one of her mother's dying wishes to Mark, that he would pass it on to their daughter when she became a mother herself.

Feen remembered the ring well. It was beautiful; a thin platinum band with three clear diamonds set in a row. Receiving another special, heart-centred part of her mother was another exciting thing to look forward to.

All in all, life had shaped up rather well so far. Gavin and Carla had also gone a long way towards reconciliation. She'd been to see him a number of times while he'd first been staying at Teapot Cottage, before he and Feen had got married, and every time she did, they seemed to make a little more progress. There was still a long way to go, but Carla had made a massive effort, and while Gavin still didn't fully trust her, he'd invited her to the cottage for a meal, once or twice, just the two of them. Their conversations had flourished there, like they couldn't seem to anywhere else.

It was the cottage itself, with its peculiar healing aura, that made things so much easier. There was no denying that a little of its magic had rubbed off on Gavin and Carla. While mother and son may never be truly close, a mutual understanding and respect was growing that had started there. Even if pleasantries were all they would ever actually manage, it was a long way forward from how things had been when Gavin had first arrived in Torley; grieving, angry, bitter, and determined to take what was his and leave again, and never look back.

Feen had been astonished when Adie told her about the conversation she'd had with Carla at her and Gavin's wedding last summer. It had seemed as if the ice might be properly thawing, largely thanks to Adie's extraordinary capacity for forgiveness and calm. She'd made the first move, and that in itself was something special, considering how much Carla had hurt her. Feen was constantly amazed by how strong and sensible, yet kind and compassionate Adie was. She'd been in Feen's and Mark's lives for less than two years, but neither of them could imagine life without her now.

Feen dragged her attention back to the road ahead. The rain was relentless. The windshield wipers automatically stepped up a notch to cope with the onslaught, which managed to cut down a little of the blinding glare from the headlights of the cars coming up the hill. It really was a filthy night. Now, on the road by herself in the cold near-dark of a miserable rainstorm, chicken cacciatore didn't seem quite so important. What mattered more was being at home with her husband. He'd eat beans on toast, cheerfully, if that was all she gave him. Feen considered turning the car around and simply heading home, wondering if it might just be more sensible to save the chicken for tomorrow night instead. But what the hell, she was halfway to the supermarket already.

I may as well see it through for the five minutes it'll take to get there now.

She gritted her teeth. As she approached the slight left-hand bend that swept down and into the town, Feen felt a momentary confusion at the sight of an oncoming car, which seemed to be on the wrong side of the road. She touched the brakes lightly and leaned forward, peering through the blinding rain, to try and make out what was happening. There was no time for her brain to register anything else as the car slammed into the front of the Cayenne with a massive, body-slamming bang, sending it spinning out of control, straight over the hard shoulder on the opposite side of the road, crashing straight through the barrier, and hurtling down the bank.

Chapter Twenty-Three

A Song of Despair

It's gotta get better, it has to. Can't take the fear anymore
I wish I'd known, would've stopped you,
before you walked out the door
Mangled metal, broken glass, your breath so fragile and weak
Never been a day in my life till now that ever felt so bleak.
Come back to me, come back to me, my beautiful, beautiful girl
Please don't leave me
I just couldn't make it without you in a broken world.

As soon as Gavin heard the first siren a dark, clawing feeling in the pit of his stomach told him that something was terribly wrong. He raced downstairs. The preparations for the evening meal were all over the kitchen table, but Feen was nowhere in sight. He knew she wasn't upstairs, and she wasn't in her workroom or in the living room either. He called her name, got no response, and quickly flung the front door open, to check if his car was in the drive. Sure enough, it wasn't, and the keys were missing from the hook. Without another thought, he started to run.

Halfway down the driveway to the main road he saw them; flashing blue lights from at least one emergency vehicle. His legs started to feel like lumps of lead as he ran, to the end of the long drive, and then all the way down the main road. It seemed *so* far!

As he approached the scene of the accident, his lungs were screaming from the long hard pull. More emergency responders had arrived and still more were pulling up. He'd never seen so many blue lights in one place before. A Toyota four-wheel-drive, with its front end smashed in and its windscreen littered with

270

cracks, was facing uphill on the wrong side of the road. Its airbags had deployed and were now crumpling. Whoever had been in it was no longer there. Two ambulances, with their lights flashing, were parked alongside it.

In an instant, he knew it had been a head-on collision, with the Toyota clearly at fault. As he looked over the bank, he was crushed to see the rear end of his own car, which was sitting with its bonnet facing downwards, about forty feet below the road. Mercifully, it was still right-side up. He could just make out his personalised numberplate as the police shone spotlights down the bank to try and see what had happened.

His blood ran cold. There was no movement from the car. Three police cars were at the top of the bank now, with their lights flashing too, and two fire engines were also now arriving at the scene, slashing the dark, rain-soaked sky and the uncompromising rock faces that flanked both sides of the pass with jagged flashes of blue. One of the policemen was talking into a radio about mobilising a mountain rescue team. Gavin ran up to him, shaking. He fought to control himself while he gave the policeman all the information he could offer.

'I'm Gavin Black. That's my Porsche Cayenne down the bank. I'm pretty sure my wife is driving it. Her name is Feen Raven-Black, and she's 28 weeks pregnant with twins.'

He ran back to the edge of the bank, and started frantically trying to find a way down. The policeman called him back, but Gavin ignored him. He had to get down there. It was a long way down, and the bank was very steep, almost perpendicular. He knew why a chopper had been called. There was next to no hope of rescuers getting down and back up again with a stretcher. Finding a way down was a treacherous prospect, but there was no way Gavin could just stand there at the top. He had to get to Feen.

Oh, God, sweetheart, what were you thinking? Why didn't you just fucking tell me you needed something?

As he slithered his way down the bank, getting caught up on rocks and brambles, he felt thorns tearing at his hands and face. He didn't care. He just had to get to Feen. It was raining so hard, the bank was like a mudslide, which actually helped him get

271

down to the car faster. As he approached it, he heard a policeman bellowing at the top of his voice from above.

'Don't touch the car! It might go down further!'

That was a good point. Gavin's first instinct had been to just yank the driver's door open and get to Feen but now, suddenly, he had to consider the very real possibility that the Cayenne might be precariously balanced, and any movement could send it plunging straight to the bottom of the valley. Its headlights were still on, throwing dim, lacklustre light around the front, but Gavin could see enough to know that it had hit a huge rock, which had clearly broken its journey down. After a cursory check, he was satisfied that the car would not be going any further, and he silently thanked a God he didn't even believe in, and roared up, as loudly as he could.

'It's safe. Stuck on a rock. Not going anywhere.'

'Don't move her! Keep her as still as you can!' the policeman bellowed again.

Gavin pulled at the driver's door handle but the door wouldn't budge.

Jammed!

Dry sobbing with panic and frustration, he managed to scrabble around the back of the car to the front passenger door, and managed to wrench it open. All airbags had deployed, and were now gradually deflating, and he could see Feen. She was conscious - just - but her eyes weren't focussed, and her head was bleeding profusely. Her teeth had gone straight through her bottom lip.

'Feen! Feen, it's me, sweetheart. Can you hear me?'

She looked at him vacantly and blinked, as if trying to focus. Gavin heaved himself into the car and picked up her hand and kissed it.

'I'm right here, sweetheart. I'm right here, and help is coming. You're going to be fine, just stay with me, okay?'

She nodded at him, blinked slowly, a few times, then closed her eyes. He squeezed her hand.

'Stay with me, baby. Stay awake, come on. Are you hurt, sweetheart? Can you wiggle your toes and fingers?'

Gavin felt foolish asking questions he wasn't even sure were the right ones, but he wanted to make sure, in his own amateur way, that Feen stayed conscious, and that her neck and back were undamaged. She nodded again.

Gavin leaned out of the car and called up the bank. Two paramedics were sliding their way down towards him. Gavin was completely unaware that he was sobbing his heart out.

'She's alive! She's alive, but she's barely conscious, and she's pregnant. 28 weeks. Please, God, please hurry. You have to get her out!' He suddenly felt himself teetering on the very edge of uncontrollable panic.

One of the paramedics grabbed him by the shoulders and ordered him to concentrate on breathing as deeply as he could. It worked. The other paramedic helped him out of the car then hauled himself into it.

As Gavin stood mutely by, shaking with fear and panic, the paramedics questioned Feen and swiftly and adeptly assessed her injuries. They decided that her neck and back were unhurt, but the job of getting her out of the car would still be a delicate one. Since the driver's door was jammed, they'd have to get her out through the passenger side, and she was in no shape to help them.

He heard the low thump of helicopter rotors. Relief flooded him, as he looked up to see a rescue helicopter hovering above the car. The paramedics told him Feen would be flown straight to Cumbria infirmary in Carlisle.

It all seemed to happen in slow-motion, but once she was safely in the chopper and it had left the scene, the two paramedics each took one of Gavin's arms and pulled him back up the bank. There hadn't been time to lift him as well; the pilot wanted to get Feen straight to the infirmary.

It was hard-going, slow and frustrating, fighting their way back up the impossibly slippery slope, in the pouring rain, but they finally made it to the top, shaking, soaking wet, and caked in mud. Gavin found the policeman he'd spoken to earlier and asked him if he could please send someone to Ravensdown Farm to tell Mark and Adie Raven what had happened, because Feen was their daughter. Another policeman stepped forward. 'I'll drive you to the hospital, Mr Black.'

He was quickly ushered into a police car, and within seconds, it set off at top speed for Carlisle. His teeth were chattering. He was soaked to the skin, filthy, and ice-cold with fear. What if

Feen was badly injured? And what about the babies? They were far too young to be born yet. If it had to come to that, would they survive? Were they alive even now?

When he arrived at the hospital, Feen was still being assessed after being hooked up to various different monitors and drips. It seemed that she had escaped serious injury to her body, but her head had taken an impact from the airbag deploying, and from the side strut of the Porsche on the driver's side that had, for some strange reason, folded like a flimsy piece of cardboard. It had buckled inward and struck the right side of her head.

Gavin was also worried about the force of the airbag against the top of her belly, and what harm it may have done to the babies. He was assured by the doctor in charge that they would let him know as soon as they had any news.

About an hour later, Adie and Mark came barrelling through the double doors, with Carla following closely behind. Their faces were white with worry, but he felt a massive rush of relief that they were finally here. He'd felt so alone with his fear. He'd left his mobile phone at home too, so he wasn't able to call anyone. The loneliness he'd felt while waiting for support to arrive, was the most profound he'd ever experienced. It was the worst thing in the world, being so afraid that someone would come and give him the worst news imaginable, while he was by himself.

'There's no news. She was conscious at the scene, but not terribly lucid. They airlifted her. I don't know what's happening. They're not letting anyone see her yet. Not even me.' He put his hands into his hair then and wept.

In an instant, Cara's arms were around him. He returned her embrace, clinging to her and sobbing like he used to do as a little boy, whenever he was afraid. She held him tightly, stroking his hair, but saying nothing. She simply let him cry, holding him safe while he did it.

After a minute or so, he managed to get himself under control, and took a couple of deep, shuddering breaths. At that point, Carla spoke. She still had her face buried in his hair, and she more or less mumbled into it.

'I know you're scared. But try not to be, at least until we know more. Ok?'

He nodded, mutely. Carla released him, and he was quickly swept into another tight hug by Adie. He felt Mark pat him on the shoulder, and when he looked beyond Adie he could see the other man's face etched with fear and confusion. Mark cleared his throat.

'I'll go see if I can find out anythin' new.'

Gavin sat down. His voice was hoarse. He sniffed hard and shook his head in frustration. 'They won't tell him anything. They won't even tell me, and I'm her husband. I'm the father of those babies.'

Carla and Adie both drew up chairs and sat next to him, one on either side. Mark came back in, shaking his head. 'They don't really know owt yet. They said they'll come an' let us know when they've got 'er stabilized.'

He went on to say that when the police came to the house and told them what had happened, they explained that the Toyota appeared to have taken the right-hand bend too wide coming up the hill in the rain and had been on the wrong side of the road when it slammed into the Porsche. That only confirmed what Gavin had suspected. Apparently, the driver and her passenger (her husband) had chest and leg injuries. They were both currently having surgery somewhere else within the hospital.

Gavin suddenly felt homicidal with rage. It must have shown in his face, because Mark quickly grabbed him by the arm.

'I know, lad. I know. I feel't same. But we 'ave to forget them bastards fer now. Your energy's needed 'ere, wi' Feen. We all 'ave to pray for 'er bein' alright, an' fer them babbies to be right. That's all that matters now.'

Gavin knew Mark made sense, but it didn't stop him from wanting to hunt down the other driver, and give her a broken neck to keep her other injuries company.

Adie was visibly upset but she spoke quietly but firmly.

'Nobody sets out to cause an accident like this. Nobody would have wanted this. That driver made a simple but catastrophic mistake. That's what it was. A mistake. As hard as it is to stomach, it's the bare truth, and Mark's right. We can't dwell on it.'

Mark sat down heavily, speaking quietly, almost to himself. 'Pissin' rain, black as bloody coal, bugger all visibility, the worst part o't road to be in, everythin' convergin' to make the worst 'appen. You couldn't make it up if you bloody tried.'

'I think it's commonly called a 'clusterfuck,' Mark,' Carla replied quietly, and he nodded in agreement.

Silence prevailed for a good half hour as each of them sat with their own turbulent thoughts. Finally, a doctor came through to talk to them.

Gavin rose to his feet, bracing himself for the worst. The doctor established who everyone was, then spoke directly to Gavin.

'Hi, Mr Black. I'm David Gray. I'm the neonatologist in charge of your wife's pregnancy. She's not in bad shape, all things considered, but she's banged her head pretty hard and her MRI scan shows a heavy concussion, so we've sedated her. We're keeping her in, at least overnight, and we're watching her very closely.'

Gavin stared at him, terrified.

'What about the babies? She's having twins. They're 28 weeks'

David Gray nodded. 'Yes, we know. Concussion is referred to here as TBI - Traumatic Brain Injury - and a TBI can compromise the viability of a pregnancy in some cases, but this stage there's no sign of foetal distress. Your wife's placentas are both intact from what we can see on the ultrasound. The babies are still doing fine, but, as I say, the team is keeping a very close eye on things. If there's any change, rest assured, we'll act accordingly.'

Carla snorted. '*'Act accordingly'*? What does that even *mean?*'

David Gray continued to direct his words to Gavin. 'It means that if the babies start showing signs of distress, we may have to consider a Caesarean section. Obviously, we want to avoid that kind of complication if we can, since your wife is under sedation with a head trauma, and that can bring complications if she goes into labour. Our aim is to keep the twins in the womb for as long as possible. We've administered some drugs to support that. I just have to make you aware of the potential for change. We're confident that the car's airbags have protected her from the worst of the trauma from the RTA, but we still have to be prepared for any outcome. '

Gavin felt hollow. *Deliver the babies now? At 28 weeks? Would they even survive that, if it had to happen?*

Mark stepped forward. 'When d'yer expect 'er to wake up?'

David Gray shook his head. 'It won't be before tomorrow morning. Serious concussion can take a while to recover from, and we can't speed up that process. It has to happen in its own time, and its different for each person. She needs to be sedated to keep the pain under control while things start going back to what they should be. I'm sorry. Obviously, I wish I could tell you more.'

'Obviously!' Carla snorted again, almost to herself.

David Gray gave them all a perfunctory smile and left the room.

Mark rounded on Carla. 'The man's doin' 'is best, woman. Can yer not be so bastard-bloody rude to 'im?'

Gavin closed his eyes. The last thing he needed now was a row between his mother and his father-in-law. That was what you got for putting them all in the same room without preparation, in a crisis, he supposed. Nobody had a chance to choose in advance, how to behave. But Adie, bless her, was not about to let an argument develop. She spoke up firmly again, in a tone that confirmed she wasn't going to take any nonsense, even from her own husband. She glared at Mark, and then at Carla.

'Ok, we're all shocked and upset. I understand that, but getting pissed off with one another won't help anything. We need to just let these people get on with their job, and trust that they're doing everything they can. Let's stop the sniping, put a lid on the anger, and work together, here.'

Mark had the grace to nod. He mumbled an apology to Carla, who responded with a tight smile.

'I'm sorry too, Mark. I'm just worried, you know? It's all a massive shock. She's not even my daughter, and I'm terrified.' She caught a sob in her throat, and sat down again beside Gavin. He put a hand on her shoulder. Adie spoke up again, a little more kindly this time.

'Of course you are, Carla. They're your grandchildren too!'

At around twenty to midnight, just as Gavin was dozing in and out of sleep, David Gray came rushing through, and informed him that the babies were in distress and would have to be delivered straight away. There was no alternative. The drugs they'd given Feen to try and prevent her from going into labour hadn't worked. They were now prepping her and taking her straight up to the operating theatre for an immediate Caesarean section.

For the second time in just a few short hours, Gavin's blood ran cold.

'No!' He cried, hoarsely. 'You can't! She's only 28 weeks! They're too young. They're too tiny. Please! There must be something else you can do!' Tears were running down his face as he cried out. He felt enveloped by white noise.

This can't be happening!

David Gray placed a hand on his shoulder.

'Look at me, Mr Black. Look at me. Please?'

Shaking with fear, Gavin dragged his eyes to David Gray's face. The man continued gently but firmly. 'We've got this, one hundred percent. We have. At 28 weeks the babies are viable. There is an excellent chance of ongoing, full development for them at this stage, outside of the womb. It's not ideal, I know. It's not what any of us want, believe me, but I'm afraid there's no alternative. Both of Feen's placentas have ruptured. The twins cannot stay inside her. We have to get them out, to give them a fighting chance.'

Gavin was struggling to accept his assurances. Carla came and put an arm around his waist, as if to hold him up. She looked squarely at the neonatologist.

'What are their chances really? Give it to us straight please. Nobody's in the mood for bullshit or false hope around here.'

'The survival rate at this stage of development is excellent. It's better than 90% with only a ten percent chance of ongoing health problems. Their lungs, brains and other organs are still developing, but we can support that with different drugs. They're definitely at a viable stage. They'll still need a lot of care for quite some time, in our SCBU, the neonatal intensive care unit, to try and mitigate ongoing health problems. There are likely to be immediate complications but we'll deal with them as best we can. We're very well set up to care for premature babies here. As a matter of fact we get quite a few transferring in from other places. It's a very specialist unit.' David Gray took another deep breath and smiled tightly at Gavin.

'There's a risk, of course. They are incredibly tiny, and there are no guarantees, but it's their only chance, I'm afraid.'

Gavin was unable to speak. He wanted to simply fall to his knees and scream. He believed though, that if he did start screaming, he wouldn't be able to stop. He fought to keep the rising tide of panic from swallowing him whole.

Carla nodded curtly at David Gray. 'Well, you'd best get on with it then, hadn't you? And don't stuff it up.'

He gave her an equally curt nod in return. 'We don't plan to.'

Everyone was fully awake again now. A nurse came in and shepherded them all to the hospital's maternity unit, to another waiting room, close to where Feen was about to undergo surgery. Everyone was terrified. Gavin still felt dazed, as if someone had hit him hard. He was still fighting the urge to lapse into full-blown hysteria.

'Gavin,' Carla prompted sharply, shaking him by the shoulders. 'You heard what Mr Gray said. The twins have better than a ninety percent survival rate! That's amazing, right?'

'That's still a ten percent chance they won't make it,' he mumbled back. 'And what about Feen? How will she ever cope, if they don't survive?'

'They will survive, Gavin. These people are competent and dedicated. You heard what they said. This is a specialist neonatal unit. They'll do everything in their medical power to make sure those babies are absolutely fine.'

Carla sounded a lot more confident than she probably felt, but Gavin was grateful for her show of strength and apparent determination to keep him from being swallowed whole by his own fear. They were *all* in danger of falling apart, all struggling not to fear the worst and eat themselves alive with worry.

The minutes dragged by, until a theatre nurse in scrubs popped her head around the door and asked Gavin if he'd like to be present for the imminent delivery of the twins. He didn't need to be asked twice.

279

'I'm Steph Jacobs, and I'm a neonatal nurse, Mr Black. I understand you've already met Mr Gray,' the nurse said to him. 'He'll be overseeing the obstetrician, Mr Hunter, in delivering the twins tonight.'

The operating theatre was busy; teeming with medical staff and jammed full of equipment. Two incubators were set alongside the operating table, where Feen lay, with foetal monitors at either side of her. Gavin reached for her hand and kissed it, then held his breath as the obstetrician held up his scalpel and made the incision across her belly.

The surgical team were talking among themselves, in matter-of-fact terms, and nobody seemed to be panicking. To all intents and purposes, it looked like a routine job they were well used to doing. Gavin felt a little calmed by that, and continued to hold and kiss Feen's hand, and stroke her hair while they worked.

He found himself crying like a baby himself, when their first twin, a son, was delivered. He was incredibly, shockingly tiny. Gavin couldn't believe something that small could even survive, but he was clearly a little fighter if the short but robust squawk he emitted was anything to judge by. The obstetrician passed him gently to a theatre nurse who carefully placed him in a plastic bag, and laid him onto a tall, intimidating machine next to Feen's head. The nurse saw Gavin looking at it anxiously.

'This is what we call a resuscitaire,' the nurse, Steph, explained. 'We use these to stabilise newborns who need to be kept warm, and who might need a little help with their breathing, before we put them in a regular incubator,' she explained.

Gavin now had the chance to see his baby son clearly. He had the tiniest scrunched up face. Gavin felt a massive surge of protective love for him, but he was desperately afraid for his survival. He seemed ridiculously, impossibly, non-viably small.

'Time of birth, 23.58 pm' Steph announced. 'A premature but potentially healthy baby boy. 1.044 kilograms, a delicate little lad!' she reported, with a beaming smile at Gavin. He leaned forward and whispered in Feen's ear.

'Sweetheart, the first one's a little boy. We have a son. Hang in there, the next one's coming up.'

The obstetrician addressed the remaining baby, still in Feen's womb. He spent a minute assessing its position, and after a couple more minutes, he pulled it clear. Again, Gavin sobbed as the ridiculously tiny baby was handed to the nurse to be wrapped and placed onto a second resuscitaire.

'Time of birth, 0.04 am. A premature but potentially healthy baby girl. .952 kilograms, a proper little pixie!' Steph proclaimed, after checking the reading. She smiled again. Gavin's heart swelled yet again at the sight of his tiny daughter, who had squawked even less than her brother, but the sound was still heartening, nonetheless.

Within a few minutes, Steph and another nurse had transferred the infants to incubators and wheeled them from the room, bound for the SCBU. A third nurse informed Gavin that he would be able to see them again after their first assessment, in about an hour's time.

Gavin struggled to wrap his head around how quickly everything had happened across the night. It had been less than seven hours since he'd been in his music room while his wife prepared their dinner, and just twenty minutes from having been told that the Caesarean had been necessary, to the process being done and dusted. In the space of a few catastrophic, crazy hours, his life had changed completely. His wife had somehow survived a horrific accident, and he'd suddenly become a father to impossibly tiny twins.

He could hardly wait, for Feen to wake up. More than anything else in the world, he wanted her to see her beautiful babies; to be there, fully present for them, as they started their battle for life.

When she was back on the ward, and he was finally alone with her, he picked up her hand and talked to her again, with tears streaming down his face at the same time as having the biggest grin imaginable, on his face. He literally didn't know whether to laugh or cry, so he found himself doing a bit of both. He couldn't remember ever having been such an emotional basket-case, before tonight.

'Oh, sweetheart. My beautiful, brave, heroic girl. You did it! You've given birth to the two most beautiful babies in the entire world. A boy and a girl. Our son came first, so I dunno what that means. Maybe he's going to be bossy and punctual. Our little girl came second, just six minutes later, so maybe our lad will always have the upper hand, and maybe our lass will always be tardy. Only time will tell, eh?'

David Gray came into the room, and he wasn't smiling. Gavin felt his heart plummet.

'Your little fighters are hanging in there. We've warmed them up, and they're on ventilators because their lungs aren't fully developed yet. That is entirely normal in preemies this young, and we're not worried about it. However, we've also done routine ultrasound scans and what we *are* a little concerned about - although it's far from rare - is that your daughter has what we call an IVH; an intraventricular haemorrhage, where blood seeps into the fluid filled areas of the brain. It's a very common condition in babies this premature, I'm afraid, because the blood vessels in the brain at 28 weeks are still very fragile. It's really only in the last trimester of gestation that they become stronger and of course they've missed out on that chance.'

Gavin felt himself going light-headed and it must have shown on his face, because David Gray put a steadying hand on his arm, before continuing.

'We have this under control, Gavin. Just trust us. We're confident that we have this, because as rare as it is to see it straightaway, that's what's happened here. IVH normally doesn't occur until a few days after delivery, but we've caught a very rare and lucky break to see it this early, and it means we can keep a very close eye on things and also monitor your son in case he develops it too, so we can be on top of that straight away too.'

'What are the complications? What can you do?' Gavin had never felt so desperate in his life.

'Luckily, your daughter's IVH is only Grade 2. It's what we call a germinal matrix haemorrhage, which involves only a small amount of bleeding, and since it normally resolves itself, we'll manage and treat any symptoms, as the most we can do, in the meantime. But it's important for you to know that we don't expect any long-term problems with it. Had it been a Grade 3 or 4, it would have been a different story. But we do expect this to resolve itself over time, with the kind of neonatal support we can offer here.' David Gray ran a hand through his shock of silver hair. He looked exhausted.

'The team will keep a very close eye on your son, and if he also develops an IVH - which I have to tell you is likely - we'll just have to hope it will be a low-grade one also. We'll keep you informed.'

'But they'll be ok?' Gavin's voice sounded, even to himself, like it was coming from a million miles away.

'We've every reason to be hopeful, Mr Black. They're in the best possible place, and they're extraordinary little fighters. The next three or four days should tell us more about how they'll develop. They'll be with us for a good while, at least a couple of months, until they're closer to their expected delivery time, so that we can ensure they continue to develop the way they would have in the womb, but you'll be able to see them as often as you like. Try not to worry.' A look of utter weariness passed briefly across his face. He rubbed his face, and his breath came out in a ragged sigh.

'Sorry. We've all been run off our feet. I've been here for forty hours myself, thanks to one crisis after another coming in. I'm getting to be a danger more than a help now, with fatigue, so I'm heading home for some shut-eye, but a Mr Pieter DeSilva will come and introduce himself to you shortly. He's a consultant obstetrician, and he'll be here all night. He'll keep you updated if required, although things do look stable for tonight. He'll be more than happy to answer any other questions you might have.'

Then with a brief smile and a nod, David Gray excused himself. Even in the midst of his own turmoil, Gavin hoped the poor man was going home to get some decent sleep.

The babies would be in the SCBU for couple of months! That seemed like forever. But at least it would give Feen time to fully recover, Gavin reasoned, and the babies would be cared for in the best way, to maximise their chances at coming out as normal infants, and leading normal lives. For now, he simply had to hope that his family would be alright. He knew that they couldn't be in a better place, or be receiving better care, and there was nothing more he could do. He had to stop panicking, and deal with the reality; that only care and time would move things forward. No amount of talking or getting hysterical would help.

He remembered that the family was all still downstairs, waiting for news, so he left the room and called softly to the nurse at the ward desk, to let her know he'd be gone for a few minutes, but would be coming back. She looked up and briefly nodded, then went back to what she was doing.

As he entered the waiting area, he could see that the night was taking its toll on everyone. They were all clearly exhausted and worried beyond belief. So, as afraid as he was for the immediate future, Gavin decided to put a brave face on and try and be upbeat. He took a couple of deep, steadying breaths.

'She's been successfully delivered of the twins. Caesarean section. We have a handsome little boy. He came first, just before midnight, and our beautiful baby girl wandered in a bit later, just after. They're perfectly formed and doing ok, but they're desperately tiny, only weighing around a kilo each. They've got a bit of black hair, they've cried, and they were put in plastic bags and then onto some resuscitation machine thing, and they're currently up in the SCBU being assessed. There are tubes and wires everywhere, and it's all a bit of a blur to me now, what they're all for, but the twins are holding their own.'

He went on to tell them about what David Gray had said about the haemorrhage and risks. Everyone gasped with dismay, but he reassured them as best he could. He tried not to let them see how worried he still was. There was no point in freaking everybody out. They all just had to hang onto the facts. He concluded by simply saying, 'Feen's still unconscious, but it all went as well as could be expected, under the circumstances. Oh, God! They're so amazing! *She* is so amazing, my beautiful girl.'

He let out a long breath and sat down. Tears streamed down his face again. He'd stopped even trying to control the turmoil of emotions. He was spent. Mark came over and clapped him on the back.

'One of each! Congratulations, man! Bloody magic, that is, and the little buggers'll both be right as rain, you'll see!'

Carla also reached over to him, drawing him into a quick hug.

'Fantastic news. Mark's right, Gavin. They'll all be just fine. Congratulations, you're a dad! And I'm a bloody granny.' She looked round at everyone, and managed a wobbly smile. 'So I guess this has suddenly turned into a grandparents' convention!'

'And great aunts and uncles!' Bob piped up. He and Sheila had arrived while Gavin was in the SCBU.

Despite himself, despite his fear, Gavin grinned at that. 'Yeah, I suppose it has.'

'And Stan and 'azel are *great* grandparents!' Mark grinned, 'along wi' Anny Gralice, as Feen likes to call me mother-in-law.'

He gently put his arms around Adie, who was sitting with her head in her hands, silently crying her eyes out. Her shoulders were slumped, and shaking with her sobs.

'Come on, lass. It's all gone as well as it could. Yer've nowt to be cryin' this 'ard over! Them babbies are as safe as they ever could be right now, an' Feen? She'll be awake in't mornin' won't she? She's alright, Adie, and she'll be there fer't babbies. Yer can stop bein' afraid.'

He looked up at Gavin and gave a rueful smile. 'Relief, I expect.'

Gavin nodded. 'We're not out of the woods yet though.'

'Aye lad. I know. But it's lookin' as could as it can do, right?'

Gavin nodded again. Sheila and Bob came over to him and offered their congratulations. They told everyone that they'd head home again, if nobody minded, but they'd be at the other end of the phone and fully expected it to ring if there were any further developments or complications. They were very firm about wanting to be kept in the loop.

Mark, Adie and Carla decided to stay. Feen was expected to wake up in the morning, and they all wanted to be there when she did. Nobody imagined they'd get a wink of sleep if they went home anyway. Adie arranged for a couple of pizzas to be delivered, and they all steeled themselves to make do with the terrible tea and coffee from the vending machines.

The night was long and agonising. Gavin spent most of it going to and fro, between Feen's bedside and the SCBU unit, where the babies were hooked up to a variety of equipment. Incredibly tiny and fragile, they were kept alive by a staggering array of ventilators, monitors, picc lines and feeding tubes. They underwent brain scans, chest x-rays, and endless other assessments.

The staff of the SCBU were incredibly encouraging and supportive. They were magnificent, and Gavin trusted them completely. So far at least, his baby son had not developed an intraventricular bleed like his sister had. More than one nurse had

285

remarked on how fortunate they'd been that the baby girl's IVH had occurred straight away. It was a rare thing for it to be present straight after a birth. It felt like a gift, in a macabre kind of way, to have received the alert so quickly.

Mark and Adie spent the entire night at Feen's bedside, just chatting to her while she slept, and talking quietly between themselves. They were determinedly positive and upbeat, although Mark seemed to have aged ten years overnight. Gavin felt like he'd aged the same amount himself, after so much shock and fear.

Carla divided her time between the SCBU and the waiting area, looking in on Mark and Adie from time to time, to see if they wanted any coffee or tea. When morning came, she went to the hospital restaurant and picked up a few breakfast sandwiches, and some decent coffee for everyone. She was turning out to be a real trooper, doing whatever she could, to help.

Chapter Twenty-Four

A Song of Hope

Everythin' looks better when the sun comes up,
and the birds all start to sing
Suddenly I'm stronger, as I wait to see
just what today will bring
Never thought we'd be here, in a million years
You never think, when your day begins, it's gonna end in tears
Life happens, we have no choice, we simply have to deal
Even when we don't know what the hell to do or feel.
But love shines through, love shines through
However tough we have to be, we can,
'cause loves shines through.

Gavin and Mark devoured the bacon and egg rolls that Carla handed to them, and both men virtually sobbed at the joy of finally getting their hands on a decent cup of coffee.

'I can't get by on the shyte that passes for tea and coffee in 'ere,' Mark growled. 'It's worse than rats' piss. Thanks, Carla. Yer a saint.'

Carla snorted at him, but she did it gently. 'Never thought I'd ever hear you say *that* to me, Mark Raven.'

Mark told Gavin that he'd already arranged for the Porsche to be winched back up the bank and taken to a compound in Carlisle, where the insurance assessors would take a look at it. But, in his opinion, it would likely be a write-off.

Even if it wasn't, Gavin was certain that he couldn't keep it. It had been Martin's much-loved car, and part of him hated the thought of letting it go, as another piece of his father that he had to say goodbye to. But how could he bring himself to drive it again, knowing that his wife and two babies had nearly lost their lives in it? All thanks to a crazy overseas tourist who'd been driving around a blind bend on the wrong side of the bloody road.

Both the driver of the Toyota and her husband had survived, but both had sustained life-changing injuries. The driver had broken five ribs and suffered a punctured lung and a shattered pelvis. Her husband, in the passenger seat, had lost his right leg from the knee down.

Gavin couldn't yet bring himself to feel any compassion yet, for either of them. Maybe in time he would but, for now, he couldn't find it within himself to feel anything other than white-hot rage, at how close he'd come to being robbed of his family, thanks to the woman's carelessness. There was apparently some concern that her fertility would be compromised because of the extent of her pelvic fractures, but Gavin wondered if maybe that was some sort of karmic justice, meted out to her for almost robbing him of his own children.

She would certainly face prosecution, and the two of them would be in the hospital for some time, before being able to go home to the United States for further rehabilitation. They had both asked to see Gavin, but he'd declined. No matter what state he'd have found them in, he really couldn't trust himself not to throttle them where they lay.

Just as he was about to leave to go up and check on the babies, Feen finally began to stir. Adie got up and went rushing down the corridor to the nurses' station, calling for them. 'Come quickly everyone, she's waking up!'

Two nurses quickly raced to Feen's room, one calling to another left behind to contact the ward doctor at once. Within ninety seconds, Feen's room was full of doctors and nurses.

She was definitely coming around, slowly, but it took her a while to open her eyes. Everyone stood around waiting, while a nurse sat her up as best she could, propped an extra pillow behind her, and tried to keep her comfortable.

Feen focussed on the nurse nearest to her. She looked confused, then looked further out, straight at Gavin. She smiled, faintly, and blinked a few times.

A nurse moved the tray table closer to her. A glass of water was sitting on it, with a straw sticking out of it. The nurse put the straw up to Feen's mouth.

'Here, love. Can you draw on that a little?'

Feen obligingly managed to draw some water through. She still looked confused, blinking and trying to focus on the different doctors and nurses. Then she looked straight at Gavin again. This time, her smile was less faint.

She recognises me!

A massive surge of relief coursed through his entire body, and he came forward to hold Feen's hand as the ward doctor gently explained to her that she was in hospital because she'd been in a car accident. He also explained, even more gently, that they'd had to deliver her of her twins, who were now safe and being cared for in the hospital's specialist neo-natal unit.

Feen's eyes widened in alarm. She looked again at Gavin, with fear in her eyes. He smiled at her.

'They're doing fine, sweetheart. But you were badly hurt, and they were in distress. They're fighters though, a son and a daughter. As soon as you're able, we can go up and see them. They can't wait to meet you!'

Feen's eyes filled with tears, which spilled out and down the sides of her face. The closest nurse took her other hand for a brief moment as the doctor explained. 'They are doing just fine,' he affirmed. 'We're taking very good care of them. The neo-natal nurses adore them. They're in very good hands up there!'

Feen put her free hand to her belly. The lost look in her eyes was almost more than Gavin could bear. He gently squeezed her hand, kissed it, and smoother her hair back from her face. He couldn't keep the emotion out of his voice.

'You had to stay asleep, sweetheart. You were badly concussed, and in a lot of pain. I know you feel robbed, and I know how unfair it must feel. But they didn't rock up alone! I was here with you, when they were delivered. Just before and just after midnight, last night. So they came into the world with me right there, watching. They are so beautiful, Feen! I can't wait for you to see them! They're gorgeous, perfect, tiny babies. Our son and daughter!'

She focussed on him again, and spoke quietly. 'What date is it?'

'April 15th. Our boy was born last night, at two minutes to midnight. Our girl rocked in about six minutes later, so today. They'll have different birthdays, which is a bit weird, but that doesn't really matter, does it?' Gavin replied. He was beaming from ear to ear, he couldn't help himself. 'They're proper battlers, Feen. Superheroes, both, and you won't believe how beautiful they are!'

'I need to see them.' She looked tiny, tired and drawn. The effort of saying just a few words was clearly exhausting. The nurse came forward again, smiling.

'I expect you could kill a cup of tea, hmmm? Shall I get one for you?'

Feen nodded, just once.

'Would you like something to eat, as well? I could get a plate of scrambled eggs sent in for you to pick at?'

Feen shook her head. Adie smiled up at the nurse.

'I don't think she's ready to eat just yet. But when she is, you'll be amazed at how much she'll put away. She eats as much as her father, and never puts on an ounce. There's no justice. I only have to *look* at what she eats and I get fat.'

The doctor spent a little more time examining Feen, showing a light into her eyes, testing her reflexes, and doing the finger test before her eyes. He asked her if she knew her name, and what year it was. He then stood back and gave her a beaming smile.

'Excellent! I'll be back soon, but please just relax, and let your brain and body rest. The kind of sleep you've just woken up from can leave you feeling a little disoriented, but that's normal. And I'm sure you have an almighty headache? We can give you some painkillers for that, but it would be helpful if you can at least eat something.'

Everyone left the room, including Mark and Adie, leaving Gavin and Feen alone. She gently squeezed his hand.

'I'm so sorry.'

Gavin shook his head emphatically. 'You've nothing to be sorry about, sweetheart. Nothing at all. It was an accident. It wasn't your fault.'

She was now looking into the middle distance, focussing on nothing in particular. He spoke again, gently. 'D'you remember any of it, what happened?'

She shook her head. 'Not much. Just rain and linding blights.'

As Gavin explained to her what had happened, she began to sob.

'Oh God! Gavin, I wanted to have them naturally, to feel them coming! I can't believe I wasn't present when they came into the world.' She took a deep, shuddering breath.

'My mother was here, she's let me know that, but I wasn't! I do feel *so* robbed,' she whispered. 'And I feel like I've let them down.'

'You very nearly weren't here at all, Feen. You've survived a terrible crash. And you haven't let our babies down! You'll see them very soon, I promise. I'll go and find out now, when we can get you up to the SCBU. Your dad and Adie were here all night, by the way, and so was Mum. You haven't been left alone for a single second.'

'Alder and Willow' Feen said, softly.

'What's that, sweetheart?'

'Alder and Willow. Their names. That has to be their names.'

Gavin felt slightly confused. 'Um, ok, I guess, but why?'

'Because of when they were born. Celtic trees. On the cusp of the two Celtic moons. The Alder and the Willow Moons.'

Gavin frowned. 'Hmmm. I was kind of hoping we could call our son after Dad. Martin?'

Feen thought for a moment. 'What about Alder Martin, and Willow Beth? Raven-Black?'

'Willow Beth Raven-Black. Alder Martin Raven-Black. Yeah, that could work. It sounds quite good, I suppose.' Gavin chewed he inside of his cheek, thoughtfully

Feen's shook her head. 'It's not negotiable. They were born prematurely, over two Celtic Moons, Gavin. In the Celtic tree calendar, Alder moon gives way to Willow moon at midnight on April 14th. Alder will shield, protect, nurture and bring peace to his sister. Willow will bring spirituality and psychic ability to her brother, and help him find the strength to withstand hardship, loss, and difficult emotions. It's destiny. It was meant to be. They must be who they were destined to be.'

She seemed very insistent, and Gavin was more grateful than he'd ever find words for, for the one random rock that had stopped her from plunging to a certain death at the bottom of the valley, and for the fact that she was awake and intact. If she wanted to call the babies Butterfly Bells and Twinkle Toes, she wouldn't get any argument from him!

'Ok. Alder and Willow it is. 'I'll let the SCBU staff know, so they can stop calling them Miss and Master Black.'

Chapter Twenty-Five

A Soul-Infusion to Strengthen Faith

As the sun sets on the day, stand beneath a tall oak tree,
with your back against its trunk. Press the full length of
your spine against the tree, and close your eyes.
Breathe deeply, in and out, until you start to see
the green behind your eyes, rising.
Keep breathing as the level increases,
and continue until green is all you see.
As you start to feel the life-force energy
that you have been filled with,
Allow your heart to overflow, with gratitude,
to the tree itself, and for all that you have today,
And step forward, in trust and love,
that you are full aligned with the universe.
Incantation (once):
'Grant me light, Great Universe, with fortitude to follow,
Bestow the strength and faith I need
to face today and tomorrow.'

Later that evening, to her immense relief, Feen was deemed fit
to be discharged from the hospital. It would be a massive wrench
to leave Alder and Willow, but she was going home for a few
hours, to hopefully get some sleep in her own bed!

She and Gavin, Adie, Mark and Carla all stopped for a quick dinner at the Beeches hotel on the way home. Bob and Sheila accepted the invitation to join them too, and met them there. It was a warm event, with Mark ordering a bottle of champagne to 'wet the babbies' heads.'

It didn't really feel appropriate to Feen, to celebrate the birth of the babies just yet, while they were still so terribly tiny, and clinging so tenuously to life but, in her heart, she knew that her family's need for a celebration of sorts was also down to the fact that she herself was alright. And, in the very *deepest* part of her heart, she already knew her valiant son and daughter were going to be okay. They would, ultimately, be absolutely fine. They were in the best possible place for now, and instead of worrying about things she couldn't control, Feen just had to trust the hospital - and she found that she did.

She couldn't remember the accident itself, but she was comfortable with that too. There was enough to deal with already, without having to suffer flashbacks or traumatic memories. An ethereal shield had been lovingly draped around her, courtesy of her mother and her other guides, and it would stay there until the time was right to remember the details of the accident that had almost claimed her and Alder and Willow's lives. Maybe the time to remember would never come at all, and that was okay too. She was at peace with all of it.

Gavin had already told her they would have their own celebration together soon, just the two of them, but for now he just wanted to thank the family for the staunch support they'd offered through the most terrifying twenty-four hours of his life.

Feen agreed. She knew how instrumental they'd all been, in keeping him sane and focussed, so treating them to a meal and a few drinks seemed like a very small thing to do, in gratitude. She wasn't ready to eat much herself, but she did manage to polish off a prawn cocktail, and half of Gavin's sticky toffee pudding.

She would quite possibly have this horrible headache for up to a week, according to the doctors, but light painkillers would definitely help and so would a few early nights. She had to avoid anything too mentally taxing, and because she'd had a Caesarean section, her belly was painful too, and she'd been given strict instructions not to drive or do anything physically strenuous.

The state she was in was one of the main reasons why she'd felt she had no choice but to fully surrender to the intrinsic conviction she had been given from her guides, that Alder and Willow would come through their ordeal. She was grateful to have that. It was a blessing, to be spared the crippling worry that other parents in the same situation must surely feel.

Carla was on her best behaviour tonight, and didn't seem to be straining too hard to be civil. In fact, Feen decided, she was better than that. She was cordial and generous with her praise of how everyone had rallied round to make the last twenty-four hours bearable for Gavin, and nobody was more surprised than he and Feen were, when she stood up at the table, declaring that she had something to say. She cleared her throat and began to speak, seeming not to care that other pub patrons would also probably be able to hear her words.

'I just want to say... I know I don't deserve the kindness you've all shown me, while we've all been so anxious and afraid. But I want to thank you for including me in all this. I know I'm not the nicest person, but I'm trying to be better, and if this ordeal has shown me anything, it's that family is the most important thing. No matter how much we might disagree on some stuff, and no matter how important those things might feel, none of it should get in the way of being there for one another when we need it.'

Carla looked around the table, but nobody spoke. She took a wobbly breath and continued.

'I've done some horrible things that I'm not proud of. In fact, I'm ashamed of how I've behaved in the past. I guess I've just felt very alone, and misunderstood, and reactive, but I think that was probably my own fault. I've created my own life, and I've alienated people along the way. I know that. But I don't want to do that anymore, so I hope you'll give me the chance to prove I can be a decent mother and grandmother, and a decent friend. I've got this nice new family, and I want to be part of it.' She wiped her eyes impatiently with the back of her hand, and sniffed hard.

'I know you'll probably want to think about whether I deserve to be included, and I'll understand if you don't, but I hope you do, because I don't want to be the person I was anymore. I need help to be better, and I think I can get there with the right support. I've never *had* any support, and I don't think I'd have known how to accept it if it was offered, for a long time. I know that sounds like an excuse, and it's not meant to be, but it's the only explanation I've got.'

Nobody said anything for a few heartbeats. Then, to Feen's utter astonishment, Mark got up from his chair, walked around the table, and gave Carla a very quick hug.

'Yer 'ave to stop beatin' yerself up at some stage, lass. Let people in. What's done is done. The only way we can go is forward, so let's leave all that dirty bloody water under't bridge an' start again. Don't look back, lass. There's nowt that way for yer now. Stop pickin' at yerself, and give the scars a chance to 'eal. Welcome to't family.'

Gavin was stunned too, and didn't know what to say. Suddenly, Carla was in a full flood of tears, Adie was in tears, Sheila was in tears, and Feen gave in and joined them. She watched, with real pride, as Gavin stood up and held his arms out to his mother, who stepped into them, shaking, and weeping gently into his hair. Like everyone else at the table, he clearly understood what it had cost her to stand up and say what she did.

He held her tightly. Feen picked up on how quickly it started to feel awkward though, and after a time they both stepped back, grinning a little self-consciously, and sat back down. With a warm smile, Adie silently handed Carla a napkin so she could wipe her eyes and blow her nose. Feen felt compelled to speak, through the lump in her throat.

'Thanks for being such a trooper, Carla. I know Gavin couldn't have got through this without *any* of you, to be honest, but you've been absolutely amazing. So supportive and encouraging. You're a better woman than you think you are. Just be your real self, would you please, from now on? Because I happen to think that's more than good enough, and I have a funny feeling everyone else does too.'

Adie spoke up. 'Feen's right, Carla. Underneath all the aggro you are a really good woman. I've watched you for long enough to know. You've had a rough time and it's changed how you've seen the world, and how you've reacted, but please know that we all understand. We've all had our demons too, to try and overcome.

'We all care, Carla, and we all do want you in the family. I know I speak for us all when I say that. Please trust us not to hurt you. Please know that whatever is said or done within this family, even if it's not always the best or the right thing, it always comes from a place of good intention. We're all a long way from perfect, but no-one wants to hurt anyone, and that includes you.'

A pregnant pause followed. It seemed that nobody quite knew what to say. Again, astonishingly, it was Mark who made the effort to lighten the atmosphere by feigning offence at Adie's insinuation that he wasn't a perfect specimen of manhood.

'Well, it's crushed, I am. *Bloody* crushed. All this time, 'ere I was, perfectly 'appy, thinkin' I were perfect! Yer've broke me 'eart, Adie.'

Everyone laughed, and not just with relief. With his broad Lancashire accent, wry observation, relentless determination to call a spade a spade (no matter who might be offended), and deadpan humour, Mark could sometimes be an absolute scream.

Feen grinned and blew him a grateful kiss. Gavin gave him a wink of thanks then reached out and squeezed his mother's hand. 'There's no such thing as the perfect family, Mum. Look at the almost-perfect Mark! Even he's got a few rust-spots on his armour. We all have to accept one another's faults and fuckups. There's a lot still to be resolved, I know. There's a lot of trust to rebuild. We all need to talk a lot more, and we will. We'll get there, in the end, though. I'm certain of it.'

Feen was certain of it too.

Carla smiled a little. 'You get that from your dad,' she said softly. 'Martin always looked on the bright side of everything. As infuriating as relentless bloody optimists aways are,' she added, with just a hint of one of her trademark sarcastic smirks. Feen just shook her head and tried not to laugh. What were they all going to do with her?

It had been a night and day night of miracles, she decided. She and Gavin had two beautiful babies that were going to be alright, despite their untimely and traumatic introduction to life. Feen herself was in pretty good shape considering she'd been pulled out of a car that had hurtled over a cliff and dangled at the top of a ravine, and Mark's previously held animosity towards Carla had dissolved after his amazing, magnanimous gesture towards her.

She was so proud of her lovely dad. To quote his own description of himself he was, in many ways, 'as rough as a badger's arse,' but he had no problem in showing the soft side of his heart when he felt the situation called for it. Feen supposed they could all thank Adie for that. Like Mark, she was one in a million, and she had certainly made Mark's world a better place, after wandering unwittingly into it, around a year and a half ago. Feen was thankful beyond measure, that Alder and Willow would have such incredible, generous-hearted grandparents.

She suddenly felt a deep wave of exhaustion. Her painkillers were wearing off now, and she needed to get to bed. Gavin took one look at her and announced that it was time for everyone to head home and get some sleep.

She didn't argue with him. Right now, she wanted nothing more than to snuggle up in bed with his arms around her, holding her tight; her gorgeous husband. He'd gone through all kinds of hell, in the last twenty-four hours. All she wanted was for them to lie in bed and hold each other, thank their lucky stars for the miracles that had rained down on them, and let the world turn without them for a little while, as they quietly dreamed of their new life, with their beautiful babies at the centre of it.

Chapter Twenty-Six

In the back seat of Mark's Range Rover, on the journey home, Carla laid her head back and closed her eyes. She was weary to her bones, from the trauma of the past twenty-four hours. Feen's instinct had apparently assured her that everything was going to be alright, and although Carla couldn't even begin to understand how that worked, she grudgingly admired how calm her daughter-in-law seemed to be about everything. Gavin was still frantic with worry about the babies, though, and how they would fare as such tiny preemies.

She'd done her best to reassure him, and was - for once - inclined to follow Feen's lead, and have faith in *her* unshakeable belief, that everything would be just fine in the end. She'd tried to get Gavin to do the same, but that was a tough call. Having his twins born months ahead of time, in such traumatic and terrifying circumstances, had rocked her son to the core.

This had been the kind of emotional rollercoaster that Carla had always struggled (and usually failed) to manage well, and had spent a lot of her life actively trying to avoid. There had been more than enough drama in the early years, when she'd been a new mother herself, and the oblivious partner of a gay man. The upheaval and heartbreak around her relationship with Martin Black had been enough to last a lifetime, and the scars ran very deep. She didn't want or need any more anguish in her life. Years ago, she'd decided she was done with drama. Yet here she was again, through no fault of her own, teetering on the edge of a savage emotional whirlpool; one that that had already grabbed hold of her son and was threatening to suck him under. In trying to keep him out of it, she was in danger of being pulled in herself.

Everything had been so straightforward, before Gavin had turned up back in her life again, almost a year ago. Life had been peaceful and uncomplicated. There hadn't been a lot to get excited about, but there hadn't been a lot to get upset about either, and that was just the way Carla liked things. She'd managed, over time, to establish something resembling a normal, quiet life.

She lived with her parents, she went to work, she had a few people she saw socially who admittedly were more like good acquaintances than true friends, but that was enough. It was a life she'd got used to and had little problem with. Sure, there were times when she thought it might be nice to have a man-friend to share her life with, or even a close girlfriend to truly be herself with. No woman was an island, after all.

But relationships were complicated, and she'd long since reached the conclusion that it was better to feel the occasional pang of loneliness than to have to deal with the continuing drama that came with families and friendships. She'd experienced and seen enough, through watching and listening to the people she worked and occasionally socialized with, to know that however tranquil the waters might appear to be, they never seemed to stay that way for long. Some people's relationships seemed so complicated, she couldn't even fathom why they actually hung onto them. Why did they fight so hard and go through all kinds of anguish just to keep a difficult marriage, friendship or family bond? What was the point of all that? Did some people really think it was better to continue to suffer in a bad relationship than not have one at all?

But it dawned on Carla now, that if Gavin hadn't turned up in her life again, she'd have carried on the way she was and lived (and probably died) without ever having contact with him again. She wouldn't have got to see how fine a man he'd become or experience the pride of being responsible for at least some of that. Although she had thoroughly despised Martin Black, she had to admit that he'd done an amazing job of raising their son. Gavin had turned out to be a truly good, kind man, full of compassion, integrity and talent. He was damn handsome, to boot. It reminded her, somewhat sadly, of what a 'looker' she'd been herself, all those years ago, before the lines of bitterness and disappointment had taken up residence on her once-pretty face and destroyed what happy expression she once might naturally have had.

No wonder Feen Raven had been smitten with Gavin. And what an odd little creature she was! She'd always given Carla the creeps, before, but since the wedding, and having seen how happy she and Gavin were together, Carla had taken time, with Dawn's help, to reflect on her first reactions. Nobody else seemed to find Feen unduly strange, at least not to the point of actually disliking her. Most people who knew much about her at all had a very positive opinion of the little woman, with her witchy ways and childlike figure. She was strange, to put it mildly. But a great many people seemed to love her, and to her credit she seemed to be as strong as an ox. The accident, and the emergency delivery of premature twin babies was enough to knock *anyone* around! But Feen had hung in there, and had woken up with nothing more complicated than a concussion and a Caesarean scar.

Carla recalled how confused, shocked and traumatized Feen had been when she was told that her babies had been born by Caesarean section while she'd been under sedation. On the one hand, it must have been great to have been spared the awful, tearing pain of childbirth, but Carla remembered the feeling of having Gavin put into her arms while she was still sweating from delivering him, how gratifying it was to have pushed him into the world all by herself, as her biggest achievement, and then to have him given straight to her. That first cuddle, she acknowledged now, had been the greatest moment of her entire life.

She tried to imagine it differently, to imagine what it must be like to be denied that. It would be a cruel blow for any woman, and then to know how tiny and fragile and at risk the baby was? That would be unthinkable. She felt an unfamiliar wave of compassion, for what Feen had missed out on, and still had to face. It would be months before the poor girl would feel the real weight and warmth of her babies in her arms.

Carla knew that she still had a lot to come to terms with, herself, and she suddenly found herself wanting to go absolutely anywhere but home. She didn't want to have to try and figure her life out, which now felt like a pressing task to be done, with her parents hovering around her. As much as she loved them, and however well-meaning they unfailingly were, Stan and Hazel could be hard work, and seldom knew to leave her alone when she needed it most. She cleared her throat and leaned forward.

'Adie, I'm wondering if Teapot Cottage is vacant at the moment? I could use some space to clear my head. I feel like I've got a lot to think about, and home doesn't feel like the right place to be right now. If the cottage is free, d'you think I could rent it for a week or two, to have a bit of space to get my head together?'

Adie checked the calendar on her phone, then turned in her seat, and smiled.

'What a great idea Carla! I think that makes a lot of sense. The cottage currently has tenants, who booked it for a full week, but they're only staying the weekend. They'll be leaving tomorrow, late in the afternoon or early evening. Since they already covered the cost for the whole week, I'm happy not to 'double-dip.' You can have it for free from Monday until next Friday, and then if you want to pay for the week after that, it would give you, what? Eleven days, with the time I need to turn it around for the next incoming tenants? Would that work? I'll have to get in there and clean it Monday morning, but you can have it from one o'clock in the afternoon. You can have the second week for half price, if it helps. The standard family discount.'

Carla nodded gratefully.

'Monday would be perfect, and thanks for the discount. That does help - a lot. I think having a bit of space will help me more than anything else right now.'

'Yes, I'm sure it will. I think we're all feeling a bit overwhelmed. I feel knackered, myself, and I know Mark does too. We're all a bit too old to be pulling these 'all-nighters' and not suffering for it, aren't we?'

Carla nodded shortly. 'I'm going to take some leave. I'm owed heaps because I never take it, and they're always banging on about me using it or losing it. I lost two weeks last year because I didn't take it. So I'll ring them first thing Monday morning and take a couple of weeks off, and I'll spend them at the cottage.'

She decided that her latest workshop venture could wait. Since initially renovating the old chair she'd found in the loft, she'd decided to give it as a wedding present to Gavin and Feen. They'd been thrilled, so she'd gone ahead and done two more. She'd sold them locally for a tidy little profit and had then found a local sellers' site on the internet where people were often getting rid of stuff, sometimes for free, other times very cheaply. She'd picked up an old sideboard from a village on the other side of Carlisle, with gorgeous carved art deco drawers, for a paltry sum. It was a peeling, rickety mess, having sat at the back of someone's garage for twenty years, unloved and forgotten. Carla had sanded it, mended the leg that was crooked, painted it a gorgeous sage green, and put new drawer handles on it. She'd been surprised and absolutely thrilled when she'd put it up for sale on another internet for-sale site and someone had paid her exactly ten times what she'd paid for it, within two days of her listing it.

At the moment she had an old Welsh dresser sitting in Stan's workshop that needed a good amount of tender loving care. It was half sanded, and Carla intended to finish that job and then paint it a matt, chalky cream. She decided she'd leave the top of the sideboard stripped and simply polished with wax. It was solid oak and had lovely lead-light windowpanes in its two top doors. It would be a stunning piece when she finally finished it and since she'd got it for free she was very excited about how it would look and what she might get for it.

Her mother had come home one day with a book on furniture repairs. It was an old book that Hazel had found in a charity shop in the town, but the principles it talked about, and the illustrations it showed, were all still completely relevant, and Carla was grateful for her mother's thoughtfulness. Stan had also spent time with her in the workshop, showing her around the tools and explaining how things like the bench vice could help when she was gluing pieces of wood back together, which types of glue would be the best to use on wood, how to choose, reload and use a more robust staple gun, and how different files could help with reshaping things. They'd gone shopping for a few more tools together, and that had been fun.

She was becoming proficient in fixing old furniture, and she was truly amazed at how much she enjoyed doing it. Her long, manicured nails had snapped off without much preamble and fallen by the wayside, but she found she actually didn't mind them looking shorter and unvarnished.

She was starting to wonder if she could make a modest living, with her new-found passion.

Even though she was regretful about having to leave her latest project behind in Stan's workshop, she felt a small frisson of excitement at the thought of being in her own space for eleven whole days, without having to think about anyone else. Living with her parents worked out fine, for the most part, but occasionally the hankering for a bit of time on her own did send her scurrying to spend a night or two in a B & B every few weeks or so.

Right now, there was a lot to process. She could feel big changes evolving within herself, and she needed time and space to acknowledge them, to learn to be less afraid of them, and work out what she wanted for the future.

She was a grandmother now! It felt as if life was steering her in a completely different direction from where she always thought she'd be going, and she wasn't at all prepared for it. She wasn't even entirely sure whether she *wanted* it, but she knew she had to try and figure everything out before it drove her crazy. The pull to do all that at Teapot Cottage had been almost visceral. She was surprised at how important it felt, to stay there for a little while.

'*You're the expert on you,*' Dawn had said to her, more than once. Carla had always agreed with the statement each time her therapist had said it, although she'd never really thought it through. But Dawn was right. When Carla chose to think about her own needs she *did* know, inside herself, what would help her most. Sometimes she refused to acknowledge what she knew in her heart of hearts, through fear or pride, or some other misplaced emotion. But she did always know, deep down, and right now she knew it was definitely time to start acting on those gut instincts. Wherever they took her, well, that's where she would end up, and she'd deal with whatever it meant when the time came.

It was time now; to own herself, and work on being the person she was *capable* of being, not just the one she'd *settled* for being. Purely and simply, she didn't want to make excuses for herself anymore. Gavin deserved better, so did her parents and the family she'd become part of. So did her beautiful new grandchildren. And - finally - Carla knew it was time to admit that she actually wanted better for herself.

* * * * *

303

Two days later, she moved into Teapot Cottage. The bright red Aga sat staring defiantly at her from its central place in the cosy kitchen. She wasn't proficient in using one, but she did remember the basics, from the old solid-fuel one they used to have in the kitchen at her parents' house. Stan had ripped it out years ago, saying that keeping the old thing going was more trouble than it was worth but, as Carla recalled, it had been quite efficient when it was working properly. She decided that the best approach was to tackle this one head-on, and master it to a level where its power to overwhelm her was gone. Adie had thoughtfully left a detailed instruction booklet sitting beside it, which would definitely help. Apparently, Adie herself had been scared to death of it once, but now used one three times the size up at the main house and declared that she wouldn't use anything else now.

Quite a transformation, Carla had thought to herself. *We'll see if I decide the same thing.*

At first, she couldn't see herself getting past the very basics of reheating, but three days into her stay, she'd already made two vegetable lasagnes from scratch. The first was burnt beyond salvage, but the second was edible. She also pulled off a passable chocolate cake, and two very decent batches of cheese and bacon scones. The second batch had been offered to the Raven family, as soon as she realised that she'd never eat them all herself. Even as she was handing them over at the door of Ravensdown House, she felt slightly ridiculous, with thoughts of hauling coals to Newcastle hovering in the back of her mind. But Adie had been genuinely delighted with the scones which had, even by Carla's own admission, turned out perfectly.

'So it looks like you've mastered the Aga! Well done!'

Carla had half-grinned at her, pleased with her own efforts. 'I don't know if I'm a true convert to it in the same way you and Feen are, but I can see why you like it, and it does make a good Victoria sponge.' She declined Adie's invitation to come in for coffee, and scuttled back down to her temporary home.

Teapot Cottage always felt welcoming and womb-like. The warmth of the Aga definitely helped, since Spring still wasn't offering much in the way of warm weather. The view of Torley valley from the multi-paned windows was stunning, and a bookshelf laden with paperbacks of every genre had promised a welcome distraction if her navel-gazing became too much for her. Her burgeoning thoughts hadn't overwhelmed her yet, but she was happy with the idea of counterbalancing inward contemplation with the odd bit of trashy fiction, and she was seriously considering attempting the jigsaw puzzle of the London Underground that was sitting on the shelf beneath the coffee table. You could, after all, have a little too much self-reflection. There was only so much of yourself you could ever really take in one hit, without it driving you mental.

Every morning she made a point of resetting the fire for the coming evening, and always looked forward to lighting it as the sun went down behind Torley valley. Then she'd curl up with a book on one of the window seats, with their sumptuous cushions and snuggly throws, until it was time to make herself some food.

Now, as she put the kettle under the tap to fill it for a cup of tea, Carla allowed herself the luxury of finally starting to relax. Before she'd arrived, Adie had stocked the little fridge for her with bacon, butter, milk and cheese, and she'd left a bottle of red wine on the table, along with a loaf of freshly baked bread and an open box of half a dozen farm eggs. A post-it note stuck to the side of the bottle had simply said 'Enjoy!'

What a nice woman Adie Raven had turned out to be. She was a good, considerate landlady, keeping a respectful distance and only enquiring occasionally if there was anything Carla needed. A fresh wave of shame washed over her at the thought of how she'd treated poor Adie when she'd first met her. At the time, it had been plain to Carla that Mark Raven had been smitten with 'the house-sitter at Teapot Cottage.' Everyone had been whispering about it at that infernal, wretched Christmas party, and Mark's actions that night had confirmed it. The knowledge had enraged Carla, since she'd thought she was a shoo-in for Mark's affections before Adie had shown up.

At least, that's what she'd managed to convince herself.

Funny, what you can talk yourself into, when you want it badly enough.

And Carla had wanted Mark Raven badly, not because he was attractive and the kind of gold-hearted rough diamond most women dream of ending up with. He was certainly good looking, but the attraction for Carla (now that she was being honest with herself) was mostly because of what he had to offer in material terms. He spoke like a hillbilly, and although that wasn't his fault, it used to make Carla cringe. She figured she could learn to live with his appalling lack of polish, though, because other things were more important. Security. Status. A rather spectacular home and enough money to never have to worry too much about anything, ever again.

At the time, the lure of those things had been too hard to resist. She'd spent far too much time on her own, to the point where she was heartily sick of the prospect of being that way for the rest of her life, waiting around for however long it would take for her poor parents to shuffle off the mortal coil so she could inherit their house with Tristan, hopefully buy him out, and have the security she felt so much in need of. That made her feel like something of a buzzard, quietly waiting for its victim to hurry up and finish dying. For all her faults, she couldn't get comfortable with the idea of simply marking time like that, and she certainly didn't want anything bad to happen to her Mum and Dad.

It mortified her now, how she'd behaved towards Mark, flinging herself at him like desperate mutton dressed as lamb. He'd been so tolerant of her advances, going along with much of it in public, to avoid embarrassing her. It wasn't far shy of pity, really, how he'd responded to her, considering how cornered he must have felt by her determination to act as if they were an item, when it was really all in her own head.

The bald truth had hurt, when she'd finally acknowledged it. Mark had never been attracted enough to even kiss her properly, let alone seduce her. The overtures of affection and attempted seduction had always come from her, and while Mark never openly rejected her, he never fully embraced her advances either, certainly not with the kind of enthusiasm a man truly interested would have done. She'd doggedly pursued him, refusing to see his persistently lukewarm responses for what they really were, telling herself that he was simply slow to catch fire, that she was so irresistible he would eventually succumb to her charms.

It was acutely humiliating, remembering all that.

She'd been kidding herself. Her few friends had warned her that she was making a fool of herself over a man who was, to all intents and purposes, still grieving for his long-dead wife, but Carla had refused to listen. Now those same friends were no longer anywhere to be found, after the way she'd behaved and the mean things she'd done in a fit of jealous rage. She didn't blame *anyone* for not wanting to know her. They could wander off into the sunset, the lucky things. She couldn't do the same; she was stuck with herself.

A romance with Mark Raven would never have worked, anyway. Even if he'd been as attracted to her as she was to him, they were too different to have ever made it as a couple. Despite being able to offer the trappings of financial security and a beautiful home, and being something of a gentleman in his own rough and ready way, Mark was a working-class farmer, a simple character, a man of the soil who liked his home hearth and a quiet life. He wasn't adventurous or overly sociable. Carla had always suspected (but had never been willing to admit it until now) that she'd have been bored to tears with the life she'd have had with him. She'd fancied herself as Lady of the Manor, all the while ignoring the persistent little voice that constantly chipped away at her, telling her how much she'd actually hate it.

But, she *was* the expert on herself. Deep down, she knew such a life, with a man like that, would turn out to be nothing more than a comfortable trap. It would have all too quickly become a life she'd have ended up desperate to escape from.

However gilded, a cage is still a cage.

No. No amount of security or status would make up for being with a man she didn't love, who didn't love her. She knew that now. She'd already lived countless lies with one man - one she *had* loved, with all her heart and soul. As mean and self-serving as she'd become through the years, the pain of being with another man who didn't love her was more than she could face again, no matter how hard she might try to convince herself that the carrots that came with it were worth it.

Carla found herself weeping in self-disgrace, over how she'd behaved and what she'd done. She'd never had a pet, so she'd never understood the anguish faced by those who did, who sometimes had to confront the horrible reality that their beloved cats, dogs, rabbits, guinea pigs, ferrets, goats, horses or even pet lambs, might die unexpectedly. Her community service at the local vet surgery had showed her, many times over, how devastating it was for an animal's owner to lose their beloved pet or - worse - to be compelled to make the agonising decision to end an animal's life.

She'd seen enough tears, enough people leaving the surgery dazed with shock and grief after losing their cherished pets, to appreciate that what she'd done to Adie Raven, and to the poor dog itself, was beyond the comprehension of anyone rational and sane. Despite the observations her therapist Dawn had offered about self-forgiveness for acts done in extreme emotional turmoil, Carla was still wrestling with that one. All she could do, for now, was give thanks every single day of her life to the gods that had allowed Sid the spaniel to survive. His poor owners, away in Australia, had trusted Adie to take care of him while they were gone. How heartbroken would they have been, as innocent victims, if Sid had died the agonising death he would have, if Feen hadn't got to him in time?

Carla had learned, during her time at the surgery, how poison affects an animal. It dies in excruciating pain as its organs systematically fail. The vets at the Valley surgery had made a definite, deliberate point of leaving her in no doubt about that.

They hadn't wanted her there, but they'd complied with the court order, hoping (as the judge himself had done) that Carla would learn something from doing her community service with them. In the end they had actually been pleased with her work. When she left, they even gave her a thank-you card, wishing her good luck for the future, and all of the staff had signed it. It meant a lot to Carla. Although she hadn't been consciously aware of the fact, she was already well on the way to reform, even then.

Her thoughts turned now, towards Martin, and she knew it was time; to make peace with what he had meant to her, and with what they had both done to one another. It was time; as Dawn had so often suggested, to acknowledge and accept that hurt, put it to bed, and properly move on. It was time; to let Martin go, to lay his memory to rest with whatever kindness she could find in her heart, and to forgive herself for what she'd said and done at a time when her very sanity could fairly have been called into question. Only then would she have a shot at finding some peace. She had been mentally unwell back then, there was no doubt about that. It was time to accept that too, without shame or anguish.

Some people said that nearly a third of all adults suffer from mental health issues at some point in their lives. Children suffered too, and maybe Gavin hightailing it to his Dad's was his instinctive way of trying to avoid being sucked into the void as well. Now, she could appreciate that it had felt to him like the only thing he could do, at the time. Now, she was actually grateful for the fact that he'd had the sense to do that for himself. He was a survivor. He had been, since day one.

Carla needed to start being a survivor too, rather than a victim. She needed to discover who she really was, to examine her real wants and needs, and work out what she really wanted from life. For far too long, she'd been coasting along, living with her parents, stuck in a dead-end job with nothing much to look forward to. Coasting was convenient, and painless; there was no need to think too hard about anything, but it hadn't occurred to her that there could be more to her life than that. It had taken Gavin's return to make her realise how unfulfilled and lonely she was, to the point where she'd started being driven mad by her own life! She barely had the energy anymore, to even be mean to people. Maintaining her trademark behaviour was actually becoming a chore and a bore. Gavin re-entering her life had given her a massive jolt, but her animosity towards him wasn't real anymore.

Carla could sense a subtle but certain sea change occurring, and she allowed the wind of it to circle her now, and gently push her forward. She wasn't sure what the true meaning of it was yet, or where it was taking her, but here in this tranquil little cottage she was amazed to discover that clarity was coming. She was already starting to figure things out. She was equally amazed to discover that the prospect of confronting herself coming around that corner, and owning her dysfunction, wasn't as terrifying as she'd imagined it would be. Here in this beautiful, nurturing, womb-like space, Carla came to understand that the future *could* be better than the past, for herself and for the family she was part of.

Hello Again (A Song for Carla)

Hello again, where have we been,
in almost half a lifetime of things unseen?
All these years and I ask myself, could I have done a lot better?
I could have picked a phone up, or even wrote a letter.

But I didn't, I didn't, and you wanna know why?
I lost myself, while I was out there learning how to fly
But I found me again, wrapped up in a song.
Took a while, for me to figure out where I'd gone wrong
The chance to say... Hello again,
It means something, You mean something,
you mean a lot to me.

Took a while, for me to work out where I'd find my wings
I've you to thank, for lots of things
It wasn't all my dad that made me, you did too
I hope I got the best of him, and the best of you
The chance to say... Hello again,
It means something, You mean something,
you mean a lot to me.

Took a while, to write a song that comes straight from the heart
Maybe you could take it, as a gift, a brand-new start
'Hello again' could mean something,
If I mean something, if I mean something,
if I mean anything to you.

ONE YEAR LATER

It had been nearly three months before Feen and Gavin were finally able to bring their babies home. Different complications had arisen, including a battle in the first few days after their birth to regulate their temperatures, and then the much-feared brain bleed for their tiny son Alder. It appeared around a week after he was born. Again, like his sister Willow's, it had been a Grade II haemorrhage, so it had resolved itself over a few weeks. The twins had also been severely anaemic and had needed regular blood transfusions during their time in the SCBU.

Other challenges also took time to resolve, such as the agonisingly slow development of their immature respiratory systems, the establishment of their weak immune systems, and getting to grips with their gastro-oesophageal reflux disease which meant they couldn't keep milk down. Feen wasn't able to breast feed them successfully, which didn't help matters, and the twins seemed to be allergic to cow's milk.

The battles had sometimes felt endless, and insurmountable, and there had been many, many days when progress had felt like two steps forward and ten steps back, but the hospital staff had been unfailingly positive about every aspect of Alder and Willow's development. They'd given both babies the utmost care, and were genuinely thrilled on the day Feen and Gavin were finally allowed to bring them home. They'd formed a farewell line, in the hospital corridor, and as Feen and Gavin each left the ward with a twin in their arms, they were clapped all the way to the elevators by the delighted ward staff. It felt like the scariest and most exciting day of Feen's life, and she knew Gavin felt the same.

The months that followed were filled with depressingly regular hospital appointments for various tests and monitoring, but halfway through the autumn the twins were officially deemed to be fighting fit and from that point on would only need to be seen by a paediatric consultant once every few months. The relief had been indescribable. Feen and Gavin, with the pressure finally

311

off their shoulders, had cried real tears, along with the rest of the family. Everyone realised, at that point, just how tense, worried and afraid they'd all been, and for how long.

But now the twins were thriving. They were of average weight and size now, babbling their first few half-coherent words, and crawling well. They were as happy and healthy as any year-old babies could be and by looking at or listening to them, there was no hint at all at of what they'd been through.

Feen thanked her and the babies' guides, every single day, for the love and support they'd offered in the aftermath of the accident and beyond. The little family had been very closely held, in an intense, ethereal embrace; she had no doubt about that.

In the weeks that followed the accident, she'd started remembering fragments of it, including the impact she'd felt when the front of Gavin's car had struck the one solitary rock on the entire hillside she'd careered down after she'd been bashed off the road. That rock, the one that saved her, was a sentinel of the angels. They had seen her going off the road. They couldn't have prevented it, but they did guide the car towards that rock, the only one on the entire hillside big enough to have stopped Feen's inexorable slide towards a certain death. Her mother's face had swum before her eyes in that split second before the body-slamming jolt. That was how she knew she'd been saved.

Beth had come to her more often, since the accident. Yet another exclusive portal had opened for Feen, in addition to the ones she already had a unique access to. Now, the ability of mother and daughter to communicate had somehow been further enhanced. Feen had always known that her mother's spirit was hovering around the fringes of her life, ever protective and encouraging. She'd always felt it, especially at the more emotional times, but her own near-death experience had brought Beth almost tangibly closer to her. Almost, but not quite. There was still usually only a *sense* that Beth was around, but it was a much stronger feeling now, less ethereal and fragmented, and more constant. Feen felt more *stable*, somehow, in the connection she had with her mother's all-knowing, grounding spirit. And, of course, Beth still whispered, like she always had, whenever the time seemed right.

The deeper and more meaningful connection had the wonderful effect of allaying many of Feen's fears about motherhood, especially when the babies first started their fight for life. Beth had come through to her, many times in those first few hours and days, to reassure and calm her.

At first, Feen had been terrified that not having experienced the birth of her children might have meant she wouldn't bond with them the way she was supposed to. Then she agonised over her inability to breastfeed them, and whether that might damage her bond with them too. She worried that the consultants might have missed something vital in their diagnoses and monitoring that could mean more health problems for the twins further down the line. She spent a lot of sleepless nights wondering if she was even *capable* of managing the responsibility of them, which had all too often felt crushing.

At those times, Beth would simply whisper to her, in a voice that only Feen could hear; *'Stop worrying! It will all be fine. They will be fine, and you will be fine, love.'* And it seemed they all really were.

And Gavin was the best father! He was very hands-on and supportive when his work schedule allowed, and even though he was getting a lot busier with his music, he always made sure he had plenty of time for his babies. He adored them, and was especially gentle with Willow, who was a slight little thing, built more like her mother.

Her dad adored them too, and made no bones about it. While he worked in the barn, Mark would sometimes have them in there with him, sitting in their highchairs with a rusk each to gnaw on. Feen would hear him chattering away to them, as if they could understand every word of his funny way of talking. It made her laugh, that they would grow up understanding a dialect that was barely still alive elsewhere in the Lancashire community.

Mark often remarked at how much like Feen baby Willow was already becoming, with the same startling blue eyes, dark hair, fine bones and deceptively strong limbs. He regularly repeated a little story about Feen that always made everyone laugh, no matter how many times they heard it;

'Little 'un may've looked like a twig that'd snap in't first big breeze, but by 'eck! She beat me at bloody arm-wrestlin' an' she were only seven! Willow'll 'ave me by't time she's four, just you wait an' see!'

Alder was a bit more solid than his sister. He was a stocky baby and it looked like he would take more after his Dad and his maternal Granddad. He had Gavin's cheeky grin and Mark's dimpled right cheek, but he had Feen's blue eyes too, to go with his shock of black hair. He would break a few hearts one day, there were no two ways about that. With the mix of Raven and Walton/Black genes, both babies were dark haired and beautiful. Feen continually marvelled at how perfect their skin was, how exquisite their little fingernails were, how long their eyelashes were, and how beautiful they smelled when they'd been freshly bathed and tucked into their special twin-sized cot. It was hard to imagine being any more in love than she was right now, with her children, her husband, and the rest of her amazing family.

As new parents, she and Gavin had been lucky to have had so much support around them, in that first year. They hadn't spent much time at the London flat in the first six months after the twins had been born, because the schedule of hospital appointments had been heavy to begin with, and Feen did need her family around her until things started to settle down. By the end of the autumn, when she and Gavin finally felt that everything was on a more even keel, it still hadn't felt quite right to move back to London so soon before Christmas. It had been New Year by the time they'd finally gone back to the flat, and that had been a massive adjustment for everyone.

Across the year, Carla had become more of a presence in their lives too, but a much more welcome one. Stan and Hazel also helped out with whatever they could, whether it be cooking a dinner for Feen and Gavin when they'd spent a gruelling day at the hospital, or babysitting on the rare nights when they felt confident enough to snatch a couple of hours away for a movie or a quick pub meal. Carla wanted to be an actively involved grandmother, and she was very good with the twins. So were 'Han and Stazel' Walton, and Feen was thrilled that the babies had such wonderful fourth-generation family members in their lives.

Feen and Gavin both continually marvelled at how far Carla had come, towards building a meaningful life for herself, with positive relationships in it. She was no longer living with her parents. She had dropped to part time hours in her job and had recently bought a vacant shop on Lanty's Walk, the lane opposite the Bull and Royal pub at the south edge of Torley town. It had space at the back that she could use as a workshop, where she'd started restoring old furniture to its former glory. The place had been empty for a long time, so she'd been able to negotiate a very good deal on the purchase price, with the help of Mark, of all people. He knew the owner that was selling it, and had used his powers of persuasion to help secure an amazing deal.

Gavin had insisted on buying it for her, as part of what he truly felt she was owed after being emotionally destroyed by Martin, so many years before. After a very strong battle of wills, where Feen had learned exactly how stubborn her husband could be when it suited him, Carla had finally given in and accepted his gift.

She fixed old furniture in the back of the shop and sold it at the front. She had a really good instinct for what could be made beautiful and her shop had the advantage of a two-faceted corner window, so that anyone driving into or out of the town could see what she had for sale. She had also bought a van, with a loan (not another gift, at her own insistence) from Gavin, and he or Stan sometimes helped her with picking up heavier items, like a sideboard or sofa, that needed fixing up. Through a part time course at a local college she had learned the art of upholstery, and she'd taken a couple of woodwork courses to help her understand how best to work with wood, which helped her to repair damaged furniture more effectively. She'd also done a couple of small-business courses, to help her understand how to make her little venture profitable.

Her shop, simply called 'Carla's,' was doing quite well. It was only open three days a week, but most weeks she sold at least two items, and usually for a tidy profit. She seemed very happy to have found her niche, something she was really good at, and she'd even been nominated for a local Inspiring Women in Business award. She hadn't won, but the publicity hadn't hurt, and she'd even been interviewed on a local radio station, to talk about her new-found passion for upcycling, and starting her own business later in life.

Feen and Gavin were proud of her, and proud that the founding piece of her new enterprise had been their little purple occasional chair, the beautiful wedding present she'd given them. The chair had become Carla's official business logo, in a kind of cartoon illustration, with her name in curved letters above it in a funky script.

The shop came with an upstairs flat that was roomy and full of lovely natural light, but it had been in dire need of an upgrade. With Gavin and Stan's help, and with her excellent eye for home bargains to decorate and furnish it with, Carla had renovated it beautifully, and made it lovely and cosy.

She'd also managed to acquire a stray black tom cat who had randomly turned up on her doorstep from out of nowhere, not long after she'd moved in. He had clearly selected her as the person he wanted to live with. She'd been resistant at first, and kept trying to shoo him away, but he'd consistently refused to budge, and wouldn't take no for an answer whenever she tried to ignore him. Eventually, she'd rolled her eyes, heaved a heavy exasperated sigh, bundled him into a box, and taken him to the vet to get him checked over. The vet thought he was probably about three years old and slightly underweight but otherwise healthy; he just needed some love and feeding up.

Carla had him neutered, microchipped, treated for worms and fleas, and vaccinated. She named him Marmite because she said, many times over, that she couldn't decide whether she loved him or hated him. But he slept on her bed beside her every night, and when she was working downstairs, or busy in the shop, or relaxing in the flat, he'd be close by, usually lying on one of the seven different luxury cat beds she'd bought for him. If he wasn't doing that, he'd be climbing all over the plushest and most elaborate cat tower that had ever been invented, playing with his vast array of top-quality toys, or picking at his gourmet food.

The Ravens, true to their word, had budged up and made room for her, and she was welcomed to every family event that was planned. She and Gavin had developed a healthy respect for one another, and while she was never going to be a gushing, 'huggy' mama, and she could still be crushingly acerbic when it suited her, she wasn't nasty with it anymore. She had a sarcastic sense of humour, and it took a while to appreciate where she was coming from with it, but she had stopped being offensive and could sometimes be very funny, witty and clever. She was head over heels in love and as soppy as a puppy with her two grandchildren, and the love she had for her son, and the love he had for her in return, was steadily growing.

It was plain for all to see, that a previously bitter and spiteful woman was becoming a lot more mellow. As much as it pained a few people to admit it, Carla Walton was actually becoming quite likeable.

She'd sought Feen out, not long after the babies had come home from the hospital. She'd brought a huge bouquet of flowers and a bottle of very good wine.

'Feen, do you have time for a drink? I'd like to talk to you.'

Feen had been happy to take some time, sensing that her mother-in-law had things to say that were important, as part of her self-healing journey.

'Of course, Carla. Please, pull up a pew. I'll grab a couple of glasses. I'm a fectacular spailure at breastfeeding, but at least it means I can have a glass of wine!'

'Feen, please stop worrying about the whole breastfeeding thing! I struggled with Gavin, too. Not every woman can make it work, but that doesn't make us bad mothers. Trust me, the fact that I was a crappy mother had *nothing* to do with the fact that I couldn't get Gavin on the tit. I know how frustrating and disappointing it is for you, that you can't feed the twins yourself, but you don't have a choice. You have to accept it, hoick the big bloody knickers up, and just get on with things.'

'I know. It's fine, really it is. They're doing absolutely fine. I just wanted to help boost them a bit, you know? They've been through so much. They heed all the nelp they can get.'

'They *are* fine, and you guys are doing great with them. Look, Feen, I wanted to apologise to you properly - you know - for the past. I know I treated you very badly when I was trying to get to know your dad. I looked down my nose at you, and that wasn't fair. I'm sorry. And I should have said all this many months ago. I'm sorry for that too. 'Courageous Carla' they call me. Except they don't, of course.'

'Well, whoever 'they' are, they bloody should! You're the bravest person I know. Look how far you've come! But Carla, it's okay. Really, it is. We were different people back then, with different ideas and goals. We wanted different things, and we didn't know each other like we do now.'

'Yeah, that's true. But I was a bitch, to most people actually, but especially to you. I've learned so much, this past year or so. I feel like a different woman. When I look back on how I was, when you first knew me, I can't believe I was such a nasty piece of work. I really was, wasn't I? It's fine for you to admit it.'

'You were in a lot of pain, Carla; pain you'd been struggling with for years, and that does things to people. It changes them, takes away their japacity for coy. You lost sight of who you really were.'

'I had no *idea* who I really was, even before I got involved with Gavin's father! I was just a naïve girl from a hick town, who didn't know shit from clay. I've never had the slightest idea who I was at all, until this last year.'

Carla had pulled a face and gone on to confess; 'I grew up in the shadow of my brainy big brother Tris, who was *always* going to be a doctor. He was only eight years old when he decided that. And, as we grew up, his ever-expanding cleverness just made me feel so inadequate and stupid. I was never going to aspire to anything as great and grand as a damn doctor! I knew it, and my parents knew it, so they never had the same expectations of me.

'But somehow that was worse, because I felt like they'd already given up on me amounting to *anything*, by the time I was leaving college without even the slightest idea what I wanted to do with my life. It wasn't like they even tried to point me in any specific direction. They more or less left me to figure things out for myself, which I didn't really know how to do. Bloody Tristan, 'Brain of Britain,' had managed to get it all figured out at the ripe old age of eight.'

'Oh, Carla! I'm so sorry. I had no idea your insecurity went back that far! Gavin told me about what happened with you and his dad, but I never knew you were already so low in self-esteem! It must've been hard growing up with such a tough comparison, without any kind of compass, and feeling like you didn't measure up.'

Carla shrugged. 'Yeah, well, it was what it was. I ended up as a shop girl, and Tris got to be a doctor. All a long time ago now, and thanks to you guys so kindly inviting him to your wedding, I got the chance to reconnect with him a little too. We're back in touch again, and Gavin's getting to know his uncle, finally. What a bloody fool I've been. I mean, it wasn't Tris' fault he got all the best brain cells, was it? How could I keep holding a grudge against him for something he couldn't help? So much of what used to make sense to me just doesn't, anymore.' Carla had shaken her head then.

'But as the years stacked up, I somehow became miserable and bitter, and I got so used to it that I forgot that it was even possible to be happy. I've had to relearn that, and even now, I sometimes feel *guilty* for being happy, like I don't deserve it, after everything I've done, and how much I've hurt people.'

'Well, that's ridiculous! Of course you deserve to be happy! You've worked really hard to get out from under all that stuff. You paid the penalty for Sid, and you've done so much work on your relationship with Gavin. He's so glad to have you in his life again.'

'That song he wrote for me? It made me cry, Feen. He came to Teapot Cottage and dropped off the stick, for me to listen to it on my laptop. There was a note, telling me that he'd written it for me, after you'd suggested it. I played it, and I couldn't stop sobbing for hours. Nobody has ever done anything like that for me, ever, in my whole life. Even Martin never wrote me a song. Both of you are so kind. I can't thank you enough, for giving me a real chance to prove I'm not a monster.'

Feen had shaken her head at that. 'I never thought you were a monster, Carla. Troubled, yes, and frustrating in the extreme, and unwilling to deal to your demons. I tried to explain that to Gavin, and he got it, and he wanted to reach out to you, but he was so tied up in knots over how to do that, because he didn't really know you anymore, to predict how you'd react. I just wondered if it might be easier for him to say how he melt through his fusic, you know, as an easier way to say everything.

'For a songwriter, he sure does find himself lost for words sometimes, especially over emotional things. And for what it's worth, that song made me cry too. The melody is so beautiful. He worked on that for a long time. And his voice isn't so terrible, really. I mean, he'll never have a career as a singer, but it's a passable voice I think, for that kind of thing at least.'

The struggle to communicate was a guy thing, Feen supposed. But there again, Carla herself had never been much good at trying to explain herself either, for a long time.

I guess the apples never fall far from their trees.

'You know, I have to apologise to you too, Carla. I wasn't very nice to you either, when you were seeing my dad for a bit. I guess, in my own defence, I knew you didn't like me much, and I knew you weren't the right woman for Daddy. No offence, I mean, but...'

Feen let the sentence taper off, acutely conscious that she couldn't end it nicely. But Carla just shrugged and pulled one of her trademark faces.

'It wasn't that I didn't like you, I didn't even know you, did I? I just found you weird, that was all. You freaked me out. I knew you were part of the package that came with Mark, but I didn't have a clue how to relate to you, so I just ignored you instead. It was easier. That's what I've always done - ignored anything in the 'too hard basket' and refuse to let it stop me. And you were right about compatibility. You'd struggle to find two people that were *less* well suited. I knew it at the time, deep down, but I couldn't admit it. At one time he was untouchable, in the community. Nobody thought he'd marry again. I was arrogant enough to think I could change that. I never read a single warning sign! But Adie is perfect for your dad. That really *is* a match made in heaven.'

'Well, if there's one thing I've learned, about this funny family, it's that we're a strong bunch. We bounce back from everything, and we're better for it. You included! To be honest, Carla, I really admire how you've pulled your life together. You've got your own place, a little business that's greadily stowing, and you've got us, whether you like it or not.'

Feen leaned forward, conspiratorially, grinning. 'And Gavin told me about that incident in Peg's café, when you were with him, and you told that woman who used to be your mum's friend that she was a who-faced old tag who knew nothing about anything and never deserved Hazel as a friend in the first place. I thought that was bloody brilliant. Good for you!'

'Well, they'd been friends for forty-odd years before I reared my head and fucked everything up for poor Mum! But I told that old tart straight, in the café, that I didn't give a rat's arse if she wanted to look down her nose and make snide remarks at *me* like she did, but she wasn't going to get away with doing the same to my poor innocent mother.

'Short-sighted, two-faced bat. You don't punish the parent for the sins of the child! Only a cretin would do that, especially when the child in question is actually a grown-up screwball with a questionably sound mind of her own, who chooses not just to *take* the low road, but to actually run hell-for-leather down it with her arms wide open.' Carla had shrugged, and pulled a face.

'I can still be pretty hard to get along with, Feen, when people piss me off. I know that, and it will probably never change, and a small part of me doesn't even want it to, if I'm honest. I don't think it hurts to have an edge, sometimes. It means people don't walk all over you.

'But my time at Teapot Cottage made me realise that a second chance at being a decent mother is the best thing that could have happened to me. It wasn't too late. As the saying goes, 'even a blind squirrel finds a nut now and then' and this was mine. I've finally been able to tell Mum and Dad everything too, which was huge, and they've been amazing; far more understanding than I ever thought they could be. I guess they've seen a lot of life, more than I've ever given them credit for. We're getting on a lot better now.' Carla had fidgeted a bit then, and smiled self-consciously.

'I must say, it's a lot more comfortable being around people nowadays, especially the ones who do understand. Letting people in hasn't been so terrible, once I got used to doing it. And becoming a grandmother has changed *everything!* I owe it to those two little monsters, to be the best I can be for them. They're gorgeous, and they deserve a decent family, on both sides.'

Feen smiled softly now, remembering that conversation. Carla really had turned things around for herself after her time at Teapot Cottage, and the transformation of a lost soul to a woman with real purpose was a wonderful thing to behold. Feel felt privileged to have witnessed the profound changes in her mother-in-law, and she knew that Teapot Cottage had been largely responsible. Carla had been pulled there, unsurprisingly, and in the ten days or so that she'd been there, she'd managed - with the help of a little bit of magic - to work through so much of what had been bleeding her dry for decades.

She was out of that desert now, with everything to look forward to. Feen knew that Carla would find love again too, sometime in the not-too-distant future. She kept the knowledge to herself, and didn't even tell Gavin what she could see in Carla's 'cards.' A nice man, with the ability to stand up to her, take no nonsense, and love and cherish her the way she deserved, was already on his way to her.

Gavin had started doing well too, with his music. In the last few months, he'd written a couple of songs for a new band that was getting a lot of attention. His work had been noticed by three (or was it four now?) bands that were already big news in the UK, and one of those had plenty of lyrics but were struggling with melodies for them. Gavin Raven-Black, as he now called himself, was becoming big news too, in the songwriting world. By his own admission, he was happier than he'd ever been, doing what he loved, and being well-paid for it. Having a wonderful family was the icing on the cake for him. Feen continually marvelled at how well he juggled his responsibilities, and always with a smile and what looked like minimal effort. He was capable, strong and generous, and intuitive to boot. She couldn't have found a better man, to share her destiny with. He really was the other half of her.

Mark and Adie were ticking along alright too. Mark had employed a farmhand, who was working out quite well, and Feen was relieved that some of the heavier work had now been taken off his hands. He'd never regained full strength after his accident in the barn, and had finally admitted that to himself, and got help. Feen knew that Adie was vastly relieved about it. Mark hadn't admitted out loud that he needed practical support. He'd used the excuse that he just wanted to spend more time with his lovely wife. Everyone went along with it, telling him how sensible it was that he devote real time to what was, after all, still a fairly new marriage. In truth, everyone cared more about the fact that he'd actually got the help he needed, than they did about the reason why.

Having help on the farm meant that Adie and Mark had been able to do a bit of travelling, to different places, and they were both very excited right now about a trip they had planned with Bob and Sheila. They were all going on a two-week safari in Africa, as a private party with a dedicated guide. Feen had never seen anyone so excited, and she was excited *for* them, especially since it had been a long-cherished dream for them all. Everyone needed something to look forward to, and Feen figured they all deserved a decent block of time away, on such a fabulous holiday.

She'd had to put her jewellery design for Gina Giordano on hold, temporarily, while she dealt with the twins and got life on a more even keel. It simply hadn't been realistic to devote the time to the work that was expected, considering how demanding the twins were with all their health concerns. Gina had been very understanding, because she was a mother herself, but she was also a businesswoman with a clearly defined seasonal timetable. She was becoming more insistent now, that Feen try to submit some designs at least, so they could know what they had to work with. Luckily, they'd been able to glide through on the previous designs for the seasons Feen had missed, but she knew they couldn't get away with doing that for a second year in a row.

She'd missed her jewellery work a lot, and had been glad to go back to designing Gina's autumn/winter line that should have been completed for the previous year. She had been working on a few samples that she'd recently submitted for Gina's approval, and was waiting to hear back. She had a good feeling about it, though. The designs were good, and because all of the pieces in the Giordano collections were all very limited edition, Feen never had to make too many of anything. She now felt it was within her grasp to get going again and make sure the collection was as robust as Gina expected it to be.

There was still a lot to be done, and some of it still felt daunting, but Feen was sure she could hold her own. The little family would be spending the summer at Ravensdown again, and Feen was looking forward to it immensely. Once the designs for Gina had been tweaked and approved, there was plenty of help to be had in Torley while she squirreled herself away in her workshop to produce the pieces. She was confident that there would be enough time to get everything done, once Gina had approved the designs she wanted.

Adie was usually on hand and more than happy to spend an afternoon playing peek-a-boo or dancing stupidly and singing, at the top of her tone-deaf voice, to make the twins laugh. As for Mark, he never needed to be asked twice, if he could entertain 'them bonny babbies.' The Waltons always made time to help out, too. Gavin could work just as well at Ravensdown and, as busy as he was, he never minded having Alder and Willow with him. He'd sing to them, in his almost-terrible voice, and plunk-play music to them on one of his keyboards. Even Josie Valley, her best friend, was a great back-up if Feen needed to concentrate on something other than the twins for a few hours.

Alder and Willow were such a delight, as babies. They had brought two warring families together, which was no small thing, and with everyone on both sides now committed to being the best they could be for one another, everything finally felt like it was heading in the right direction.

So much had changed in the past year. Feen herself had grown, beyond belief. She was a million miles away now, from that immature, freaked-out girl who'd bolted at the sight of Mr Right. She was a wife and a mother now, and she'd been through a terrible fire. Often, in waves that came and went, she felt wise beyond her years and so much more aware now, of the wisdom of aeons past.

She knew her astrological challenges would start soon enough too, with the children. They were Aries fire-babies; the astrological arch-enemy of her own water sign of Cancer. They also had little in common with their father's earthy Capricorn. Put simply, using Anny Gralice's Astro-logic and good grasp of physics, earth can be scorched by fire, but earth can put fire out. Fire can evaporate water, but water can drown fire. The bottom line was that relationships beset by elemental challenges would require careful nurturing and blending, with compromise on all sides.

Feen was grateful for the roadmap she had, in Alice's early teachings, and she and Gavin had already discussed how they would tackle the inevitable discord that would arise. Between her own mutable moods and 'bizarre' behaviours, his tendency to sometimes be over-organised and ploddingly methodical, and the twins' predicted impulsiveness and impatience, they'd all have their work cut out for them. But after doing all their astrological charts, Feen had discovered that although the challenges were clear, there were also some excellent compatibilities lurking in the wings.

Her little fireballs would be inspiring, creative, sunny, and deeply driven to succeed. She would always nurture them fully, but would lovingly take a backseat when the time came for them to shine, and Gavin would guide them gently and with infinite understanding and patience, in all the ways that mattered, as they started to learn about the world and their own successful place in it. If everyone concentrated their energies on being and giving their best, and teaching the twins to do the same, they would grow and thrive as a loving family.

Feen also knew that her mother was ever-present, and every bit as proud. Sometimes, when it was quiet, usually when the rest of the household was asleep, she would hear Beth whisper, *'Well done. You're doing fine. You're all doing absolutely fine. All is well. Sweet dreams, love.'*

And Feen would whisper back, into the night, 'Thank you so much Mum, for everything. I couldn't do this without you. I'm glad I'll never have to. Goodnight, and sweet dreams to you too.'

Annie Cook's Debut novel is available now…

No Small Change
A Teapot Cottage Tale (#1)

**The 'change of life' means menopause.
But what if it also means reinvention,
with the help of a little bit of magic?**

Adie Bostock is a self-confessed 'basket-case.' She's fifty-two, at the mercy of her haphazard hormones, and struggling to face the end of her marriage. Alone for Christmas and fed up with family drama, she lands at Teapot Cottage where she plans to wallow in guilt and self-pity in private.

But the cottage, with its mysterious healing energy, has other plans for Adie and she soon finds out that it takes more than one person to make things fall apart, and more than one to put them back together.

Confirmed widower Mark Raven is a rough-edged farmer determined to hide his heart. He's battling with grief and ageing, and keeping his rather dreamy daughter at least partly in the real world. Romance is not on his radar.

Adie and Mark want to keep things purely platonic, but an unseen influence is nudging them in a different direction. Then Adie's husband decides he wants her back. It's what she's been praying for, but is it still what she really wants?

*Escape to the Lake District with this magical,
life-affirming story about overcoming adversity
and finding love again later in life.*

Coming soon…

WHEN IT'S MEANT TO HAPPEN
A Teapot Cottage Tale (#3)

**Having a baby is something most women
dream of and plan for. But what does it mean if you can't
make it happen, no matter how hard you try?**

Debby Davies longs for a family of her own. She is desperate to have a baby with the husband she adores, but fruitless years of trying to conceive have left her feeling like a failure. It's starting to make her crazy, that she can't seem to achieve the one thing she always felt destined to do.

Darren Davies is at his wits' end with his wife. Her simmering resentment is changing her in ways that really scare him, and the horrible way her parents treat him is starting to take its toll. He's beginning to question whether their marriage can survive what feels like a never-ending series of storms.

As their doubts take hold, that their love can survive, they know they're in the last chance saloon. But Teapot Cottage, with its mystical ability to pour balm on battered souls, has plans for Debby and Darren that show them what's possible in ways they could never have imagined.

Can they stay together and face a very different future from the one they had planned, or will they find the challenges too great, and go their separate ways?

*Run away from home for a while! Come to the Lake District, to a
place where miracles can happen, with the help of
a little bit of magic!*

www.Anniecookwriter.com

Milton Keynes UK
Ingram Content Group UK Ltd.
UKHW051232010224
437047UK00003BB/5